"MEDICINE, STRONG MEDICINE . . ."

The old Indian paused, and looked at Cory expectantly.

"I didn't know that was in the hole. I didn't mean to do anything wrong. I brought it out in the light just to see what it was."

"You held it—this medicine! You touched. Very wrong. Now must be made clean again. Take medicine bag, hold it in smoke, hold tight."

Cory could not disobey. Taking the bag, he edged forward until he could hold it into the full stream of the smoke. He smelled a strange scent as the smoke grew thicker and thicker until it rose in a straight column, a signal column. He reached out his hands. . . . But they were no longer his hands, they were paws, with claws, and with fur covering them! Where had the Indian's magic transported him—and what had he become?

ANDRE NORTON is one of the true masters of science fiction and fantasy, the author who, perhaps more than any other, is responsible for luring generations of readers into the tantalizing worlds of fantasy and the future. THE MAGIC BOOKS, with its three classic tales of enchantment, provides a wondrous opportunity to explore the many worlds of Andre Norton.

THE MAGIC BOOKS

◆

ANDRE NORTON

A SIGNET BOOK

NEW AMERICAN LIBRARY

A DIVISION OF PENGUIN BOOKS USA INC., NEW YORK
PUBLISHED IN CANADA BY
PENGUIN BOOKS CANADA LIMITED MARKHAM ONTARIO

Copyright © 1965, 1967, 1968 by Andre Norton

SIGNET, SIGNET CLASSIC, MENTOR, ONYX, PLUME, MERIDIAN
and NAL BOOKS are published by New American Library,
a division of Penguin Books USA Inc.,
1633 Broadway, New York, New York 10019

First Signet Printing, March, 1988

3 4 5 6 7 8 9 10 11

PRINTED IN CANADA

FUR MAGIC

⤜ CONTENTS ⤛

AUTHOR'S NOTE

NORTH AMERICAN INDIANS, no matter of what tribe, have many legends of the Old Ones, those birds and animals (all greater than their dwarfed descendants we know now) who lived as men before the coming of man himself. Some of the furred or feathered people had strange powers. Foremost among them was the Changer. To the Plains Indians he most often wore the form of a coyote, an animal noted even to this day for its intelligence and cunning above the ordinary. To other tribes he was the Raven, or even had the scales of a reptile.

One of his many names was the Trickster, since he delighted in practical jokes and in outwitting his fellows. The Changer aided as much as he harmed, turning the course of rivers to benefit the Old Ones, altering their lands for their profit. His were the powers of nature. And widely separated Indian nations agreed that he at last created man—some say as an idle fancy, others that he wished to make a new servant. Only it did not work out as he had planned.

The legend that the Changer "turned the world over" is current with the Indians of the far Northwest.

One version of the story states that he at last defied the Great Spirit, and through the Thunderbird (that awesome winged messenger, the greatest of totems) was sent into exile. But a day for his return has also been decreed. Where upon he shall come forth to turn the world back again. Man will then vanish and the Old Ones will once more live to fill the woodlands, the prairies, and the deserts from which man has so long hunted them.

WILD COUNTRY

IT WAS COLD and far too dark outside the window to be really day-time yet. Now if he were back home this morning—Cory sat on the edge of the bunk, holding the boot he was sure was going to be too tight, and thought about home. Right now he would be willing to sit out in the full blaze of Florida sun if only all could be just as it had been before Dad went off with the Air Rescue to Vietnam. Aunt Lucy would be downstairs in the kitchen getting breakfast and all would be—right. Only Dad was gone, to a place Cory could not even pronounce, and Aunt Lucy was nursing Grandma in San Francisco. So Florida was not home any more.

"Cory!" It was not a loud call, nor was the rap on the door which accompanied it a loud rap, but Cory was startled sharply out of his daydream.

"Yes, sir, Uncle Jasper, I'm coming!" he answered as quickly as he could, pulling on first one boot, then the other. With speed, though the buttons did not slip very easily into their proper holes this morning, he fastened his shirt and tucked the tails into his jeans.

He longed to roll back beneath the covers on the bunk, maybe even pull them over his head, and forget all about yesterday. Horses—

Cory winced, rubbing aching bruises. Riding— But at least they were going in the jeep today. Only he did not want to face Uncle Jasper this morning, though there was no hope of avoiding that. He stamped down hard on each foot, the unfamiliar height of the heels making him feel as if he tilted forward, so different from Florida sandals.

Horses— Cory had found out something about himself yesterday which made him drag his booted feet now as he opened the door and went reluctantly down the ranch-house hall. He was afraid, not only of the horse Uncle Jasper had said was old, and tame, and good for a beginner to learn to ride on but of—of the country—and perhaps a little—of Uncle Jasper.

Last night he had lain awake and listened to all kinds of disturbing noises. Of course, he had told himself over and over that there was *nothing* to be afraid of. But he had never lived out in the open before, with not even a paved road, and with all those mountains shooting up to the sky. Here there were just miles and miles of nothing but wild things—tall grass no one ever cut and big trees and—animals— Uncle Jasper had pointed out a coyote track right beside the corral last night.

Corral— Cory's memory switched again to his shameful performance at the corral yesterday afternoon. Maybe it was true, what he had once read in a book, that animals knew when you were afraid of them. Because that tame old horse had bucked him right off. And—and he had not had the real guts to get back up in the saddle again when Uncle Jasper said to.

Even now, though it was so cold in the very early morning, Cory felt hot all over remembering it. Uncle Jasper had not said a thing. In fact he had talked about something else, brought Cory back here to the ranch-house and showed him all the Indian things in the big room.

Indian things— Cory sighed. All his life he had been so proud of knowing Uncle Jasper, boasting about it at school and in the Scouts, bragging that he had a real live Indian foster uncle, who had served with Dad in Korea and now lived in Idaho and raised Appaloosa horses for rodeos. Then Uncle Jasper had come to

Florida just about the time Dad got his orders to ship out and Aunt Lucy was called to Grandma's. And he had offered to take Cory to his ranch for the whole summer! It had been such a wonderful, exciting time, getting ready to go, and reading about the West—all he could read—though it had been tough to say good-bye to Dad, too.

He stood in the doorway looking out into the early morning, shivering, pulling on his sweater. Now he could hear men's voices out by the jeep and the moving of horses in the big corral.

Horses. When you watched the cowboys on TV, riding looked so easy. And when Dad and Uncle Jasper had taken him to the rodeo—well, the riders had taken a lot of spills—but that had been watching, not trying to do it yourself. Now when he thought of horses all he could really see were big hoofs in the air, aiming straight at *him*.

"Cory?"

"Coming, Uncle Jasper!" He shivered again and began to run to the jeep, resolutely not looking towards the corral. There had been a couple of stories he had read about devil horses and cougars and—

The hills were very dark against the greying sky as he reached the jeep. Uncle Jasper was talking to Mr. Baynes.

"This is Cory Alder," Uncle Jasper said.

Cory remembered his manners. "How do you do, sir." He held out his hand as Dad had taught him. Mr. Baynes looked a little surprised, as if he did not expect this.

"Hi, kid," he answered. "Want to see the herd, eh? Well, hop in."

Cory scrambled into the back of the jeep where two saddles and other riding gear were already piled, leaving only a sliver of room for him. Two saddles—not three—one for Uncle Jasper, one for Mr. Baynes— He felt a surge of relief. Then Uncle Jasper did not expect

12

him to ride! They would be at the line camp, and maybe he could stay there.

He tried to find something to hold on to, for Uncle Jasper did not turn into the ranch road, but pointed the jeep towards a very dark range of hills, and cut off across country.

They bounced and jumped, whipping through sagebrush, around rocks, until they half fell into the dried bed of a vanished stream, and used that for a road. Once they heard a drumming even louder than the sound of the motor. Uncle Jasper slowed to a stop, his head turning as he listened so that the silver disks on his hatband glinted in the strengthening light. Then he got to his feet, steadying himself with one hand on the frame of the windscreen, his face up almost as if he were sniffing the wind to catch some scent as well as listening so intently.

Cory studied him. Uncle Jasper was even taller than Dad. And, though he wore a rancher's work clothes, the silver-studded band on his wide-brimmed Stetson, and the fact that he had a broad archer's guard on his wrist, made him look different from Mr. Baynes. The latter was tanned almost as dark as Uncle Jasper and had black hair, too.

Then Cory forgot the men in the front seat as he saw what they watched for, a herd of horses moving at a gallop. But the wildly running band passed well beyond the stream bed and Cory sighed with relief.

"Cougar started 'em maybe," Mr. Baynes commented. His hand dropped to the rifle caught in the clips on the jeep side as men had once carried such weapons in saddle scabbards.

"Could be," Uncle Jasper agreed. "Take a look when we come back—though cougar is more interested in deer."

The jeep ground on. Now Cory thought of cougar, of a big snarling cat lying along a tree limb, or flattened on top of a rock such as that one right over there, ready to jump its prey. He had read about cougars, and bears, and wolves, and all the other animals of this country when he was all excited about coming here.

But that had been only reading, and now that he was truly living on a ranch—he was afraid. One could easily look at the picture of a cougar, but it was another thing to see shadows and think of what might be hiding in them.

Cory stared at the rocky ridge they were now nearing, really coming much too close. Was that a suspicious hump there, a hump that could be a cougar ready to launch at the jeep? Cougars did not attack men, he knew, but what if a very hungry cougar decided that the jeep was a new kind of animal, maybe a bigger species of deer?

The trouble was that Cory kept thinking about such things all the time. He knew, and tried to keep reminding himself, of what he had read in all the books, of stories Dad had told him of the times he himself had stayed here with Uncle Jasper—that there was nothing to be afraid of. Only now that he was here, the shadows were too real, and he was shivering inside every time he looked at them. Yet he had to be careful not to let Uncle Jasper know—not after what had happened yesterday in the corral.

They bounced safely past the suspicious rock, and the jeep pulled up the bank to settle down again in a very rough and rutted way. Uncle Jasper guided the wheels into the ruts and their ride, while still very bumpy, was no longer so shaky. The sky was much lighter now and those big, dark shadows, so able to hide anything, were disappearing.

Save for the ruts, they might have been passing through a country where they were the first men ever to travel that way. Cory saw a high-flying bird and thought, with a thrill not born from fear this time, that it must be an eagle. It was the animals possibly lurking on the ground that scared him, not birds.

The rutted way swung around the curve of a hill and they came to a halt before a cabin. Cory was surprised to see that it looked so very much like those he was familiar with in the TV Westerns. There were log walls, with the chinks between the logs filled with clay. A roof jutted forward to shelter the plank door, and there were two windows, their shutters thrown open. To one side was a pole corral holding several horses. And a stone wall, about knee-high, guarded a basin into which a pipe fed a steady flow of water from a spring.

In a circle of old ashes and fire-blackened stones burned a campfire. There was a smoke-stained coffee-pot resting on three stones, with the flames licking not too far away.

Cory sniffed. He was now very hungry. And the smell from a frying pan, also braced on stones, was enough to make one want breakfast right away. The man who squatted on his heels tending the cooking stood up. Cory recognized Ned Redhawk, Uncle Jasper's foreman, whom he had seen only at a distance a couple of days before.

"Grub's waitin'. Light an' eat," was his greeting. He stooped again to set out a pile of aluminium plates, and then waved one hand at some logs rolled up at a comfortable distance from the fire.

"Smells good, Ned." Uncle Jasper uncoiled his long length from behind the steering wheel of the jeep. He stood for a moment breathing deeply. "Good mornin' to hit the high country, too. Baynes is ready to pick him out some prime breedin' stock."

"White-top herds most likely," Ned returned. "Saul says they're movin' down from Kinsaw now at grazin' speed. You should be able to take your look 'bout noon, everythin' bein' equal."

"Been huntin', Ned?" Uncle Jasper nodded towards

15

the still-barked tree log that formed one support for the porch roof of the cabin. Cory was surprised to see what hung there—an unstrung bow, beneath it a quiver of arrows. Of course, he knew that that big bracelet Uncle Jasper wore was a bow guard, and he had seen bows in a rack at the ranch. But he thought they were only for target shooting. Did Uncle Jasper and Ned still use them for real hunting?

"Cougar out there has got him a taste for colt. Plenty of deer 'bout, no need for him to use his fangs on the herds," Ned said. "He's a big one, front forepaw missin' one toe, so he marks an easy trail. Found three or four kills this past month, all his doin'—two of them colt."

"Should take a rifle," Mr. Baynes cut in. He pulled the one from the jeep clips as if ready to set off hunting the big cat at once.

Uncle Jasper laughed. "You know what folks say about us, Jim. That we're too tight with pennies to buy shells. Fact is, we like to use bows, makes things a little more equal somehow. Killin' the People goes against the grain, unless we have to. Anyway—this is our way—"

What did he mean by "the People," Cory wondered. Did he mean that he and Ned hunted *men*? No, that could not be true. He wished he dared to go over and examine the bow. And the quiver—he could see it was old, covered with a bead-and-quill pattern just like the very old one back at the ranch. And there was a fringe of coarse, tattered stuff along the carrying strap. He had seen something like that in a picture in a book—scalps! That was what it had said under that picture—scalps! Cory jerked his eyes from the quiver and sat down beside Uncle Jasper on one of the logs, determined not to imagine any more things.

"Here you are, son." A plate of bacon and beans, a mixture he would not ordinarily consider breakfast, was offered him.

"Thank you, sir. It sure smells good!"

Ned looked at him with some of the surprise Mr. Baynes had shown. "Cliff Alder's boy, ain't you?"

"Yes, sir. Dad's in Vietnam now."

"So I heard. But there was something in that bare statement of fact which was better than any open concern.

"This all new to you, eh?" Ned made a sweeping gesture which seemed to include the hills and the beginning of the valley in which the cabin stood.

Before Cory could answer, there was a sharp yelp from farther up in the heights, which was echoed hollowly. Cory did not have a chance to conceal his start, the quick betraying jerk of his head. Then he waited, tense, for Uncle Jasper, someone, to comment on his show of unease.

But instead, Uncle Jasper set down his coffee cup and looked up the slope as if he could see who or what had yelped. "The Changer is impatient this mornin'."

Ned chuckled. "Takes a likin' for some plate scrapin's, he does. Wants us to move out and let him do some nosin' 'bout."

"The Changer?" Cory asked, his shame in betraying his alarm lost for a moment in curiosity.

It was Uncle Jasper who answered, his voice serious as if he were telling something that was a proven fact. "Coyote—he's the Changer. For our tribe, the Nez Percé, he wears that form, for some other tribes he is the Raven. Before the coming of the white men there were my own people here. But before them the Old People, the animals. Only they were not as they are today. No, they lived in tribes, and were the rulers of the world. They had their hunting grounds, their war-paths, their peace fires."

"But the Changer," Ned was rolling a cigarette with loose tobacco and paper, and now he cut in as Uncle Jasper paused to drink more coffee, "he never wanted things to be the same. It was in him to change them

17

around. Some say he made the Indian because he wanted to see a new kind of animal."

"Only he tried a last change," Uncle Jasper took up the story again, "and it was the Great Spirit who defeated him. So then, some way, he was sent out to live on an island in the sea. When enough time passes and the white man puts an end to the world through his muddlin', then the Changer shall return and turn the world over so the People, the animals, will rule again."

"Could be that story has somethin'," commented Mr. Baynes, "considerin' all we keep hearin' of world news. Most animals I've seen run their lives with a lot more sense than we seem to be showin' lately." He raised his own cup of coffee to the direction from which the coyote yelp had sounded. "Good mornin' to you, Changer. Only I don't think you'll get a chance to try turnin' the world yet a while."

"When," Cory asked, "is he supposed to turn the world over?"

Uncle Jasper smiled. "Well, you may just be alive to see it, son. I think the legend collectors have it figured out for about the year 2000, white man's time. But that's a good way off yet, and now we have some horses to look at."

Cory's fork scraped on his plate. Horses—but there were only two saddles in the jeep. He glanced—unnoticed, he hoped—at the rail beside the corral. One there—that would be Ned's. Maybe—maybe Uncle Jasper would not force him to say right out what he had been trying to get up courage enough to say all morning—that he could not, just could not, ride today.

But Uncle Jasper was talking to Ned. "Seen any more smoke?"

"Not yet. But it's time. Sometimes he just rides in without warnin'—you know how he does."

Uncle Jasper looked down now at Cory. "You can help me, Cory."

"How?" the boy asked warily. Was Uncle Jasper just making up some job around here to cover up for him? He felt a little sick—after all his big plans and wanting to make Uncle Jasper glad he had asked him—and Dad proud of him—

"Black Elk is due about now. He is an important man, Cory, and he generally stops here before goin' on to the ranch. There's a line phone in there." Uncle Jasper nodded at the cabin. "But Black Elk keeps to the old ways, he won't ever use it. If he comes, you can phone in and they'll send the other jeep up to drive him down. He does like a jeep ride."

"You mean the old man still travels around by himself?" demanded Mr. Baynes. "Why, he must be near a hundred!"

"Close to that," agreed Uncle Jasper. "He was with Chief Joseph on the Great March. His uncle was Lightning Tongue, the last of the big medicine men. And Black Elk was his pupil, made his fastin' trip for a spirit guide and all. He says it's his medicine that keeps him young. Ned sighted a smoke from the peaks three days ago, which means he's on the trail. And he likes to spend a little time at the spring." Uncle Jasper nodded to the bubbling water. "Place means a lot to him, though he's never said why. Has something to do with the old days. He may stay to inspect any colts we bring down. Still has a master eye for a horse. They used to pay him well, our breeders, to pow-wow for them. Most of the old ones believed he could get them a five-finger colt every time. But that's something else he won't talk about any more. Says the old times are slippin' away and no one cares—makes him disappointed with us." Uncle Jasper finished his coffee.

"What is a five-finger colt?" Cory wanted to know.

"A perfectly marked Appaloosa has five well-placed spots on the haunches, and that makes a five-finger horse. Not all of them have it, even if they are carefully bred. They give us Nez Percé the credit for developin' the Appaloosa breed, but whether that's just legend or not"—he shrugged—"who knows. We did and do have good luck raisin' them. And now they're in big favour, for which we can thank fortune.

"So, Cory, if you'll stay here and wait for Black Elk, phone in if he wants to go on down to the ranch, that will be a help. If he wants to wait, tell him we'll be back before the sun touches Two Ears. He doesn't hold with watch-measured time."

Mr. Baynes and Ned had already gone on to the corral, making ready to rope out their mounts.

"All right, Uncle Jasper." Cory stood up. "I'll stay right here."

But as the men saddled up and prepared to ride for the high country, Cory had to struggle not to call out that he wanted to go with them, that somehow he would stick on a horse, that he was willing to walk all the way, but that he could not stay here alone.

Uncle Jasper rode over with a last message. "Don't forget the phone. And your lunch is in a box in the jeep. Don't wander off—this country can be tricky when you don't know it. But you've got good sense, Cory, and I know you can be depended upon not to get lost."

At least Uncle Jasper gave him that much credit, thought Cory, and tried to take some comfort from that. But he knew that he had fallen far below the standard Cliff Alder's son should have kept.

After they were gone, Cory went and sat in the jeep. Somehow, with the sun-warmed seat under him, he felt more secure. He had thought that once the men were gone it would be quiet. But now when he listened he heard all kinds of other sounds. A bird flew down from the roof of the cabin and pecked at some of the crumbs from breakfast. And some brownish animal shuffled around the far end of the cabin, plainly intent upon its own affairs, paying no attention to Cory. But he watched it carefully until it disappeared.

Finally he got out of the jeep, to gather up the plates and pans and carry them to the spring basin, scrubbing them clean with sand. It was something to do. Ned had taken the bow and quiver— Cory thought again of the cougar.

What if it hunted, or wandered, up this way? Would the cabin be a safe place to hide? But if there was a phone inside—

He pushed open the door, wanting to be sure. After the bright sunlight of the clearing, the inside was dusty dark. Cory stood blinking on the threshold until his eyes adjusted to the gloom. Two bunks, now stripped to their bare boards, were built against the far wall. A stove was to one side, a box half full of wooden lengths beside it. There was a wall cupboard, its door open to show another pile of plates, a row of cans, and some tin cups.

In the centre of the room was a table with four chairs. But on the wall to the left, stretched out tightly by pegs, was a skin. Of what kind of animal Cory did not know, but it was large. It had been scraped free of hair and on it were paintings. He moved closer. The paintings had been drawn in red and yellow and black, all colours so faded now that in the half-light he could hardly make them out.

There were horses with the spotted hindquarters of the Appaloosa breed. There were men, some with feathers on their heads, others wearing crude little hats. The hatted men carried guns, while the feathered ones were armed with bows and only a few guns. Cory realized that this was meant to tell the story of some old battle.

As he came out into the open again, he heard once more the challenging yelp of a coyote, and he wondered if it was angry because he was there—that, as Ned had said, it wanted to come down looking for camp food. A fresh wind blew, but it was warmer than it had been at dawn. He pulled off his sweater and dropped it on the back seat of the jeep.

This Black Elk, Mr. Baynes had said he was very old. And Uncle Jasper had said he had been with Chief Joseph on the retreat when the Nez Percé had been driven from their lands and had fled towards the Canadian border.

Cory had read about that. He had always wanted to know about the Nez Percé, because of Dad and Uncle Jasper. But Uncle Jasper had never lived on a reservation, because his father, too, had had this ranch. And Uncle Jasper had been in college when the Korean War broke out, and then he enlisted in Dad's outfit.

Somehow he found it hard to think of Uncle Jasper as a real Indian. When they had come through town to the ranch four days ago, Cory had seen other Indians. Most of them were dressed like ranchers. There had been just one old man with grey braids falling from under his hat.

If this Black Elk was so old, maybe *he* wore braids and looked more like the Indians in the books. Cory tried to imagine how Uncle Jasper would appear if he were dressed as his ancestors in bead-and-quill-trimmed buckskin, with his hair long, and scalps on his quiver.

Scalps— Cory thought of the ragged fringe on Ned's quiver strap. Had those really been *scalps*?

STRONG MEDICINE

CORY HAD NO desire to wander far from the cabin; Uncle Jasper need not have worried about that. But as the morning grew late he walked along the cliff behind the cabin out in the bright sun. Thus he discovered a crevice behind the spring. Or rather he fell into it, his boots slipping on the rock as he climbed for a better look at the valley stretching on from the line camp.

A small bush that guarded the entrance to the opening broke under his weight, and his head and shoulders were suddenly in darkness as he lay on his back, kicking in surprise and shock. He threw out his arms and they struck painfully against rock walls, scraping off skin against those rough surfaces. As he fought to sit up his struggles grew wilder, for he felt as if he were caught in a trap.

Then he pushed against earth under him, and sat up, facing out into the open. There was a queer smell here and he rested on something soft that moved under his hip as if it were alive.

He jerked away as far as he could, and felt under him fur and skin. Had he landed on some animal? No, this was more like a bag.

Edging forward, Cory came into the open, bringing his find with him. It was a bag of yellowish-brown skin, strips of fur dangling from it. There were pictures on the bag, like those on the skin on the cabin wall, and some feathers tied to the strips of fur. Though it was shaped as a bag it had no opening, Cory discovered as he turned it around in his hands.

He got to his feet stiffly, the tumble having started all of yesterday's bruises aching again. Bringing the bag with him, he went to the jeep to hunt in the storage compartment for a torch. With this in his hand he returned to the crevice, shining the light into the rock-walled pocket.

Against the back leaned a wooden pole from which hung feathers on bead-sewn strings. And there was a covered basket of woven grasses. Suddenly Cory remembered something Uncle Jasper had said about Black Elk, that there was a place here he visited. Maybe this was it. These things looked new, or at least not as if they had been here for years and years from the real Indian days. Perhaps he had better put everything back just as he had found it. But the top of the basket was squashed in; he must have broken it when he landed.

Cory tried to pull it loose. Inside was a turtle shell broken straight across. And when he picked it up some pebbles fell from it. Nothing was going to fix that again. He would just have to tell Uncle Jasper about it later. But at least it was an accident. And if he put everything back—

He went to the jeep for the skin bag. And he had that strange feeling for an instant as he laid his hand on it that it was alive in some way. Maybe this was just because it had been warmed by the sun. But he was glad to get rid of it; he laid it beside the smashed turtle shell in the basket, then pushed the broken bush as a cork to stopper the crevice.

Here the overflow of the spring basin trickled into a thread of brook. Cory knelt to wash his hands, and saw the flick of a fish tail going downstream. He wiped his palms on the sun-warmed grass and looked at a tall rock. At least that had no breaks in it, and if he climbed to its top he would have a good view of the valley.

From the jeep he got the field glasses he had brought this morning. These in hand, he climbed to the top of the rock.

The stream from the basin joined a larger rivulet and finally a wider flow of water. Grass grew high and there were clumps of tall bushes or low trees. From one of these copses below moved brown animals. Cows? But this was a horse ranch. Cory adjusted the glasses. Out of the distance moved great shaggy bodies burdened with coarse tangles of hair on their shoulders and heads—buffalo!

Unbelieving, Cory watched the big, horned head of the first animal he had focused upon rise, a wisp of grass now hanging from the powerful, bearded jaws as the bull chewed with satisfaction. One, two, three of them, then a smaller one—a calf. But buffalo had been gone from this country for a long time. They were only to be seen in parks or zoos. Could some have hidden out wild in the hills?

Grazing their way slowly, the buffalo reached the water, stood to drink their fill, the water dripping from their throat hair as they raised their heads now and then to look about. Suddenly the big bull moved back a length, faced the way they had come, his head dropping lower, horns ready. The other two adults copied him, setting the calf behind the safe wall of their own bodies.

Cory turned the glasses in the direction the bull faced. He saw movement in the tall grass. Wolf?

Whatever was there was certainly larger than the coyote Uncle Jasper had pointed out to him when they had driven to the ranch from the airport. Yet it looked like that animal.

Then—

Cory blinked.

The coyote-shaped head rose higher than that of any animal. It was not a coyote at all but a mask worn by a man, an animal hide over his head and shoulders. Yet, Cory would have sworn that at first he had seen a very large but real coyote.

As the man in the mask moved forward, Cory saw that he wore not only the furred hide about his head and shoulders but that below he had on the fringed buckskins of a history-book Indian.

He did not carry a gun or even bow and arrows as Uncle Jasper and Ned used. Instead, in one hand, he held a feather-trimmed pole such as Cory had seen in the crevice, the feathers fluttering in the breeze. In the other was a turtle-shell box, just like the broken one, mounted on a handle, and this he shook back and forth. He was not walking directly forwards, but taking quick, short steps, two forward, one back, in a kind of dance.

The uneasiness Cory had felt in the crevice returned. He had a strange, frightening feeling that though the man in the mask had no field glasses, though he had not even looked towards Cory huddled on the sun-warmed rock, he knew the boy watched him and for that he was angry.

Was—was this Black Elk? But Uncle Jasper, Mr. Baynes, they had both said Black Elk was an old man. Somehow Cory did not think the masked dancer was old; he moved too quickly, too easily, though of course Cory could not see his face.

Now the boy could hear a low murmur of sound, and a sharp click-click. Cory wanted to slide down the rock, put it between him and the dancer. Yet at that moment he could not move; his arms and legs would not obey his frightened mind.

The feathered pole in the dancer's hand began to swing back and forth and Cory watched it, even though he did not want to. His fear grew stronger. Back and forth, back and forth—now that murmur of sound was louder and he thought he could almost distinguish words, though he could not understand them. And he must—not! That much he was now sure of.

He fought against what seemed to keep his hands holding the glasses to his eyes. He must not watch that swinging pole—With a jerk Cory managed to drop the glasses. He sat there in the strong heat of the sun, cold and gasping, as if he had just crawled out of the chilled water of a mountain stream where he had come near to drowning.

Now when he dared to look again, the buffalo were only brown lumps. And he could not see the coyote-masked dancer at all. With a choked cry of relief, Cory slid down on the opposite side of the rock, glad to have that as an additional wall between him and the valley, and ran for the jeep.

Once more he climbed into its seat, his fingers curling around the steering wheel, shivering all through his body. But this—this was real! Slowly he began to feel warm inside again, and he relaxed.

Cory did not know how long he sat there. But the sun was high and hot on his head, and he was hungry when he finally roused himself to reach into the back and get his lunch box. In his mind he had gone over and over what he had seen, or thought he had seen. Buffalo—three big ones and a calf, and then the man in the coyote mask dancing. He was sure, almost, that he had seen it all. Yet, was any of it real?

There was only one way to prove it—go down there and look. Even if they had all gone by now, they would have left tracks. But—could he?

Cory's head turned slowly from right to left, once more that chill crept up his spine. It was all very peaceful—ordinary—right here. He had unwrapped one of the big meat sandwiches and sat with it as yet untasted in his hand. If he did not go down there— right now—he never could.

And if he did not, then he would have this to remember—that Cory Alder was a coward. What he would not quite admit to himself yesterday after the horse had thrown him, what he had felt in the dark of the night when he heard all those strange sounds, was very plain. Cory Alder was a coward—a boy Uncle Jasper would be ashamed to have around. And what about Dad—Dad who had two medals for bravery— what would he think if he knew what Cory felt right now? Afraid of a horse, of the dark, of animals, of the country?

Dad would be on his way downhill right now. He would look for tracks. He would even stand right up to face a buffalo, or that dancer with his feather-strung pole and his coyote mask. That is what Dad—or Uncle Jasper—would do.

Cory dropped the sandwich on the seat and crawled stiffly out of the jeep. His lower lip was caught between his teeth, his hands balled into fists. He began deliberately to walk back towards the rock, but he did not take the field glasses this time. No, he would not sit far off and look through those, he was going—down there!

His walk became a run as he knew that he must hurry before he lost the will to go and would have to return to the jeep. He ran with his head down, his eyes on the ground, with the small brook from the spring to guide him to the larger stream.

He was past the rock now, and the taller grass whipped against his legs. All the time he listened for that sound that the dancer made. But what he heard was just the distant call of some bird.

Cory dodged about a tall bush and nearly fell as his toe caught against a root. He managed to keep on his feet. But that taught him caution and he slowed, made himself look around. Somehow, even though he was now away from the jeep, which had seemed the only anchor in a suddenly threatening world, he felt better. The sun was bright as well as hot and the quiet promised that perhaps the dancer was gone.

He came out between two bushes on the stream bank and knew that chance rather than any plan of his had brought him out just across the water from the point where the buffalo had drunk. The water looked shallow. It was so clear he could see a fish below. And there were some stones in it standing dry-topped to offer a bridge.

Cory sat down and pulled off boots and socks, wadding the socks into the boots. Gripping those in one hand, he jumped to the first of the stones. Water lapped up a little over his toes, so cold he gasped. But the next stone and the next were wholly dry. Then he was on the other side.

There was a clay bank with tracks cutting it. He did not wait to put on his boots, but padded on, stepping gingerly as sharp bits of gravel made him hop, to look at those tracks. They had been made by hoofs, he was sure, though he was no tracker. And not too long ago. But he could not have told whether a buffalo or a steer had cut them.

Cory sat down on a weathered log to put on his boots again. He took a long time, but at last he could stall no longer. There had been hoofed animals here, but would he find any traces of the masked dancer if he looked farther?

He did not want to. But he got to his feet, made himself face in that direction, take one step, then another—

The grass was so tall—Cory halted. That grass was waving, and not because of any wind. Something was moving through it towards the river, towards him! He took a step backward and his feet slipped in the clay. As he had fallen before into that crevice beside the spring, so now he went down into the river, the flood of cold water splashing up and about him as he sat in it waistdeep just below the bank.

For a long moment he was shocked into just sitting there. Then a sound from the bank brought his attention back to the hoof-scarred rise. Yellow-brown head with sharply pricked ears, yellow eyes fast upon him, a muzzle open to show a tongue lolling from between fanged jaws—

Cory yelled. He could not have bitten back that cry. He threw himself away from the bank and from what stood there, flopping back into the river, somehow getting to his feet and splashing on, to put the width of the water between him and that animal.

He fought his way up the opposite bank and ran, not daring to look behind to see if that thing followed. It was no masked dancer; his glance, hurried as it had been, told him that. A wolf—a coyote—a huge four-footed hunter had stood looking down at him. The worst his imagination had pictured for him now seemed to have come alive.

Cory's breath whistled in gasps as he took the rise

into the narrow end of the valley where the cabin stood. The phone in the cabin—what had Uncle Jasper said—that someone would come if he called?

Water squelched in his boots, and he found that the unaccustomed high heels made it hard to balance as he fought his way up the slope. He grabbed at bushes, even at large tufts of grass, to pull himself ahead. Then he rounded the rock from which he had used the glasses, saw the cabin and the jeep ahead, and threw himself at the promised safety of both with all the strength he had left.

But as he brought up with force against the side of the jeep, he heard the nicker of a horse. He turned his head to look wildly at the corral— Uncle Jasper—Ned— somebody—

There was a horse standing there right enough. The vividly marked spots of an Appaloosa were half hidden by a brilliant Navajo blanket, draped over the saddle instead of under it. The horse was not tied, but stood with dangling reins.

Cory, panting, turned his head farther. The rider of the horse rested on the beaten earth of the cabin porch. In spite of the heat of the day, he had another brightly coloured blanket folded cloakwise about his shoulders. He was sitting cross-legged and there were moccasins on his feet, the sun glinting on their beading, fringed buckskin leggings showing above them.

The dancer?

But when Cory looked beyond the clothing to the man's face, he lost any certainty. He had never seen such an old man before. The dark skin covering the prominent bones was seamed with great ridges of wrinkles, the chin jutting out in a sharp curve that matched the heavy rise of the big nose above.

Hair, grey and long, had been reinforced with bits of furred skin into braids that hung forward on the blanketed chest, each braid ending in a beaded tassel of yellowish fur. On the deeply wrinkled face were dabs of yellow-white—could it be paint?—that stood out sharply against the weathered skin.

The eyes, which were so hidden among the wrinkles that Cory could not really see them, seemed to be turned on him. And under that regard Cory tried to pull himself together, a hot flood of shame, worse than any he had known before, flushing through him. He stood away from the jeep very conscious not only of the way he had burst into the clearing but also of his drenched clothing.

But the old man on the porch said nothing, made no move. He must see Cory, but it was as if Cory had to make any first advance. Very hesitatingly the boy moved forward. This must be Black Elk, but what was Cory to do or say now? For want of any guide, Cory finally spoke first.

"I am Cory Alder. Uncle Jasper—he said to phone for the jeep, for Black Elk. You are Black Elk, sir?"

The old man did not reply and Cory stopped. He would have to walk around him to get into the cabin and phone. And supposing this was not Black Elk? How could he be sure if the old man would not answer?

"Please," to Cory his voice sounded very weak and unsure, "are—are you Black Elk?" It was almost, he decided, like trying to talk to Colonel Means. Only somehow this old Indian was even harder to face than Colonel Means, who had once come home with Dad.

"Black Elk—yes."

Relief flooded through Cory at that answer. So he *had* understood! Why, then, all Cory had to do was call for the jeep, and maybe he could ride back with Black Elk and whoever drove it to the ranch, leaving a note for Uncle Jasper. That would work out all right. And he would not have to stay here any longer.

"I'll call the jeep from the Bar Plume." Confidence returned and Cory started on, but a hand of brown, wrinkled skin drawn tightly over bones came from under the blanket and gestured him back.

"No. I stay here. Eat—drink—"

"Yes—yes, sir." Cory looked to the seat of the jeep where he had left his lunch—how long ago?

There were crumbs and smears on the seat, but no sandwiches. And ants were thick about a blob of spilled jelly. Had Black Elk helped himself? No, there was a piece of ragged bread on the ground between the jeep and the nearest tree, as if the food thief had been frightened off, perhaps by the coming of the Indian.

Cory remembered the cupboard in the cabin; perhaps there was something there. At least he knew how to make coffee and fry bacon, if he could find coffee and bacon somewhere inside. He made a careful detour about the visitor, who did not move either head or body, and entered the cabin.

To his relief there was food in the cupboard. He chose quickly: tinned corn, bacon, a tin of peaches, some coffee in a sack. Not much, but maybe enough. He returned to the open, to build up the fire and turn out bacon in the skillet he had earlier washed by the spring. He could not tell whether Black Elk was watching his every move; the old man might just have gone to sleep. But at last Cory was so intent upon his cooking that he was startled when a shadow did fall across the stone where he had set out plates, and he looked up to see the blanketed figure.

Perhaps once Black Elk had been as tall as Uncle Jasper, now he was bent forward and the blanket fell about him in heavy folds, hiding most of his body. Cory, wiping the back of his hand across his sweaty forehead, wondered how the old Indian could wrap up so in this heat. His own clothes were almost dry now, though they felt uncomfortably wrinkled. And his wet boots pinched his feet.

He hurried to pour out a tin cup of coffee and offer it to Black Elk. Once more that skeleton hand appeared, to accept the cup.

"It's pretty hot," Cory warned. But if Black Elk

understood him, it did not matter, for the old man gulped it down in two long sucks, then held the cup out for more.

He drank the pot dry while Cory sizzled the bacon, added drained corn to the fat, and piled the result on their plates. Then he ate, not greedily, but steadily, not only the contents of the plate Cory gave him but reached out and took Cory's portion also, while Cory was busy making more coffee.

Then Black Elk finished by cleaning up the whole tin of peaches. Cory, licking his lips and more aware than ever of his own hunger, gathered the empty plates together and stood up, to head for the cabin and the phone.

"No jeep now." The old man, who had not spoken during the meal, leaned forward to face the fire now dying back into ashes. The forefront of his blanket fell open and Cory saw what must have been hidden there earlier. Held in his hands, almost as if it were a living animal that must be restrained from escape, was something Cory had seen before—the bundle of skin he had put back into the broken basket in the crevice.

He did not know whether Black Elk heard his small gasp as he recognized it. But he was sure that the other was watching him intently for some purpose.

"Medicine." The old man's voice was thin and high. "Strong medicine." He waited as if for some comment from Cory, and minutes dragged on while Cory felt more and more uncomfortable.

"I fell," he said at last in a rush of words "I slipped and fell. I didn't know that was in the hole, and I didn't mean to break the basket—or do anything wrong!" This was like watching the masked dancer all over again, Cory thought. And he was afraid again—just as much as he had been before.

"You held it—this medicine!"

He thought that was meant as a question and he answered, "Yes, I didn't mean to do anything wrong, sir! I fell, and then it was under me. I—I brought it out in the light, just to see what it was. But then I took it right back again and put it in the basket—honest, I did."

"You touched. Very wrong. Now must be made clean again."

Black Elk held the bag against his chest with his right hand. The left disappeared inside the shield of blanket, to emerge with the fingers tightened into a fist—a fist which was first shaken and then opened over the fire. He must have thrown something into the midst of the coals, Cory thought, for there was a puff of smoke that shot up and then became a column.

"You"—Black Elk looked to Cory—"touched. Now you make clean. Take medicine bag, hold it in smoke, hold tight. You do wrong; now you do right."

It was an order Cory could not disobey. He came reluctantly to Black Elk, accepted the bundle, edged forward until he could hold it into the full stream of the smoke. It broke and eddied about the bundle, floating around Cory's head. He smelled a strange scent, tried to jerk his head one way or another to rid it from his eyes and nostrils. But he could not, and the smoke grew thicker and thicker until he could see nothing at all but its billows.

WAR PARTY CAPTIVE

CORY BLINKED, AND blinked again. There was still smoke before him, but it no longer filled his nose or smarted his half-blinded eyes. This vapour rose in a straight column to the sky—a signal column.

And he had something very important to do. His

hands moved and a thick branch of pine cut across that column, purposefully breaking it.

His hands!

But those were not hands holding the branch, those were paws—with claws and a coarse brown fur covering them! And his body— He was no longer standing on his two feet; he was squatting back on rounded haunches, his hind feet big paws with webs between the toes. Over all his body was thick fur.

Frightened, he tried to screw his head around farther to see over his shoulder. There was a broad, flat tail lying in the dust behind, balancing him as he stood, or rather crouched, before the fire. It had no fur, but was scaled instead.

Cory dropped the branch of pine, put his paw-hands to his face—to touch great teeth in an animal's jaw.

"What—"

He had said that, but the sound in his own ears was a kind of chirp. And he was alone—no Black Elk, or cabin, or jeep, or corral, or horse. Even the valley was not the same. He was up among some rocks with a small pocket of fire before him that was again sending its unbroken thread of smoke into the sky. What had happened to him, and to the world he had known?

Cory dropped down, to plant his forefeet against a rock. Suddenly he felt so frightened he was weak, unable to move. He shut his eyes, keeping them so with all his strength. Now, when he looked again everything would be all right—he would be safely back at the campfire. He was afraid to open his eyes, to take the chance that this was no dream but somehow real. But it could not be! It just could not be!

At last he counted, to fifty, to one hundred, to one hundred and fifty, telling himself each time that when he reached the last number he would look. At two hundred he fought his fear to the point where he could open his eyes.

There was the same rock before him, and the two

furred paws resting against it. If this was a dream it still continued. A scream was in Cory's throat, but the sound he uttered was not a boy's cry; it was a guttural animal noise.

Bracing himself back on those forepaws, he tried to look about him once more for some clue as to what had happened. Staring down at his plump body, he noticed for the first time that there were things that did not belong to an animal. He was wearing a band of skin that crossed from one shoulder to under the opposite foreleg. It was covered with small, overlapping scales that glittered in the sun, and it supported a kind of box made from a pair of shells fitted together. In addition, from the outer edge of the shell container dangled short strings of colourful seeds.

By the fire was a pile of pieces of wood, all showing marks, not of an axe, but of having been gnawed to the proper length. And by them was a spear with a wooden haft and a point of bone, sharp and dangerous looking.

That, too, was ornamented below its head with some small shells threaded on bits of grass or reed. When Cory reached for it, he discovered it was just the right length and shape for his paw to grasp easily. It must be a weapon intended for this animal body to use.

But whose body? Not his!

Once more fear churned in him and he wanted to run as he had from the river when the coyote had stood on the bank watching him.

River—water— He must have water! That was safe, a place to hide. Water!

Cory, still holding the spear in his paw, turned away from the signal fire, padding around the pocket among the rocks, hunting an open way through which he could reach the safety of the river. He did not know how he was so sure that it was near him; he was just certain that it was and that he must reach it soon, or a greater danger than any he had yet faced would catch up with him.

He found at last the narrow space that formed a gateway, and scrambled through. He discovered now, somewhat to his surprise, that he did not naturally walk four-footed as his animal body might suggest was the proper way to travel, but that he stumped along on his hind legs, his heavy tail held a little aloft to keep it from dragging, though now and then it thumped against the ground.

Certainly the brush and scattered trees were all much taller than he remembered. Or was it that he was smaller? But he was following a trail in the earth which bore the print of many paws and hoofs which led down the slope.

Water— He could smell it! Cory's shuffle became what was for this new body a high burst of speed. Smell *water*? asked one part of his mind. You cannot *smell* water. You can hear it, see it, taste it, but not smell it. Yes, you smell it, replied this new body firmly.

The trail led to water and seeing that before him, Cory's new body took command, plunging him forward in a dive. Then he was swimming effortlessly under the surface with more speed and ease than he had known in travel ashore. The feeling of danger was easing. He broke surface again and climbed out where a small side eddy of stream formed a pool in a hollow, the surface of which was troubled only by the skating progress of water insects and the occasional bubble blowing of some underwater dweller.

The pool provided a mirror for Cory to see himself.

"Beaver!" Again the word emerged as only a chitter of noise, which he understood. He leaned closer, straining to see, to know that this was indeed what he had become.

Beaver, yes, but Cory's zoo-remembered image did not quite match the reflection in the water. Gauging his size by the trees and the rocks, while he was smaller than the boy Cory Alder, he was still about twice the size of the beavers he had seen at the zoo. And in addition to the skin strip with the shell box, he wore several strings of small shells and coloured seeds fastened around his thick neck, while on top of his head was a net of them anchored by his small ears. His eyes were ringed with circles of yellow, undoubtedly paint—though why had that not washed off in the water?

He laid down the spear, which he had carried without being really aware of it all through his swim across the river. Using his claws as wedges, Cory pried open the shell case. There was charred moss inside, and from it the smell of burning, around a small coal. He snapped the shell shut again. So he was a beaver, but one who was armed with a spear, carried fire, and wore paint and strings of beads. How—and why?

The Old People! The story Uncle Jasper had told— about the animal people and the Changer. Animals who had held the world before the white man or even the Indian—who had lived in tribes, gone on the warpath, hunted, and—

Somehow the thought of hunting brought with it an instant feeling of hunger. Cory remembered the lunch he had not so much as tasted, the plates of hot food, both of which had been cleaned up by Black Elk. What did beavers eat? Wood, or bark, or something of the sort? He looked around him, wondering what thing growing along the pool side might be best, and thought that he would have to let this new body decide for him, just as it had when it brought him down to the river.

It pointed him now to a low-hanging willow, and shortly Cory was relishing bark his strong front teeth stripped from the branches. He ate well and heavily, intent for a moment on the filling of his too empty stomach. And it was not until he was finished that he began to think again.

What had happened to him, he could not guess, unless he was dreaming. If so, this dream was not only longer than any he could remember, but far more real. He could not recall any dream in which he had eaten until comfortably full, or gone swimming and actually felt the touch of water. Now, though, the fright that had sent him running to the river was fading. What he felt was more curiosity as to what was going to happen next.

Absent-mindedly he kicked some remaining shreds of willow bark into the pool and looked around him. The need to explore was part of his curiosity. He would travel by river, instead of clumsily waddling on land. It only remained to decide which way, up or down.

Perhaps it was a desire to make his travel as easy as possible that sent him finally down. But he soon discovered that the waterway was not lonely. It had its own population, and he watched the life he met there carefully.

Fish wriggled about, and there were birds that skimmed above the water or waded out to hunt frogs. There was no sign of any animal, until he came to an untidy mass of dead twigs and the like wedged against a hole under the water line of a clay bank.

"Muskrat!" Cory could not have told how he knew this, but know it he did. The lodge in the clay bank was deserted, however, more so than if deserted by chance. His lips wrinkled back from his chisel teeth as he tracked a scenting of the story to be read there. Death—and something else—

MINK!

His beaver paw closed tightly about the haft of his spear.

Mink and danger . . . but not recently. . . . The war party that had raided here had been long gone—at least two suns, maybe three dark times. Without realizing how or why, Cory's thoughts began to follow another path. And then, it was almost as if he had opened a door—or perhaps it would be better to say the cover of a book—so that he could read—not much, but enough to warn him.

Mink warriors raiding upriver. And a beaver scout—that was he—questing down. Not in advance of a war party—no. Rather to seek out a new village site because a shaking of far hills had opened a path in the earth to swallow up the pond that had held their lodges for a long time.

Mink—one mink he, Cory-Yellow Shell could grapple with—could gain battle honours perhaps just by touching without danger to himself. But a war party of them—that brought the need to go softly and avoid notice. And he had been in the open, swimming as one of the finned ones with no need to fear except from the long-legged walkers.

He raised his head well out of the water, shadowed by the mass of bedding that had been cast forth from the muskrat den. Some of that had been clawed over by the mink; their scent was all through the top layer. And the strong musk of the lodge's rightful owner did not hide it completely. Now Yellow Shell listened and a distant cawing made him tense, very still.

The Changer! Or rather one of his crow scouts. The beaver did not so much as twitch a whisker until he heard a second call, farther from the river and to the north. When he took to the water again, it was with all of Yellow Shell's skill and not Cory's blundering. Yet Cory's wondering, his fear, his need for knowledge was still there, sharing the beaver's memory.

Yellow Shell worked his way along the riverbank, using every bit of cover. Twice more he scented mink. And then another and more pleasing and friendly odour—otter. There was a slick mud slide down the bank and to that the otter scent clung, though over it the mink taint was strong as if the enemy had nosed up and down that clay surface for some time.

Half buried in the mud at the edge of the water, Yellow Shell nosed out a broken necklet of shell beads. There was a spot of blood on its stringing thong. So the mink had counted coup, killed or taken a prisoner here. He climbed out on the bank and went scouting.

One otter, he decided. Perhaps young. And the minks had lain in ambush beside the slide. They had rolled in sage to cover their scent. He finally found the scuffed marks of battle, two more splashes of blood, and followed that trail back to the water's edge. They had taken a prisoner, then.

Again Yellow Shell snarled silently. Slinking mink! He dug the butt of his spear into the soft earth of the bank with a quick thrust. By now the otter was dead, or had better be. The mink had evil ways of dealing with captives.

This was no beaver affair. Only mink was enemy all along the river, for long ago beaver and otter had smoked a pipe in a lodge they had both had a share in building and made peace, which had thereafter lain between their tribes. They were no menace to each other, though both were water peoples. For the beaver liked roots and bark, the otter hunted meat. And sometimes it chanced that they camped together and had gift givings and song dances.

Cory stirred. How did *he* know all this—what otter smelled like, or mink? And those scraps of memory about things that seemed to have happened to Yellow Shell before he became Cory, or Cory him? This was the strangest dream—

He turned his spear around in his forepaws. Maybe if he went upriver again, right back to the place where the fire had been—he could wake up in the right world, stop being Yellow Shell, be Cory Alder again.

Then a shadow swept overhead, making a dark blot first on the bank and then on the water. Again, for the third time, that chilling fear gripped Cory. He screwed up his head, which was never meant to rise at such an angle from a beaver's shoulders. A big bird—black— coasting along—crow!

And with that recognition his fear grew stronger. He was no longer the beaver Yellow Shell with powers of scent, hearing, sight. He was Cory in a strange body and in a frightening world.

And he was Cory just long enough to be betrayed.

Out of nowhere—for he still watched the crow wheel over the river—fell a rope of twisted hide. It looped about his chest, jerked tight enough in an instant to pin his forelegs to his body, and dragged him back from the water towards which he made an instinctive start. The force of the pull overbalanced him so that he toppled on to his back, scraping across the ground, striking the slick clay of the otter slide, up which he was drawn, still on his back.

Before he could gain his feet at the top or make use of his quite formidable beaver weapons of teeth and tail, he was struck on the head, and both sun and day vanished completely in the bursting pain of that blow.

It was with Cory's bewilderment that he awoke again. His head ached and there was a sticky mass on one cheek that his exploring tongue was able to touch enough to tell him it was blood. His forepaws were tightly roped to his sides, his tail fastened with a loop the other end of which was about his throat, so should he try to use his tail as a weapon the movement would strangle him.

He lay on his side under a bush and there was the stink of mink all around. Also, there *was* a mink curled up not too far away, a plaster of fresh mud and leaves across foreleg and shoulder. The warrior faced away from Cory. He had several thongs around his neck, now pushed to one side by the plaster on his wounds, and those were strung with rows of teeth, among which—Yellow Shell brought his front teeth together with an angry click—were several from beaver jaws.

The mink kept shifting position and it was plain that his wound pained him. Now and then he turned his head a fraction and snapped at the edge of the plaster, as if that gesture gave him some relief from his misery.

By the wounded guard's side Yellow Shell counted at least five war pouches, three of them fashioned from turtle shells. This told him that he faced an experienced and wily adversary. For those who counted turtles among their dead enemies were the best of their tribe. As well as he could, Cory tested the strength of the cords that held him. They were of hide, braided, and there was no breaking them. Now his fate would depend upon chance and upon the very important point of how far they were from the mink village. For it was apparent he was not to be killed at once, but saved for some unpleasant later purpose.

It must be, beaver knowledge told Cory, close to evening. And night was mink time, even as it was normally for beaver also. If they went on by water in the dark, his captors might have to loosen him to do his own swimming, and that would give him a chance—

But he was not to be so lucky. The wounded mink suddenly raised a war club, a knot of stone tied to a shaft, the ball having several ugly, stained projections. Perhaps that was what had brought Yellow Shell down. Crouching, the mink listened.

Beaver ears caught what human ones might have missed, a stealthy slithering sound. Then three more minks appeared, as if they had risen out of the earth.

They did not speak to the guard, but half ran to their prisoner, the last one dragging something. What that was, Cory discovered a moment later when he was roughly rolled on to a surface made of saplings still studded with branch stubs. To this his captors made him fast by vicious pulls of rope. Then he was dragged along and dropped, to land with punishing force at the bottom of a cut, again to be pulled along.

Here the drag did not catch so easily, but slipped better behind the two minks pulling it, giving the two coming from the rear little need to lend a push. The sled balanced on the top of another incline, was given a vigorous shove by the minks behind, and plunged on down what could only be the otter slide, to land in the stream.

Travel by land became travel by water, and the push and pull of the mink party appeared to be taking them along at a swift pace. Cory, unable to move, the painful up-twist of his tail beginning to hurt almost as much as the pounding in his head, felt himself borne along on the surface of the river, eyes up to the night sky. Though he could not turn his head far enough to see, he was aware, shortly after, that the first party of his captors had been joined by more of their kind. He wondered if they had an otter in their paws also.

A moon rose soon and its clear light on the water did not appear to alarm the mink party. If they had any enemies in this part of the country, they did not fear them. Perhaps they claimed this whole section of the river as their territory and had long since cleared it of any who might dare to challenge their rights to it as a hunting ground.

Cory was carried on under a place where long willow branches hung close to the water, reminding him that it had been some time since he had eaten. A long— How long *would* this dream last?

Dreams—what had someone said way back at the beginning of this day which had ended so strangely— about dreams? Something about someone who dreamed? Oh, Uncle Jasper— He had said it about Black Elk. Medicine dreams— Didn't the Indians believe that a boy must go out and stay without eating until he dreamed about an animal who was to be his guardian for the rest of his life?

Black Elk—and that bag he had said was strong medicine. The bag and the fire and the smoke, and Black Elk making him hold the bag into that smoke. This dream had started with that—as if it were a medicine dream. Only Cory was not an Indian boy, and these minks were certainly not guardian spirits out to help him. What he had of Yellow Shell's thoughts told him that they were exactly the opposite.

And what about the black crows and the Changer, who could change animals, and tried to make man, or had made him, and who was finally beaten because he could not change or move mountains?

The ache in Cory's head grew worse. The brightness of the moon hurt eyes that could not turn away. He shut his eyes and tried to put all his strength into a desire to awaken from this dream. Only—how could you *make* yourself wake up? Usually a bad dream broke of itself and you found yourself lying in bed, with your heart pounding, your hands wet, and your stomach twisted inside you. He felt as scared and unhappy now, only he was not truly Cory but a beaver and a prisoner.

The raft on which he was tied continued to whirl along, and he felt rather than saw that two of the minks swam, one on either side, giving it a steer now and then, keeping it steadily moving. Then he heard a distant roaring and beaver mind told Cory that it was bad water—a fall, or perhaps a rapid.

His raft turned in the water as the minks shoved it out of the current. A little while later it was in the shallows, bumping around stones while the war party scraped, tugged, and lifted at it.

"You"—a mink head twisted on a slender neck was held closer to his so that he could see the glinting merciless eyes of the warrior—"walk. Stop—we kill!"

The sounds were so gabbled and ill-pronounced, it was as if the mink spoke beaver but not well. But Cory felt the freedom as the cords that had held him to the raft were loosened. Then they boosted him to his hind feet, leaving his tail still fast to his neck. The line about his forepaws was grasped at the other end by the mink who had hissed the order and warning, and a sharp pull at that started him on.

It was a rough way, and twice Cory lost footing and fell among the rocks. Both times he was prodded to his feet again by his own spear in the hands of a mink; once he was beaten on the haunches by a club. Somehow he got on, but he no longer tried to think. There was only one thing left, to watch the barely marked trail and try to keep walking it.

They had left the riverbank, but the roar from that direction grew louder. Then they turned again, and Cory, struggling to keep alert, believed that they now paralleled the water. Twice they rested, not for his sake, he knew, but because two of their own company had leaf-and-mud-plastered wounds.

The second time they pulled off the trail, Cory saw that he was not the only captive. Ahead was another wounded, bound with ropes—an otter. But that animal seemed hardly able to move, and two of the minks pushed and shoved him along.

At last they returned to the riverbank and the minks brought up the raft to which Cory was once more tied. By that time he was so tired that when afloat on the water he fell into a state that was neither sleep nor a faint, but a combination of the two.

BROKEN CLAW

A SERIES OF wild screams and cries rang in Cory's ears. He tried to move, but he could only turn his aching head a little. And when he did that, he looked into the narrowed eyes of a mink swimming beside the raft to which he was bound. Those eyes were ringed with red paint, which added to the hatred in them.

Beyond the mink's head, he caught sight of a river-bank where there were more of the furred warriors slipping now into the water to head for the incoming party. Then the raft under Cory gave a leap forward as if hurled by the push of a new energy, bumped out of the water up and down over gravel and stones, adding to the aches in his helpless body.

So, still bound, Cory was towed on into the mink village. It was no small gathering place, as his Yellow Shell memories told him that of a beaver clan would be, but a number of lodges.

Sheets of bark had been set up on end, bound together with saplings, all made into cone shapes, not unlike the tepees Cory remembered from the pictures of the Plains Indian villages of his human past. To the front of most of these were planted poles from which dangled strips of fur, strings of teeth, a feather or two. No two of them were alike and perhaps, Cory thought, they stood for the owner of that particular lodge.

But he was not given time to see much, for a flood of minks—squaws and cubs—closed about him. Armed with sticks, clods of hard earth, they struck at him, all the time keeping up that horrible squalling until he

47

was deafened as well as bruised by their blows. But finally the minks of the war party, perhaps fearing that their captive might be too battered before they were ready to deal with him themselves, closed about the raft and drove off his tormentors.

They came to one lodge set a little apart from the rest and sharp teeth cut speedily through those cords that kept Cory on the raft, though not his other bonds. He was pushed, rolled inside, and then his captors dropped the door flap and left him in the dusk of the interior. For it was not yet dawn and very little light entered. Perhaps not for Cory eyes, but for Yellow Shell it was enough to see that he was not alone, that another securely tied captive lay on the other side of the bark-walled shelter.

It was the otter, his fur bedabbled with blood, his eyes closed. So limp and unmoving was he that Cory thought perhaps he was already dead; though why the minks would leave him here in this way if that were so, he could not tell.

Yellow Shell memories frightened Cory; he tried to push them out of his mind. He did not *want* to think about what minks did to their captives; he wanted to get out of here, and as soon as he could. But all his pulling and twisting only made those hide ropes cut the more sharply into his flesh, sawing through fur to the skin underneath. He had been very skilfully roped; nowhere was he able to bend his head to get at the cords with teeth that could sever them in a moment, for the loop tying head to tail stopped that. To try was to choke himself.

After several moments of such struggling Cory lay still, looking about him in the tepee to see what might be put to his use.

Around the sides, except near the door opening, dried grass lay in heaps as if to serve as beds. But the two prisoners had been dumped well away from them. Some pouches or bags of skin hung from the upper walls, far above the reach of his head. There was nothing else—except the otter.

Cory turned his head as far as he could, to watch the other captive. He saw that the otter's eyes were now open, and fixed on him. The otter's mouth opened and clicked shut twice. The Yellow Shell part of Cory's mind knew that signal.

"Enemy—danger—"

Such a warning was not needed. Both the boy and beaver parts of him knew that minks and danger went together. But the otter was not yet finished.

As with Yellow Shell, the otter's forepaws had been lashed tightly to his sides, but he could still flex his claws and those nearest the beaver now moved—in a pattern Yellow Shell also knew. Finger talk was always used by tribes that were friendly but whose speech was too different for either to mouth.

"Mink and—other—"

Other? What did the otter mean by that?

Yellow Shell's paws had been so tightly tied they were numb; he could hardly flex them now. But he was able to give a small sideways jerk expressing the wish to know more.

"Crows come—with orders—" The otter strained, but the effort was so great that he lay panting and visibly weakened when he was done.

Crows? Cory thought back to the river where he had watched the crow and so had been easily captured by the minks. The Changer? A crow, or crows, carrying orders to the minks? The Yellow Shell part of him was almost as frightened as Cory had been when he first found himself in this strange world.

And, Yellow Shell's fears warned, if this was some matter of the Changer, it was worse than just minks at war. There was even more need to get out of here. Cory looked at the otter again. That animal lay with his eyes closed, as if the energy he had used to sign-talk had completely exhausted him.

Cory tried to squirm towards the otter, but the way his neck and tail were tied prevented him, and his faint hope of having the otter chew through his bonds was gone. If the otter could roll to him—? But he could see that a second loop about the otter's hind feet, lashed to a stake driven into the ground, kept him tight.

The beaver's struggles had brought his shoulder against a lump on the ground, painful under him. He twisted his head as far as he could and saw that the lump was his own shell box. He wondered why his captors had not taken it from him. Then he remembered what it held—the small coal. He had fire, if the coal were still alive. And there was the dried grass of the beds. Could he make use of that? No, said the beaver part of him. But Cory's mind said yes to a desperate plan. Only how could he open the box with his forepaws tied?

Cory began to wriggle, trying to lift his shoulder under which the box lay. For long minutes he was unsuccessful; the box moved when he did, remaining stubbornly under his body in spite of all his efforts. Then it gave a little as he tried harder to raise his weight from it. He did not know how long he would have before the minks might burst in. And every time that fearful thought made him move faster, the box seemed to slide back farther under him.

At last it was free of his shoulder. Now began the strain to turn his head far enough, to roll so that he could reach the box with his chisel teeth. Again that seemed impossible, and so hard was the task that he could hardly believe he had succeeded when he did get the shell between his teeth and held it there firmly. Now to reach the bedding at his left. To move caused agony in his tail, or else choked his throat. He could only do it by inches. But at last, with the shell box between his teeth, his nose nudged against the heap of dried grass.

What he was going to do now was very dangerous. To loose fire where he and the otter lay so helpless— But Cory's desperation was greater now than Yellow Shell's shrinking, and he would not allow himself to think of anything beyond trying to do this.

Those strong teeth, meant for the felling of trees, crunched together on the shell, and he smelled the smouldering coal inside. Then, with all the force he could muster, Cory spat the broken box and the coal in it on to the grass, saw it catch with a small spurt of flame. He gave an upward heave of his hind feet and tail so that the flame could eat at the cord holding so cruelly tight. He could smell singed fur now, feel the burn, had to fight Yellow Shell's fear to hold steady. For while animals knew fire and used it gingerly, they still had greater fear than man of what was to him the most ancient of tools.

Just when he was sure he could no longer stand it, the pressure on his throat was gone and he was able to bend his head forward far enough that his teeth severed in one snap the ties about his forelegs, gave another to cut those holding his hind legs.

He felt the pain of returning circulation, stumbled when he wanted to move fast and easily. But he staggered to the otter, bit through the cord that fastened him to the stake. Then, dragging the smaller animal with him, Yellow Shell reached the rear of the bark tepee. He thrust the bedding away from the wall with great sweeps of his paws, throwing it towards the entrance to make a wall of fire between them and any mink trying to enter.

Luckily the grass did not burn as fast as Yellow Shell had feared it might, but rather smouldered, puffing out smoke that made him cough, hurt his eyes. But teeth and claws were now at work on the rear wall. And before his determined assault the wall split.

What would he find awaiting them outside? Armed minks? But this time he would be ready for them, with punishing tail, claws, teeth. And he, Yellow Shell, was the better of any mink or two or three. Even if they jumped him as a pack, he could give a good account of himself before they pulled him down.

It was the smoke whirling out with them that masked their going. And the nature of the minks was an aid. For they were of the same nature as beaver and otter; they had to be close to water. And, though the village was on the bank of the river, it was still too far from water to suit the furred raiders. As Yellow Shell made for the stream, with the otter he dragged along, he fell into a water-filled cut running between the tepees. How that had been made was a wonder to him as he plunged beneath its surface and struck out in the direction of the river. The minks did not try to control the flow of water as did his own people. They built no dams, or any ditches down which to float the wood, bark, and leaves that meant houses and food. But this cut was the saving of Yellow Shell and the otter now.

The passage was narrow for a beaver, having been made for the lighter bulk of minks. For, while the warriors who had captured him were much larger than any mink of Cory's world, they were still less in size than Yellow Shell. In spite of the tight fit at some parts of the way, the beaver won through and brought the otter with him.

He surfaced to breathe at last, turned the otter around to brace the smaller animal's wounded body against the wall of the ditch while he cut through his bonds. The otter's eyes were open and he was now aware of what went on about him. As soon as the cords fell away, he brought up his forepaws in an urgent signing:

"To the river!"

Yellow Shell needed no urging. He went under water, keeping one forepaw on the otter until that animal gave an impatient wriggle and freed himself from the beaver's hold, passed him, and slid from the ditch into deeper waters.

Able as the beaver and otter were in the river, yet the minks, too, could follow them there with deadly ease. They would be more wary of attacking either animal in the water, however, where both were more at home than the minks. Yellow Shell noted that while the otter moved quickly at first, he soon lagged, and it was plain that his wounds, which began to bleed again, were slowing him down. One was on the back of his head, proving, Yellow Shell thought, that he must have been struck with a club. The other hurt was on his forepaw, which the otter kept tucked against his chest as if to shield it from even the slight pressure of the water.

A discolouration from blood tinged the water, leaving a trail to be followed by the enemy. Yellow Shell dared not take the time to scout behind to see whether the minks had yet discovered their escape. He could only hope to be on their way in what small time they had left before the hunt started behind. With any luck the burning tepee could hide their escape for a time.

Cory did not try to struggle now against Yellow Shell for command of the beaver body. He only wished that this too real dream would end and he could wake up once more into the world he had always known.

Upstream or down? The beaver hesitated. It was the otter who waved with his undamaged paw that they should go up, against the current. Yet, would that not be the very way the minks would expect them to go—back towards where they had been captured?

The otter signed again, impatiently. "Upstream— hurry—" He tried to follow his own directions, but swam clumsily, and an eddy pushed him towards the bank. Yellow Shell easily caught up with him, shouldered him on, across the river, towards the opposite bank. Along that they made a slow and painful way, keeping under water where they could, pausing for rests where roots or brush overhung the water to give them a screening shadow.

For it was day now and a bright one, with sunlight glittering on the surface of the river, insects buzzing above, water life to be seen. Yellow Shell ate willow bark within his reach without leaving the stream. The otter clawed aside water-washed rocks with his good paw, aided by the beaver when he understood what his companion wished, and snapped up the crawfish hiding under such roofing.

He was, the otter signed, named Broken Claw; he looked ruefully at his torn paw as he gestured that. And he was of the Marsh Spring tribe, though this was the season when his people split into family groups and went off for the summer hunting. Since he had no squaw or cubs in his lodge as yet, he had been on a solitary exploring trip when he had been trapped by the minks. And at that, Broken Claw showed shame at his failure to be alert. He had come upon a slide, he told Yellow Shell frankly, and had tried it out. Absorbed in the fun of the swift descent, he had gone up and down more times than he could remember now, the result being that he lost all caution and had at last slid directly into a net trap of the minks.

It was not the minks he feared most, however, but the fact that he must have been spied upon by crows who reported him to the mink raiders.

"The Changer—"

"What does the Changer?" Yellow Shell asked in the beaver language.

"Who knows?" The otter seemed to understand enough of those guttural sounds to sign an answer. Perhaps he understood beaver even if he did not speak it. "But it is bad when the Changer comes. The world may turn over—as it is said that in time it will."

The world may turn over—that touched another and frightening memory for Yellow Shell. There would come a day—all the medicine makers said it, sang it, beat it out on drums when the People came to dance big medicine—that the world *would* turn over, when nothing would be as it now was. And all that was safe and sure would be swept away, and all that was straight would become crooked, all that was light would be dark. And the People would no longer be People, but as slaves.

"As slaves—" Yellow Shell's paws moved in that sign and Broken Claw nodded.

"Already that begins to be. You saw the waterway of the mink village. That was dug by slaves, beavers they took as cubs and made work for them."

"And what becomes of them?" Yellow Shell's teeth snapped, his strong tail moved through the water, sweeping a stand of reeds into a broken mass. "What happens to them after they so work?"

"They go, none know where," Broken Claw answered. "But the crows of the Changer carry many messages to that village."

"If the Changer meddles—" Yellow Shell shivered. Again Broken Claw nodded.

"True." His good forepaw moved in a gesture of agreement. "It is best that our peoples know of this. Mine are scattered, which is evil. We must gather together again, although this is against our custom in the days that are warm. What of yours, Elder Brother?"

"They move village. I am a scout for them."

"It would be better for them not to find new water in this land," replied the otter. "The sooner you say that to your chief, the better it shall be for your people."

"And you?"

"To the lodge of our chief Long Tooth, who stays in a place appointed where our people may gather in time of danger. He will then send messages, signal fires, to draw our people there."

"Yet the minks will be behind us now—"

Broken Claw nodded. "The minks, yes. If they listen indeed to the words of the crows and those who fly scout for them in the sky, then we must both travel with the ever-seeing eyes of the war trail. In the water we need not tie fringes to our feet to wipe out the trail we leave, but they are also of the water and they will know." He looked about where they had eaten, and Yellow Shell saw the foolish way they had behaved in their hunger.

It would be a very stupid mink who would not see the stripped willow, the overturned rocks, and not know that a beaver and an otter had halted here to rest and eat.

The otter signed. "Yes, we have been as cubs untaught, my Brother. Let us hope that this does not lead to evil for us."

At first Yellow Shell thought that some of the traces could be hidden. A moment's study told him that was impossible. All they could do now was to put as much space between them and this breakage as they could.

But while his powerful beaver body had almost recovered from the rough handling given him by the minks, though his head still ached and his exploring paw touched a tender swelling on his skull where the war club had fallen, the otter was less able. And though Broken Claw tried valiantly to swim forward on his own, at last he fell behind. When Yellow Shell realized that and turned back, he found the otter drifting with the current, almost torn away from a feeble claw hold on a river rock.

"Hold this." Yellow Shell took the other's good paw and worked it into a loop of necklace about his own shoulders. The otter seemed almost unconscious again. He watched what the beaver did, but did not say anything as the other made preparations to tow him.

Putting out a forepaw to hold the otter's head so they could look at each other, Yellow Shell signed slowly.

"Where—is—your—chief's lodge?"

The otter blinked. Then his injured paw moved in a short answer.

"Stream—into—river—big stone—painted rock—follow stream."

"How far?" Yellow Shell next asked.

But Broken Claw's eyes were closed, his head lay limply back against the paw that the beaver used to brace it higher.

So, with the weight of the otter now dragging against him, Yellow Shell paddled along the bank, still keeping to the protection he could find there against sighting from the sky. He found that swimming with Broken Claw as a helpless burden tired him quickly, and he had to rest more and more often, pulling the otter out of the stream under some overhang so he could breathe. Twice he cowered in such a hiding place as the shadow of wings fell on the water. Once he could not be sure whether that was a crow or some hunting hawk. But the second time he caught sight of black feathers and was sure.

For a long time after that the beaver crouched over the otter in a cup beneath the overhang of bank, not sure as to what to do. If they had been seen by that dark flyer, then the minks would speedily know where they were. But if they had not, and took to the water now, then the crow might be perched in some tree, watching for them to do just that.

But the minks did not arrive and he guessed he was only wasting precious time in hiding. Yellow Shell ventured out again, still towing Broken Claw. At their next rest, however, the otter roused and seemed better able to understand what they were doing. He agreed that he was weak enough to need Yellow Shell's support. But he urged that the beaver help him now up on to the bank between two rocks.

From that point he made a long and searching study of the river. Yellow Shell did the same, but could see nothing except insects, birds—including two of the long-legged stalkers of fish and frogs. And no black-winged ones. Then below them, a little ahead, the grass parted and a deer trotted out to dip muzzle and drink.

Broken Claw crowded against him, using contact of shoulder against shoulder to catch Yellow Shell's full attention. With his good forepaw the otter pointed upstream and to the opposite bank.

The beaver recognized what must be the landmark Broken Claw had told him about. But to reach it they must cross the open river, in full sight of the sky. And on the other side he could sight no bushes or overhang of bank to cover them.

A cawing flattened both animals between the rocks where they sheltered. Crows—two of them—wheeled above the river. One of the long-legged waders called in return, challengingly, in warning against such an invasion of his territory. Of him the crows seemed to take little heed.

Then the wader took to the air and Yellow Shell did not mistake the purpose with which the larger bird set out to clear away the black-feathered invaders. They fled south, the wader winging after them. But in the time when they had been above the river, had they sighted the two among the rocks? There was no answer to that, no answer but again to make such speed as they could, to get away from that point before the crows could report them, or manage to elude the wader and return.

BEARERS OF THE PIPE

TAKING ADVANTAGE OF the retreat of the crows, they crossed the river at once and rounded the base of rock that divided the other stream. Yellow Shell halted in surprise as he glanced up at that pillar of stone. For set as a deep hollow in it, well above the level he could reach, even standing as erect as he could, was the mark of a paw. It was not, he saw upon closer inspection, the track of a beaver, or of an otter, or a mink. Yet it was clearly an animal sign, left imprinted in the rock as if that had been soft mud.

Around it were traces of old paint, and some of that rubbed into the hollow of the track itself, indicating that it was indeed mighty medicine and such a mark as would be a boundary to a territory.

"The paw—" He swam on to catch up with Broken Claw, who was heartened to the point of travelling by himself again.

"Mark of a Great One, a River Spirit," Broken Claw answered. "It is big medicine. If it were otter, or beaver, then the mink could not pass it. But it is for all water dwellers and so cannot aid us now."

The stream, once they were beyond where it split about the pillar to enter the river, was what Yellow Shell would have selected himself if he could have picked their means of escaping observation.

For it was a narrow slit, much overgrown with bank-rooted bushes and willows. Also it was plain that this was otter country. They passed otter marks on other stones, not pressed into rock, of course, as the river spirit had set its print, but left in pictures of coloured clay above the high-water mark. These were not of his tribe and Yellow Shell could not read them. But twice Broken Claw paused by some that looked fresher than the rest and at the second such he signed:

"Many return to the tribe. There is danger—already they may know that."

Again his spirit was more willing than his body. And, although he had seemed strong enough to enter the stream on his own and swim therein for some distance unaided, he began to slip back, and finally clung to a water-logged tree root until Yellow Shell once more lent his strength to the smaller animal.

The stream entered a marsh where there were tall reeds and a series of pools. Some farther off were scum-rimmed and evil-smelling. But along the brook the water was clear and Yellow Shell felt safer than he had since his capture by the mink war party. Then the otter pulled against him and the beaver came to a halt where the stream widened to a pool, a pool half-dammed by a fallen tree and some drift caught against that.

At the otter's gesture, Yellow Shell aided Broken Claw to the top of the tree log. Pressing his wounded paw tightly against him, he used the other to beat upon a stub of branch still protruding from the log. It gave off a sound that carried out over the marsh. And then Broken Claw paused, for from far in the water-soaked land before them came a pound-pound of answer.

"They know we come," he signed, slipping from the tree to the water. And Yellow Shell saw marks on the log that said that this signal must have been so given many times before.

So they continued, and the beaver was not surprised when an otter suddenly arrived out of a reed bed, to look at them and then be gone again, giving Yellow Shell only a swift glimpse of a painted muzzle, a head-dress of feathers and reed beads. But there had been a spear in the otter's paw and he had carried it as one well used to that weapon.

At last they came out into what must have been the centre of the swamplands, a core of dry land rising as a mounded island, well protected from discovery by the watery world around it. Earth, which was mostly clay in which were many stones, had been heaped and plastered together, perhaps on a foundation of rocks. On this were the lodges of brush, also plastered with mud that had hardened in the sun. The lodges were smooth-walled and wholly above water, but with something of the same look as beaver lodges—as if they might have been copied from the larger homes of Yellow Shell's people.

There were otters awaiting their coming, the warriors in front, squaws and cubs behind, but only a handful compared to the number of lodges. If, as Broken Claw had believed, the tribe was assembling again, not all had yet reached this swamp stronghold.

Coup poles stood in front of about five of the lodges, their battle honours dangling—not strings of teeth as in the mink village, but here bunches of feathers or coloured reed chains. The waiting warriors made way for Yellow Shell to climb up on the island. For these last few feet Broken Claw shook free of his aid and walked alone. Two of the foremost of those who waited hurried to his side, giving him support and leading the way through the almost deserted village to a middle lodge that was larger than all the rest, its clayed sides covered with pictures, and coloured marks drawn in the soft substance and then filled in with black or red paint. As on the rocks some of the marks were weathered, but others stood out brightly as if only recently done. And Yellow Shell knew these for tribe and clan records, so this must be the lodge of not only a tribal chief but one who also held the rank of medicine singer.

A warrior pushed past Yellow Shell to loop aside a curtain knotted out of dried reeds. And the beaver paused, allowing Broken Claw and his two supporters to enter first. There was a small fire in the centre of the lodge and from it came a thin blue thread of sweet-smelling smoke. To one side squatted a very old otter, his muzzle white. As his head swung towards them, Yellow Shell saw that he had but one eye, that the other side of his head was scarred with long rips that were well healed. Before him was a small ceremonial drum made of a tortoise shell with the skin of a salmon dried tight across it. On this the old otter beat softly from time to time, using only the tips of his claws, making a kind of muttering sound, as if something deep within the earth whispered to him.

Facing him across the fire was a younger otter, but one who had yet more years than Broken Claw, or even the warriors who had brought their wounded comrade into the lodge. He was the largest otter Yellow Shell had ever seen, fully as big as a beaver. Around the eyes he had painted black circles, and on his chest hung a disk of bone carved and painted—the badge of a high chief. Thrown over one foreleg and trailing out behind him on the floor was a square of reeds woven together, with feathers tucked into that weaving to make a bright robe of ceremony.

There was a burst of otter talk that Yellow Shell could not understand, and then the chief reached under the edge of his feather-patterned robe and brought out a long-stemmed pipe. With two claws he skilfully brought up a burning twig from the fire and set it to the bowl. With a puff of fragrant smoke rising from it, he raised the pipe towards the roof of the lodge, the sky, pointing it again down to the earth, then east, north, west, and south, finally offering the stem to Yellow Shell.

Taking it carefully into his forepaws the beaver drew a deep breath and then puffed it out slowly, turning his head meanwhile in the same order as the otter chief had presented the pipe.

As he passed the pipe to the left and so into the waiting paws of the old otter who had stopped his drumming to take it, the chief spoke in swift sign language.

"The lodge of Long Tooth is our brother's. The food and drink that are Long Tooth's are our brother's. Let him rest, and eat and drink, for the trail behind him has been long and hard."

The reed matting that was the door of the lodge was drawn aside as a squaw almost as old in years as the drumming otter brought in a bowl, which she set before Yellow Shell, and with it a gourd that now served as a cup and from which came the scent of some stewed herb. The beaver dipped into the bowl and found fresh alder bark, sweet to the taste, and with it bulbs of water plants.

As he ate and drank, courteously ignored by all, Long Tooth talked to Broken Claw. Then the young otter was taken away by his friends and the chief sat staring into the fire, the pipe now resting under his paws but no longer burning. The ancient otter went back to the low drum of claw on stretched fish skin.

But at length he said something to the chief, and Long Tooth nodded slowly. The old otter reached into the edge of the fireplace and scooped up a pawful of grey-white ash. He scattered this over the surface of the drum, adding a second pawful to the first, so that there was now a thin coating of powder on the drum top.

Then, putting one paw on either side of the drum as if to hold it very steady, he threw back his head, so that his grey muzzle pointed almost straight up to the roof over their heads, and began a chant in a voice that was thin, and old, and quavery. But, as the old one continued, Yellow Shell, listening, knew he was hearing a medicine singer of power, one who could control great forces. And so the beaver sat quietly, not daring to stir.

Cory felt that he had been shut tight into a small part of Yellow Shell from which there was no escape, and this was frightening. Yet with that fear was the feeling that something important was going to begin right before his eyes, and he gazed as intently upon the medicine otter as the rest.

The quavering chant died away and the otter was visibly taking a deep breath, drawing air into his lungs as if about to plunge into water and stay thereunder for a long time. Holding that breath, he leaned forward over the powdered drum. And then he blew his lungs empty, straight over the ashes.

Cory expected to see them all disappear, but they did not. What was left made a pattern, an outline, crude but recognizable, of a bird. And Yellow Shell knew that symbol, for it was one common with all the river tribes, and perhaps with the plains tribes also, though with them the river peoples had little dealings. It was the mark of the Eagle, or rather of the Eagle's totem—the Thunderbird.

The old otter and Long Tooth looked at each other and nodded, then the otter chief signed to Yellow Shell:

"This is a bad thing now on the river. The minks move here and there. They raid, they take prisoners, and always the crows fly before them, spying. Other things move—perhaps they are spirits—but who sees spirits except when he dreams a medicine dream? It is not wise of such as we to look upon the ways of spirits. Yet the Changer is both spirit and of the People, and what he does can mean much evil to all of us. We do not know what he would do. They say that in some time to come he will turn the world over and the People will be slaves if they live. Though slaves to what—we do not know—perhaps evil spirits. Perhaps the time comes now when he would do this. And we cannot tell if there are any we can call upon who are strong enough to stand against the Changer.

"But of all of us the Eagle lives the highest, the closest to the Sky World. And if he will aid us, then—"

What he might have added he did not, for in that moment the old otter uttered a sharp cry. Yellow Shell had been so intent upon what the chief was saying that he had been staring straight at the otter's paws, with only a glance now and then to the face of the speaker. Now he jerked his head around and saw that the old otter was eyeing him, Yellow Shell, with a searching stare.

Now the old one's withered paws moved, shakily, with less ease than Long Tooth's, but with the same authority the chief used.

"The mark of the Changer is on you! You are and you are not beaver!"

Cory did not know the proper signs, but his beaver paws moved in an answer that was the truth.

"I am and I am not beaver. But," he hastened to add, "I am no enemy."

"No," the medicine otter agreed. "You are a friend to us, to all who stand against the Changer. Listen well: if you would find what will defeat him, perhaps make you not beaver-with-another but wholly beaver, wholly other again, then go you to Eagle. For this is a spirit thing and Eagle knows more than we do—or else Raven does, Raven who shakes the dance rattle, who sings the songs-of-great-power for Eagle's tribe."

Cory was eager. "You mean Eagle—he can change me back?"

But the medicine otter shook his head. "Only the Changer can change. But there are ways, powers, to make him—sometimes. And from Raven, who is Eagle's holder of spirit power, you can perhaps discover that which shall be as a spear for the hunting of the Changer."

"We send a pipe to Eagle." Long Tooth spoke now,

his claws glistening in the firelight as his paws moved. "If you wish, you may go with the pipe bearers. You have earned much from us by bringing Broken Claw back, but this is a spirit way and so not to be followed unless one has great need. If your need seems so to you, go with our pipe people into the mountains."

"Yes." Yellow Shell's answer was swift and sure.

"Rest you then," the old otter signed. "For the way is long and hard. And it will take time for the pipe medicine. There are songs and dances of power to be used to make it ready."

The beaver was shown a heap of bedding grass at the back of the chief's own lodge for his resting and he curled upon that thankfully, so tired that he could no longer hold his eyes open. But even as he fell asleep he wondered that one already asleep in his own world—as Cory must be—could also sleep in a dream.

Sound awoke him and for a moment or two he could not remember where he lay, but the dried, sweet-smelling grass was under his nose and as he moved, it rustled, making him remember. So the dream was not yet finished and he was still the beaver Yellow Shell; he did not need to look upon the paws that were his hands, or the fur on his body, to be sure of such knowledge.

He turned his head. The old otter had put aside his drum, was squatting hunched forward closer to the fire. Before him lay a bundle tied with thongs that were threaded with beads of cut reeds and seeds, and bits of feathers. Over this the otter held his forepaws and Yellow Shell knew that this was a medicine bag and one his hosts considered to possess great power. The medicine otter was now drawing forth a portion of that power into himself. He chanted, but in a very low voice, using otter language that Yellow Shell did not understand.

With the tips of his claws, the old otter placed

around and over that decorated bundle a covering of skin, pieced-together fish skin, and over that a second cover of woven grasses that was painted brightly and heavily with power signs of coloured clay. Then he arose, with a stiffness that suggested that he moved only with great pain and effort, to place the bundle back in a sling hung from the roof of the lodge.

Squatting again, he sat nursing his forepaws against his chest, singing in a low mumble. But he did not wait for long. The curtain door of the lodge was pulled aside and Long Tooth entered, carrying a long bundle painted half red, half black, so that Yellow Shell knew that this, too, was a medicine thing.

Two more otters followed him. Both wore ceremonial paint and each carried a coup stick that he planted in the earth before the fire on the side where he took his place.

The chief laid his bundle on a decorated mat and untied the first of its wrappings while they all chanted. There was a second wrapping painted blue and yellow, a third that was all red, and a last that was white, each unfastened with great care by Long Tooth. Then there was exposed a pipe.

It was a pipe of great ceremony and a very old one, Yellow Shell knew. Its bowl was of red stone that had been chipped with patience into the shape of an otter's head. The long stem was decorated with reed and seed beads and painted black.

Once the pipe was free of its wrappings, the old otter leaned forward to hold his wrinkled paws over it, giving to it the power he had drawn from the medicine bundle. Cory noticed that he did not touch it, nor did any of the other otters, including Long Tooth.

After some minutes the chief again covered the pipe with the wrappings that had lain loosely under it, one, two, three, four. When the last and outer one was securely tied, he slipped the whole into a case of oiled fish skin, a final protection for the bundle. And to this was made fast a carrying strap so that he who bore it would still have his paws free.

Yellow Shell sat up on his haunches and the grass of the bedding rustled, sounding very loud in the lodge where the chanting had now ceased. The old otter had wavered back to the bedding on his side of the fire and curled up there, as if what he had just done had exhausted his store of energy.

"A sun and a sleep have you lain here, Brother," Long Tooth signed to Yellow Shell. "It is now well with you?"

"It is well, Elder Brother. My feet are ready for the trail."

"And the trail awaits the feet of those who bear the pipe," returned Long Tooth. "Fill yourself from our bowls, drink from our stores, Brother, then go with our good will."

He must have made some sign or sound Yellow Shell did not catch, for the old squaw came in once more with a steaming bowl of drink, a newly culled bunch of water roots and alder bark. And Yellow Shell ate all he could stuff into him, knowing that it was well to depart for a long journey with a full stomach, for that was an honour to the owner of the lodge.

They set out at sunset. The bearers of the pipe were the same two warriors who had shared the ceremony in the chief's lodge, only now their paint-of-ceremony had been washed from their fur and they went with only the sacred white colour circling their eyes, and in bars on their foreheads. Nor did they carry spears, for even the mink must respect an enemy who travels with a medicine pipe, lest raising paw against such travellers bring the wrath of all spirits down upon the attacker.

Yellow Shell had gone to the lodge where Broken Claw lay, his wounds packed with healing mud and herbs. The younger warrior, his eyes dulled by fever, had looked longingly at the beaver.

"I—would—I could—take—this trail—" he signed with slow sweeps of his uninjured paw.

"So it is known, Brother," Yellow Shell returned. "But if this time you do not take this path, there shall come another when you do. Know this, between you and me there is blood shared and we are as two cublings of the same litter."

"It—is—so—and together we shall take the war trail against the mink!"

Yellow Shell nodded. "The spirits willing it, yes, my Brother!"

The three left the swamp by a waterway so over-hung with reed growth and brush that Yellow Shell guessed it had been purposely hidden. In places it was almost too narrow for the bulk of his beaver body, but the otters skimmed through it with ease.

Before dawn they were well away from the swamp and had travelled overland, which was the greater danger, through a woodland, heading for a stream that would lead them into the mountains. His companions seemed so sure of the trail that Yellow Shell followed them without question. But they went most cautiously through the forest, sharing out, before they ventured into that dangerous territory, the contents of a fish-skin packet that had sage and other strong-smelling herbs worked into oil, to hide their scent from the flesh eaters.

Once they crouched together in a well-rotted hollow log to watch the passing of a cougar. He was snarling softly to himself as he went, and, though Yellow Shell did not understand the great cat's language, he could guess that he must have missed an early kill and was now intent on making up for that loss. Whether it was the pungent stuff with which they had smeared their bodies, or else the spirit power of the pipe, the green eyes did not turn in their direction. And death on four padded feet went back and away from where they sat in hiding.

Yellow Shell found it difficult to keep up with the otters, though they all dropped to four feet. They ran with an up-and-down humping movement whereas he waddled at an awkward shuffle. And he knew that he was delaying them, though they did not say so.

The forest lay at an upward slope and they were heading in the direction of the heights. Cory found himself listening for the call of a crow even as he had during their flight upriver. At the same time he was aware of seeing more about him than he had ever noted before. To look at things through Yellow Shell's eyes was indeed to see a new world. The range of sight was closer to ground level, in spite of the beaver's large size, but at that range it was much keener than a boy's.

They did not pause to eat; in fact they carried no food with them. Yellow Shell had only the spear Broken Claw had urged him to take, shorter and lighter than the one he had carried before, but with a very sharp point. And his two companions bore only the pipe in its wrappings, taking it in turn with its carrying strap about a shoulder.

At dawn they came out of the forest on the edge of a drop, below which, in a canyon, ran the stream for which they searched. They made their way cautiously down the rise and all three splashed thankfully into the water, the otters straight away turning over stones in search of their favourite food—crawfish.

Yellow Shell was not so lucky. There was only rocky ground here, no willows, alders, or water plants. He would have to hope that up ahead he could find something to fill his now empty stomach. Or else, if the otters were planning to rest through the daylight hours and travel at night, perhaps he could prospect downstream and return.

He signed a question and the elder of the two pipe bearers replied. There was a deep overhang ahead, if the bank had not collapsed. Scouts from the village had long ago established a resting place. As for casting downstream for food—perhaps Yellow Shell was wise to try. There was little ahead in the way of growing things and he might go hungry if he could not share their hunting.

The overhang was still there and the otters whisked into its shadow, pulling up out of the water to roll in a patch of sand, drying their fur. Yellow Shell looked around carefully, setting landmarks in his mind. Then he plunged back into the water, this time swimming with the current downstream.

For a space there was nothing but rocky walls, and his hunger grew the keener because he began to fear that he would have to go so far hunting food that he would have a long trail back. At last he came out from between those walls as one would emerge from a gate and was in a small meadow-like pocket.

A deer snorted and stamped, startled, as he edged along the bank towards a good stand of willows. But there were no wings in the early-morning sky and he crept from the water to examine the possibilities of breakfast.

In the end he was able to eat his fill, though the food was not as good as that of the otter village. And, having done that, he set about cutting such lengths of bark as would not be too difficult to carry, tying them together with twists of tough root. With the otters' warning in mind, he thought he would do better to carry food with him up the mountain, and he hoped what he could take would be enough.

EAGLES' BARGAIN

WHEN THEY STARTED on at nightfall, Yellow Shell found his bundle of bark something of a hindrance, but as they went farther and farther upstream, twice having to leave the water and climb around small falls, he was glad he had it. For this was a waste land of rocks and stones and they seldom saw a green thing. When such did grow, it was only a wind-twisted cedar or the like, which was no fit food for him.

Dawn found them high in the mountains, with one giant peak standing directly before them. The otters, Red Head and Stone Foot, signed that that was their goal and they would have to leave the stream ahead and climb that wall in order to reach the eagles' tribal grounds.

Again they found shelter for the day. Yellow Shell ate sparingly of his food and saw that the otters were following his example, hunting for crawfish, but killing more than they ate and tying those up in thongs of fish skin.

"Where is Eagles' lodge?" Yellow Shell signed when they returned with this food supply.

"Up and up and up—" Red Head replied.

"There is a trail?"

"Part way only, then we light a signal fire," it was Stone Foot's turn to answer. "If Eagle will speak with us, he will send warriors to carry us the rest of the way."

Yellow Shell did not like the sound of that. Earth or water safely under one was one thing. To be borne aloft by an eagle who might or possibly might not be friendly was something very different. But he did not say so to the otters, since it appeared that this was a usual way of visiting Eagle as far as they were concerned—*if* they had visited Eagle before. But if not his present companions, someone from their village must have done so, or they would not be so sure of how one got there.

Again he slept. But this time he kept waking, and raising his head to listen. For what he was not sure but there was a strange feeling that the three in their hollow between the two rocks were not the only ones on this mountain side, that other animals—or things— moved here with some purpose. Though for all his watching, and straining his ears to hear what he might not see, the beaver sighted or heard nothing, save a flying insect or two, and once a bird that skimmed low over the water but did not wear the black feathers of a crow.

If he was uneasy, so were the otters. Twice Stone Foot, the elder of the two, slipped away from their crevice into the water, but not to swim on the surface with a flick of the hind foot to send him driving ahead as was the usual way of his clan. He vanished, diving under with such power as to hide him from sight almost instantly. Once he cast downstream, once up, and both times he returned after a short space, to sign that the river was empty of any travellers save fish. They kept watch on the land, but did not venture from the stream side, napping in turns, one always on guard.

With the coming of dusk they left the water and began the last portion of their climb. Land travel was a slower progress and both the otters and the beaver disliked it. Already clouds were blacking out what remained of the grey sky of evening, seeming to pull in a tight circle about the top of the very mountain that they climbed. Rain came, hard and fast, so that at times they had to take cover as best they could from its fury, waiting until it slackened somewhat so they could cross some open space that provided only poor footing.

Flashes of lightning were bright and sharp.

Thunderbird. His Yellow Shell mind drew a strange picture for Cory, that of a giant bird perching on a mountain top or winging in the clouds above such a peak, shooting those blasts of fire from the fanning of its sky-wide wings.

By one such flash he saw that Stone Foot had smeared mud across his muzzle below his eyes, and knew that the otter had taken the precaution of claiming protection from the earth. Now Yellow Shell reached out a paw to scrabble in a small hollow by a boulder and pick up enough of the wet soil to do the same. For earth stood fast against the force of wind and water, and to claim such protection now was what they must do on this mountain side where wind and water attacked.

At length Red Head, who was in the lead, turned from a last straining climb, and they came out of the full force of the wind into a cup-like space between two rocks, part wall of the mountain, and a spur that shot out from the cliff. Water ran in a steady stream through it, but as the otters hunkered down in that hollow, Yellow Shell followed their example.

The dark was so thick that even his night sight could no longer serve him. Now the lightning ceased and the storm began to slacken so that the runnel of water became a trickle and then vanished altogether.

Yellow Shell had held his paws in that water as long as it had lasted. Never meant for such hard scrambling over a rough surface, the pads on all four feet were scraped and raw, but the water eased their hurt. He expected the otters to move on, but they did not, and he began to think that perhaps this was the place where they must signal for aid into the eagle country.

For what was left of the night they dozed together in the cup, sheltered from the last of the storm, the bundles of food at their feet, the well-wrapped pipe safe between the two otters. But at dawn they stirred, and Red Head brought out just such a shell fire-box as Cory had used to escape the minks.

Yellow Shell looked about for wood. If Red Head wanted a fire they must have some. But he could see nothing save a withered-looking bush fighting hard to keep its hold against a steep slope.

"That?" he signed and pointed to the bush.

The otter nodded and Yellow Shell pulled out of the cup to go and cut it down, an action he did not find easy since he feared starting a landslide that would take him with it. But sharp teeth served him well, and by patient effort he brought down a tree. In two trips he had dragged back all that piece of growth to the crevice.

Just as Red Head had produced the coal of fire to start new flames, so did Stone Foot now bring out a small pouch that he held waiting in his paw. The first otter took bits of branch and twig that Yellow Shell had sheared off for him and with care built them into a tripod of small sticks. It was small, too small, Yellow Shell thought, to last long, but he could see nothing else usable anywhere about them now.

As the clear light of morning finally touched the mountain side where they had sheltered, Red Head set the coal within his tepee of brush and they saw a curl of smoke wreath up. When the first small flame broke, Stone Foot reached out to quickly dump the contents of his pouch on it. The answer was more smoke, but much thicker and darker, with a reddish colour such as Yellow Shell had not seen before. Channelled by the rock walls of the crack in which they crouched, it rose up and up. There was no wind this morning, as if the storm last night had exhausted it. And the smoke trail was like a ladder climbing into the Sky Country itself.

Yellow Shell remembered old tales of such ladders

and how the people of under earth had sometimes climbed them, not many finding the Sky Country ready to welcome such intruders. Did—did the otters believe that Eagle indeed lived in the spirit world?

But his companions were making no effort to climb any such way. Instead they ate from their packets of crawfish, and with appetite, as if they saw no use now in saving any of the food for later. Following their example, Yellow Shell finished the last of his now dried bark and withered leaves, and found it not nearly enough to satisfy him.

The beaver had no way of measuring time in a world where watches and clocks were unknown. But the fire burned itself out swiftly, he thought. Yet the otters made no move to travel on, or to hunt more wood for another fire. Having eaten all their food bag, they settled back again, one on either side of the pipe, as if to sleep away the day.

Yellow Shell was restless, wanting either to go on ahead or to retreat down the mountain. Retreat was possible, for he could see their back trail plainly by day. But the otters were right, there was no way ahead. They were faced with a sheer wall of cliff, as if some giant had at one time used his knife to cut down a slice through the mountain.

A shadow swept across the cliff. Yellow Shell froze as that winged shape wheeled about, circling, and, at each circle, dropping closer to where the fire had burned.

Out of the crevice came the otters. Still guarding the pipe between their bodies, they reared up on their haunches to their greatest height. The beaver did the same. The winged shape came in, to perch upon a pinnacle of the spur that had been part of their shelter.

It was an eagle and, though Cory had never seen one so close, he thought that this one was far larger than the birds of his own world—as were also the beaver shape he wore, and the otters.

It turned its head from side to side, looking down at them, its wings still a little out-held and not folded against its large body. Yellow Shell had to tilt back against the firm support of his tail to see it well. But now he noted that around its feet it wore bindings of coloured stuff from which hung seeds and the rattles cut from snake tails.

The eagle carried no weapon. Cory thought that it did not need any but its own cruel-looking beak and talons. And now it opened that beak in a screaming cry that shook Cory, and that was echoed faintly from the heights behind from which it had come.

The otters used sign language, taking turns. And Yellow Shell read those signs. They were few and plain, telling that they were pipe bearers, on a peaceful mission from tribe to tribe.

Done with that, they sat waiting. The eagle appeared to be thinking, as if he were making sure of the truth of their statement. Then once more he gave that piercing scream. And, in answer, more shadows flapped down along the face of the cliff, two of his fellows.

The otters, as if this were the most natural welcome in the world, moved out into the open, and Stone Foot made the cord of the pipe package tight to him, using as an additional lashing the thong that had tied his crawfish bag.

Then the eagle who had first arrived pounced, and Stone Foot was borne aloft. A second came for Red Head, and the third black shadow was over Yellow Shell. In that moment the beaver wanted to flee. This was too like real dangers he had known in the past, not an act of any friendship. But he had no time to move. The claws closed about him and with a lurch, sickening to him, he was in the air, the safety of the ground left rapidly below.

There was a vast difference, Cory speedily discovered, between travelling in a comfortable plane in his own world, and by eagle power in this. He closed his eyes, trying not to feel the tight and painful grip of the claws, the rush of wind, only hoping that the journey would be a very short one.

He was dropped, rather than set down, rolling over in a painful half bounce. Opening his eyes, he struggled to his feet—to face what he was surprised to find lay at the crest of that tall mountain.

Perhaps the tower of rock and earth had been born a volcano, and they were now where the inner flames had burned. For this was a basin sloping from ragged stone edging. There was a lake in the centre around an island of stone outcrops. About the outer edge of that body of water were trees and grass, a miniature woodland.

It was the island that Yellow Shell now faced, having been dropped with the otters on a sand bar reaching into the water. And the island was the eagle village, their bushes of nests mounted on blocks, broken pillars, and mounds of stone.

It was a crowded village, and there was much coming and going—mostly of parent birds supplying their screaming young with food. But those eagles who had brought the animals did not stop at the village, rather they spiralled up to the wall of the basin valley where Yellow Shell caught sight of other birds moving in and out of fissures in the rock.

The otters were busied with the pipe bundle, loosing its wrappings, pulling off the fish-skin protective covering. But still the four layers of painted skins were about it as they laid it carefully out on the sand, the bowl end pointing towards them, the stem to the village on the lake.

However it was not from the village that the chief came. He wheeled from the crags, circling down to perch on a big rock by the shore, one worn in hollows where his huge feet rested, as if generations of eagles had sat there before him.

Tufts of weasel fur, for the weasel is a valiant war-

rior and skilful in evading pursuit, hung from a necklace about his throat, together with the tooth of a
cougar, as if he had indeed counted coup on that
mightiest of four-footed enemies. He was a proud and
fierce chief, more for leadership on the warpath than
on the peace trail, Yellow Shell thought, as he looked
upon him with awe.

Several lesser eagles settled down on lower rocks.
And every one of them wore coup necklaces laced
with that which told of their past victories. But the last
comer was no eagle.

At first Yellow Shell flinched at the sight of those
dead black wings—a crow? Then he saw that this was
a raven, larger than the crows he had seen scouting
when he fled upriver with Broken Claw.

No coup necklace was about the Raven's throat.
But the rattles of a rock rattler were tied to his legs,
and he carried on a thong a small drum, hardly larger
than Yellow Shell's hind paw. He did not have the
painted circles of red or yellow that marked the eagles
about their eyes. A dab of white, spirit white, made a
vividly plain mark just above the jutting of his beak.

The eagles and the Raven folded their wings as the
otters moved with a slow ceremony to unveil the pipe,
wrapping by wrapping. They worked in silence, nor
was there any sound from the birds who sat in such
quiet that they might have been carved of the very
stone upon which they now perched. Even the noises
from the village lessened and Yellow Shell saw that
there were fewer comings and goings from there. Many
of the parent birds settled down on the nests, all facing
towards the shore and the meeting between the animals and their chief.

At last the pipe was fully exposed and lay in the
sunlight. It seemed to shine, as if the sun put fire to
the red of its bowl. For the first time Stone Foot
spoke, his voice rising and falling in a chant that the
beaver, while he did not understand it, recognized as a

medicine song, and not addressed to the eagles but to some protective spirit.

When he had done, Red Head, moving with care, dropped a pinch of tobacco into the bowl and brought out his shell box with its smouldering tinder. But he did not light the pipe as yet. He waited.

Again a long period, or it seemed long to Cory, of just waiting. Then the eagle chief moved from his rock perch to a lower stone set closer to the otters. From that he stretched forth his leg, his claws closing about the pipe stem. Red Head lit the pipe, and the eagle chief raised it to the sky, pointed it to earth, and then to the four corners of the world, even as Long Tooth had done with that other pipe when he welcomed Yellow Shell to the otter village.

The chief smoked, expelling a puff from his bill, passed the pipe to the Raven. And the Raven in turn gave it to Stone Foot, Stone Foot to Yellow Shell, and then to Red Head. Having blown the last ceremonial curl of smoke, the otter tapped the tobacco ashes from the bowl and laid the pipe back on its wrappings, the stem still pointed arrow straight at the chief.

A great clawed foot rose so that the claws could move in signs.

"I am Storm Cloud of the Swift Ones, the Mighty Wings."

Stone Foot signed in answer. "We are Stone Foot, Red Head, bearers of the pipe. And this is Yellow Shell, who is—"

The Raven hopped down from his stone perch. Among the eagles he had seemed small. Standing thus on the ground to face the beaver, he proved to be almost as large as Yellow Shell. He moved with a lurch and Cory saw that his left foot had lost a claw. But he steadied himself well on it as he signed:

"This is a beaver, yet not a beaver."

"That is true," Yellow Shell spoke for himself.

"You bear a pipe?" The Eagle looked at him. "Do you speak for the beavers?"

"For myself only. The medicine otter said that the Raven had great power, that he could aid me in becoming all beaver, all other once more."

"But this is not a matter of the pipe." The Eagle's sweep of clawed foot was impatient. "It is the matter of the pipe to which Storm Cloud has been summoned. What speak the otters?"

Stone Foot's paws moved deliberately, giving to his signs the dignity of a ceremonial speech in his own tongue.

"There is much trouble along the river. Those who serve the Changer fly and raid. The minks take prisoners for him, and we know not what becomes of them. Our spirit talker has sung and his dreams have been ill ones. We would know what the Swift Flyers, the Mighty Wings, have seen in the land. For even the edges of the Sky Country are theirs and little can be hidden from their strong eyes."

There was another pause before the Eagle made answer. "It is true there is a new coming and going. The Changer's village has moved close to the place of Stone Trees, though the hunting there is poorer. It is as if they must wait there for someone, or something to happen. Spirits walk by night; you may sense their passing. But to know more than that, we must search—and we have left well enough alone."

The Raven bowed his head in a vigorous up and down. "Yes, yes, it is better not to draw the eye of the Changer, lest he be minded of one. But does your spirit talker fear that the time spoken of is near—that the world is about to be turned over?"

Cory saw all the eagles shift uneasily, their heads turn from the Raven to the otters. He could see that the bold question disturbed them.

"There is always that to be feared," Stone Foot returned.

"So. Well, the Thunderbird dwells yonder. We shall burn sweet smoke such as he loves to have blown into his wings, and cry aloud to the wind what we fear. But also, tell your chief," Storm Cloud continued, "that we shall search from the air and learn what we may. None of those who serve the Changer can out-climb or out-fly us, as they shall learn if they match their powers against ours."

Again there was movement among the eagles as they drew themselves tall on their perch rocks with their pride as strong to see as their war shouts would be heard.

"The Swift Flyers, the Mighty Wings, are great ones, undefeated in any battle," signed Stone Foot. "If this they will do, then all along the river shall know that we will be prepared for any war, if war is what they should bring upon us."

Together with Red Head he began to rewrap the medicine pipe, securing each fastening. But the Raven turned his attention now fully on Yellow Shell.

"You have come to Raven," he said. "Raven's ears are open to hear what you would ask."

"It is as I have said—the medicine otter told me that if I would be as I was before the Changer looked upon me, I must come to the Eagle and the Raven."

But the Raven was shaking his head. "I hold the calling of spirits, yes. They are sky spirits, and wind spirits, and a few earth spirits. But the powers of the Changer they cannot break. They can only tell you where to seek an answer, they cannot give it to you."

"And will you ask them for me?"

Storm Cloud's beak clicked together in a sharp sound, drawing Yellow Shell's attention. As the beaver looked to him, he signed:

"To do that requires a mighty singing. Such singing is not done for nothing. We have no old peace with your people, nor have we any friendship or brotherhood with you, Beaver-who-is-not-wholly-a-beaver."

"Friendship is a matter of giving as well as taking." The Yellow Shell part of him made a bolder answer than Cory might have used. "I ask not to be given where I do not give. What would you want of me as a price for such a singing?"

The Raven did not answer; it was as if he believed this a matter of bargaining between Yellow Shell and the chief. He himself was content upon Storm Cloud's decision.

"You are of those who master water," the Eagle said after a long moment's pause. He might have been trying to determine some manner of payment of benefit to his tribe, thought Cory. "This, our lake, is sometimes too full. Rocks tumble from the cliffs and close the stream that empties it, and then there is much hard labour to clear them free. Twice have storms so filled it that lower nests have been washed away. Dig you a way for water to run, one that we may use at such times, and this singing shall be yours."

"I am but one beaver," Yellow Shell countered. "This may be such a task as would need a whole clan to do."

Storm Cloud's bill clicked again, impatiently. "A whole clan does not ask for spirit singing, but you do. Therefore it is your task. And perhaps only you can find a way to use the stream that is, clear it more easily of rocks."

"What I can do, I shall," Yellow Shell promised.

The otters had the pipe recovered, were ready to be gone, and Storm Cloud had already assigned two of his warriors to fly them down the mountain. But Yellow Shell had a few moments to talk with them. He signed a wish that they might find his own people and warn them against marching south into these river lands where trouble was gathering. And this, Red Head agreed, they would do, sending their best scout north. Then the otters were snatched up by the eagles, who seemed to want to rid themselves of their guests as soon as possible, and Yellow Shell was left behind.

Storm Cloud, too, was a-wing, heading back to the crags, and only a young eagle swooped about the beaver. Even as Raven signed, "Split Bill will show you the waterway," the eagle's clutch was hard upon him, and he, too, was borne skyward in a fearsome soaring.

RAVEN'S SING

YELLOW SHELL LOOKED over the terrain when the eagle warrior dropped him at the outlet of the lake. There was a stream that fed through a narrow gap and the beaver could see how a fall of rocks from above would dam it. But this was not a trouble his people had had to face before, for their task was usually the making, not the clearing, of dams.

He swam along the river outlet, nosing at both banks, trying to find some way to deepen the flow of water. But he could not see any method of tunnelling through the stone of the cliffs.

Since the present outlet was so banked with rock, he returned to the lake and began to explore its banks at this end. The eagle who had brought him grew bored and flew away, and Yellow Shell was left alone to face what seemed a hopeless task. But the beaver stubbornly refused to admit defeat.

In the end his forelegs and head suddenly broke through a screen of brush into a hole in the mountain cup. If all the basin had been formed by a volcano in action, then this crack had come at that time, with a later spread of molten rock to roof above it. When

Yellow Shell padded into it, he found not the crevice he had first expected but a channel, which brought him, by a very dark way, out on the open mountain side on the other side of the basin wall.

He went back to the valley of the lake and squatted down at the edge of the water, eating a hearty meal of freshly stripped bark while he studied the bank by that fissure. It was a big job for one beaver working alone, but he could see no other possible way to provide the eagles' lake with an emergency overflow exit. By mid-afternoon he was at work.

The bank of the lake must be undermined, cut through so that there was an open spillway into that crack. He dug with his forepaws until they were as sore as they had been from travel over stone. Rocks had to be loosened and pushed from side to side, then firmly embedded again to make a kind of funnel into the spillway.

He worked through the last of the daylight, keeping on into the night, stopping only now and then for a much needed rest or to eat again from the food about him. Now he had a raw gash in the earth, partly walled in with stones and such pieces of hard saplings as he could pound and wedge in for security. Mud mixed with broken brush was then plastered over that foundation, all to form a channel. The whole thing was the height of his body above the present level of the lake, and at that end he built another wall of small stones, to be easily shifted by the strong claws of the eagles when the need arose.

He was lying with his sore feet in the lapping waters of the lake at the next sunrise, so tired he thought that he could not easily move again. But to the best of his beaver skill he had provided the eagles with the safety they needed. Let the river leading from the lake again be sealed by falling stones and they need only pull out the thin dam corking this outlet, and the flood would pour through the new channel. Of course there was no way of testing it until such a calamity occurred, and Yellow Shell wondered dully if they would demand such proof before they fulfilled their part of the bargain.

There was the whir of wings in the air above him and the eagle who had brought him there, or one enough like him to be his twin, landed on the edge of the restraining dam Yellow Shell had built. He teetered there as he looked down into the channel the beaver had cut and walled.

Yellow Shell was too tired to lift his paws in any language sign. But he nodded, first to the lake and then to the spillway he had made, hoping that the eagle, if he were a messenger, would understand that the task was done.

The bird's sharp eyes shifted from the animal to the cut leading to the dark hole in the basin side. Then his claws formed a series of signs.

"This is a way through the rock?"

Yellow Shell pulled his sore paws from the soothing water to sign back:

"A way through the mountain wall. When the water rises, pull the stones now under you. There will be a new way to drain—"

The eagle bent his head to survey the dam on which he perched, touched his beak to one of the topmost stones as if testing its stability, or else estimating his chance of being able to move it when the need arose. Apparently he was satisfied, for without another sign to Yellow Shell he took wing and was out over the lake in a couple of sweeps, heading, the beaver noted, not for the village on the island but up to the crags where Storm Cloud and his escort of warriors had gone the day before.

Yellow Shell combed at his muddy fur, wincing when his sore paw hurt, but intent on making himself clean if the eagles were to come to inspect his handiwork. Their pride was known to all the tribes, but the beavers were certainly not the least among the People. He wished he had his boxes of paint, his ceremonial beads and belt, that he might make a proper showing. For, looking at his work of the past hours, he thought he could take pride in it.

The eagle who had come to inspect did serve as a messenger, for more mighty wings were visible in the morning air and very shortly Storm Cloud, together with those who must be his subchiefs and leading warriors, settled on the dam. They looked at the dam, at the cut behind it, at the crevice into which the waters would be funnelled when the need arose. Yellow Shell signed to the eagle chief the purpose of each part of the spillway.

Now—would the eagles demand from him a demonstration—one which would mean that he must somehow dam that other river outlet and turn the water into this? At the very thought of such labour, his paws burned and his back ached. But it would appear that Storm Cloud was not so suspicious of the beaver's skill.

The eagle chief himself walked along the now dry funnel, thrust his head and shoulders well into the hole of the crevice. But he did not go all the way through. Perhaps he could see the light at the other end, which was now more visible since Yellow Shell had also cleaned the exit to allow easy passage.

The eagle chief came back to face the beaver.

"It is well," he signed. "You have made what was needed. Therefore we shall now do as we promised."

He must have given some signal that Yellow Shell was not aware of, for one of the waiting warriors suddenly caught the beaver and rose into the air. Yellow Shell closed his eyes against that fear of being so far from the safe ground and hung motionless in his bearer's hold as the wind blew chill about him.

They did not return to the shore across from the village island where he and the otters had been deposited before. Rather they climbed up to the crags from which Storm Cloud had come. Here was a flat shelf on which the beaver was dropped and he sat carefully as close to its middle as he could without his distrust of these heights being visible to his hosts—or so he hoped.

The rock about him was cracked and broken and these holes and crevices seemed to serve the birds as lodges. One such opening faced Yellow Shell now. They were all patterned with drawings to celebrate coups and deeds, not only of the living warriors who now inhabited them but those of their ancestors, for the eagles must have lived here a long, long time. But the lodge of stone that Yellow Shell faced was very different from the others in that its painted border was all of pictures showing strong medicine. And, as Yellow Shell hunched there looking at those, Raven hopped forth from the crack of the doorway. He clapped his wings vigorously and, at his summons, two young eagles came from behind him, one carrying a small drum painted half red, half white, the other a bundle that he put down carefully beside a spot on the rock stained black by many past fires.

The eagle who had brought out the bundle now went to one side, pulling back to the fire site in three or four trips short lengths of well-dried wood that he built up into a tepee shape. This done, he went to perch with the other eagles, except for the one with the drum. There were rocks for their sitting all around the open space. Yellow Shell turned his head from right to left and saw that all the birds had settled down quietly in a ring, though he did not turn his back on Raven to see if they were also behind him.

Now the drummer began to thump with the claws of his right foot, first gently, then with more force, so that it sounded at the beginning as might the mutter of thunder as yet far off, growing stronger and stronger.

Raven took a coal from a firebox, set it to the tepee

of wood, tossing into the flames that followed sub-
stances he took from his bundles.

Smoke came, and it was coloured, first blue, then
red—and there was a mingling of strange odours to be
sniffed. The puffs of smoke did not spread, but rose in
a smooth, straight pillar to the clouds as had the signal
fire of the otters. Yellow Shell, straining back his head
on his thick neck to watch them climb, thought that
this looked more and more like a rope reaching to the
Sky Country—which, here on the mountain top, could
not be too far away.

Was Raven planning to use that to reach the Sky
World and talk there with the spirit peoples?

It would seem not. Once the smoke was thick and
climbing well, Raven fastened dance rattles to his feet,
took up turtle shells filled with pebbles. Then he began to dance about the fire, and as he danced he sang,
though the words he croaked had no meaning for
Yellow Shell.

Tired as he was, the beaver tried to fight sleep; yet
in spite of all his efforts, his head would nod forward
on his chest and his eyes close. Then he would straighten
up with a start, glancing around hurriedly to see if the
eagles or Raven had noticed.

But they were watching only Raven. Finally the
fight became too much for Yellow Shell and there was
a moment when he did not wake again, but went
further into sleep.

And he dreamed, knowing even as he dreamed that
this was a spirit dream and one he must remember
when he awakened.

He was flying high in the sky, not borne so by one
of the eagles so that the dread of falling was ever with
him, but as if he, too, had wings and had worn them
all his life.

Below him stretched all the world as was known to
Yellow Shell. There was the lake from which his clan
had begun their march south. And he saw them now,

recognizing each and every one of them. They had an otter in their midst and were watching that animal's flying forepaws. So Yellow Shell knew that the warning against the south had reached them and they would now turn back, or perhaps east or west, to safety.

And he saw the river, and the swamp marsh of the otter village where warriors now made new spears and squaws were working on a mighty gathering of food, as if they thought that their island home might be under siege.

There, too, was the mink lodge where he and Broken Claw had been held captive, and there he saw the minks lashing beaver slaves, thin, worn, undersized, to work building new canals. And Yellow Shell ground his teeth together in hot anger at the sight.

But all this was not what the spirits wished him to see. He was swept along, rather than flew, to the southeast, with the mountains of the eagles now at his back. So he came to a land that was prairie, changing to desert in places. There was a village and he saw that it was one of the coyotes, and now he knew that what he was to be shown was the stronghold of the Changer.

Down and down he dropped over that village, until he feared that any one of those there would raise head to the sky and see him. But none did, for the spirit dream was his protection. And he came to ground before a skin-walled lodge set a little apart from the rest. On it were pictures of great and strong medicine, so that he feared to put out a paw to raise the flap of the doorway. Yet that he must do, for the need that had brought him there so ordered him.

Thus he came into the lodge and recognized it for one of a great medicine person. But the spirits of his dreams raised his eyes to the centre pole of the lodge and to the bundle hanging there, and he knew that this was what he must have for his own if he would be only Yellow Shell again. But when he reached up his forepaws to seize it, there was a billow of dark and stinking smoke from the place of fire and he leaped back, a leap that took him through the door flap into the open again. Then he found that he could not return, rather he was again soaring into the air, heading away from the coyote town, back to the eagle mountain. And at last he sat in the rock crags, across the smoking fire from Raven, who no longer danced. The drumming had stopped and the drummer was gone, so were the eagles who had watched. It was the beginning of night.

"You know," Raven did not sign that but croaked the words in beaver, which, though harshly accented, were plain enough for Yellow Shell to understand.

"Yes, I know," the beaver returned.

"To that place you must go, and the medicine bundle you must take, then shall you be able to force the Changer to make the wrong once more right. For that bundle is his strength and without it he is but half of what he wants to be."

"A long way," Yellow Shell said. "It will take much time."

"Not too long by wing," Raven replied briskly. "Four feet would make much of it, but we shall do better for you."

"You are kind—"

Raven opened his beak in harsh laughter. "I do not do this for kindness, Beaver. I do it because the Changer and I have old troubles between us. Once we were friends and made medicine together. Then he learned secretly that which he would not share with me, and he walked apart, daring to laugh when I asked that we should do as brothers and have no knowledge held one from the other. Thus, bring the Changer to humbleness and I shall be glad. I would ask you for his medicine, but the spirits have foretold that that must serve another purpose. However, without it he shall suffer and that shall be as I wish it."

He got up and the dance rattles about his feet gave off a faint whisper of sound.

"I cannot ask you into my lodge, Beaver, for there is much there that only I can safely look upon. But you will find shelter in that crevice over there, and food. Rest for a time, and then there shall come one to see you on the first part of your journey."

Yellow Shell crawled out of the wind, which now blew very chill about him, into the opening Raven had pointed to. There he found some bark one of the eagles must have brought from below. It was not what he would have chosen for himself, and it tasted bitter. But he ate it thankfully and curled up to sleep.

Before there was any light a clawed foot shook him awake. It was the young eagle drummer who stood over him. Seeing Yellow Shell's eyes open, he signed swiftly that they must go. He did not give the beaver any time to protest or question, but, as soon as Yellow Shell crawled from the crevice, he seized him, and they were off into the dark clouds and the wind. For the third time that flight was a frightening thing and the beaver shut his eyes to endure it. To make it worse, this was a longer flight than that up the mountain or to the end of the lake. Those now seemed to have been only short moments of danger.

Over him the powerful wings beat steadily and Yellow Shell guessed that, as in the spirit dream, they were heading southwest, away from the mountains and over the prairie desert land where he had seen the coyote village. He tried to think what he would do when he got there. To secure such a precious thing from the lodge where it was hung, in the midst of an enemy village, was so dangerous an undertaking that he could not hope to be successful. Yet the spirit dream had made most clear that that he must do.

Suddenly he guessed that the eagle was descending and he opened his eyes. Being held as he was face downward, he could indeed see the earth racing up to meet him. But morning could not be too far distant as the light was now grey—yet it was still dark and shad-owed on the ground.

The eagle did not set him down gently, but loosed his grip, so that Yellow Shell fell into the midst of a bush and was fighting against its thorned branches all in an instant. When he had battled his way free of that, his bearer was only a very distant moving object in the sky, and he had no chance to thank him, if one could truly offer thanks for being dumped so unceremoni-ously in an unknown land, perhaps very near an en-emy village.

Yellow Shell sat up on his haunches and looked about. This was plainly open prairie land and not too rich, for the only bushes he could see were stubby ones with a starved look as if good soil and much water were things they had never known since their seeding. There were patches of bare sand here and there that gave rooting to nothing at all.

He turned his head slowly. The coyote village, wher-ever it might lie, could not be set too far from some source of water, for water all animals must have. Now he sniffed each puff of wind that reached him, drew in deep breaths in every direction, hoping to pick up the scent of water.

Not only must he find water as a probable guide to the village but as a source of food. The withered stuff the eagles had supplied the night before had blunted his hunger, but it had not really satisfied him, and now he wanted, needed food, and must have it.

He was facing south when the very faint scent he hunted reached him. There was no help for it, he must walk, over a country that was not meant for his kind, awkward and slow on land. His only hope of ever reaching that water was to be always alert to all that lay about him.

The sun was rising as he thumped along, his paws beginning to hurt again as they met the hot, hard surface. He kept when he could to the patches of coarse grass that offered cushioning. There was life here; he saw birds, a lizard or two out in the early morning before heat drove them into cover. And once he made a wide circle around a place where the hated, musky scent of snake was a warning.

His only relief was that the odour of water grew ever stronger, drawing him forward with longing to plunge into some river, even into a pool, with cool wet all about him. Then he stiffened and crouched low in the shadow of a bush, hoping he had taken to that cover in time. The loud, ear-hurting call of a crow, of more than one, sounded clearly across the land.

Turning his head up and back, Yellow Shell was able to sight them as they passed overhead—three of them, southbound as himself but angling a little more to the east. If he dared believe they were on their way to the coyote village, then there was a hope that he could still reach water some distance away from the enemy, for the scent seemed to run from east to west.

Making very sure that the crows were well away before he left his bush shelter, Yellow Shell stumbled on. He marked ahead every bush or stand of tall grass in which he could crouch if the need for hiding arose, and he made the best speed he could in a zigzag path from one to the next.

The water scent was so strong now that he had a hard time keeping from breaking into a run. But he held to his caution and kept up his move from cover to cover, waiting in between times. The sun was growing hotter and there were more birds, but no lizards, to be seen. Once he sighted a pair of rabbits. They were painted for a raid, and were moving with caution like him. Young bucks, he thought, perhaps out in a daring attempt to count some coup in coyote country—though he thought that their daring was that of young fools and that any coups counted in that way should be their shame and not their glory.

Beavers counted bravery a virtue as much as any

other of the People, but a brave fool got no praise from them for his folly. Yellow Shell kept carefully out of sight of the pair, when in other times he might have asked for directions. If they did fall to the coyotes, which was only too possible, he wanted no tales told about his presence in a place where a lone beaver could be so noteworthy a happening as to attract instant attention and investigation.

The ground suddenly ended in a sharp-edged drop and he looked down into a gully. Perhaps at other times of the year the stream at the bottom of it was a sizable river. But now it had shrunk into hardly more than a series of pools, all shallow—too much so, at least the ones he saw, for swimming. But it was water and his whole body longed for its touch.

Only the gully was so open. To venture down there where there was no shelter was only asking to be sighted by crows, by any coyote on scout.

Yellow Shell angled along the bank, looking longingly at the pools that at another time would have disgusted him by the murkiness of their water. As he went, the pools did grow larger and joined with one another, and there were actually signs of a sluggish current. Perhaps closer to the source of this dying river there was more water.

At last he caught sight of greenery growing in the gully and, with a thankful sigh of relief, he half tumbled over the edge, to slip and roll down to the stream's edge. But he was not so forgetful of danger not to turn and hide as much of the signs of his passing as he could by wide sweeps of his tail.

The growth was scrub alder and he feasted upon it. But he was careful to take his twigs and bark from spots where the breakage would not be easily seen. And he also cut a small bundle for future use as he had before they had climbed the mountain. In a semi-desert land one could not depend on too much to be found.

There was one pool that gave him a chance to sink deep beneath the surface, wet through his sand- and soil-burdened fur, ease the smarting of his paws. He dove and swam, always staying in the shadow the growth threw across the water, until he felt almost his old strong self again.

By the measurement of the sun's path, it was now past noon. He half floated on the water, trying to plan. As with most of the People, the coyotes preferred the night to the bright of day. And dark would find their camp alert and awake. To push on now for a first look around, if the village did not lie too far ahead, might be wise. He tightened the reeds binding his bundle of food and began to swim, taking to the bank again only when the water grew too shallow. But there were not many such places now. In fact the stream soon became a river instead of a series of pools, and he was able to make faster time than he had all the earlier part of this day.

FOREST OF STONE

I T WAS SUNSET, the sun having already dropped behind the mountains to the west. Yellow Shell crouched in a thicket while he rubbed vigorously into his coarse upper fur pawfuls of bruised, strongly scented leaves. His hope that this might cover his own musky odour was perhaps wrong, but it was the only protection he now had. And to get into the coyote camp, to that lodge that stood just a little apart but was the same one he had seen in the spirit dream, was now necessary.

He had watched it for a long time. But the door flap had remained down, whereas those in the others of the camp were propped open, lashed to small sticks to keep them so. This could mean one of two things— that the lodge was indeed empty, or that its owner was at home and desired no visitors. And for the beaver's purpose there was a vast difference between those two facts.

It had been late afternoon when he had found the village on the north side of the shallow river. On the south bank were more patches of sand until the land began to be true desert country.

Yellow Shell had not had much time for exploring or scouting the camp, for the coyotes were already stirring. Young squaws came down to the water's edge, bringing skin bags rubbed with fat to make them water-tight, taking the liquid back to their tepees. Cubs ran about, playing wild pounce and chase games. And the beaver watched yawning warriors come out of their lodges, stretch, grimace to show long fangs, snap at flies, rouse for the night's hunting hours. He wondered then about the two rabbit braves—would they be caught in this territory before they could retreat?

One coyote, or two, or even three, he would dare to face by himself. His teeth, his tail, his spear were deadly weapons. But to be set upon by a pack—that would be like the ambush of the minks all over again. So Yellow Shell prudently withdrew downriver into hiding, to consider what must be done.

He might, of course, go into hiding to wait out the night, try to reach the lodge again the next morning when the village was once more asleep. But time was important. He could not be sure how he knew that, only that it was so.

There was this—he could watch for his chance, and after the hunting parties had left and the life of the village began to follow the usual pattern, he might be able to reach the medicine lodge unseen. He was lucky in that it was not the chief's, which was set in the middle of the circles of tepees, but apart on the northern edge. And perhaps, though he dreaded leaving the water, he could work his way around to it, using the tall grass for cover. If there was no one inside, he could get in easily enough, for the skin wall at the back would split under his teeth.

So, patiently, Yellow Shell lay in the water, only his head, under the shadow of a willow, above the surface of the stream, watching carefully all he could see of the camp.

Someone beat a drum with quick, sharp taps, and then a howling call rang out in a summons. He saw braves trotting towards the centre of the village to answer. Not a war party. There had been no dancing, no singing. No, he must have been right in his guess—a hunt was now intended. And by the numbers in the pack so assembled, the prey to be was no easily attacked beast. Could they be after the horned ones of the prairie? Yellow Shell gave a short snort at the thought. What powerful medicine *must* hang in their midst if these thought they could bring down a buffalo! Yet so large a gathering of hunters could not be aimed at any lesser game.

He saw a part of the pack as they trotted out. At the fore went a mighty coyote with lighter fur that showed almost white in the twilight where it was not dabbed with paint. He was flanked by the seasoned warriors of the village. Trailing this impressive van were younger hunters, some hardly out of cubhood, bringing up the rear. These did not prance or bark, but padded humbly in their elders' wake as if deeply impressed by the task now before them.

Yellow Shell waited until they were long gone, for they headed north into the grassland, thus verifying his suspicion that it was indeed buffalo they were going to run. And he wondered at the daring of the chief who had planned this hunt, which even the Wolf Tribe would think twice of attempting, old enemies of the horned ones that they were.

By the rise of the moon the camp was not quite so busy. Many of the cubs were down splashing in the river. Yellow Shell had edged back into the grassland, his nose wrinkling when the smell of meat from the tepees reached him. As he went deeper into the prairie, he used his keen scent to find certain leaves, pleased when he came across a sage bush very aromatic in the night wind.

Now he smeared more of the crushed leaves well into his coat, along the scaly skin of his powerful tail. As a cover it might not be all he could wish, but the coyotes were so keen of nose that he needed all the protection he could find. The wind blew now from the east, which was a small thing in his favour. But he hated to travel on land, which was always hard for him.

Once again he scuttled from bush to bush, working around in a wide half circle that he might approach the camp from the north, and thus be closest to the medicine lodge. To get right against its back was his hope. He could listen at its wall, and if he heard no movement within, he would take a chance and slit the skin.

What he would do with the bag he sought once he had it in his paws. Yellow Shell did not yet know. The spirit dream had shown him that this he must do in order to help himself, and so he would follow its direction.

When the leaves were only green-grey smears on the pads of his paws, he gave a last wipe of those paws on his haunches and moved out. There was a stir in the village, but it did not reach the medicine lodge. Perhaps the coyotes had good reason to be in awe of the Changer, though all knew that he favoured the coyotes as brothers and wore their shape more often than any other, dwelling among them for periods of time, to their great joy.

Now and again Yellow Shell gave an anxious glance to the sky. He had not forgotten the crows he had seen flying in this direction, though in all his scouting of the village he had not seen them here. Perhaps they had brought sóme message, and, that task done, had left again.

With a last burst of the best speed a beaver could summon on land, Yellow Shell reached the position he had aimed for, right at the back of the medicine lodge. He edged as close as he could, laying his ear against its surface, trying to hold his breath and still a little the fast beating of his own heart, so that he could listen the better and catch any small sound from within.

The noises of the camp were annoying; he could not block them out well enough to be sure that there was not a sleeper inside. But after a long wait, the beaver knew that he could not remain there, doing nothing. He would have to make up his mind before the return of the hunting party. They must pass close to where he crouched and he had little hope that his smearing of sage and other scented leaves would cover him from their keen noses.

He began to dig a little with his forepaws, pausing fearfully after every scoop or two to listen. But there was no sound. At last his fear of being discovered by the hunters' return grew stronger than his caution, and he snapped at the skin wall of the tepee near the bottom where he had made a hollow in the earth. Three such slashing attacks and he had an opening large enough for his head and shoulders.

Immediately before him, tickling his nose and providing a screen, was a heaping of dried grass and sage twigs for a bed place. There was no fire in the circle of ash-smeared stones in the centre of the lodge. No one was there.

Yellow Shell wriggled all the way in, to sit up on the bed and look about. There were no food-storage bags or water carriers hanging from the poles set up against both sides of the lodge to support such, on the right and left of the front flap door. And under him the bedding was dusty dry, crunched as he moved, as did stuff long gathered that had not been lately put to use.

He could smell coyote, yes, but not as strongly as if one had recently lived here. And he began a wary circuit, using his nose to tell him what might have happened here.

The smell of dried meat clung faintly to the poles for the storage bags. And there was also the scent of herbs, which might be part of medicine. But he was not ready for the disappointment that awaited him as he straightened to his full height under the centre pole of the tepee and stretched back his head to see where the bundle had hung in the dream. There was nothing there.

Of course, the Changer would have taken the bag with him when he went. But where—where now must Yellow Shell follow or search? The beaver slumped to all fours, the pain of his sore feet, the aches in his body suddenly the sharper. And the misery of not knowing what to do next was a dark shadow over his mind.

As he so crouched closer to the beaten earth, he caught sight, very plain in the gloom of the lodge, of a small bit of white—a piece of eagle down. And he knew it for a thing of power. His dream—the bundle—it had been wrapped in a skin bag with tassels of fur and feathers dangling from it. This would seem to be a part of one such tassel. Carefully Yellow Shell picked it up between two claws.

The White Eagle! Not the mighty Storm Cloud of the heights, but a far greater chief than he. Because the White Eagle truly ruled the sky below the Sky Country, and only by his will might one pass safely from the world below to the world above. Forever did he sit on a far higher peak than any Storm Cloud knew, a peak in the north. Always he faced the sunrise, but on his right and to his left sat two younger eagles. And he on the right was the Speaker who faced north, and he on the south was the Overseer. Those flew at intervals high above the world so that they might see all that happened, reporting to the White Eagle how it fared with land, water, beasts and growing things.

So this white down was the sign of the White Eagle and a precious thing of much power. Holding it so, Yellow Shell knew a slight spurt of hope, knew what he could now try. So when he crawled out of the lodge, he took with him that wisp of feather.

Now—to find a high place. He hunched up to look about him. The river had rocks along its banks farther to the east. At the moment those were the highest spots the beaver could sight. There was no hope to return in time to the mountains, or even to the foothills. He had this to encourage him—a rising and a strong wind that now tugged at him.

In his haste to try out his plan for finding where the Changer had gone with the medicine bag, Yellow Shell almost lost his caution. It was only a series of sharp barks from the direction of the prairie that reminded him that he must still be alert to what lay there, to the hunters who might at any moment return. And it seemed that that was just what was happening now. For at that barking there were more echoes from among the lodges and he saw the squaws and older cubs gathering in excitement, the younger of them heading out, in his direction, as if to meet the returning warriors.

With a burst of speed difficult for his heavy body, Yellow Shell scuttled as fast as he could towards the river, putting such a screen of grass and brush between him and the village as he could find, hoping to reach the river to the east well beyond the village.

He was soon almost winded, for this was rough ground and his fear pushed him to greater and greater efforts. The barking chorus behind him took on the measure of a song and he thought he read triumph in it. The warriors of the camp might be back from a battle or successful raid—anyway, it was plain they had accomplished something of which they were proud.

Yellow Shell did not pause to look back, nor had he any eyes for anything but the ground immediately around him. If he could but reach the water—As it had been yesterday, the need for water was now like a whip laid across his haunches.

Here was a rise of rocks, those he had picked out as a good base for his try at using the eagle down. But he had no thought of that now; even in the night he could be sighted by those hunters from the plains. Instead he plunged into the first opening he saw between those rough stones, scrambling up and down, sometimes slipping painfully on pebbles and gravel caught in the hollows between them, until he came once more to a drop, with the stream lying below.

Taking the precious feather carefully into his mouth, Yellow Shell thankfully dived in, allowed the water to close over him, hardly daring to believe even now that he had managed to leave the village without raising an alarm. Could it be that the power of the spirit dream somehow clung to him, so that just as he had visited the lodge by dream undetected by the coyotes, so he was now also able to go in body?

He swam upstream, ready to duck beneath the surface of any pool if the need arose. The river-bed was narrower here, channelled between steadily rising banks of stones embedded in sun-hardened clay. He put as much distance between him and the camp as he could, alert to any sound from behind that would warn that he was being trailed.

But perhaps whatever success the hunters had had so satisfied the coyotes that they were aware of nothing else. Again he wondered if they had indeed brought down a buffalo, for to those whom the Changer favoured, such a coup might well be possible.

Dawn found him on much higher ground, the stream

now running swiftly and with a force he found increasingly difficult to battle against. He pulled out of its grip at last. There were no alders, willows, or edible roots here, and he regretted not having brought supplies with him. But hunger could not turn him back now.

The feather plume, when he took it carefully out of his mouth, was almost as wet as if he had switched it through the river. He held it up with great care to where the breeze blew, trying to dry it. And as he did so, he chanted, though he did not raise his voice above the mutter of the water behind him:

> "Eagle, hear me—
> Let your power be with me.
> White Eagle, hear me.
> Speaker, hear me.
> Overseer, the seeker, hear me.
> White is this,
> Of your medicine.
> Let the wind that is the beating
> Of your wings in the sky
> Carry this, which is of your own power,
> To join with that which is of its own.
> Carry high, and carry far,
> To join again that which is its own!"

He pulled from around his neck what was left of his necklaces and looped them with one paw about the haft of his spear, for this was all he had to offer. Then he threw the spear and the dangling ornaments up into the sky with all the force left in his tired foreleg. It rose, swept on and on and was gone beyond the rocky wall. And Yellow Shell was heartened, for it had not tumbled back into the stones where he could see. But as long as he was able to watch, it had gone up and up. Perhaps White Eagle would be pleased to notice his offering, and would listen with an attentive ear to his singing.

Holding the feather still in the drying breeze with one forepaw, Yellow Shell scrambled up and up to follow the general direction of his vanished spear. It was not an easy climb and he was puffing hard through a half-open mouth as he reached the top.

Dawn was grey in the sky, the sun's day paint beginning to show on the eastern sky. The river had made a wide curve and now he could see that its source lay somewhere to the north, not the east, perhaps in the very mountains where Storm Cloud's tribe nested.

Once more the beaver chanted his petition to the White Eagle. And out of the river valley, or so it seemed, curled a breeze that although not forceful enough to be termed a wind, yet blew steadily.

Into this Yellow Shell loosed the feather. It was caught up in the breeze, to be borne southward into the desert waste on this side of the river. And with firm faith that he was indeed following a sure guide, the beaver set out after it.

It was light enough to see the feather clearly, to be able to follow its flight. So small a thing to trust to—For the first time in many hours, Cory thought as himself and not as Yellow Shell. Surely he could not depend upon such a thing as this!

But because the faith of his Yellow Shell self was so strong, Cory did not struggle against it.

To his surprise, it almost seemed that the feather *was* indeed a purposeful guide. Twice, Yellow Shell tired and crouched panting, unable to keep on. Then the feather was caught temporarily, to flutter on the top of some sun-dried, leafless piece of dead growth, only to be torn loose and carried on when the beaver was ready to shuffle ahead. Finally a last gust whirled it up and up into the bright blue of the cloudless sky as the beaver came to the edge of a basin.

This might be twin to that cupped-mountain stronghold of the eagles. But whereas that had been green and held water, this held sand, with strange, rough columns rising out of it, some of which had been toppled to lie full length.

Set up in the heart of this was a small skin shelter before which crouched an oddly shaped figure. It was busy, its forepaws patting and pulling at a mass of clay on the ground before it. Now and then it sprinkled water from a gourd on to that mass, always returning to its pinching and pulling, kneading and rolling.

The feather was like a snowflake, drifting through a winter day. As the beaver watched, it floated downward once more, heading straight for the worker. And Yellow Shell knew that he had found the Changer, though what he did here, the beaver could not guess.

Carefully he climbed down the basin wall, scurrying as fast as he could into the shadow of the nearest of those pillars, putting it between him and the Changer. As he set a paw on it, he found it was stone, yet once it must have been a tree, for it had the look of bark and wood. And if so, this must have been woodland changed to stone. Another trick of the Changer? If so, for what purpose? How could trees of stone serve anyone—Unless the Changer had been merely using his power for sport and to see what he might accomplish.

Yellow Shell crept on, though under his thick coat of fur he felt cold enough to shiver. The sun might be beating hotly down on his slowly moving body, yet the closer he drew to that absorbed worker, the more he felt a deep chill of fear.

Perhaps the Changer would catch sight of the eagle down, know that it had guided someone to spy on him. And what would be the fate of such a spy? To be changed—perhaps to such stone as these trees? Go back, said his fear. Yet Yellow Shell shuffled on, from one patch of shadow to the next.

He could hear the faint murmur of song now, and

he guessed that the worker strove to sing into his
fashioning of the clay some power. Yet it would seem
that he was not accomplishing what he wished. For
time and time again he would bring the full weight of
his forepaws down on the clay, smashing it all flat
again, growling over the destruction of his efforts.

Forepaws? Yellow Shell blinked (Cory would have
exclaimed aloud had he then his human lips and voice).
Those paws had looked like yellow coyote paws from
a distance. But now—now they seemed to be human
fingers busy once again at pushing, pinching, rolling—

He saw that the squatting figure was neither wholly
an animal nor a man, but a strange combination of the
two, as if someone had started to make a change from
beast to man and the experiment had been only half
successful.

Hands were at the end of furred forelegs, and the
head was domed, as a human skull, though large ears
pricked on either side. It was as if a man wore a
beast's mask over his whole head. The hind legs were
still pawed, but the shoulders under the yellow-brown
hide were those of a man.

To Cory-Yellow Shell the combination was worse
than if one wholly coyote or wholly human had been
squatting there. To Cory the beast-human was all wrong
and to be feared, while his Yellow Shell self found the
human-beast unnatural and frightening. Yet the beaver could no longer retreat; he was held where he was
as if bound to the column behind which he hid. And
that realization came with such a shock that he whim-
pered aloud.

The singer's head lifted, green beast's eyes looked
straight at the stone tree behind which Yellow Shell
crouched. The Changer made a swift gesture, a beckoning. Against his will the beaver's body obeyed that
summons, creeping out into the sun, treading straight
to where the Changer worked in clay, with no hope of
escaping that powerful pull.

About the Changer was a wide patch of dug-up earth, pocked with holes out of which he must have scraped his clay. A big mass of it was directly before him, having no form at all now, for he had just once more pounded what he shaped into nothingness. He sat, his man's hands resting upon its surface, watching the beaver. And he no longer sang, but rather he studied, as if he saw a use in Yellow Shell, as if some missing part to what he would shape had come to him.

Seeing that look, the beaver's terror grew, and with it an inner stir in his human self also. Cory must now break through this nightmare, awake into the real world before something worse happened. He could not guess what that something was, but the beaver's fear was a warning and he knew it too—as great as the terror that had touched him when he had watched the buffalo and the dancer.

A SHAPING OF SHAPES

"**W**HAT HAVE WE HERE?" The Changer spoke, and it seemed to Yellow Shell that his words were beaver, but to Cory's ears they were human. "You have come here to take the wood-which-is-stone for the making of spear points?" He nodded to one of the fallen pillars where its side had been chipped and broken, shattered lumps lying in the sand. "But, no, I think you have come for another reason, and it is one that can well serve my purpose. Now sit you and watch!"

And with those words he seemed to root Yellow Shell to the ground, for the beaver could not move, nor was he able to turn his eyes from the Changer's hands.

Once more the Changer mixed a little water from the gourd into the pile of moist clay, and his fingers pushed and pulled at the stuff. What arose from the muddy mixture under his coaxing was a small figure that very roughly resembled a man. There were two legs, two arms, a squat body, and a round blob ball for a head. But it was very crude, and plainly its maker was dissatisfied, for with his fist he impatiently smashed it back into the clay once more.

Cory came fully to life in the beaver body, aroused to take control at the sight of the manikin that had so disappointed its maker. And he spoke, though the sounds he made were a beaver's gutturals.

"You are making a man!"

The Changer stopped kneading the clay, his head swung up so those green eyes stared at Cory, or the beaver Cory now was. Very cold, very frightening were those eyes. Yellow Shell, the beaver, might not have been able to meet that stare for long, but Cory, the boy, somehow found courage and held steady. Slowly that gaze changed from cruel menace to surprise, and then speculation.

"So—you are that one," the Changer said.

What he meant by that, Cory did not know. But he continued to face the half man, half coyote with all the will he could summon to his aid. And now he had an idea. He did not know how such a thought had come, but he grasped it with a new boldness, as if to beaver stubbornness he added what only a human could know. He did not reply to the Changer's half question, but he said:

"You are trying to make a man."

Once more those green eyes were chill with anger— Cory did not know whether it was his guess or the Changer's own failure. A mud-spattered hand half rose as if to aim a blow at the beaver. Then it fell back on the clay, which he began to pinch and twist again in moist chunks, though now his attention was more on Cory than on what he was trying to do.

"You would bargain—with *me?*" There was a challenge in that demand.

"I offer you a model," Cory returned and waited in suspense, but with some hope. Would the Changer accept, turn him back to his human self for the sake of a model to copy for his manikin?

And if he were once more a boy, could he stay that way? Could he find his way back to his own world and time? The medicine bundle was what he needed to bargain with the Changer—Raven and the spirit dream had made that plain. And the medicine bundle was gone from the lodge in the coyote village. The Changer was working, or trying to work, strong magic here, so he must need that powerful bundle. As yet Cory had had no chance to look around, but perhaps if he got the Changer to believe he would be willing to aid in this present task, he could be given that chance.

The Changer's fingers were still now. He began to wipe the mud from them by scraping one hand over the other, until they were clean of most of the moist mass. All the time he eyed Cory as if he were measuring, weighing, turning the beaver inside out to get at what might lie beneath his furry hide.

Would he get out the bundle? Did he need to bring it into the open if he were to make Cory human once more? But the Changer was apparently in no hurry. He still rubbed his hands together, but absently now, as if his thoughts were very busy elsewhere.

Then he began to sing, a low-voiced chant. Cory could not understand the words, but the beaver's body began to shiver, chills ran along his spine, down forelimbs and back legs. The broad, powerful tail twitched, rose a little to beat up and down, hitting the ground in a thumping he could not control. The bond that had tied Yellow Shell in place no longer held. Instead the beaver began to dance, against his will. He moved to no familiar beat of drum or ankle rattle, no sounding of turtle shell filled with pebbles, but to the song the Changer sang. Faster and faster he danced, whirling about in a dizzying circle that made his head spin so that he felt he could no longer see, or think, or breathe.

On and on he spun in that bewildering circle until there was nothing left in the world but that singing, loud as the crackle of lightning, the roll of storm thunder across mountain tops. Still Yellow Shell danced.

As suddenly as he had begun, the singer stopped. Once more Yellow Shell—no, not the beaver but the boy Cory—stood foot-rooted to the ground directly before the pile of mud from which the Changer was trying to shape his man. But Cory no longer wore Yellow Shell's thick fur, his paws, his tail. In so much had he won—he was a boy again.

However, he could not move, as he speedily discovered. He was as much a prisoner standing here as he had been when tied by the mink ropes. And now fear returned to him as he saw the animal jaws of the Changer open in a knowing grin, as if the other could read his thoughts and took pleasure in defeating his hopes. Perhaps—Cory shivered in spite of the sun's heat on his head and shoulders—perhaps this strange creature could do just that.

Still keeping his green eyes on Cory, the Changer began to work again with the clay, pinching, prodding, pulling it into shape, not looking at what he was doing at all, but rather at the boy's body. But it would seem that this method worked, for the manikin that now grew under his fingers was no rough figure but far more of a human shape. And he sang as he worked, words that Cory did not understand, though he recognized quickly that it was a song of power.

Up and up rose the figure the Changer made. Now it was as tall as Cory's knees, as his waist, and still it grew as the Changer's hands moved faster and faster, his singing grew louder. Never did he look at what he fashioned, but always at the boy, though once or twice he leaned over to spit into the mud, and again he threw into the clay pinches of some dusty stuff he took from a small pouch belted around his misshapen, half-beast body.

Now the manikin stood as tall as Cory's shoulder. As yet the head remained only a ball, but the body was clearly done. And Cory's fear deepened, for there was this about the Changer's work—as it grew more human, so did Cory hate it more. It was as though it might be a great enemy, or the sum of all his own fears from both worlds.

The Changer dropped his hands and for the first time his eyes left Cory, so the boy felt a sense of relief, as if that intent stare had held him prisoner. Now the shaper looked from Cory to the image of mud and back again with long measurement, though the ball head of the figure remained unfinished.

Apparently satisfied with his work, the Changer edged backward without rising to his feet, putting his hands to the ground on either side to pull himself along. Again Cory felt relief from some loosening of the will that held him. But he guessed that it was best not to betray he had that small freedom, lest the Changer turn his full attention once more on his prisoner.

Now the Changer pulled sticks before him, so that they lay between him and the image he had created. He set these up for a fire as the otters had their signal, in the form of a tepee. But he did not touch light to it at once. Instead he took from his belt pouch some small packets of leaves folded in upon themselves, each fastened with sharp thorns into tight packages. These he unpinned one by one, to display small amounts of what might be dried herbs or dust.

Cory was deeply afraid now, though as yet he had not been openly threatened. If he could have done so he would have run, just as he had from the buffalo and the dancer. But, though he was somewhat freed from the bonds the Changer had so mysteriously laid upon him, he was not free enough to leave. He knew, he could not tell how—unless that was part of Yellow Shell's beaver memory still lingering with him—that if he could not fight now, it would be the end of him. For the Changer's full medicine would be too strong for him to withstand.

Too strong for animals—but what about man? How had that thought come to Cory? Animal—man. Man *was* an animal, but also more, sometimes only a little, but still more. Thoughts raced in his mind. If he let the Changer complete the magic he would do here— then perhaps man would never be that little bit more, though he could not tell how he knew that.

Suddenly, as clearly as if his eyes actually saw it before him—a picture formed in his mind—the head of a black bird. Crow—such as served the Changer? No! There were white circles about the eyes and the bird's beak opened to voice a medicine song—Raven!

And it seemed to Cory that when he thought the name Raven, the picture in his mind turned its eyes on him and a new picture formed, by the will and power of Raven. Another bird head—this one white—Storm Cloud? No, it was a greater eagle. And he remembered the White Eagle to whom Yellow Shell had appealed when he loosed the bit of down that had guided him here.

But what had the White Eagle to do with—? Again as he identified the picture, that majestic bird also turned to look squarely at him and once more came another picture. But this one was vast, clouded, he could see only a bit of it, and he sensed with awe that it was given to no one to see the whole of what stood there.

And perhaps it was the remnants of Yellow Shell's memory that gave an awesome name to that half-seen shadow. For that it was awesome even the human

Cory recognized. Thunderbird! And when he named it in his mind it became clearer for a single instant. But Cory could never afterwards recall just what he had seen then, or if he had seen anything at all, but had only been blinded by the appearance of something it was not given to his kind to understand.

But Thunderbird's shadow remained with him. And to that vague picture Yellow Shell's memory added some words that were strong medicine—very strong. Cory did not repeat them aloud, but he turned his head to look at the mud image, which moment by moment grew less and less like clay, more and more like brown skin laid over firm flesh, upheld by solid bone.

Cory studied the ball of a head that had never been truly finished, and in his mind he repeated the medicine words, trying to shut out all but those words and the need for saying them over and over. Why it was necessary to do this he could not say, only that it was all he *could* do to prevent the Changer from completing his purpose.

Smoke with a strong smell puffed up around him, but drifted more towards the image, clinging to the mud. Then hands reached out to grasp the clay body on either side of its slender waist, lifted it up. Cory, still watching, repeated the words in his mind now with all his energy. He saw the Changer set the mud man down with its feet in the blazing, smoking fire, so that the flames rose up about it.

Then the Changer stood up, his half-man, half-beast form even stranger looking when he was erect. And he began a medicine song. But Cory tried to shut his ears to the sound, to think only of the words that would call the Thunderbird. While his feet could not move from where they appeared to be fixed to the ground, he found he could raise his hands somewhat. And they moved now in signs following the words in his mind.

At first the flames rose very high, shoulder high

around the image, and the smoke veiled it from view. There was a feeling of triumph, of success in that smoke, and in the singing.

Still Cory's hands moved to match the words in his mind and perhaps the Changer was so intent upon his own magic that he did not see what Cory did.

Then the smoke rippled and a wind rose out of nowhere. The sun was clouded and a chill edged the breeze. The dance and song pattern of the Changer altered. He took a step or two more, then stood, looking about him with quick wariness, as if he had been shocked out of a dream.

The wind not only whipped away the smoke but it pulled at the live brands of the fire, whirling one up in a shower of sparks, carrying it away, to be followed by a second, a third. The Changer cried out, but his voice sounded more like the howl of a coyote. He flung up his hand as if to stop one of those flying torches, and the fire of it must have singed him painfully, for again he howled in rage.

His eyes flamed yellow-green, turning from the wind-driven fire to Cory, and his lips drew back to show the fangs of a hunting beast. He vigorously made signs with his man hands. For a moment the wind died a little, the showering sparks did not fill the air.

Only now the clouds had so darkened the sky that they made a low ceiling. Cory felt that if he reached up his arm he could touch them. From those clouds broke flashes of lightning and the Changer whirled at the first brilliant crackling, as if he could not believe in this sudden storm.

He snarled at the flashes, again showing his fangs, and voiced a long, wailing howl. He might have been ordering those clouds to clear, the sun to shine again. But only for a moment he stood so, looking up into the gathering fury. Then he turned, his anger visible in every upstanding hair on his shoulders, in the prick of his ears, the wrinkling of his lips.

Once more his hands moved in signs. The bit of Yellow Shell still in Cory cringed at the sight of those. For, not being a medicine beaver, he could not read the signs, yet in them he saw great power.

Cory's thoughts faltered; he could no longer remember clearly those words that had spoiled what the Changer meant to do here. But his failure to keep up the fight did not seem to matter. Perhaps he had only prepared the way for another force that would now take over, whether he continued to call it or not.

His hands fell heavily to his sides, as if once more chained there. And he could not move, even when one of the wind-blown brands burned his neck with its sparks, singeing his hair.

For if the wind had subsided a little at the Changer's retort, it rose again, scattering the fire as if a broom had been used for that purpose. And the flames were almost gone as huge drops of rain fell with the force of blows on the ground, on the dying coals, on the mud image, and on Cory.

Now the Changer stood to his full height, his Coyote head flung back on his man's shoulders, his eyes searching the sky as he turned his head slowly. It was as if he looked to find his enemy above, searched there for a target against which to loose his powers.

For a long moment he stood so, while the coals of fire hissed black and dead under the pelting of the rain and it grew colder and colder. Cory, who only moments earlier had felt the terrible heat of the sun in this desert place, now shivered and shook under the blast of the chill.

Seeming at last to have made up his mind, the Changer turned his back on the now dead fire, on the image standing in what had been its heart. He went to one of the dead bushes nearby and, stooping down, laced the fingers of his right hand among its branches, bringing it up out of the ground in a single pull.

Its roots made a tangle from among which he plucked

a bag. Cory, seeing it, knew that this was what Yellow Shell had hunted. This was the Changer's great medicine; with it in hand he was armed, ready to stand firm against all the spirits of sky, earth, water, and air.

With both hands he held it aloft, into the full force of the storm, shaking it from side to side as if it were a dance rattle, or as if he wanted the spirits in that punishing wind to be well aware of with what he threatened them.

The wind died, the rain ceased, the clouds began to split apart. All the while the Changer, holding high his mighty power, danced and sang. That singing was not for the ears of man, it was stronger than any lightning crackle, any cruel roll of thunder.

Still the Changer danced and sang, and held the medicine bundle as one might hold a spear against an enemy, driving away the storm that had spoiled all his plans. For how long he danced so, Cory could not have said, for time no longer had a meaning.

But at last even the Changer must have grown tired, for Cory could see again, hear again. And the beast-man sat upon the ground even as he had when first Yellow Shell had looked down into the forest of stone trees. There was now only a shapeless mass of clay where the image had stood, flowing down from a blob supported on two legs that the fire had baked into a more enduring substance.

The Changer lifted the hand holding the medicine bundle and tapped that mass lightly, and straightway even the legs became mud again. He looked down for a long time at that sticky pile. Then he roused, threw back his head, and gave one of those far-sounding howls. Having done so, he stared at Cory and there was such an evil glint in his narrow beast eyes that the boy tried vainly to fight the bonds laid upon him.

For a time the Changer made no move, though now and then he turned his head with the coyote ears a-prick as if he were listening. The sun went down, to leave them in the night. No fire burned and Cory's human sight could not pierce the darkness as Yellow Shell's had done. But, almost as if he wanted to prove to Cory that he had won, the Changer rebuilt the fire, though it was not in the same place as the other and he did not toss into it the contents of leaf packets.

There came a fluttering out of the dark, and feathered shapes lit on the ground, hopped into the circle of light about the fire. Crows—ten—twenty—more—coming and going so that Cory could not count them, or even be sure that they were not the same ones over and over. As each hopped past the Changer, he spat out on the ground a mouthful of yellow-brown clay, which the beast-man mixed with the other mass. And that grew taller and taller. Now he scraped and mixed it well, working the new and old clay together as he sang in a voice hardly louder than a murmur, as if he feared being overheard.

Some of the crows settled down on the other side of the fire. Cory noted that they showed interest, not in what their master was doing but in the medicine bag that lay close to him, for he had not returned it to hiding after using it to drive off the storm. And the boy knew that if he could but get it out of the Changer's reach, he could put an end to all that was happening here. But he could see no chance of that.

Knead, pinch, pull, shape—the Changer's human hands moved faster, with a greater sureness than they had before, as if, having once made the manikin, his fingers remembered their task. But this time the figure he wrought was larger, was as tall in fact as a man, as Uncle Jasper.

Uncle Jasper. Cory blinked. That other world seemed so far away, so lost to him now. Yet, when he had thought of Uncle Jasper—Yes! His hands had been able to move: Uncle Jasper, the ranch—Dad— Just as he had seen the Raven, White Eagle, and that shadowy other in his mind, so now he tried to picture all he

118

could that was most important to him of his own world
and time. But, as he felt his bonds loosen, he did not
try yet to move. Patience he had learned from Yellow
Shell, and the determination to fight for survival, but
some of this stubborn will to face danger was now
Cory's own, either newborn or simply newly roused
from a spark that had always been there, but that he
had not known he had.

Let the Changer become so interested in his "man"
that he would forget Cory. Even now he seldom looked
at the boy; he appeared no longer to need him as a
pattern.

And the birds— They had eyes only for the medicine
bag. To reach it Cory would have to half circle the
fire, but in a second, before he got so far, the Changer
could snatch it to safety. His only hope was to wait for
some chance.

Again the body stood finished, the head remaining a
round ball. But this time the Changer went to work on
that. He made no attempt to give it a human face.
Instead the clay moved under his fingers into the shape
of a long narrow jaw and nose, pointed ears—the head
of a coyote, twin to the one on the Changer's own
shoulders. He stood back at last to study it critically.
Then, with finger-tips, went to work again, modifying
the beast look somewhat. Still it was far more an
animal's mask than any face. But that apparently was
the result the Changer wanted.

Now for the first time in hours he looked directly at
Cory with a tooth-showing grin.

"How like you my man?" he barked.

"It is not a man." Cory told him the truth.

"But it is the new man," the Changer told him.
"For this is a man as he should be for the good of the
People. And for the good of the Changer." Again he
laughed, though it was more of a yapping.

"Yes," he continued, "this is man as the People
need him, for to us he shall be a slave and not a

master. These—" he touched the dangling mud hands almost contemptuously, "shall serve the People as sometimes paws cannot. These—" now he rapped the wide mud shoulders, then stooped to run a finger-tip down the clay legs, "shall bear burdens, run to our command. This is man as the Changer has made him, shaped from the earth, hardened, as he soon will be, by fire, made ready for the life—" now he turned to look at Cory with those evil, narrow eyes, "you shall give him!"

Cory cried out; he thought he screamed. And in that moment he was answered out of the dark, out of the sky—with a shriek that set the very earth trembling under them.

THE CHANGER CHALLENGED

ONCE MORE THE sky was torn by broad purple flashes of lightning and a chill wind blew about them. In a half crouch, snarling, the Changer turned to face the dark beyond the fire.

Something moved there. Cory could not see it plainly; the clouds were so thick, the night so very dark. But he thought that great wings fanned, that a head as large as his own body turned so that burning eyes might look upon them. And the boy wanted to throw himself to the ground, dig into the sand, as if he were Yellow Shell diving into the river water.

The crows cried out, but they did not take to the air. Instead they cowered close to the ground, as if seeking shelter where there was no cover left. But the

Changer now stood tall, his back to the fire and to his man of mud, facing the fluttering in the night.

"Hear me." He spoke as he would to Cory, yet even above the noise made by the crows, the drumming of the thunder, he could be heard. "I am He Who Shapes, and this is my power. You cannot deny it to me for it is mine!"

And he spoke as if he knew very well who or what was in the dark there, and felt confident that he could safely face it so.

Who—or what— This was the shadow that had risen behind the White Eagle in Yellow Shell's vision—this was the *Thunderbird!*

To Cory, Yellow Shell's memory supplied the rest— this was the Thunderbird whose presence was in the storm, the wind, the lightning, the pound of thunder, the rise of wind. The Thunderbird spoke for one being only—the Great Spirit.

"I am He Who Shapes, who changes," the Changer repeated, still confident, but faintly angry now. "This is my power and I hold it against all the spirit ones, great or small!"

The crows cawed together harshly. Then, instead of taking to wing, they scuttled out of the circle of light, taking shelter in the shadow of one of the trees lying prone. If they could dig their way into the sand, thought Cory, seeing their flight, they would be doing that right now.

There was a fanning of wings, so huge they could be felt as a rippling of the air, and after that a new crackling of lightning. But as yet no rain had appeared.

"Elder Brother, listen. We have no quarrel, no spear, no claw or fang now bared to make a red road running between us. You lead the storm clouds into battle, as was given you to do. I but do as was given me, I shape and change, shape and change. And now it is in me to shape one who will serve the People, who will not say 'Do this, do that,' 'Come be my meat and let me eat,'

121

'Come be my robe and let me wear.' For if I do not breathe life into this one, there shall come another somewhat like him but of another shaping, and then it shall be ill for the People, and all their greatness shall be gone. They will dwindle into less and less, and some shall vanish from mother earth, never to be seen again. I, the Changer, have foreseen this evil thing. And because I *am* the Changer, it is laid upon me to see that it will not come to be so."

"The time is not due, the shape is not right. It is not for you, Younger Brother, to do this, which is a great, great thing that none but the ONE ABOVE may do." The words rolled out of the dark with the beat of thunder, as if they were a chant sung to a drum.

"I am the Changer, Elder Brother. So was the power given me in the First Days, so it has always been. Such power once given cannot be taken away. That is the Right and the Law."

"That is the Right and the Law," agreed the voice from the dark. "But also it is the Right and the Law that one may challenge you, is that not also the truth?"

The Changer laughed in a sharp, yelping sound. "That's the truth, Elder Brother. But who can do so? For mine alone of the earth spirits is the shaping power. You, Elder Brother, can control the wind, the clouds, the lightning and thunder, the pound of rain, the coming of cold moons' snow. But can you shape anything?"

"The power is yours only—on earth," again agreed the shadow.

"And it is on earth now that we stand, Elder Brother. Therefore, I say that this shall be done—that I shall shape this 'man' to be a servant to the People. Nor will you again raise a storm to stop me, for when I have so spoken, then it becomes my right."

"It becomes your right," again echoed that mighty voice. "But still you may be challenged—"

"Not on my making of this thing," returned the Changer quickly.

"Then otherwise," replied the Thunderbird. "For it is this message that I bring—there shall be a challenge, and, if you lose, then you shall with your own hands destroy this thing you have shaped, and you shall forget its making and not so shape again. Instead you shall be guided for a space by the will and wishes of he who challenges."

"And if I win?" There was such confidence in the Changer that he seemed to be growing taller, larger, to match the shadowy giant Cory could more sense than see.

"And if you win, then it shall be as you have said. Though this thing is wrong, yet it shall live and be all you have promised, a servant to the People, never more than that."

"So be it! Such a tossing of game sticks pleases me. But since I am the challenged, I say that this testing shall be rooted in mother earth, for I am *her* son and not one who commands air, wind, and water as my right."

"So be it," agreed the Thunderbird in turn. "You have the choice that this contest be of the earth. Mine is the second saying, which is this—"

There was movement in the night as if mighty wings were spread, and Cory felt those eyes burning not only on the Changer and the image of mud but on him also. And in that moment he guessed that soon, if ever, would come his chance, and he must be ready to seize it. That binding the Changer had laid upon him still held in part, but suppose the Changer would be so occupied with this contest that he must use all his power for it? Then Cory would be wholly free. He could see the medicine bag still lying beside the fire, very plain in the light.

The Thunderbird had paused for a long moment, as

if he were turning over in his mind several different possibilities of a challenge. At last he spoke.

"Of the earth, yet in a manner of seeing of my sky also. Look you to the north, Younger Brother. What see you?"

There was a vivid flash of lightning to tear aside the night, holding steady as no lightning Cory had ever witnessed before had done. Against it stood the black outline of a mountain, one of lesser width but greater height than the eagles' hold.

"I see earth shaped as a spearhead aimed at the sky," replied the Changer. "This is a piece of medicine to be thought on, Elder Brother. Perhaps it does not promise good for you."

"A piece of earth," answered the Thunderbird. "As you have asked for, Younger Brother. Now this be my challenge—which is not really mine but that of One Above speaking through me—that you take this earthen spear and without changing its form you lay it upon the ground so that it no longer aims its point to the sky, but into this desert country, even at this fire where you would harden your shaping into life."

Still that lightning banked behind the mountain, showing it plainly. And the Changer looked at it steadily, nor did he show that he thought the task impossible.

"It is of the earth," he said, "and so must obey me." And to Cory he sounded as confident as ever.

Facing the mountain, he uttered some sharp howls, as if the huge mound of earth and stone were alive but sleeping, and must be so awakened to listen to his orders. Then his feet began to stamp, heavier and heavier and heavier, as he put his full force into each planting of those coyote paws.

Stamp, stamp, right paw, left paw—

Under his own feet Cory felt an answering quiver in the earth, as if the force of that stamping ran out under the surface.

Stamp, stamp—those paws were now digging holes

into the ground where the Changer brought them down with all his might. At the same time he began to sing, pointing his human hands at the mountain peak against that light which could no longer be considered lightning, for it remained steady and clear.

And having pointed out the mountain, the Changer now went through the motions of hurling at the peak, although his hands held nothing Cory could see.

Stamp, hurl, stamp, hurl. Cory watched, yet the peak remained unchanged. And the boy wondered if there was any time limit placed upon this contest.

With a great effort he dragged his eyes away from the Changer and looked to where the medicine bundle lay. Now he began to try his strength once more against the spell the Changer had held him in. His hands moved to answer his will, and then his arms, stiffly, with pain, as if they had been cramped in one position too long. He tried not to flinch lest the Changer notice him. But the coyote head remained steadily facing the mountain.

Cory glanced up to see that the hurling motions had come to an end. Now the Changer moved right hand and arm in a wide, sweeping, beckoning. It might be that in answer to his signal he expected that distant humping of earth to take to itself legs or wings and come forward at his gesture.

If he expected such, he was doomed to disappointment. But Cory gave only a short glance at what the Changer did. He was edging, hardly more than an inch at a time, out of the place where he had been rooted for so long at the other's pleasure. Now the image stood between him and the Changer, and he had yet some feet to go around the fire to get his hands on the medicine bag. So much depended upon whether the Changer would remember him, or whether he would need the bag for his present magic. Cory could only try, for he believed that he would not get a second chance.

He stooped a little to flex his stiff knees, then stood erect several times, remaining still when it seemed that prick-eared head was about to turn. The crows had left off cawing, almost as if they feared they were distracting their master's attention at this great testing of his power. But they watched from where they were and perhaps they would betray Cory.

And what of that great shape? Had it indeed come to his call that first time when the storm had destroyed both the fire and the image baking in it? Yet Cory was sure, though he could not have said how he knew, that that shape was not really concerned with him at all, but only with what might happen when the Changer shaped his mud and thought of giving it life.

So Cory kept to his own purpose, to reach the medicine bag. With his hands on that, could he indeed escape the Changer's spells—return himself to his own world and time?

Still the Changer sang his song, beckoned to the mountain. Then, from far away, there was a rushing that became a roar and Cory, startled, looked round.

Where the mountain had stood stark and clear, shown only by the light the Thunderbird had summoned, now shot a red column of fire. A volcano?

And that fire climbed into the sky, as might a fountain. As the spray of a fountain falls, so did a shower of giant sparks come, together with brilliant streams channelling the earth of the peak's sides. The peak was being consumed. As its sides melted, so clouds gathered above it, dark and heavy. From them poured streams of rain, so that steam arose. And underneath him, as far from the mountain as he was, Cory could feel the ground weave and shake, move as if some great explosion tore under its surface.

Cory was thrown forward, his hands out, and the fire the Changer had built was scattered in brands that glowed and sputtered. Even the Changer was down on his hands and knees, and now he looked more animal than man. He was snarling, snapping at a flaming bit of wood that had seared against his upper arm.

The image he had made tottered back and forth, though it did not fall. And the Changer, seeing it in danger, made a sudden leap to steady it, brace it up against the continued shaking of the ground.

At the mountain the flames tore up and across the sky as if more than just one peak was now burning, or as if earth itself, and rock, could burn as easily as dried wood. But the flood from the sky poured steadily on it, drowning that fire bit by bit. Though they were miles away, they could hear the noise of that mighty battle between fire and water.

Under Cory's hand as he pushed against the ground to gain his feet was a smooth object. The medicine bag! He had the medicine bag! But where could he go—what could he do with it? He had no doubt the Changer could get it away from him with ease if he remained nearby.

A glance told him that the Changer was still occupied with saving his clay figure from breaking. Whether or not he could claim any victory in the contest, Cory did not know. The Changer was lowering the mountain, but not as the Thunderbird had directed—moving the point undisturbed out to lie pointing into the waste. And the storm the Thunderbird had summoned was putting an end to the fire.

Cory held the bundle tight against his chest. Then he scrambled to his feet and began to run, without any goal, just out into the desert, towards the wall of the basin that held the wood of stone. If the crows gave warning of his going, he did not hear them, for that roaring in the earth, in the sky, was a harsh sound filling the whole night.

Panting, he somehow got up the ridge, pausing there for a moment to look back. The fire had caught the small hide shelter of the Changer. From this point Cory could not see the shadowy form of the Thunderbird, only the beast-man steadying his image against one of the stone trees. Around and around above flew a wheeling circle of crows. And seeing that, Cory began to run again.

When he had first picked up the medicine bag, it had seemed very light, as if it were stuffed only with feathers. But as he went it grew heavier and heavier, weighing against him so that at last he was drawn towards the earth. And he ran as if a prisoner's chain were fastened to his feet; his flight became a trot, and finally a walk. Now he was in the dark, though from behind, the glow of the melting mountain was like a sun rising, only in the north instead of the east. It sent his own shadow moving before him—and that shadow changed.

It had been a boy's as he left the hollow. Now it grew hunched of back, thicker— Cory looked down at his own body. There was fur, there were the webbed hind feet, the clawed forepaws, behind him a scaled tail dragged on the ground. His pace was the shuffle of a beaver. He was Yellow Shell again!

The heart almost went out of Cory. He had been sure he had won back his own body, if not his own world—but now— Now he had the medicine bag, yes, but he had lost himself again. And in a clumsy beaver body, in this desert place, he would have so little chance to escape—for this was coyote land and he did not doubt that the Changer would have the advantage.

Yet he continued to shuffle on, the heavy bag clasped tight to his chest with one forepaw while he walked on the other three with what speed he could make. Water—if he could only reach water! But this was desert. There was no water here.

Unless—unless the storm would have given some to the land, even if only for a short time before the sand drank it up!

Yellow Shell's sense, his quivering nose in a head thrown as far back on his bulky shoulders as he could raise it, sought water. And the scent of it came to him—south and west. Unhesitatingly he turned to find that water.

He humped along at the best speed his beaver body was capable of making. And the bag grew ever heavier, chained and slowed him more and more. Yet he did not put it down, even for a breath of rest. He had a feeling that were he once to let it out of his hold, he would not be able to pick it up again.

The false sun of the blazing mountain was dying now. Perhaps the storm the Thunderbird had raised to quell the flames was winning. So his path grew darker. He now entered a world of sand dunes. To climb up and down carrying the weight of the bag was more than Yellow Shell dared attempt. He had a vision of being buried in some slip of a treacherous surface. So he had to turn and twist, push along such low places as he could find. As Cory he would have had no guide and might have become hopelessly lost. But as Yellow Shell the scent of water found him a path.

There came a cawing overhead. He did not have to look up to know that one of the crows must have sighted him, that even if the Changer had lost him for a time, now he was trailed again. That the beast-man would be after him at once, Yellow Shell did not doubt. His only hope was based on the fact that the scent of water was now stronger and that the dunes among which he slipped and slid were growing smaller and farther apart.

He came around a last one, was out on a stretch of rocky ground, great masses of it towering into the sky. The cawing over his head echoed and re-echoed. More of the crows joined in a flock. He expected them to attack him, to try to force him to drop the bag that now weighed upon him as if he had his foreleg around a big stone. But they only circled in the sky and called to their master.

With a last burst of the best speed he could make,

Yellow Shell stumped across the stony land and came upon what he sought, a cut in the earth with the silver of water running through it. Though it was no true river, yet now it had a current that whirled along pieces of uprooted sagebrush and the long-dried remnants of other storms, so that to plunge blindly in with the weight of the bag was a dangerous thing. But not as dangerous, the beaver thought, as to remain on land where he was so clumsy and slow.

Without stopping to think or look behind, Yellow Shell dived, and the bag pulled him down and down, as if it would pin him to the bottom of the cut, hold him anchored so that the rush of the water, the beating of those floating pieces in it, would drown or batter him to death.

Yet Yellow Shell held to his stolen trophy, swimming along with the current with what strength he had, dragging the bag with him. It caught on rocks embedded in the bottom, on pieces of the drift, and he fought it almost as if it were a live enemy determined to finish him. But never did he loosen his hold upon it.

Then he was caught in a sudden eddy of the current. The bag loosened in his grip, almost whirled away. He fought to retain it but had to crawl half out of the water to do that. And at that moment he heard a noise that froze him where he was.

The howl of a coyote sounded so loud and sharp it seemed as if the hot breath of that hunter were able to dry the fur rising in a fighting ridge on the beaver's back. Baring his murderous teeth, Yellow Shell turned in the mud, tucking the bag under his body, Cory's determination strengthening the animal stubbornness at facing old enemies.

Across the water was the Changer. But he himself had changed. There was nothing of man left in the great yellow-white beast who stood there. It was all animal, and the yellow eyes, the teeth from which the snarling lips curled away, promised only death.

Yellow Shell snarled back. His forepaws were set tightly on the medicine bag, and now he lowered his head, nipping the taut surface of the bundle with his teeth, his intent plain. Let the Changer move at him and he would destroy what he had taken.

The coyote watched him. As the fire on the mountain had paled, so now the first streaks of dawn lighted the sky. And once more in Yellow Shell's mind came a faint and ghostly vision of Raven, behind him the White Eagle, and farther yet—the Thunderbird. Somehow, from them, added knowledge came to his aid.

Hold—if he could hold here and now until the sun rose. And then let the sunlight touch upon the bag, so would the Changer's power be broken. For he had used much of it, too much of it, upon the mountain, which had not answered his call but been consumed in part. In this much he had lost the battle, but he would try again—unless his medicine was also destroyed.

Knowing this, Cory-Yellow Shell crouched low above the bag, sheltered it with his body. None too soon, for if the crows had held off attack before, they did not do so now, but flew down and against him, striking with punishing beaks at his head, his eyes, stabbing his body painfully, though the thickness of his fur was some armour. Using his tail to defend himself as best he could, Yellow Shell stayed where he was, covering the bag.

With the attack from the birds there came also a different attack, aimed not against his body but his mind. A strong will battled against him, sought to make him give up what he had stolen. First it promised what he wanted most, his own body, return to his own world. Yet Cory-Yellow Shell did not yield. Then it threatened that he would never again be Cory, never return to the world he knew, while the crows dived and pecked at him until he was bleeding from countless small wounds on his head and shoulders.

The first red was in the sky, and that grew while the

131

coyote prowled up and down the bank of the now fast-drying stream, and the crows cawed their hatred and rage overhead. Why the Changer did not attack in person, Cory did not understand. But the running water seemed to form a barrier he could not cross. Only the water was shrinking fast, and then—

It was a race between the coming of the sun and the vanishing of the water. If the water failed first, then Yellow Shell had no hope at all. Yet the beaver crouched and waited.

Sun—a first beam struck across the ground. Yellow Shell cried out as one of the crows struck viciously at his eye. He did not hesitate or try to protect himself, but used all his remaining strength to push the bundle out into that weak beam as it became stronger and stronger.

As if the sun had lighted a fire, smoke rose from the bundle, puffed out and out—

Cory coughed, coughed again, staggered back a step or two. He stood on two feet, he was a boy again. And in his hands he held the bundle—or was it the bundle? For it crumbled as might dried clay, sifting through his fingers in the fashion of fine sand. Then there were only particles of ashy dust left. The smoke blew away from him and he looked about as one just awakened from sleep.

Sleep—dream— He was at the line camp! There was the jeep, the corral, the horse and—Black Elk.

The old Indian sat with his blanket wrapped around his shoulders in spite of the heat. It was not dawn but late afternoon.

"What—what happened?" Cory's voice sounded small, frightened, and he was then ashamed of that sound.

"World turned over," Black Elk answered.

"The Changer—"

"He was." Black Elk looked directly at Cory for a

second. Was there, or was there not (for a moment Cory felt the old chill of fear) a yellow glint in those eyes? If it served as a reminder of the Changer himself, it was gone in an instant.

"He was, he will be," Black Elk spoke. "Medicine things, they are not for the white man."

"No." Cory was eager to agree. He wiped his hands vigorously against his jeans, trying to smear off the last of the clinging dust that had been the bag.

"World turn over again," Black Elk continued. "Time coming—"

"It was a dream." Cory backed away from the fire and the old Indian. "Just a dream."

"Dreams spirit things, sometimes true," Black Elk said. "Indian learns from dreams—white man laughs, but Indian knows. You not laugh now, I think."

"No," Cory agreed. He certainly did not feel like laughing. He glanced at that safe anchor to the real world, the jeep. But now, somehow he had no need for such an anchor. The horse whinnied and Black Elk spoke again.

"Horse wants drink. You take—down to river—now!"

Cory moved without hesitation to obey the order. He laid his hand without shrinking on the curve of the Appaloosa's neck and the horse blew at him, snorted. But Cory felt light and free inside, and knew that he had lost the tight burden of his fear. No—he did not need the jeep as an island of safety in a world that had been so strange and dark and threatening, but was now more like an open door to the learning of many things.

He led out the Appaloosa. When he passed Black Elk, the old Indian's eyes were closed as if he slept.

The river was where he had seen the buffalo and the masked dancer. Were those, too, part of the dream, of the world that had not yet turned over? He did not know, but with every step he took, Cory began to understand that what he had learned as Yellow Shell was now a never-to-be-forgotten part of Cory Alder.

Had the Changer (he could see him—the Raven, the Eagle, the misty shape which was the Thunderbird—now in his mind for an instant), had the Changer indeed really reshaped him? Not into a beaver, but into someone stronger than he had been before he had worn fur and stood in a stone forest daring to summon a power greater than himself?

The horse had raised his dripping muzzle from the water. Almost without thinking, Cory guided him to a fallen tree trunk, using that for a mounting block to scramble somewhat awkwardly but with determination into the saddle. He gathered up the braided leather thong of the Indian halter, and with growing confidence turned his mount's head by a steady pull.

He rode up the slope, his pride growing. And now he suddenly heard thundering hoofs, saw the running of some free colts, and behind, the dusty figures of three riders.

Fur Magic—he could not tell why it had been his. But he sat quietly in Black Elk's saddle to face Uncle Jasper, the western sun warm on him, feeling very much a part of a new world.

STEEL MAGIC

For Stephen, Greg, Eric, Peter,
Donald, Alexander, and Jeffrey.
And for Kristen and Deborah,
who love stories of fairy worlds.

∽ CONTENTS ∽

THE LAKE AND THE CASTLE

THE ADVENTURE BEGAN with the picnic basket that Sara Lowry won at the Firemen's Strawberry Festival at Ternsport Village. Because it was the first time any of the junior Lowrys had ever won anything, they could hardly believe it when Chief Loomis called out the number of the ticket Sara had knotted into one corner of her handkerchief. Both Greg and Eric had to hustle her up to the platform where Chief Loomis waited beside the loud-speaker.

The basket was super, the boys agreed as soon as they had a chance to examine it. Inside the lid, fastened in a piece of webbing, were forks, spoons, and knives of stainless steel, and there was a set of four cups—blue, yellow, green, and fire-engine red—with matching plastic plates. Sara was still so surprised at her luck that she would not have been astonished if the basket had vanished completely before she carried it back to Uncle Mac's station wagon.

When Uncle Mac slowed down for the sharp turn into the Tern Manor private road, Sara clutched the basket handles tighter. Greg's sharp elbow dug into her ribs, but she did not try to wriggle away. This place was spooky at night, and she did not wonder that Greg moved back from the window when ragged branches reached out as if they were trying to drag the car off the narrow road into all those shadows. At night you had to keep thinking about how this was still New York State, with the Hudson River only two hills and three fields away—and not a scary country out of a fairy tale.

Now they were passing the dark place where the big house had once stood. Twenty years ago it had burned down, long before Uncle Mac had bought the old carriage house and the ground with the gardens for what he called his hideaway. Uncle Mac wrote books and wanted peace and quiet when he was working—lots of it. But the old cellar holes still marked where the house had stood, and the Lowrys had been strictly warned not to explore there. Since Uncle Mac was perfectly reasonable about letting them go everywhere else through the overgrown gardens and the little piece of woodland, the Lowrys were content.

They drove into the old stable yard. When the big house had been built fifty years ago, there had been horses here, and people had actually ridden in the funny carriage the children had found crowded into part of an old barn. But now the station wagon occupied the main part of the barn and there were no horses.

Mrs. Steiner, the housekeeper, was waiting on the doorstep of the carriage house and she waved an air mail–special delivery letter at Uncle Mac the minute he got out of the car. She was also wearing one of her own special "past-your-bedtime-and-hurry-in-before-I-miss-my-favorite-TV-program" looks for the Lowrys. Mrs. Steiner spoke with authority, whereas Uncle Mac, especially while writing, would sometimes absent-mindedly agree to interesting changes of rules and regulations. Uncle Mac was not used to children. Mrs. Steiner was, and an opponent to be respected in any tug of wills.

On the whole the Lowry children had been looking forward to a good summer. In spite of Mrs. Steiner there were advantages to staying at Tern Manor. Since Dad had been ordered to Japan on special service and had taken Mother with him for two months, Uncle Mac's was far better than just second best.

When one was used to towns and not the country, though, what was left of the old estate could be frightening at times. Greg had gone to scout camp, and Eric had taken overnight hikes in the state park when Dad was stationed at the big air base in Colorado. But this was Sara's first visit to a piece of the outdoors that had been allowed to run wild, just as it pleased. She was still afraid of so many big, shaggy bushes and tall trees, and managed to have one of the boys with her whenever she went too far from the stable yard or the road.

Mrs. Steiner spoke darkly of snakes, but they did not frighten Sara. Pictures of snakes in library books were interesting, and to watch one going about its business might be fun. But poison ivy and "those nasty bugs," which Mrs. Steiner also mentioned at length, were another matter. Sara did not like to think about bugs, especially the kind that had a large number of legs and might investigate humans. Spiders were far more unpleasant than snakes, she had long ago decided. She was really afraid of them, though she knew that was silly. But to see one scurrying along on all those legs—ugh! As they climbed the stairs to the small bedrooms in the top story of the carriage house, Eric joggled the basket Sara still carried.

"Let's fill this up tomorrow and really go exploring—for the whole day!"

"Might be a good time to hunt for the lake," Greg agreed. "We'll ask Uncle Mac at breakfast—after he's had his third cup of coffee."

"Mrs. Steiner say there's liable to be snakes there," Sara offered. Please, she added to herself, just no *big* spiders, little ones were bad enough. Greg snorted and Eric stamped hard on the next step. "Mrs. Steiner sees snakes everywhere, when she isn't seeing something else as bad. Water snakes, maybe, and I'd like to get me one of those for a pet. Anyway, we've wanted to find the lake ever since Uncle Mac told us there was one."

This was perfectly true. The legend of the lost lake as Uncle Mac had told it was enough to excite all three Lowrys. The gardens were now a matted jungle, but they had been planned to encircle an ornamental lake. Mr. Brosius had bought the land more than fifty years ago, throwing three riverside farms together and spending a great deal of time and money developing the estate. He was a legend, too, was Mr. Brosius, a stranger with a long beard, who had paid for all the costs of the manor's building in gold coins. Then he had gone and the house had burned.

Nobody had been quite sure who really owned the manor, and finally it had been sold for taxes. Farmers had bought the fields, and the part with the gardens had gone to a real-estate man who finally sold it to Uncle Mac. And Uncle Mac had never cared enough to plow through all the brambles and brush to see if there was a lake any more. In fact he said he was sure it must have dried up a long time ago.

Sara wondered if that was true. She paused in her undressing to open the picnic basket and gloat over its contents just once more. What if Uncle Mac had not taken them to the festival tonight, or if she had not had her allowance in her purse and could not have bought that dime ticket? Maybe if she had not won the basket the boys would not have included her in the lake hunt. This was going to be a fine summer!

After she had turned off the light, she sat up in bed. This was the first night she had not stood by the window listening to all the queer little sounds which were a part of the night outside. It was so easy to believe that there were things out there which were never to be sighted by day, things as lost as the lake and maybe even stranger. . . .

But tonight she thought instead of packing the picnic basket. And with plans of peanut-butter sandwiches and hard-boiled eggs, cookies and Cokes, Sara lay back at last to pull up sheet and quilt.

Their plan went well the next morning. Uncle Mac's letter had summoned him to New York City, and Mrs. Steiner drowned out the crackles and pops of rapidly disappearing breakfast food with the statement that she would give the house a really good cleaning.

When Sara produced the basket and asked for the raw materials of picnicking she met no opposition at all. Mrs. Steiner even made up a Thermos of frozen lemonade. Luck was on their side and it was the perfect day to go lake hunting.

Greg used a compass and led the way in what he claimed was the proper direction to reach the center of the wild gardens, but as they went the basket began to prove a nuisance. When it was necessary for the explorers to wriggle on all fours through thickets, it had to be bumped and pushed along in a way which Sara was sure mixed its contents more than was desirable. And she stoutly protested the frequent suggestions that she alone carry it, since it belonged to her anyway.

They were wrangling loudly on this point when they came, quite unexpectedly, to the top of a flight of crumbling, moss-greened stairs and saw the lake below—but not only the lake!

"It's Camelot!" Eric cried first. "Remember the picture in the Prince Valiant book? It's Camelot—King Arthur's castle!"

Sara, who had different reading tastes, dropped down on the top step and rubbed a brier-scratched hand back and forth across her knee. Her eyes were round with happy wonder as she half whispered, "Oz!"

Greg said nothing at all. It was real, it must be. And it was the most wonderful find the Lowrys had ever made. But what was it doing here and why hadn't Uncle Mac ever told them about it when he spoke of the lost lake? Who had built it and why—because real castles, even if very small ones, didn't just grow on islands in the middle of lakes these days!

Part of Uncle Mac's prophecy that the lake might be

dried or drying was true. Shore marks showed it had
shrunk a lot, and a stretch of sand and gravel made a
bridge between the island and the shore. As he studied the building, Greg could see the castle was a ruin.
Part of one tower had fallen to choke the small courtyard. But maybe they could put the stones back and
rebuild it.

Excited as they all were, they descended the steps
slowly. Eric looked at the murky water—it might be
deeper than it looked. He hoped no one would suggest
swimming, because then he might just have to try and
he didn't want to, not in this lake—or, to be honest,
not anywhere. He pointed into the water as he caught
sight of something else. "There's a boat sunk there.
Maybe they had to use that once to get to the island."

"Who built it?" Sara wondered. "There never were
any knights in America. People had stopped living in
castles before the Pilgrims came."

Greg teetered from heels to toes and back again.
"Must have been Mr. Brosius. Maybe he came from a
place where they still had castles, and wanted a little
one to make him feel at home. But it's funny Uncle
Mac didn't say anything about a castle here. You'd
think people would remember that if they remembered the lake."

Sara picked up the basket. "Anyway we can walk
right out to it now." It seemed almost as if this really
were Oz and she were Dorothy approaching the Emer-
ald City!

"We sure can!" Eric jumped a short space of green-
scummed water, giving himself a good margin for landing on the shelf of gravel. He kicked a stone into the
lake, watched the ripples lap back. Water could never
be trusted, there was nothing safe or solid about it. He
was very glad they had that sand-and-gravel path. This
lake was unpleasantly full of shadows—shadows which
might hide almost anything.

Although the castle was a miniature, it had not been

built for a garrison of toy soldiers. Even Uncle Mac, tall as he was, could have passed through the front gateway without having to stoop. But when they got beyond the pile of stones fallen from the tower, they faced a blank wall. Greg was surprised—from his survey taken from the stairs he had thought it much larger.

"What a fake!" Eric exploded. "I thought it was a real castle. It sure looked bigger from the shore."

"We can pretend it is." Sara refused to be disappointed. Even half a castle was much better than none. "If we pull all these blocks out of the way it will seem larger."

Eric kicked, sand and gravel spurting from the toe of his shoe. "Maybe."

Clearing out all those stones seemed to him a job about equal to running the lawn mower completely around the piece of garden Uncle Mac was trying to retame.

Greg moved slowly along the walls, studying the way the stones had been put together. Had the castle just been built to look pretty—something like the summer-house, which was not too far from the stable yard but which they could not play in because of the rotted floor?

The part of the wall directly facing the entrance was largely concealed by a creeper that had forced its way through a crack to stretch a curtain over the stone. But when he parted those leaves in one place, he made a new discovery which suggested that his first impression of the castle's size might not have been wrong after all.

"Hey! Here's another doorway, but somebody filled it up!"

Sara's hands gripped the handles of the picnic basket so tightly that the wood cut into her palms. "Maybe—" she wet her lips "—maybe that's where he went—"

"Who went?" Eric demanded.

"Mr. Brosius—when he disappeared and they never found him at all—"

Greg laughed. "That's silly! You know what Uncle Mac said, Mr. Brosius was drowned in the river, they found his boat floating."

"But they didn't find him," Sara said stubbornly.

"No, but it was his boat and he went out in it a lot. And the river's bad along there." Greg piled up the evidence. "Remember how Mrs. Steiner harped about its being dangerous, even on the first night we came, and Uncle Mac made us promise not to go there at all?"

Eric came to Greg's support. Sure, that was the story and Mrs. Steiner had been quick to tell it to them, one of her awful warnings. Uncle Mac had even driven them down to the water and pointed out where the current was so strong and tricky. Eric shook his head to spill the picture of that rolling water out of his mind.

Last summer, and the summer before, he had had swimming lessons. And, well, it had been easy to go in with Dad, or with Slim, the instructor at the beach. But even so he didn't like or really trust a lot of water. He never had.

Maybe Greg felt the same way when he sometimes got all stiff and quiet in the dark. There was that time when they broke the flashlight going downstairs to fix a burned-out fuse and Dad had finally come down to see what was keeping them. Greg hadn't moved from the last step of the stairs at all. Well, now it wasn't dark, and they didn't have to get into the dirty old lake, so why think about things like that?

Greg was tearing away a big handful of creeper, leaving the wall bare but speckled with little patches of suckers from the vine. Whoever had sealed up that doorway long ago had been in a big hurry or careless. Because at the very top one of the filling stones was missing, leaving a dark hole.

Greg scrambled up a tottery ladder of fallen rubble and thrust his hand into the hole, which was still well above eye level.

"There's a lot of space beyond," he reported eagerly. "Maybe another room."

"Do you suppose we could pull out the rest of the stones?" Sara asked. But she was not too happy. She had not liked seeing Greg's hand disappear that way, it made her feel shivery—but excited too.

Greg was already at work, ripping free more of the creeper. Now he picked at some more of the blocks.

"Got to have something to pry this mortar loose."

None of them wanted to make the long trip back to the house for a tool. It was Eric who demanded that Sara hand over one of the forks from the picnic basket.

"They're made of stainless steel, aren't they? Well, steel's awfully tough. And anyway there're only three of us and four of them. Won't matter if we break one."

Sara protested hotly, but she did want to see what lay behind the wall and finally she handed over a fork. The boys took turns picking out crumbling mortar and, as the fork did the job very easily, they were able to pass the loose stones to their sister to stack to one side. Midges buzzed about, and some very hungry mosquitoes decided it was lunch time. Spiders, large, hairy, and completely horrible, ran from disturbed homes in the creeper and made Sara a little sick as they scuttled madly by.

At last Greg pulled up to look through the irregular window they had cleared.

"What's inside?" Sara jerked at Greg's dangling shirt tail and Eric clamored to be allowed to take his place.

There was an odd expression on Greg's tanned face.

"Answer a person, can't you? What's there?"

"I don't know—"

"Let me see!" Eric applied an elbow to good purpose and took his brother's place.

"Why, it's all gray!" he cried out a moment later. "Maybe just a sealed-up room without any windows— the kind to keep treasure in. Maybe this is where Mr. Brosius kept all his gold."

The thought of possible treasure banished some of Sara's doubts. It also spurred the boys on to harder efforts and they soon had a larger space cleared so Sara could see in too.

It *was* gray in there, as if the space on the other side of the wall were full of fog. She did not like it, but if it was a treasure place . . . Mr. Brosius had always spent gold in the village. That story was true; people still talked about it a lot.

"I'm the oldest." Greg broke the silence with an assertion that had led them into—and sometimes out of—trouble many times in the past. "I'll go first."

He climbed over the few remaining stones and was gone. It semed to Sara that the gray stuff inside had wrapped right around him.

"Greg!" she cried, but Eric was already pushing past her.

"Here goes!" As usual he refused to admit that a year's difference in age meant any difference in daring, strength, or the ability to take care of oneself under difficulties. He also vanished.

Sara gulped, and backed away a step or two from that grayness. Her foot stuck against the picnic basket and she caught at the double handles, lifted it over the barrier, and scrambled after, determined not to lose the boys.

BEYOND THE WALL

IT WAS LIKE walking into the heart of a cloud, though the gray stuff about Sara was neither cold nor wet. But to be unable to see her feet or her hands, or anything but the whirling mist, made her dizzy. She shut her eyes as she stumbled forward.

"Greg! Eric!" She had meant to shout at the top of her voice, but the names sounded like weak whispers. She choked, shivered, and began to run, the basket bumping awkwardly against her legs.

There was a bird singing somewhere and the ground underfoot felt different. Sara slowed down, then stood still and opened her eyes.

The fog was gone. But where was she? Surely not inside a room of the small castle. Timidly she reached out to touch a tree trunk and found it to be real. Then she looked back for the wall and the door. Trees, just more trees, all huge and old with thick mats of dead leaves brown and soft under them. And sunshine coming through in ragged patches.

"Eric! Greg!" Sara was screaming and she did not care. Now her voice sounded properly loud once more.

Something stepped into the open from behind a tree trunk. Sara's mouth was open for another shout. A red-brown, black, and white animal with a plumed tail and a thin, pointed nose sat down to look at her with interest. Sara stared back. Her fright was fading fast, and she was sure that the animal was laughing at her. Now she knew it was a fox. Only, she was puzzled. Were foxes always so big? The ones she had seen in

148

the zoo were much, much smaller. This one was as large as the Great Dane that had lived two houses away on the post in Colorado. He was very like, she decided, the picture of Rollicum-Bitem in *Midnight Folk,* a favorite fictional person of hers.

"Hello," she ventured.

The fox's mouth opened and his pointy tongue showed a little. Then he snapped at an impudent fly. Sara put down the basket. Would he like a peanut butter sandwich? There *were* the cold ham ones, but only three of them. Before she could move, the fox stood up and with a flick of his plumed tail was gone.

"Sara! Where are you, Sara?"

Greg dodged in and out among the trees. When he caught sight of her he waved impatiently. "Come on. We've found a river!"

Sara sighed as she picked up the basket again. She was sure that the fox wouldn't come back, not with Greg yelling that way. Then she began to wonder about the river. What was a river doing on a small island? When they had seen that dab of land from the top of the stairs, there had not been any big trees or river.

As she caught up with Greg she asked, "Where are we, Greg? How did all these trees and a river get on a small island?"

He looked puzzled too. "I don't know. I don't think we're on the island any more, Sara." He took the basket from her and clasped her arm above the elbow with his other hand. "Come on. You'll see what I mean when you get there."

They trotted in and out among the trees, which then grew farther and farther apart, and there was a lot of green-gold sunlight in the open spaces with grass and little plants.

"Butterflies! I've never seen so many butterflies!" Sara dragged back against her brother's pull. What she had first thought were flowers rose on brilliant wings to fly away.

"Yes." Greg walked more slowly. "A lot of birds here, too. You ought to see them down by the river. There was a heron fishing and we watched him catch a frog." He made a stabbing motion with two fingers held tightly together. "He used his bill just like that. This is a grand place."

They walked down a gentle slope to where a bar of gravel ran out into a shallow stream. Eric sprawled there, grabbing beneath the surface of the water. He sat up, his face red with his efforts, as they joined him.

"Fish," he explained. "All over the place. Just look at them!"

Shoals of minnows were thick along the edges of the bar, while water bugs skated on the surface and a dragonfly spun back and forth.

"I saw a fox in the woods," Sara reported. "He sat and looked at me and wasn't afraid at all. But where are we?"

Eric rolled over on his back, looking up into the blue of the cloudless sky, still dabbling one hand in the river.

"I don't care. This is a keen place, better than any old park—or any old scout camp either," he added for Greg's benefit. "And now I'm hungry. Let's see what's in that basket we've been hauling around all morning."

They moved into the shade of a stand of willows where the slightest breeze set the narrow leaves to fluttering. Sara unpacked the basket. It was Greg who pointed out that she was counting wrong.

"Hey—there're only three of us. Why put out everything for four?"

Yes, she had put out all four of the plastic plates, set a cup beside each, and had been dividing up the sandwiches. Greg had the red plate, Eric the yellow, the blue was for her. Why had she set out the green one also? Yet for some reason she was sure that it would be needed. "We may have a guest," she said.

"What do you mean? There's no one here but us." Eric laughed at her.

Sara sat back on her heels. "All right, Mr. Smarty," she snapped. "Suppose you tell me where we really are, if you know so much! This is no little island in the lake, you can't make me believe that! How do you know there's no one else here?"

Eric stopped laughing. He looked uncertainly from his sister to Greg. Then all three of them glanced back at the shadowy wood through which they had come. Greg drew a deep breath and Sara spoke again:

"And how are we going to get back? Has either of you big smart boys thought of that?" She reached for the basket as if touching that would link her with the real world again.

Greg frowned at the river. "We can get back to where we came from," he said. "I blazed trees between here and there with my scout knife." Sara was surprised and then proud of him. Greg had been clever to think of that. And, knowing that they had that tie with the castle wall and its door, she felt more at ease. But now she gathered up a sandwich from each plate and returned them to the basket. If Greg could think ahead, so could she.

"Hey!" Eric's protest was quick and sharp. "Why are you putting those away? I'm hungry!"

"You might be hungrier," she countered, "if we don't get back in time for supper."

Greg was unscrewing the top of the Thermos when he suddenly got to his feet, looking at a point behind Sara. The expression on his face made Sara turn and stopped Eric in mid-chew.

As silently as the fox had appeared back in the forest, so now did another being come into view. And, while Sara had accepted the fox as a proper native of the woods, none of the Lowrys had ever seen a man quite like this one.

He was young, Sara thought, but a lot older than Greg. And he had a nice face, even a handsome one, though it wore a tired, sad look. His brown hair, which had red lights in it under the sun's touch, was long, the side locks almost touching his shoulders, the front part cut off in thick straight bangs above his black eyebrows.

Then his clothes! He had on tight-fitting boots of soft brown leather with pointed toes, and he wore what looked like long stockings—tights, maybe—also brown. Over his shirt he had a sleeveless garment of the same green as the tree leaves, with a design embroidered in gold on the breast; it was drawn in tightly at the waist by a wide belt from which hung a sheathed dagger and a purse. In his hand was a long bow with which he was holding back the willow branches while he looked at the Lowrys in an astonishment that matched their own.

Sara got to her feet, brushing twigs and dust from her jeans.

"Please, sir—" she added the "sir" because somehow it seemed right and proper, just as if the stranger were the colonel back at the post "—will you have some lunch?"

The young man still looked bewildered. But the faint frown he had first worn was gone.

"Lunch?" He echoed the word inquiringly, giving the word a different accent.

Eric gulped down what was in his mouth and waved at the plates. "Food!"

"Yes," Sara stooped for the green plate and held it out in invitation. "Do open the lemonade, Greg, before Eric chokes to death." For that last bite appeared to have taken the wrong way down Eric's throat and he was coughing.

Suddenly the young man laughed and came forward. He leaned down to strike Eric between his shaking shoulders. The boy whooped and then swallowed, his eyes watering. Greg splashed lemonade into a cup and thrust it toward his brother.

"Greedy!" he accused. "Next time don't try to get

half a sandwich in one bite." He squatted down to fill the other three cups and pushed the green one toward the stranger.

Their guest took the cup, turning it around in his fingers as though he found the plastic substance strange. Then he sipped at the contents.

"A strange wine," he commented. "It cools the throat well, but it seems to be squeezed of grapes grown in snow."

"It isn't wine, sir," Sara hastened to explain. "Just lemonade—the frozen kind. These are peanut butter," she pointed to the sandwiches. "And that one is ham. Then there're hard-boiled eggs and pickles and some cookies—Mrs. Steiner does make good cookies."

The young man regarded all the food on his plate in a puzzled manner and finally picked up the egg.

"Salt—" Greg pushed the shaker across.

Eric had stopped coughing, though he was still red in the face. Somehow he found breath enough to ask a question.

"Do you live around here, sir?"

"Live here? No, not this nigh to the boundary. You are not of this land?"

"We came through a gate in a wall," Greg explained. "There was a castle—"

"A little castle on an island," Sara broke in. "And in the wall was this gate, all filled up with stones. The boys pulled those out so we could get through."

He was giving her the same searching attention he had given the food. "The boys?" he repeated wonderingly, "but are you not all three boys?"

Sara looked from her brothers to herself. Their jeans did all look alike, so did their shirts. But her hair—no, her hair wasn't even as long as the young man's.

"I'm Sara Lowry, and I'm a girl," she stated a bit primly, for the first time in her life annoyed at being considered one with Greg and Eric, a mistake she had hitherto always rather enjoyed. "That's my older brother, Greg." She pointed with a total lack of good manners. "And this is Eric."

The young man put his hand to his breast and bowed. It was a graceful gesture and did not in the least make Sara feel queer or foolish, but rather as if she were important and grown-up.

"And I am Huon, Warden of the West." His forefinger traced the design pictured in gold thread on his green surcoat. Sara saw the scales of a coiled dragon with menacing foreclaws and wide-open jaws. "The Green Dragon—as Arthur is the Red Dragon of the East."

Greg laid down the sandwich he had been about to unwrap. He stared very hard at Huon and there was a stubborn line to his lips—the way he looked when he thought someone was trying to make fun of him.

"You mean Arthur Pendragon. But that's a story—a fairy tale!

"Arthur Pendragon," the young man nodded encouragingly. "So you have heard of the Red Dragon, then? But not the green one?"

"Huon—there was Huon of the Horn." To Sara's vast surprise Eric said that. "And I suppose Roland's back in there?" He pointed to the wood.

But now the young man shook his head and his smile vanished.

"No. Roland fell at Roncesvalles long before my wardship here began. I wish we *did* have his like to back us now. But you have named me rightly, young sir. Once I was Huon of the Horn. Now I am Huon without the Horn, which is a bad thing. But still I am Warden of the West and so must inquire of you your business here. This gate through which you came—I do not understand," he added as if to himself. "There has been no summoning on our part. That portal was made and then sealed when Ambrosius returned to us with the knowledge that our worlds had moved too far away in space and time for men to answer our calling.

Yet you have come—" Now he was frowning again. "Can it be that here also the enemy meddles?"

"I wish somebody would explain," Sara said in a small voice. More than ever she wanted to know where they were. It seemed that the young man understood, for now he spoke directly to her:

"This land"—his hand made a wide sweep—"once had four gates. That of the Bear in the north has long been lost to us, for the enemy has occupied the land where it exists for a wealth of years. That of the Lion in the south we have closed with a powerful spell so that it is safe. That of the Boar, which lay in the east, has been forgotten so long that even Merlin Ambrosius cannot tell us where it was—or may still be. And that of the Fox here in the west. Some years ago Merlin reopened that, only to discover that there was no longer any way he could touch men's minds. Then did our fears grow—" Huon paused and sat looking down into his cup, not as if he saw the lemonade there, but other things, and unpleasant ones. "And the door was sealed—until you opened it." He fell silent.

"I saw a fox there," Sara did not quite know why she said that.

Huon smiled at her. "Yes, Rufus is a good sentinel. He marked your coming and summoned me. The creatures of the wood aid us gladly, since our lives move along the same paths."

"But what is this country and who are the enemy?" Greg asked impatiently.

"The country has many names in your world— Avalon, Awanan, Atlantis—almost as many names as there were men to name it. Have you never heard of it before? Surely you must if you know also the tale of Arthur Pendragon!" He inclined his head courteously to Greg. "And of me, Huon, once of the Horn. For this is the land to which both Arthur and I were summoned. Or is that now forgot in the world of men?" He ended a little sadly.

Arthur Pendragon—that was King Arthur of the Round Table, Sara now remembered. But Huon—she did not know his story and wished she could ask Eric about him.

Greg was scowling not at Huon but at the ground between his feet where he was digging holes with one of the spoons from the basket.

"It's completely cockeyed," he muttered. "King Arthur is just a legend. The real Arthur, he was a British-Roman who fought the Saxons. He never had a Round Table or any knights! Mr. Legard told us all about him in history last term. The rest of it—the Round Table and the knights—that was all made up in the Middle Ages, stories they told at feasts—like TV."

Huon shook his head. "Story or not in your world, young sir, you are now truly in Avalon this day. Just as I am eating your food and drinking this strange but refreshing wine of yours. And Rufus passed you through the Gate of the Fox without challenge. Thus it is meant that you should come here."

COLD IRON

"THAT YOU HAVE come through our gate without hurt or challenge," Huon continued, "means that you have not been sent or called by them." He held up his hand in a swift sign the children did not understand.

"Them?" Sara asked before biting into her sandwich. This talk about a gate was reassuring because they could go back the same way they had come through.

"The enemy," Huon replied, "are those powers of

darkness who war against all that is good and fair and right. Wizards of the Black, witches, warlocks, were-wolves, ghouls, ogres—the enemy has as many names and faces as Avalon itself—many bodies and disguises, some fair, but mainly foul. They are shadows of the darkness, who have long sought to overwhelm Avalon and then win to victory in other worlds, yours among them. Think of what you fear and hate the most, and that will be a part of the enemy and the Dark Powers.

"We lie in danger here, for by spells and treachery three talismans have been lost to us: Excalibur, Merlin's ring, and the horn—all within three days' time. And if we go into battle without them—ah, ah—" Huon shook his head "—we shall be as men fighting with weighty chains loaded upon arms and limbs." Then abruptly he asked a question: "Do you have the privilege of cold iron?"

As they stared at him in bewilderment, he pointed to one of the basket knives. "Of what metal is this wrought?"

"Stainless steel," Greg replied. "But what has that got to do with—?"

"Stainless steel," Huon interrupted. "But you have no iron—cold iron—forged by a mortal in the world of mortals? Or do you have the need for silver also?"

"We do have some silver," Sara volunteered. She brought out from the breast pocket of her shirt the knotted handkerchief which held the rest of the week's allowance, a dime and a quarter.

"What's all this about iron and silver?" Eric wanted to know.

"This." Huon drew the dagger from his belt sheath. In the shade of the willows the blade shone as brightly as if he held it in the direct sunlight. And when he turned it the metal gave off flashes of fire, as a burning log might spit sparks. "This is dwarf-forged silver—not cold iron. For one who is of Avalon may not hold

157

an iron blade within his hand lest he be burnt flesh and bone."

Greg held up the spoon with which he had been digging. "Steel *is* iron, but I'm not burned."

"Ah," Huon smiled, "but you are not truly of Avalon. As I am not, as Arthur is not. Once I swung a sword of iron, went battle clad in iron mail. But here in Avalon I laid aside such gear lest it do sad hurt to those who follow me. So I bear a dwarf-made silver blade and wear silver armor, as does Arthur. To the elf kind, cold iron is a breaker of good spells, a poison giving deep, unhealing hurts. In all of Avalon, there were once only two pieces of true iron. And now those have been taken from us—perhaps to our undoing." He twirled the flickering dagger between his fingers so that sparks dazzled their eyes.

"What are the two pieces of iron you lost?" Sara wanted to know.

"You have heard of the sword Excalibur?"

"Arthur's sword—the one he pulled from the rock," supplied Greg and then saw that Huon was gently laughing at him.

"But Arthur is only a story, have you not said so? Yet it seems to me that you know much of that story."

"Sure," Eric said impatiently, "everybody knows about King Arthur and his sword. Gee, I read about that when I was just a little kid. But that doesn't make it true," he ended a little belligerently.

"And Excalibur was one of the things you lost?" Sara persisted.

"Not lost. As I said, it was stolen through a spell and hidden by another which Merlin cannot break. Excalibur has vanished, and Merlin's ring—that was also a thing of iron and of great power—for its wearer may command beast and bird, tree and earth. The sword, the ring, and the horn—"

"Was that iron, too?"

"No. But it is a thing of sorcery, given to me by the

elf king Oberon, once high lord in this land. It can both aid and destroy. Once it nearly destroyed me, many times it came to my aid. But now I am without the Horn, and much of my power has departed—which may be an ill, ill thing for Avalon!"

"Who stole them?" Eric asked.

"The enemy, who else? They gather all their strength now to come down upon us and with their witchery nibble away at all our safeguards. It was laid upon Avalon at the Dawn of All that this land was to stand as a wall between the dark and your own mortal world. When we drive back the dark and hold it firmly in check, then peace reigns in your world. But let the dark surge forward here, winning victories, then in turn you know troubles, wars, evil.

"Avalon and your world are mirrors for each other in some fashion even beyond the understanding of Merlin Ambrosius, who knows the heart of Avalon and is the greatest one ever to be born of mortal woman and elf king. What chances with us must follow with you. And now the dark rises high. First it seeped in silently, an almost unmarked flood, now they dare to challenge us to open combat. But with our talisman gone what man—or wizard—can foresee what will chance with Avalon and her sister world?"

"And why did you want to know if we could handle iron?" asked Greg.

For a moment Huon hesitated, while his gaze went from the boys to Sara. Then he drew a deep breath as if he were about to dive into a pool.

"When one comes through the gates, it is because he has been summoned and some destiny awaits him here. Only a very great magic can reopen the way for him to go forth from Avalon again. And cold iron is your magic, just as we have other sorcery for ours."

Eric jumped to his feet. "I don't believe it. It's all a made-up story and we're going right back where we came from. Come on, Greg—Sara—let's go!"

Greg rose slowly, Sara did not move at all. Eric pulled at his brother's arm. "You blazed the trail from the gate, didn't you?" he shouted. "Show me where. Come on, Sara!"

She was repacking the basket. "All right. You go on."

Eric turned and ran. Sara looked straight into Huon's brown eyes. "The gate is really closed, isn't it?" she asked. "We can't go away again until your magic lets us, can we?" She did not know how she knew that, but Sara was sure she spoke the truth.

"I have naught to do with it." Huon sounded sad. "Though I have powers of a sort, none of them controls the gates. I believe that not even Merlin can open them for you—if you have been summoned—only when *you* make your choice—"

Greg moved closer. "What choice? You mean we have to stay here until we do something? What? Maybe get back Excalibur, or that ring, or the horn?"

Huon shrugged. "It is not for me to say. Only in Caer Siddi, the Castle Foursquare, may we learn the truth."

"Is that a long way from here?" Sara wanted to know.

"If one goes afoot, perhaps. For the Horse of the Hills it is no journey at all."

Huon stepped from the shade of the willows into the open sun of the river bank. He put his fingers to his mouth and blew a shrill whistle.

He was answered from the sky overhead. Sara watched with round eyes and Greg cried out. There was a splash, as water washed about hoofs, and the flapping of huge wings. Two black horses stood in the shallow river, the cool water eddying about their legs. But such horses! Ribbed wings like those of bats were folded against their powerful shoulders as they shook their heads and neighed a welcome to the man who had summoned them. They wore neither saddle nor bridle, but it was clear they had come to serve Huon.

One bent its head to drink, snuffling into the water, raising again a dripping muzzle. The other trotted to the bank and stretched out his head toward Greg, eying the boy with what could only be intelligent interest.

"This is Khem and that is Sitta." As Huon spoke their names, both horses bowed their heads and whinnied gently. "The paths of the upper air are as well known to them as the roads of earth. And they will bear us to Caer Siddi before sundown."

"Greg! Sara!" That was Eric shouting as he burst from the grove. "There's no gate. I followed the blazes back—no gate—only two trees standing close together!"

"Did I not say the time for return is not yet?" Huon nodded. "You must find the right key for that."

Sara gripped the basket tightly. She had believed that from the first. But somehow, to have Eric say it was sobering.

"All right." Greg faced the winged horses. "Let's get going then. I want to find out about the key and how to get home again."

Eric fell in step beside Sara, banging his hand against the basket. "You can't drag that along, too. Leave it here."

Huon came to her aid. "The maid is wise, Eric. For this is also one of the spells of Avalon: those who eat entirely of her food, drink only her wines and water, cannot easily escape her borders once again, unless they take upon themselves some grave change. Treasure the rest of your food and drink and add it to ours when you break your fast."

Greg and Eric mounted on Sitta, Eric's arms tight about his brother's waist, Greg's hands twined in the horse's mane. Huon took Sara up before him on Khem. The horses began to trot and then to gallop and their

161

wings snapped open. Then they were mounting up above the sunlit water and the lacy green of the trees.

Khem circled once and headed southeast, Sitta matching him wing to wing. A flock of large black birds started up from a field and flew with them for a while, calling in cracked, shrill voices, until the horses outdistanced them.

At first Sara was afraid to look earthward. In fact she shut her eyes tight, glad of Huon's arm about her, the solid wall of his body at her back. It made her giddy to think of what lay beneath . . . and then she heard Huon laugh.

"Come, Lady Sara, this is not so ill a way to travel. Men have long envied birds their freedom of wings, and this is the nearest mortals can come to such flight, unless they be under some enchantment and no longer men. I would not trust you to some colt fresh out of the cloud pastures. But Khem is a steady mount and will not play us any tricks. Is that not so, Father of Swift Runners?"

The horse neighed and Sara dared to open her eyes. It was really not so bad to watch the passing of the green countryside. Then from ahead there was a flash of light, rather like the sparks from Huon's dagger, but much, much larger. It was sun reflected from the roofs of four tall towers linked in a square by walls of gray-green stone.

"That is Caer Siddi, the Castle Foursquare, which is the western hold of Avalon, as Camelot is its eastern. Ha, Khem, take care in your landing, I see a muster within the walls!"

They circled well above the four towers of the outer keep and Sara looked down. People were moving below. A banner flapped from the tallest tower, a green banner of the same color as Huon's surcoat, and worked upon it in gold was a dragon.

Tall walls rose about them, and Sara shut her eyes

again quickly. Then Huon's arm tightened, and Khem was trotting, not flying. They were on the ground.

People crowded around, so many of them that at first Sara noticed only their odd dress. She stood on the pavement, glad when Greg and Eric joined her.

"Boy, oh boy, some way to travel!" Eric burst out. "Bet a jet would beat 'em, though!"

Greg was more interested in what lay about them now. "Archers! Just look at those bows!"

Sara followed her brother's direction. The archers were dressed alike, much the same as Huon. But they also wore shirts of many silvery rings linked together and over those, gray surcoats with green and gold dragons on the breasts. Their silver helmets fitted down about their faces so that it was hard to see their features. Each carried a bow as tall as himself, and slung across one shoulder was an arrow-filled quiver.

Beyond the lines of archers were more men. They, too, had ringed shirts and dragon-marked surcoats. But long green cloaks fastened at their throats. And instead of bows they had swords belted about them, while their helmets were topped with small green plumes.

Behind the men with the swords were the ladies. Sara became acutely conscious of her jeans, of the shirt which had been clean that morning but was now dirty and torn. No wonder Huon had believed her to be a boy if this was the way women dressed in Avalon! Most of them had long plaits of hair with sparkling threads braided into them. And the flower-colored dresses were long with gemmed girdles at the waists, while their loose sleeves hung in points to touch the ground.

One of the ladies, her hair dark and curling about her face, her blue-green dress rippling about her as she moved, came toward them. She had a circlet of gold and pearl on her head, and the others made way for her as if she were a queen.

"Lady of Avalon," Huon came up to her, "these are three who have entered through the Fox Gate, by let and with no hindrance. This is the Lady Sara, and her brothers Greg and Eric. And this is the Lady Claramonde who is my wife, and so High Lady of Avalon."

Just to say "hello" seemed wrong somehow. Sara smiled timidly and the lady smiled back. Then the lady's hands were on Sara's shoulders and, because the lady was small, she had only to stoop a little to kiss the girl on the forehead.

"Welcome, three times welcome." The Lady Claramonde smiled again and then turned to Eric, flustering him greatly by greeting him with the same kiss, before facing Greg. "May you all rest well within these walls. And peace be yours."

"Thanks," Eric blurted out. But to Sara's astonishment Greg made a quite creditable bow and seemed very pleased with himself.

There was another personage to greet them. The crowd of knights and archers opened a path for him as the ladies had done for Claramonde. Only this was no man-of-arms who walked toward them, but a tall person in a plain gray robe on which lines of red twisted and coiled in strange patterns. His hair was as gray as his robe and lay on his shoulders in thick locks which mingled on his breast with the wide spread of his beard. He had the brightest eyes Sara had ever seen— eyes which made one think he was looking straight into one's mind and reading everything which lay there, good or bad.

For a belt he had a sash of the same dull red as the patterns on his robe. And when one watched it closely it appeared to move, as if it possessed some strange life of its own.

"So at long last they have come." He surveyed the Lowrys with a somewhat stern look.

Sara was uncomfortable at first, but when those

dark eyes were turned directly upon her she lost her fear, if not her awe. She had never seen anyone like this man before, but she was sure he meant her no ill. In fact, quite the contrary, something reached out from him to her, giving her confidence, taking away the faint uneasiness which had been with her ever since she had passed through the gate.

"Yes, Merlin, they have come. For good reasons, let us hope, for good." Huon's voice was low and Sara thought that he too, for all his lordship, looked upon Merlin as someone greater and wiser than he.

MERLIN'S MIRROR

"I DON'T LIKE this. We've got to get away before something happens." Eric was looking out of one of the narrow castle windows. "It can't be far from sundown. What'll happen if we don't get back to Uncle Mac's for supper?"

Sara, seated on a velvet-cushioned stool, the picnic basket between her feet, laughed. "Mrs. Steiner will have a fit, that's what. Anyway Huon and the Lady Claramonde are nice and I don't think they'd let anything bad happen. And how would we get back with the gate gone? Besides, that's miles and miles away from here and we don't know the way back."

"No? Well, I bet those flying horses know it. We could get a couple of them and—"

"And how are you going to do that?" Greg came out of the shadows at the door of the chamber. "There're umpteen people around and they'd ask questions if we tried to walk out. Also, what makes you think the horses would fly for us? Sara's right, what would be the use of going back to the gate anyway, if it's no longer there?"

Greg was no taller than he had been that morning. There was a smudge of dirt on his chin, and his thick light hair needed combing. But he was different, maybe different inside, Sara thought. When he talked quietly like that, he sounded almost like Father in a serious mood.

"You mean we have to stay here until they let us go?" Eric exploded.

Sara turned on him indignantly. "That's not fair and you know it, Eric Lowry! They're not keeping us prisoner. Didn't Huon tell us right at the start that he had no way of opening the gate for us?"

Eric strode over to stand before her, his hands on his hips. "And you're ready to believe everything they tell you!"

"Be quiet!" Greg cut in, sounding more like Father than ever. Eric half swung around ready for an angry retort, but his brother continued, "Sara's right. If part of what they've told us is true, all must be. We are in a castle, aren't we? A regular King Arthur castle. And how did we get here, by riding on a pair of winged horses. Also," he ended thoughtfully, "Merlin is no hoax. And he said he had to talk with us."

"I don't trust him either!" Eric snapped defiantly.

"So, you do not trust me, young sir?"

Sara started and Eric jumped. They had been facing the room's one doorway, but they had not seen Merlin enter. Only now he was standing there, his bright eyes on them.

"Eric didn't mean that," Sara began hastily.

"Oh, but I think he did." Merlin combed his beard with the fingers of his right hand, while those of his left patted his sash belt. In the stone-walled room he seemed even taller than he had in the courtyard, and the gray of his robe blended into the gray of the walls until he might have been part of the castle itself. Now he seated himself in a high-backed chair and surveyed the Lowrys as they stood uneasily before him.

"Eric is entirely right," Merlin continued after a pause during which their discomfort grew. "Yes, he is entirely right not to trust me, Sara."

"Why?"

"Because to me the good of Avalon lies above all else. For more years than there are blocks in these walls about us, I have been one of the three guardians of this land. Arthur wields sword, mace, and lance in the east, Huon stands with his elf knights, a wall of fighting men, in the west. And I bend other powers and forces to strengthen them both. It was not so long ago that I crossed the gulf of time and space to open the Fox Gate—I, Merlin Ambrosius, the only man to walk that way in a long tale of centuries."

"Then you're Mr. Brosius!" Greg interrupted.

Merlin pulled at his beard. "So, I am still remembered? Time is not so well matched between our worlds—here it flows much faster than in yours. Yes, I opened the gate and sought those who would aid us in the coming struggle. But," his voice sounded sad now, "there were none of the right spirit and mind, none we could summon as once the powers of this land summoned Arthur and Huon and me. Now it seems the gate has done its own selecting, just as we face a newer, stronger attack from the forces of evil."

"Huon told us about losing Excalibur, your ring, and the horn," Greg said.

"So?" Merlin's bushy eyebrows lifted. "Then you can understand why we are so excited at your coming. We lose three talismans, and then you arrive. What else can we believe but that your fate is tied to our loss?"

"We didn't steal your things!" Eric sputtered.

"That we know. But you may aid in their return, if you will."

"And if we don't—then you won't let us go home again—that's it, isn't it?" Eric demanded rudely.

Merlin only looked at him and Eric flushed. It was Greg's turn to ask:

"*Is* that true, sir? We can't go home?"

Merlin was quiet again for a long moment, and suddenly Sara had a queer shamed feeling, as if she had done something wrong, although she had not spoken at all. And Eric's face was now very red.

"There is a spell which will force the gate open, yes. If you truly wish that."

"But you believe that we were meant to come here to help you, don't you, sir?" Greg persisted.

Merlin nodded. About his waist the colored lines of his sash twisted and spun until they made Sara so dizzy she had to close her eyes and turn her head away.

"You have a choice, young sirs, Lady Sara. But I must also tell you that, if you choose to give us your aid, the roads set by the mirror are never easy to follow, and he or she who travels them does not return unchanged from such journeying."

"Is it also true that when your enemy here wins a battle, then our world is endangered too?" Greg continued.

Again Merlin inclined his head. "Does your world now rest easy, my son? For the evil tide has been rising here, growing ever stronger through the years. I ask you again, does your world rest easy nowadays?"

Sara shivered. She was not quite sure what Merlin meant. But she remembered all the talk back on the other side of the gate, the things she had heard Mother and Father say.

"No," that was Greg answering, "there's always talk about another war and the Bomb."

"Avalon still holds fast, though how long we may continue to do so"—Merlin's eyes were so bright it hurt to look at them, Sara thought—"no man, mortal or elf kind, can say. It is your choice to aid us or no."

"Dad's a soldier in our world," Greg said slowly. "And if another war comes—the one everyone has been afraid of—would it come there if the enemy wins here, sir?"

"The enemy is never wholly defeated, neither in Avalon nor in your world," Merlin sighed. "He wears many surcoats, marches under many different banners, but he always exists. It is our hope to keep him ever on the defensive, always to face him squarely and never allow him a full victory. Yes, if he wins here, then well may he win in your time and space also."

"Then I choose to do as you wish," Greg answered. "It's for Dad, in a way." He looked questioningly at Sara and Eric.

"All right." Eric's agreement was reluctant. He looked as scared and unhappy as Sara felt inside.

She held to the basket which was the only real thing now in this mixed-up dream. And her voice was very small and thin as she said, "Me, I'll help too," though she did not want to at all.

Merlin straightened in his chair and now he was smiling. Sara was warmer, seeing that smile, and almost happy.

"Then do you search out our talismans, wheresoever they may lie and whosoever may guard them. Remember, cold iron is your servant and your magic—call upon it when you must—and change is the pattern of your going. And the time to begin is now!"

His voice rang as loud as a trumpet blast. Sara cried out as she had when the gate mist had wrapped her in. Then the roaring was gone.

They were still three together. She caught Eric's and Greg's hands. Neither boy pulled away from her. But this was a new place—there were no windows in this room and the light came from five globes of pale green fire set in a star overhead. Three of the walls were covered with hangings of cloth such as Sara had once seen in a museum. There were pictures on the cloth, which moved as if a current of air blew behind it. Strange men with hairy legs ran races there with unicorns. Birds flew and the leaves of the trees seemed to rustle, or perhaps it was the air which made that sound.

The fourth wall was very different, a vast shining surface reflecting all within the room. Of Merlin there was no sign. Sara's grip on her brothers' hands tightened. Now she wished they had asked to go home.

"I don't like this place," she cried and the words re-echoed—"place-place-place."

Greg pulled free and walked to the mirror wall. When he stood before it, he put out his hands so they lay palm flat on its surface. The other two followed him hesitantly.

"Greg, what do you see?" Sara crowded in on one side, Eric on the other. Both of them looked over his shoulders into the strip bordered by his hand.

They might have been looking through a window out upon open countryside. Only what lay beyond was not the green and gold land over which the wingèd horses had carried them, but a very different country.

Nor was it day, but night. Moonlight showed a wandering road just outside, climbing up and up until it was lost to sight on a mountainside. It was bordered by thickets of stunted trees, most of them leafless, and many of them twisted into queer, frightening shapes so their shadows on the ground looked like goblins or monsters. That was all—just a white road running on into dark and gloomy mountains.

"This is the road for Greg. Let him arm himself with cold iron and go!"

Was that order voiced by the people of the tapestry, or did it come from the air?

"No!" Sara cried out. "Eric, stop him!" She tried to hold Greg's arm. "It's so dark." Greg hated dark—maybe that would stop him.

But for the second time he broke her hold. "Don't be silly! If we want to help, we'll have to follow orders."

"That's a bad place, Greg, I know it is!" She turned to look at the road again. It was gone and in the mirror she could see only the reflection of the room and the three Lowrys.

"Arm himself with cold iron," Eric repeated, puzzled.

"Cold iron." Greg went down on one knee beside the picnic basket. "Remember what Huon told us about the power of iron. The same thing must be true of steel." He opened the basket to show the forks, the knives, and the spoons.

Sara sat down beside him, trying hard not to show her fright.

"Remember what he said about the magic in the food also? That we must always eat some of our own along with theirs? You must take something to eat." Her hands were shaking as she put a sandwich, an egg and some cookies into a napkin and made it into a packet. Greg took one of the forks from the webbing.

"You call that a weapon?" Eric jeered. "I think you'd better ask for a sword, or one of those big bows. After all, if you're going to help Avalon, they ought to give you something better."

"Cold iron, remember? And this is pointed, sharp." He tested the tines on his finger. "This is what I'm to take, I knew it the minute I touched it. Thanks for the food, Sara."

With the napkin packet in one hand and the fork in the other, Greg walked once more to the mirror.

"Hey, Greg, wait a minute!" Eric tried to intercept him and Sara cried out a despairing "Greg!" But at the same time she knew her protest was useless, for Greg was wearing his "do-it-now-and-get-it-over-with" expression.

They reached the mirror too late. Greg had already touched its surface. He was gone—though Sara believed that she saw for an instant a shadowy figure on the mountain road.

171

Eric ran his hands over the surface through which Greg had vanished. He pounded on it with his fists.

"Greg!" he shouted, and the tapestries stirred, but there was nothing to be seen now but the reflection of their two selves. Sara went back to the basket and then heard an exclamation from Eric.

As his brother had done before him, he was leaning close to the glass, his hands flat against it. And he was watching something.

"Is it Greg? Can you see him?" Sara flew to the mirror. Maybe they could go through, be with Greg—

But over Eric's shoulder she saw no moonlit road or high mountains. Instead there was a stretch of sea-shore, a beach of sand, with tufts of coarse grass in dark green blots. White birds coasted over the rolling waves and it was day, not night.

"This is the road for Eric. Let him arm himself with cold iron and go!"

Were those Merlin's words? Both children pushed back from the mirror. Sara looked at her brother. He was chewing his lower lip, staring down at his hands.

"Are you going?" she asked in a small voice.

He scowled and kicked at the basket. "Greg went, didn't he? If he can do it, then I can—I will! Give me some food, too, Sara, and one of those forks."

But when he took the fork, he hesitated, and slowly slid it back into the webbing loop again.

"That doesn't feel right," he said. Even more slowly he pulled out the spoon in the next loop. "This is better. Why?"

"Maybe you take what is going to help you most," suggested Sara. She was making up a second packet of food. Though she wanted to beg Eric not to go, she knew that she could not keep him from this adventure, not after he had watched Greg go before him.

"Good luck," she said forlornly as he took the food.

Eric was still scowling as he faced the mirror and his only answer was a shrug. "This is crazy," he complained. "Well, here goes!"

As Greg had done, he walked to the mirror and through it. Sara was left sitting on the floor in a very empty room.

She studied the mirror. It had made a door for Greg, another for Eric. And she knew it was only waiting to make a door for her.

"I wish we could all have gone together," she said aloud, and then she wished she had not, for the echoes rang until it sounded like people whispering behind the tapestry.

Sara picked up the basket and went to the mirror. Then she said determinedly:

"Show me my road, I am ready to go."

There was no mirror at all, but green and gold and sunshine. She marched ahead and her feet passed from floor to the softness of earth. For a moment Sara was bewildered. Here was no mountain road, no seashore. She was in the middle of a woodland glade. Could it be the same wood as held the gate?

This was so different from Greg's dark and lonesome road, from the wild seashore where Eric had gone, that Sara could not help being a little cheered. Only now that she was here, what was she to do?

"Kaaaw—"

Sara looked up. On a branch of tree which hung overhead teetered a big black bird. The sun did not make its feathers look shiny and bright, but dull and dusty. Even its feet and bill were black, but, as it turned its head to one side and looked down at her, its eye glinted red. Sara disliked it on sight.

"Kaaaw—" It spread wide its wings, and, after a few vigorous flaps, took to the air, diving at her head. Sara ducked as it circled her, its hoarse cries sounding like jeering laughter.

Sara ran back under the tree, hoping the thick branches would keep the bird off. But it settled on a limb above her, walking along the bark and watching her all the while.

"Go away!" Sara waved her arm.

"Kaaaw—" The bird jeered and flapped its wings, opening its bill to a wide extent, ending its cry with a hiss which was truly frightening.

Sara, holding to the basket, began to run. Once again the bird took off into the air and streaked down at her head. She jumped for the shelter of a bush, caught her foot on a root, and sprawled forward, scraping her knee painfully.

"Kaaaw—"

This time there was a different note in that sound, the jeer was gone. Sara sat up, nursing her skinned knee. The bush met in a green canopy over her head, and she could not see the bird, though she heard its cries plain enough.

Pattering into sight was the large fox she had met by the gate. With his attention fixed upon some point well above her head, he was snarling ferociously.

MOUNTAIN ROAD

G REG STOOD SHIVERING in the middle of the moon-lit road. He glanced back. Behind him was a dark valley, with no sign of the mirror through which he had come. A wind blew through the branches of the misshapen trees, finding a few leaves to move. It was a cold wind when it pushed against Greg. He hunched his shoulders against it and began to walk forward.

The road was not often used, he judged. In some places it was almost hidden by drifts of soil and in others the stone blocks of its surface were tilted up or down, with dried grass bunched in the cracks between them.

Now the road climbed, curving about the side of the rise. When Greg reached the top, he turned once more to look back. Only the road, running across a wasteland, was to be seen. No sign of any house or castle, nor could he sight any shelter ahead.

His legs began to ache with the strain of the steep climb. Now and again he sat down on one of the boulders brought down in old landslides. But while he rested he could hear nothing save the moan of the wind.

There were no more trees here, only small, thorny bushes without leaves, which Greg avoided after one bad scratch. He was sucking his hand when he heard a faint howl with a dim echo, coming from some place far ahead.

Three times that chilling cry sounded. Greg shivered. Wolf? He swallowed and strained to catch the last echo of that wail.

Now he looked down at the fork he was carrying, wondering what sort of defense that small weapon could be against a wolf attack. As he held it in the moonlight, testing the sharpness of the tines with his thumb, it glittered as had the dwarf-made blade Huon carried.

"Iron, cold iron." He repeated the words aloud without knowing just why. "Cold iron to arm me."

Greg stood up. Again he did not know why he must do this, but he tossed the fork from one hand to the other, and each time he caught it anew it was heavier, longer, sharper, until at last he was holding a four-foot shaft ending in four wickedly sharp points. Maybe this was another of Merlin's spells. It was a queer-looking spear but one which, added to the thought of Merlin, gave Greg confidence in spite of that distant howling.

The road was more and more broken. Sometimes the blocks were so disturbed Greg seemed to be climbing the steps of a stairway. And twice he edged about falls of earth, digging the fork-spear into the ground as support and anchor.

The moonlight, which had been so fresh and bright, was beginning to wane. Greg, seeing how bad the footing was here, and disliking the growing pools of shadow about, decided to camp until morning. He crawled into a hollow between two boulders and put his spear pointing out to seal the entrance.

He awoke stiff and cramped, so cramped that it hurt to move as he wriggled out of his half cave. It must be day but there was no sun. The world was gray, cloudy, but lighter than night. Greg found the trickle of a spring and sucked water from the palm of his hand, taking care to eat bites of his own food with the drink.

The road appeared to lead nowhere except up and up. There were no tracks in the patches of earth covering it, no trace that anyone save himself had been foolish enough to go that way for years. But, though no sun rose, the gray continued to lighten. Greg topped a narrow pass between two huge pillars of rock and gazed down into the cup of a valley, where a river ran fast under a humpbacked bridge. About that bridge, on both sides of the stream, were clusters of stone cottages, patches of green growing about them.

With a cry Greg hurried forward, half sliding down one slope, running down the next in his haste to reach the village and to see another person again.

"Halloooo!" He cupped his hands about his mouth, called out with all the force of his lungs.

The sound rolled about the valley, magnified and bounced back at him from the mountain walls. But there was no answer, no stir on the crooked street of the village. Alarmed now, Greg slowed his headlong pace, bringing his spear before him as he had the night before when he had taken refuge in the cave. He studied the huddle of dwellings with greater care. Most of them were small stone huts with thatched roofs. But now he could see that the thatch was missing in ragged patches, so that some of the houses were almost roofless.

However, just on the other side of the bridge, standing apart from the smaller buildings, was a square tower three stories high, with narrow slits of windows. And this did not seem so weatherworn.

Although Greg decided that the village had been long deserted, he was still alert. The green spots about the tumble-down cottages were rank with huge weeds with fat, unpleasant-looking leaves and small, dull purple flowers which gave out a sickly scent.

He hesitated on the bridge and then glanced quickly at the nearest cottage. The doorless entrance gaped like a toothless mouth, the window spaces were eyeholes lacking eyes. Yet Greg could not rid himself of the feeling that he was being spied upon, that someone or something was peering from that doorway, or from one of the windows, slyly—secretly—

As he moved, his spear struck against the stone parapet of the bridge with a clank of metal. And that sound, small as it was, was picked up, echoed through the empty village. Greg knew in that moment that he should never have shouted from the ridge, that perhaps he had drawn attention to himself in a manner he would regret.

Better to get out of the valley as quickly as he could. He tried to keep all those cottages in sight, sure that, if he were lucky, or fast, or clever enough, he would sooner or later catch a glimpse of what must lurk there.

Crossing the bridge, Greg came out on a stretch of moss-greened pavement about the base of the tower. As he drew level with the door, his spear turned in his hands in spite of the firm grip with which he held it, hurting his skin with the force of the movement. Armed, he stumbled forward a step or two, drawn against the wall toward the interior of the tower by some force that seemed to guide his spear.

Then he discovered he would either have to abandon his weapon or continue on inside. And since he dared not leave the spear behind, Greg advanced reluctantly, the odd weapon light and free in his hold as long as he followed its direction.

Within the tower the light was dim, for it came only through narrow slits of windows. All the lower story was one square room, empty except for powdery drifts of old leaves. Against the far wall was a stairway leading to a hole in the ceiling. This Greg mounted warily one step at a time, still urged along by the spear.

At last he reached the third and top room, which was as bare as the other two had been, and he was completely bewildered. There were three windows here, one in each of the three walls at his sides and back. In the wall fronting him there was the outline of a fourth window which had been bricked up, as had the gate through which they had come to Avalon.

Moved by the power against which he no longer struggled, Greg went to the fourth wall and pried at the sealing stones with his pronged spear. The mortar which had bound the stones must have been very weak, for at the first slight push they gave way, falling outward one after another.

Greg swung around to face the stairwell, sure that if any enemy lurked in the village the crash of the falling stones would bring him—or it—into the open.

But the echoes of the crash faded and there was no other sound. Was the blocked window another gate? But it couldn't be—there was only sky to be seen without.

Greg put his hand on the wide sill and pulled himself up for a better view. The ruinous state of the village was even more apparent from this height. There was not a whole roof on any of the cottages, no signs of cultivation in the old fields beyond.

The puzzle of why he had been brought here—for

Greg was certain he had been guided—was still a mystery. He studied the ground below and saw a ragged bush tremble where there was no wind, as if something crept beneath its masking.

From the village he looked to the far wall of the next mountain. The cloudiness of the day made it difficult to locate any landmarks ahead. Then Greg gripped his fork-spear tighter, for there was something —a pinprick of light far up, far beyond—a light which flickered as though it came from the leaping flames of a distant fire.

He realized that that distant gleam could not be sighted from any other point in the valley than where he now stood. And so it was easy to understand that that light was what he had been brought here to see, that it must be the mysterious goal of his journey.

And now as Greg went downstairs and out into the open, his spear did not resist his going. Only three houses stood between him and the open country, and he was eager to be away from the dead village. However, that was not yet done, as he discovered when he rounded the last hut.

Between him and the first scrubby growth of trees masking the upward slope of the road were what had once been fields. When he had inspected these from the tower, they had appeared to be only weed-grown spaces bordered by the rotting remains of ancient fences. And between them the road ran straight, walled by borders of half-dead hedges.

Greg halted and lowered the fork. For, flowing out of the hedgerows now, was a company of animals. They moved silently, every head swung so that eyes, yellow and green and red, were on him. Wolves—certainly the larger shapes of silver-gray were wolves— minks, weasels—all hunters, all gray of coat.

They stood in a dead tangle of grass, their heads showing above it, the bolder creatures crouched at the verge of the road. But they did not advance any farther. The wolves sat on their haunches as if they were hounds, their pink tongues showing a little. Greg gained confidence. Step by wary step he passed along the lane they had left open for him.

He watched those beads of eyes move as he moved, he held his breath as he stepped between the two wolves. Not daring to quicken pace lest he provoke them into attack, he kept on walking slowly through that strange company. But when he had reached the edge of the wood and dared to look back, the fields were as barren of life as they had been earlier. Whatever had been the purpose of that queer assembly, it had not meant danger for him.

Tired and hungry though he was, Greg began to climb again. He disliked that valley so much he did not want to pause again until he was safely out of it. But soon he ran into thickets of ripe berries and clipped them off in juicy handfuls, munching dry bits of sandwich between.

He spent that night in a rough lean-to he made by stacking branches together. And he slept soundly, though with troubled dreams. Then he awoke to another gray day.

Before he had gone a quarter mile the road forked. The wider, paved way he had followed since he had come through Merlin's mirror angled to the left. Another path, far less well marked and beginning with a very steep climb, went on ahead. And it was the latter which pointed in the direction of the spark he had sighted from the tower.

Greg studied the path. Up and up it angled, ending in the dark mouth of a deep cleft or cave. Again the fork-spear in his hands urged him up and into the very heart of that black opening. He tried to find a path around, but there was no possible one and the pull of the fork would not let him turn aside—unless he dropped it.

Greg crept forward and chill stone walls closed in on

him far too quickly. Somewhere ahead he could hear the distant lap of water. He began to sound his way, rapping the fork against the rock flooring lest he fall into some underground stream.

The dark was so thick Greg had a queer feeling he could gather up its substance in his hands, hold it. When he glanced back, the entrance was a tiny glimmer of gray, so he could hardly distinguish it—then the passage climbed and there was only the terrifying dark, a dark which swallowed you up. He felt as if he could not breathe, that he was trapped. His heart pounded heavily. He wanted nothing so much as to turn and run and run—

Now he was listening, listening for all the things his imagination told him might lie in wait here. But somehow he kept going, his head swimming with the effort that determination cost him, not daring to pause lest he would hear something indeed.

"Iron, cold iron." First he whispered those words and then said them aloud in a kind of chant. And the fork-spear swung in time to that. The feel of it in his hands began to give him confidence—until at last he saw another gleam of gray light and came out on a ledge a few feet above a wide plateau down to which he could easily leap.

At the far side of the level plateau was a paved surface, and Greg saw that it was a sort of road that wound about a series of strange pillars. At first Greg thought they might be columns of a ruined building. Then he saw that they were clustered in irregular groups or scattered singly with no plan.

In the midst of these was the remains of a fire. The huge logs which had been piled to burn there were full tree trunks, and to transport them to this barren waste must have taken a great deal of labor. But he could see no carts, no men, though the fire was not quite dead. A thin trickle of smoke still curled, and the bitter tang of it hung in the air.

Greg dropped to the plateau and walked among the pillars toward the fire. Somehow, deep inside him, he knew that this was the goal of his journey and that he was now about to do what he had been sent to accomplish. That he was to recover one of the talismans, he did not doubt. Which treasure it was and whom he was to take it from still remained mysteries.

He was one pillar away from the fire when he put his hand against the last column. But there was no rock under his fingers—he touched something else! Greg snatched his hand away. Somewhere behind or above him he heard a chime as if a cord of silver bells had been shaken with warning vigor.

SEA ROAD

S AND MOVED UNDER Eric's feet. And a sea bird screamed as it swooped to snatch a wriggling silver fish from the waves. Wind which was crisp and fresh blew against his face and pulled at Eric's hair.

He climbed to the top of the tallest dune to view the scene. The beach was wide. Behind the dune it rippled back to a point where dark patches might mark trees and bushes, but too far away for Eric to be sure. However, he was certain that his path, which was not a real one such as Greg had followed, lay seaward across the water.

So he faced in that direction, to sight a dark blot bobbing up and down, being brought to land by the breaking combers. A boat? Perhaps, though he could not be sure at this distance.

Farther out there was a smudge of shadow on the horizon. Since it did not move and was darker than any cloud, Eric thought it might be land, maybe an island. And because it lay directly ahead of the point where he had entered this country, he was sure that it was his goal.

No one could possibly expect him to *swim* way out there! Could he make it by boat—a good, steady boat?

Eric coasted down the seaward side of the dune and trotted on to the damp sand where the waves broke. Slowly he pulled off his shirt and jeans and waded out. The water was cool, stinging where the briers had made scratches on his legs and arms. Before him, just out of reach, the boat drifted. Eric took another step or two and the footing dropped sharply away from beneath him. He splashed in over his head with a cry, thrashed out wildly. He was right—water could never be trusted—try that and you were lost! Then a remnant of Slim's patient drilling at the camp swimming lessons last year returned to him and he floundered as far as the boat. Steadying himself with a hand on the gunwale, Eric looked the craft over. It was half full of water, which made it ride low, but there appeared to be no break in its sides and he thought if he could tow or push it ashore he could inspect it carefully and make sure.

That was easier to plan than to do. The boat was unhandy and sluggish, and Eric had to exert a great deal of effort to get it ashore. As its blunt bow thrust into the sand, he collapsed quite worn out.

He stumbled up after a while and rubbed himself dry on his shirt. More than anything else he wanted to stretch out and sleep, but the boat was waiting there and he had a queer feeling that time was important and he had none to waste.

Luckily it was a small boat and the material it was made of was very light so he could handle it alone. Upon closer examination Eric discovered that what covered its curved ribs was scaled skin. A giant fish might have been skinned to cover it.

Once the water was spilled out, the craft was buoyant and he pulled it all the way out of the water. Turned upside down so he could look for any breaks in its hull, it resembled a huge turtle with head, tail, and legs tucked into the shell. Dried by the sun the scales had a rainbow sheen, but they were as harsh as a file when Eric ran his hand across the surface.

Sure that it was intact, Eric sat down in the sand and ate a little of the food Sara had given him. He was thirsty, but nowhere on the dunes could he hope to find fresh water to drink.

Then he put the food packet and the spoon into the boat and pushed it afloat before climbing in. The weight of his body sank it into the waves, but it was only at that moment he realized he had neither oars nor paddle.

He was about to go ashore again to search for a piece of driftwood which might serve that purpose when his foot touched the spoon and he picked it up.

"Cold iron," he said aloud, not knowing why.

Then he watched, round eyed with amazement. From a teaspoon it grew swiftly to ladle size in his grasp, then larger, until he was holding an object, spoon-shaped still, but as big as a small spade. Magic, real magic, he thought with a small thrill of excitement.

Large though it now was, the spoon's weight could still be handled easily. Not without fear that it might shrink as suddenly as it had enlarged, Eric dipped it overside experimentally and, using it as a paddle, headed out to sea, his goal that offshore island.

Eric was not an experienced boatman, nor were the skin boat and the spoon the best equipment for such a voyage. But he dipped the improvised paddle with energy, and the temporary smoothness of the water surface was in his favor. As he drew away from the beach the sea birds gathered above him, screaming to one another, and continued to escort him out to sea.

Practice helped. His first clumsiness lessened and

his speed picked up, though he had difficulty in keeping the boat headed in the right direction. And, if he paused to rest his arms and shoulders, the incoming waves bore him back, to lose the painfully won distance. To Eric, the impatient one of the Lowrys, the very slowness of his advance was an added trial, but he continued on.

Slowly the island rose higher out of the water. There appeared to be no shore beach there. Cliffs rose directly from the sea to afford no landing place to anyone but a bird. The flock of birds that had been following Eric's slow progress now flapped ahead of the cliffs and settled down there.

As he drew nearer, inch by weary inch, Eric saw that even if some scrap of beach did exist at the foot of those rock walls there would be no way from it to the heights above. However, there were openings in the cliffs themselves, vast waves into which the sea pushed exploring fingers. Painfully Eric paddled his light craft around the end of a rocky point, hoping to find on the seaward side some landing place.

He circled the entire island, which was a small one, without finding what he sought. Yet he was certain that he *must* land here. And until he did so, and accomplished the task which had been assigned him by the mirror—or by Merlin—there was no going back.

Underneath his outward impatience Eric possessed a core of stubbornness. It was this that now held him to his weary round of paddling, though his shoulders ached and his arms felt leaden. If there was no beach, then he must find another way in—perhaps through one of those gaping caves. He chose the largest and paddled toward it.

The curve of the roof was high above his head, and for about three boat lengths the daylight lasted to guide him in. Eric used all his small skill to keep directly in midchannel, well away from the ledges of rock from which trailed lengths of green weed. The smell of the sea was strong, but with it also came another odor, not as pleasant.

As the light grew dimmer the walls began to draw together, and Eric feared his choice had not been a good one. But still he sent the boat on, even when the ledges came within scraping distance. For he believed he could see a wider area ahead. So sure was he of this that he poled the boat for the last foot or so, pushing the spoon against the rocks for leverage. There was a scrape and then he floated into a lighted space.

Far overhead a break in the rock framed the sky, and the sun shot dusty rays to a pool of quiet water. To Eric's left was the beach he had sought, showing dry white sand well above the water line.

When the keel of the boat grated on the miniature beach, Eric crawled over the blunt bow, pulling the light craft up behind him. The smell of the sea was strong here, as it had been in the outer cave, but with it was that other odor.

Eric drew the boat entirely out of the water before he explored farther. There was no way of reaching that hole far above. But the beach sloped up, and since there was no back wall to be seen as yet he started to walk on it.

He was really thirsty now, his longing for a drink increased by the sound of the sea's wash around the rocks. And he hoped to discover a spring or fresh-water pool on the surface of the island. The memory of the lemonade he had drunk so long ago made him run a parched tongue over his dry lips.

The beach slope continued upward, bringing him to a dark crevice. Eric hesitated. It was so dark in there and the thought of pushing on was not a happy one.

At last, extending the spoon before him to test the footing, he advanced. The crevice proved to be a short corridor, ending in a well. Only now, against the circle of free sky above, could he see the rough projections and hollows which provided holds for the hands and feet of a determined climber.

Fastening the spoon to his belt, Eric began to work his way up. Had it not been for his thirst he would not have found this a difficult venture. But now all he could think of was the need for fresh water—lots of water—and quickly found.

He made a last hard pull and was out, to lie panting on a mat of coarse grass. The cries of the sea birds were loud and shrill, their screams rising to a deafening din. And the odd smell which had hung in the cave was much stronger here. He sat up to look around.

The cliffs which were the sea wall of the island were, in fact, the outer sides of a giant bowl. By a series of ledges the land within descended to a valley, the center point of which could not be far above sea level.

Those ledges were covered by patches of rank green grass, but they also afforded lodging places for hundreds of nests—old nests, Eric decided, after examining the nearest. If this was the community nursery of the sea birds it was not in active use at present.

In the very center of the round valley was a vast mass of sticks and rubbish which might have been gathered by some giant among birds. Or did it mark where the refuse of years of nests had been brushed and wind-blown?

What interested Eric far more at the present was the sight of a small trickle of water splashing from ledge to ledge on the far side of the cup-shaped valley. He was sure such a tiny rivulet was not born of the sea, and it was what he wanted most at that moment.

He started around the valley, not wanting to take the more direct route over the odorous mass in the center. The birds continued to wheel and call about him, rising into the air as he passed, settling down on the ledge behind him.

They seemed, he thought once, rather like spectators gathering for a promised show. And he was sure that more and more of them were winging in from the sea to settle about the upper rim of the bowl. But none of them flew at him or tried to defend the old nests. And he did not fear their presence.

Only—there was such an attitude of waiting that Eric's uneasiness increased. He now noticed that though all the upper ledges were thick with nests the fresher masses of dried materials there were based on moldering remains of earlier building; yet, for a good space about the mass in the center, there were no smaller nests at all and the wide ledges were bare.

Eric made the journey to that thread of stream and drank from his cupped hands, taking a bite of bread with the welcome water. Then he splashed handfuls of it over his hot face and neck. From this point he had a good view of the stuff in the center of the dip. And the longer he studied it the stronger grew that unpleasant suspicion that it was not driftage from the old nests on the upper ledges but a huge nest in its own right, entwined and woven in its present state and size with purpose.

"For an eagle?" Eric wondered, wishing he knew more about birds. He remembered some pictures in an old *National Geographic* of a bird in South America—a condor. Yes, that was it—a condor! Those grew to be so large they could carry off a sheep. Was this the nest of a condor?

Judging by their condition, the other nests were all last season's; perhaps the same was true of the large one. Eric sat gazing down. The last thing he wanted to do was to descend and rake through that mess. Yet, just as he had been drawn to the island from the shore, so was he being drawn to that big nest.

He hunched forward, his elbows planted on his knees, his cupped hands supporting his chin. There were strange things caught in that tangle. He was sure that he had seen the glint of sun reflected from metal.

But the present odd behavior of the birds kept him from exploring. The upper ledges were now packed almost solid with them. And their cries and calls were dying away. They perched there, one folded wing against the next, all eying him. Eric did not like it. He wanted to retreat to the sea cave, to the boat waiting there. Only, he could not.

Then the spoon, which had been fastened to his belt, slipped free. Eric grabbed for it without success. It clattered down on one of the lower bare ledges, gave a bounce, and flew out into the very heart of the massive nest. There it stood, handle up, bowl buried deep.

He could not go back to the boat without it. Eric stood up. The birds were so quiet they all might have been holding their breath to watch some important action. Within him Eric feared that once he touched that giant nest he would provoke some unheard-of danger. He had to get the spoon and yet he dared not!

Fighting his fear Eric dropped from one ledge to the next, descending to the mass of withered sticks and other material. In order to reach the spoon he must jump out into the very center of the mess.

Now not a bird called, there was no sound at all in that queer valley. Eric jumped. From far off there came a shrill scream as he crashed down, waist-deep, in the stuff of the nest.

WOODS ROAD

IN THE WOOD where Merlin's mirror had brought her, Sara pushed back into the shelter of the bush and watched the fox anxiously, not sure that he was friendly. But she was certain that his anger was for the bird hidden somewhere in the branches above her. She hoped that his coming would drive the vicious crow—or whatever it was—away. She could still hear the bird moving about. It no longer called, but the scrape of claws on bark, a rustle as if it fanned its wings, reached her.

The fox was now gazing straight at her. Meeting that intent regard, Sara was no longer frightened. She wriggled forward out of the bush and got up, brushing dirt and dead twigs from her shirt and jeans. There was a flutter in the tree and the fox snarled menacingly. Then the bird flew out well above them and circled.

"Kaaaw—" But it was a scream of anger and defeat.

The fox answered with a sharp bark, and the black bird soared, vanishing above the treetops. Sara thankfully watched it go. Its harsh croaking could be heard dying away in the distance, and the girl sighed with relief. True, it had been only a bird, but there was something in its attack upon her which had been the more frightening because it *was* a bird, a creature so much smaller than herself, that had wanted to hurt her.

The gentlest of tugs at the bottom of her jeans drew

her attention from the treetops to her new companion. The fox was mouthing the fabric as might an affectionate dog, first pulling and then trotting a few paces on, looking back in invitation. Sara picked up the basket to follow.

The red tail with its pointed white tip waved briskly from side to side as her guide led her between two bushes and so into a path where the saplings and undergrowth reached higher and higher until they met in a green arch overhead. They were not alone in this green world. Although Sara saw no one but the fox, she could hear all kinds of small squeakings, rustlings, and patterings behind the leaf walls, as though a crowd of small forest people were gathering to watch them pass and talking in their own language.

The green road was growing dusky as light-leaved bushes gave way to dark-needled evergreens. And the pleasant, spicy odor, as well as the spring carpet of castoff needles underfoot, made the journey pleasant, in spite of the increasing shadows.

Now that they were among the evergreens, these sounds made by the unseen watchers died away, and the fox slowed his pace. His pointed ears pricked forward and, seeing his caution, Sara felt uneasy again. The darkness was full of menace and she pressed on until she felt the reassuring brush of the plumed tail against her legs.

For how long they followed the road, Sara could never afterward tell. She only knew that when they came to a clearing she was very tired and hungry, glad to sit down on a mat of pine needles and moss. The fox sat down also, his tongue lolling from his jaws.

"Are you hungry?" The three words sounded very loud in the dim place, making Sara sorry she had spoken. She opened the basket and took out a sandwich, carefully breaking it in half. The bread was beginning to dry and curl up at the edges and the peanut butter was all caked. Ordinarily she would have thrown it away, but now she ate it eagerly, offering the other half to the fox.

He eyed it curiously and then, slowly and unmistakably, he shook his head. Sara tried to eat slowly, making each bite last as long as possible. But she could not deny that she was still hungry, even after picking up the last crumb.

The fox was on his feet again, plainly waiting for her. Then they could both hear, faint and far above, that "kaaaw." This time it came from more than one bird. The fox backed against Sara, forcing her by the pressure of his body into the shadows under the trees. His head was up as he gazed into the circle of sky above the clearing.

Sara saw a line of birds skimming across the open. They were high above the clearing and none of them appeared to notice the two standing there.

"Kaaaw—"

The last bird in line fell away and swooped down. The fox ushered Sara into a hollow between two trees. Once they were safely under cover, the fox turned his head to her. He was laughing in his own way and Sara managed a small answering smile. The more she saw of those black birds the less she liked them.

The trail brought them to a brook, but the fox would not let her approach the stream until he had prowled along the bank, pausing to listen and peer up into tree branches. If any of the black birds were hidden there to spy, they were cunning enough not to betray themselves. The fox went down to lap water and Sara joined him. But he was impatient, mouthing her sleeve in warning before she had had more than a few sips to drink.

They traveled across a fallen log bridge and into the path on the other side. Then the fox came to an abrupt halt, one front paw slightly raised. Across the path, stretched in unbroken perfection, was a gauzy circle of spider web. It was the largest one Sara had ever seen and she stood very still, her heart beating fast. How large was the spider that would spin a web like that?

The fox whined softly as might a dog faced by some problem it could not solve. Plainly he did not want to touch the web. Hating the thing herself, Sara picked up a dried branch and thrust it at the lacy circle, expecting it to break into a few floating strands.

To her horror the branch bounced back. With more caution Sara brought the branch against one of the threads anchoring the web to the ground, with no better result. Delicate though the web seemed, it could not be so easily broken. And she could not bring herself to touch it with her bare hands.

They could not go around it, for here the bushes and trees so walled them in that they could not break through. Also, and this worried Sara most of all, how could they be sure that the spinner of that rubbery web was not lurking somewhere off the trail to meet them?

The web might be cut with a knife—if she had one. If she only had the fiery silver blade Huon wore! But what had he said—iron was poison to the creatures of Avalon? Iron . . . the steel knives in the picnic basket!

Sara took one out. It was a rather blunt-edged blade, made more for spreading than cutting. But maybe she could saw through the strand of web with it.

Twice only did the steel touch the web. Sara sat back on her heels with a cry of amazement. From the spot where she had tried to cut through, the threads were shriveling. In a matter of seconds the web was gone and the path open. The fox barked in approval and Sara flung her arms about his neck, hugging him while he politely touched his nose to her cheek.

She kept the knife ready in her hand, but they came

upon no more of the elastic webs as they started to climb a gradual slope. Though the trees became smaller and fewer there were still many bushes and the fox kept close to these, pushing Sara into their shadows time and time again.

At last they were faced with a wide space where only grass grew. The fox barked twice and crouched low, wriggling forward a length or so, demonstrating caution to the girl. So, worm-fashion, hot and scraped, Sara was guided to the top of a small knoll from which the fox indicated they were to spy out the country ahead.

From the knoll the ground sank once again. Sara, seeing what lay in the hollow, could not help shuddering. There was a wood of trees. But they were all stark and dead, pointing leafless branches to the sky. Around the outer edge of the wood, bands of gray stuff reached from tree trunk to tree trunk, as if lengths of material had been tightly stretched into a wall reaching higher than Sara's head. And that gray stuff was spider webs, hundreds, millions of spider webs, woven one above the other into a thick blanket.

Where were the spinners of those choking strands? Sara tried hard not to think about what they must look like, how big they would be. Surely the fox did not mean for them to go in there! Only, inwardly, Sara was sure that was just why she had been brought to this place.

The knife had broken one web. But would it work as well against that wall binding the whole dead forest? And if she did cut a path for them would they then be faced by some kind of creatures who *liked* to live in a dead wood protected by a spider-web wall? For that wall must have been fashioned to protect or imprison *something*, something Sara did not wish in the least to meet.

However, the fox did not urge her forward to attack

194

the sticky wall. Instead he retreated, working his way back to the wood from which they had come. When they were once more in the cover of the forest, the fox lay down, his head resting on his outstretched forepaws. He closed his eyes slowly and then opened them.

They were to stay there and rest, she translated. A nest of dried leaves against a fallen tree trunk seemed very soft to her as she curled up in it. She was sure her companion would not allow either bird or spider near her, and she was very tired indeed.

Something soft, maybe the blanket, moved against her chin. . . . Sara opened her eyes. The fox stood over her, the paw with which he had roused her still raised. He whined very softly deep in his throat, and she took that as a warning, pulling out of the leaf nest with as little noise as possible.

It was close to sunset. The shadows under the trees had grown long. From the top of the fallen log the fox whined again. Sara climbed up beside him and on the ground ahead saw a strange sight.

The dark soil had been cleared of leaves and sticks. In the middle of the space sat the picnic basket, and ranged out from it were stones of all sizes and shapes laid out in the form of a star within a circle. At the five points of the star small piles of green leaves were heaped.

Again the fox whined and pushed against her. Sara walked forward until she stood beside the basket. As she looked back at the animal his head bobbed up and down in approval. She was doing as he wished.

Completely puzzled she waited, watching as he trotted purposefully from one small pile of leaves to the next. He shoved at each with a forepaw, having first nosed it. What he was doing, or why, she could not guess.

When he had completed his circle he sat down on

his haunches and then reared up, holding his front paws into the air. As he barked and whined he moved his paws, and for some reason Sara found it necessary to sit down. No, not really to sit down, but to kneel, her hands on the ground as if she must copy the usual four-footed position of the fox.

Thin trails of mist rose from the leaf piles, though Sara was sure they were not afire, for she could see no flames. She smelled a wonderful spicy scent, like a combination of pine needles warmed by the sun and the cloves Mrs. Steiner used in cooking. The smoke from the little piles of leaves grew thicker and thicker, closing about her. Now Sara could not see the fox, nor anything outside the star and circle.

The smoke had made her head dizzy and queer. She wondered if she was dreaming all this, for everything looked so odd. A little frightened, she tried to get up. But her hands did not push properly—in fact, she no longer had hands!

Paws covered with gray fur rested on the ground. And there was the same gray fur up her arms! Sara swung her head about—gray fur all over her body—a gray tail behind her. Who—what was she?

Sara tried to scream. But the sound she made was very different indeed—

"Merrrow!" That was the wail of a terrified cat!

The smoke was lifting. She could see the star points, each marked by a cone of white ash where the leaves had been. And, as that curtain disappeared, she saw the fox, now looming well above her in a very disturbing way.

"Come!" The word might have been a bark to Sara-the-girl's hearing, but to Sara-the-cat it made sense. However, she remained where she was, letting the fox kick and paw inside some stones of the pattern to approach her, her protests and demands for explanation expressed in a series of yowls and hisses, while the hair stiffened along her humped spine and her tail lashed angrily.

"Come!" The fox stood over her. "The shape-changing does not last past tomorrow's dawn and there is much to do."

"What have you done to me?" Sara demanded. "I am not a cat!"

"That is true. But as a human you could not enter the Castle of the Wood. And that you must do, lest all of us of the woods and fields of Avalon be put to the service of the Dark Ones."

"How?"

"Did not Huon tell you of Wizard Merlin's ring? He who wears it upon his hand can shape and make animal and bird, tree and bush, either for good or ill. While Merlin wore it, it was used only for good—the good of all good things—the ill of all evil things. But now it has fallen into the hands of evil, so will its use be wholly to the ill of all. But evil does not yet dare to use it openly. So it has been hidden away in the Castle of the Wood, where only one armed with cold iron and the magic of cold iron may enter to bring it forth. Since evil knows at once when a human approaches its secret places, you must put on the guise of one of us. The shape you now wear will last until the rising of tomorrow's sun. So you must hurry, taking with you that iron which is your own magic."

He nosed the basket open and pointed to the knife Sara had used against the web. Bracing her paws against the edge of the basket, Sara pulled it from the webbing. It was an awkward thing to carry in her mouth as now she must.

Her earlier fright and anger were ebbing. Somehow the longer she wore the cat body the more natural it seemed. And this was going to be an exciting adventure. She was eager to be off.

The fox gave a last warning. "You must return here,

to this place, and enter into the circle and star before you change, lest you be given another shape which is not of my choosing. If evil flows behind you, it cannot follow here. Be on your way now, gray sister!"

Sara skimmed up the hillock once more. She found she could run without a sound and that her new body was good for such sly work. It was already dusk in the vale, and in that gloom the spider-web walls had a soft glow of their own.

THE SWORD

IN THE STONE wasteland of the mountains Greg felt so alone. As the chime of the bells sounded he stood very still, his head up, looking about. The stretch of mountain wall was far away and none of the strange pillars were crowned with belfries. Some thin and lazy wisps of smoke rose from the charred logs of the fire, but there was nothing else to be seen.

The pillars! While the bells still clamored, Greg returned to the pillar he had leaned against. To the eye it was a tall, rough, column of stone. Yet to the touch it was far different.

Once more Greg put out his hand, and the tips of his fingers moved not over stone but over the smoothness of metal and the soft texture of leather. For the second time he jerked away from that contact. Why should stone feel like a body dressed in scaly armor and leather? Why did his eyes tell him one thing, and his fingers another?

"Is—is there anyone here?" He meant that call to be louder than the bells, but it came from his lips hardly above a whisper. The rock pillar remained a rock to his eyes. Nothing moved. But now the sound of the bell, instead of chiming from all parts of the plateau, centered on one point across the dying fire. And more smoke puffed from the ashy brands, although no more wood had been added.

"Who is there?" Greg called again.

"There is no need to shout, sir squire."

Greg gaped. One moment the space across the fire had been empty, now someone stood there. For a second he thought it Merlin, for the person wore the same long gray robe he had seen on the wizard. Then, perhaps because his fears made him more alert, Greg knew the difference. Merlin's gray had been patterned with threads of red and it had been a silver-gray, the color of a sword blade.

But this newcomer was cloaked, and hooded as well, in the dull gray of winter storm clouds, and the patterns were in black thread, as was the girdle. Greg had felt awe for Merlin, but this stranger aroused fear. And instinctively Greg raised his fork-spear with the tines pointing to the other.

The stranger laughed gaily. White hands threw back the hood and a woman faced Greg. Her hair tumbled out of the sack of the hood and fell about her shoulders, its ends reaching below her girdle. The locks were not dark, nor fair, but the color of the silver blade Huon had shown them. And they appeared to throw off sparks of glittering light, as the dagger had drawn and reflected the sunlight.

She gathered up a handful of hair and spread it wide across her palm, then broke loose one, two, three of the long hairs. And, as she stood smiling at him, she rolled these together between thumb and forefinger.

"Why do you come here, sir squire?" she asked softly. "Also, it would seem that you do not like the open road, since you crept upon me by a back way." Her tone was that of an adult reproving a naughty child. But it was a tone Greg had heard many times in the past and it did not shame him. In that the witch made her first mistake, for he was not thrown off guard in confusion.

"I came by the road shown me," Greg answered, not knowing just why he chose those particular words, but knowing that they did not please the witch.

"Oh, and who guided you on that road?" It was a sharp demand.

Again Greg found words which were strange to him. "That which shines across stone—stone of body—stone of mind—"

"So! You are of those, are you!" Her eyes blazed green at him and her fingers moved very fast, weaving the cord she had spun of her three hairs into a net. "Then join your fellows!"

She cast the net at him over the charred logs and it expanded in the air as if to engulf his whole body. Greg thrust at it with the spear. The tines tangled in the mesh, wrapping it about the spear. One strand whipped about Greg's hand and wrist, clinging tightly.

But in seconds those strands which had caught on the prongs lost their silvery gleam, blackened, withered away to threads, and fell harmlessly to the ground. The bells shrilled in a wild clamor and the woman retreated a step or two, her clenched hand at her mouth, staring at him.

"Iron—a master of iron!" she half wailed. "Who are you who dares bring cold iron into the Stone Waste and takes no harm from it? Whom do you serve?"

"Merlin sent me."

"Merlin!" she spat the name in a snake's hiss. "Merlin, who is between the worlds so he can touch iron, and that silly boy Huon, who was born a mortal so he can wield iron as a sword, wear it as a shield, and that Arthur, a stupid, roaring bully of a king, who brought iron with him into Avalon—to poison those greater than he dared dream of being! May they rot and perish, may iron turn against them and sear the flesh from their crooked bones, may they be eaten up by the demons of the night! And you," she stared at Greg, "you are not Merlin though he is a master at shape changing. But with his ring gone from his hand" —she laughed harshly—"he could not put on any disguise which would hide him from me. And you are not Huon, and certainly not Arthur! So I command you, boy, tell me your true name?" She was smiling and her voice had grown soft again.

"Gregory Lowry," he replied, in spite of himself.

But that answer did not appear to please her in the least. She repeated the name, her hands moving in complicated gestures as they had done when she had woven the net of hair. Then she threw them up in a movement expressing impatience and defeat.

"You hold iron, against that I may not set any spell. Well, what do you want of me?"

"That which is hidden." For the third time Greg spoke words someone, or something, else had put in his mouth.

She laughed loudly. "That you shall not have! Look about you, rash child. Where will you find that which is hidden? If you search here for forty days and forty nights, still will it remain safe for me!"

The pronged spear moved in Greg's hold, as it had moved to draw him into the tower in the deserted village. Slowly the points reversed, heading earthward. Greg had a flash of memory—people hunting water with a forked stick which turned to the ground where a well might be dug—he had read about that. Could the fork-spear guide him to what must be found? He would try.

But he did not have to move far in his quest, for the weapon nearly flipped out of his grasp as he approached the fire, thrusting the tine tips into the mass of burnt wood and ash. Greg, kicking aside charred ends, began to dig.

The bells were no longer silver chimes, they were a

harsh clamor beating in his ears, making him deaf and dizzy with their din. And the witch sped around and around the fire, though she prudently kept beyond spear reach, shouting strange words and making those patterns in the air with her hands.

A fearsome scaled thing, neither snake nor crocodile but a nasty mixture of both, squatted near, reached out claws to menace him. Greg swung the spear, brushed those claws, and the thing was gone. Other horrors gathered to ring him in, but Greg, feeling secure in the power of iron, did not even try to get rid of them. He continued to fork away earth from where the fire had burned.

It was slow work, for the fork did not serve well as a shovel and he was afraid to put it down and use his hands. In the end he squatted, holding the fork with one hand and shoveling out the loosened soil with the other. Then his groping fingers found something to tug at—

The object came up and it was so heavy he had difficulty in shaking it free of the dirt. But what he held was a sword!

Greg had seen its like in a museum and he had wondered then how any man had had strength enough to swing it. For its broad blade and heavy cross hilt weighed down hand and arm. A sword—the missing talisman—Excalibur!

He put the spear between his knees for safekeeping and brushed the clay dust from the hilt and glimmering blade of the sword. It was very plain, bearing no bright gems, no wealth of gold, but he was sure this was what he had been sent to discover. Greg held it tight to him in his left arm as he looked up at the witch.

She no longer strove to weave spells, but stood quietly, eying him narrowly in return. And, as he backed away from the hole, Greg had the feeling that while she had lost the sword, she still believed that she had a chance for victory. Was it chance, or some more of Merlin's long-distance magic that had solved part of her secret for him?

For, as he backed away, the tip of the sword struck hard against one of the pillars. And that blow was answered by a choked cry!

Where the pillar had been stood a man, or rather swayed a man, his eyes closed, his face very white. He wore armor and leather like Huon's elf knights, but his surcoat was white with a red dragon for its device. He moaned and his eyes opened.

" 'Ware the witch!"

A net of hair whirled through the air. Greg caught it on his spear before it could touch the man and it withered away.

The witch screamed and the sound was not a human cry. In her place, a huge gray bird fluttered wings in rage and ran at Greg with cruel curved beak wide open. The boy swung the spear and the creature dodged, scurried on for a few feet, and took to the air, disappearing over the mountain. Then there was utter silence, for even the bells had ceased to chime.

"The sword!"

The man who had been a pillar was on his knees, his eyes wide and happy as they rested on the blade Greg held. "Sir, I beg of you, free this company. And then let us ride fast and hard. For Arthur's sword must rest in Arthur's hand before the enemy strikes into the very heart of Avalon! Time is passing very fast."

One by one Greg touched the pillars on the plateau and then the larger boulders which lay among them, until a company of men wearing the badge of the Red Dragon and their horses were living creatures once again. They left, two of the guardsmen riding double so that Greg might have a mount to himself.

The road was too broken to allow them a fast ride, but the knight Greg had first freed kept them to the best pace they could. They rounded the mountainside to the meeting of the cliff road, and before them now was the valley of the deserted village. It was close to sundown and Greg's dread of spending the night in that haunted place grew with every horse length they advanced. He tried to argue his companions into a night halt where they were, but to that they would not agree.

"You do not understand, youth. Now that the sword is out of their hands, they dare no longer hesitate in the attack. They must move before we reach Arthur or fail—and they still have the horn and the ring to hold against us. Thus if they can strike before we return Excalibur to the king, they will have some chance of victory, since only he dares carry the blade into battle. We must ride by night and day lest that chance be proven true."

"Huon's horses are winged. If we had those—" Greg said.

"The Warden of the West is served by the Horses of the Hills. But those are few in number and answer only to the call of the Green Dragon, not the Red. Most strongly do I also wish they were with us at this hour!"

Greg could see the buildings of the village now, the tower, the humpbacked bridge. They had ridden to the edge of the fields where the road ran between hedgerows and he had walked through the lines of animals. What had been the purpose of that gathering? Where now were the wolves, all the rest?

He did not see the thing that scuttled out of the bushes. Greg's first awareness of danger came when the horse he was riding reared high and he was nearly spilled from the saddle. Greg was no horseman and it was all he could do to cling to the saddle horn with one hand and the precious sword with the other, while his fork-spear fell to the ground.

That which had halted in the road before his mount had been no larger than a small dog, but it was growing fast into a scaled thing such as the witch had summoned on the plateau. Its taloned forepaw arched up above mount and rider, then flashed down.

Greg let go his hold on the saddle horn. With both hands he raised the sword; it was far too heavy for him to swing. The paw of the other came down, was impaled. The creature screamed and tried to jerk back; Greg was torn from the saddle. As he fell, in spite of his efforts, he lost his grip on the sword. Defenseless he faced the full fury of the giant dragon-thing.

The horse bolted, scattering the men who were fighting the frenzied fear of their own mounts. Greg saw the knight who led them trying to reach him.

Excalibur! Where was the sword? It had fallen from the thing's paw and lay in the road dust between Greg and the monster. The wounded limb of the reptile was shrunken and powerless, and perhaps the blade between Greg and the dragon prevented a second attack. Greg tried to look for his spear and watch the monster at the same time. Suddenly a gray shadow leaped from the hedge and slashed at the scaled tail, and Greg heard the howled challenge of a wolf. As the spined head of the thing flashed around to this new annoyance, Greg caught up his spear.

A second wolf howl rent the air, but it was a cry of anger and not of fear. Up over the road rose a wave of animals, large and small, all heading for the dragon-thing, their teeth gleaming as they came. The monster stamped its feet, swept with its tail, shrilled red rage.

Then it leaped high, springing over the sword, looming above Greg. But excited though it was, the dragon flinched from the spear prongs. Greg lunged and the monster gave way, making a fatal mistake, for on its second retreat the bulk of its underbody came down on the sword.

Its head cracked skyward and it bellowed, twisting back and forth, but seemingly unable to move from that spot, as if the blade upon which it now crouched was a trap. The outlines of its body wavered, grew smaller. Greg saw that it was no longer a dragon but the gray-robed witch of the plateau. She shivered and shuddered, but her two feet were locked to the blade of Excalibur and there she was held fast.

On her robe the black lines rippled and ran, her silver hair writhed about her as if every strand had a life of its own. Then there was a flash and the woman was gone. A column of smoke wavered, sinking lower and lower. Save for the sword the road was now empty.

But only for the moment. From the hedges and fields there were rustlings, the sounds of many voices crying out in surprise and thanksgiving. Where the animals had swarmed to help in Greg's battle now moved men and women who stared dazedly at their own hands and feet, felt their bodies, looked at each other in amazement and joy.

The knight, his horse once again under control, came pounding up. On his face there was a wild elation.

"The Witch of the Mountains is naught!" he shouted. "Behold the ruler of the Stone Waste is gone from Avalon and with her dies the evil she has done! One of the enemy is vanquished. Rejoice you people, freed from the spell of the night."

THE HORN

ON THE SEA island Eric stood with his feet deeply buried in the mass of dried stuff which formed the huge nest. He had to flounder a step or two farther to lay hands on the spoon. And it was tough wading, for his weight broke through the brittle stuff easily and gave him no steady footing. All he wanted to do was retrieve the spoon and get back to the safety of the ledges.

But Eric could not help noticing that there were odd things caught in the material of the untidy nest. A chain of gold was laced back and forth in a bundle of dried grass. Near it was a piece of tattered and faded cloth still bearing an embroidered device.

He had hold of the spoon now and tried to work it free of the sticks. But its bowl seemed to be so wedged into a hollow that he could not pull it loose. At last he was forced to tear at the mass with his hands, throwing aside wads of grass and broken branches.

It was very hot in the cup-shaped valley under the full rays of the sun and Eric paused now and again to rub his sleeve across his sweating face. The dust and grit he had stirred up in his job of destruction powdered his sweaty skin, got in his eyes and mouth. But he worked on, determined to free the spoon.

At first he thought there was a cloud lowering overhead when a shadow crossed the nest. But a sense of danger warned him and he looked up, only to cower frantically down into the wreckage he had made.

Earlier he had tried to imagine what kind of bird had built that nest. Now he knew. But to see it alive was worse than to picture it in his mind. And could that monster be only a bird? For what kind of bird had a scaled rather than a feathered head? Yet it did have feathers, black feathers, on its body, and those giant wings which flapped in thunderclaps of sound as it circled the island were fashioned like a bird's, if on a huge scale.

Eric dug at the mass of nest under him, hoping to burrow into hiding until the bird was gone. For he was very sure if he attempted to reach the open ledges he would be exposing himself to instant attack. That scaled head was armed with the curved beak of a hunter, and the feet, drawn up to its body as it flew, were taloned.

He was holding to the spoon, and at last at his

frantic tug it loosened, uprooting a vast heap of the nest material. Eric threw himself into that evil-smelling hollow. The original foundation of the huge nest had been laid across a depression. As he jumped, this foundation splintered, disclosing a small cleft in the rock floor beneath. Eric poked the spoon into this, having no wish to fall to the sea caves below. But the metal rang on rock, finding a bottom to the crevice a few feet down.

A screech from overhead—a shriek such as a diving jet might have made—set Eric to pushing and squeezing into the hole, raking his shoulders, tearing his shirt. But he was safely flattened in the rock-walled crevice when the bird-thing landed, deafening him with wild squawks.

It was the very fury of the bird which saved Eric. For it tore at the nest, and the mass of stuff it dislodged fell across the hole, covering him. He lay there, his mouth dry, his hands shaking on the handle of the spoon. Shivering, he waited for the covering to be scratched aside, and claw or beak to pluck him out. Once a talon scraped across the rock surface just above him. But the crevice saved him from discovery.

Only, how long could he stay there? The loose stuff was being torn and tossed about, so a measure of air reached him. But that was limited. And if he moved he would be seen.

With his hands Eric began to explore the narrow space in which he lay. Its width was hardly more than that of his shoulders, but it was longer than he was tall. Deeper, too, than he had first thought, for small trash from the nest had sifted into it. He was pressed down upon small branches, powdery vegetation which smelled of decay.

Eric began to dig this from under him. From sounds he could tell that the bird was still searching for him, but in such a mindless way that Eric began to believe it was a stupid creature. If that dim wit led to its forgetting him quickly, he had a good chance at escape.

Meanwhile he cleared a passage along the crevice, pushing the loose trash behind him with his feet. Then his head bumped an obstruction not so easily moved. Eric explored by touch, discovering this was no branch, for he fingered the smoothness of metal which curved sleekly.

When he tugged, the object yielded, but also he brought disaster on himself, for the whole brush heap heaved. And the bird could not have been as stupid as Eric hoped, as there was an answering flurry above. Eric gasped and choked as dust filled his mouth and blinded his eyes.

Then the whole mass over him was raked away. Eric blinked watering eyes up at the bird head curving down to him the beak open. Fortunately the head had to turn to one side before it was in striking range. Eric swung up the spoon in a last wild try at defense.

That beak struck the metal bowl with enough force to smash it back against Eric's body, driving most of the air out of his cramped lungs. He lay scarlet-faced and gasping, waiting numbly for a second blow.

When that did not come he edged about, trying to rise from the crevice. Though his eyes smarted from the dust, he could see more clearly now—until a violent flapping of the wings stirred the litter into a murky storm cloud.

The bird, its wings beating frantically, was shaking its head from side to side. And there was something odd about that head, too, though the creature's jerky movements kept Eric from a close examination. He got to his feet, the spoon held up before him.

A second time the head darted down. Eric, with all the energy he could summon, swung the spoon as he might a bat. The improvised club met the head squarely with an impact which crumpled Eric to his knees. Then the wings beat, lifting the creature into the air above the bowl. It made no sound and its head bobbed limply on its breast. Up and up it climbed and Eric stood to watch it. Was it going to strike at him from that height? Only the loosely dangling head, the now faltering beat of the wings, made him hope he had had the better of their meeting.

The birds were rising from the ledges to join the creature. But not for long did they escort it. The great wings clapped for the last time, closed against the half-feathered, half-scaled body, and the thing fell toward the sea. That it was dead, or at least mortally wounded, Eric no longer doubted.

Keeping the spoon in the crook of his arm for safety, he wiped the dust and dirt from his face. He was not sure yet just how it had happened, or why the bird had died. What Huon had told them of iron being poison to those of Avalon must be true. And he was grateful for that.

The walls of the crevice, uncovered for a good length by the bird's last efforts, were waist-high about him and Eric started to climb out, eager to reach the spring on the ledge and rinse the dust from his mouth and throat. But there was something looped about his ankle and he stooped to free it.

He was holding a strap of leather, old, but well oiled and still limber, and it had small gold stars and symbols he did not understand set into it. It could not have been hidden there long. When he pulled he discovered it was anchored to something still wedged in the wreckage of the nest.

Eric scooped away the sticks with the spoon handle. Metal gleamed up at him, not gold this time but silver, banding a duller white. He had uncovered a horn of ivory and silver.

Shaking it free, Eric held his find up to the light of day. It could not have lain long in concealment for the silver was not tarnished. A horn! Huon's horn! He had found one of the lost talismans.

Tempted, Eric rubbed the mouthpiece on his sleeve and put it to his lips. But he did not blow. There was something about the horn which was not of the world he knew. Telling himself that a call might bring another of the giant birds, Eric slung the strap over his shoulder and clawed his way back through the debris to the ledge spring where he drank deeply and ate of his food packet.

How long he had been on that island he could not have told. And time in Avalon and his own world ran differently—had not Merlin said something like that? It seemed as if he had been there for hours, yet just now it was drawing close to sunset.

Dared he try the trip back to shore by night? Eager as he was to be away from the nesting place, Eric was reluctant to set forth from the island. There was too much chance of being carried seaward in the boat. And he was too tired to paddle back. Every bone in his body ached with weariness.

Where *could* he spend the coming night? Eric shrank from the destroyed nest and the ledges about it. Better return to the sea cave and sleep in the boat, fearful though he had always been of water. And he had also better climb back before night.

Eric began the descent of the well which he had earlier climbed. He had believed the horn safe on its carrying strap. But when a handhold slipped, the strap slithered down from his shoulder and fell free, the horn with it.

Tense, Eric clung where he was, listening for the smash which would mark its landing. But he heard nothing. The thought of the horn's destruction made him so weak he was unable to move, his eyes watered, his stomach churned. What had he done in his carelessness?

All the many times in the past when Mother and Dad, Mrs. Steiner, Uncle Mac, yes, and Greg and Sara, too, had scolded him for being too fast, too impulsive, sang now in his spinning head. If the horn was broken what would happen? What could he say to

Merlin and Huon? He had failed in his part of the quest.

Because he could not remain where he was, Eric hunted for the next hold on the wall. The spoon fastened to his belt clanged against the stone, but he did not care. The sky circle above him was dimming rapidly, cutting the light.

Eric descended slowly. If the impossible had happened and the horn had not been splintered to bits when it struck the ground, he had no wish to land on it himself. He clung tightly to the wall as his toes touched the bottom and then looked down and around eagerly.

But here those dim rays from the sky were gone. Eric went down on his knees and felt about him—then moved his hands faster, sifting sand, coarse gravel between his fingers, finding and discarding stones, until he had searched the whole floor of the well. Nowhere did he touch the leather strap or a battered curve of ivory and metal. The horn had completely disappeared!

Twice he searched the space, unable to believe that the horn was gone. Had the strap caught on some projection of the well wall, he would have brushed against it during his descent. So—

Eric's head was spinning, he was sure of nothing now. After one last sweep of his hands across the floor of the well, he headed back down the narrow passage to the sea cave.

The moist, salt-scented air of the cave puffed in his face, welcome after the ordeal in the nest. At the end of the short passage before he scrambled down to the beach, Eric lingered, peering out. The lapping of sea water against rocks was loud, but he was sure he heard another noise—a click—a grating.

Eric could make out the blot which was his boat, still out of the water as he had left it. He stood quite still, trying to keep the sound of his breathing to the faintest whisper. Although he could see nothing but the bulk of the boat, he believed there was another thing out there, a living creature with perhaps the power and will to attack—or damage—the boat on which his escape from the island depended.

Once again that sound—louder now as if who or what was making it had no reason for concealment. Eric saw a dark shape flip into the air, outlined against the faint glimmer which marked the sea inlet.

That line ended in a monster claw, a claw which slowly opened and then snapped shut, as if its owner were flexing it before use. Then the clawed limb fell against the boat, and the light craft stirred in the sand, pushing toward the water. Eric knew he must act or the boat would be out in the pool beyond his reach.

His trust lay in the power of iron and he held the spoon as though it were a spear, the end of its bowl the point. Then he rushed that dark thing.

The spoon struck the side of the boat, bouncing off to a dark bulk which flinched and whipped away as if the tool were a branding iron. A jointed leg with its fearsome claw flashed up at Eric. The boy went down on one knee, holding the spoon to counter the blow, as he had held it to ward off the bird's beak. The claw struck forcibly, jamming Eric against the boat where his cheek rubbed raw on its scaled substance.

He cried out in pain, but there was no answer from the thing he fought. Eric could see only a black lump humping to the water. If it were able to escape into the sea, he could expect another attack.

Desperately Eric got to his feet, and holding the spoon over his head he ran forward, bringing the odd weapon down with all his might on the shambling creature. It slumped under the blow. He felt a stinging slash across his leg just below the knee. But he had won; the thing was no longer trying to reach water.

There were scrabbling sounds, as if many legs tried to lift a helpless weight of dying body. Then all was quiet.

Eric could not bring himself to touch the thing; he shrank from knowing what manner of creature he had fought. Sliding the spoon bowl under its bulk, he levered it into the pool. Then once again he felt the tangle of a strap about his foot, and eagerly he dug into the sand where the monster had lain, recovering the horn from where the dead thief had dropped it.

THE RING

THE WOOD WORLD awaited Sara now. As she sped toward the spider-web walls of the Castle of the Wood, strange new scents, smells which made her cat's nose twitch with excitement, arose from the ground under her paws and filled the air about her. She had never known before what it was really to be able to smell! Just as she had never known what it was to see. To her human eyes it had been dusk, a dimming of all color, a thickening and spreading of shadows. But now she could see into the heart of those shadows and so lost any fear of them.

But, though she was excited and pleased with her new body, her uneasiness returned in part as she neared the weirdly glowing spider webs. When she was still several feet away, she dropped the knife, planted both forefeet upon it for safety, and held her head as high as she could for a better look at the dead forest.

Sara shrank from touching the web. She had hoped to find a place where her cat's body might spring over the sticky band. But nowhere in sight was there any section where the outer trees were not coated from roots to lower branches with the stuff.

She must use the knife—but where? Some of the

inborn caution of the animal whose shape she now wore came to her. She slipped through a growth of tall grass and crept on, the knife again gripped in her teeth.

Fearing unpleasant sentries, she dared not make too large and easily discovered a hole in the wall. So Sara hunted until she discovered a place where two mighty tree roots stood half out of the ground. Strands of web closed the gap between them, but it was a small gap. She crouched low and used her paws as well as her mouth to guide the knife. It was a clumsy business and took much longer than it would have done had she used hands and fingers. But the strands withered away and she had a free passage into the forest.

As she entered, flattening her body between the roots, Sara could see well enough. Very luckily the web did not extend beyond the first line of trees, and there were blobs of greenish-yellow light ahead.

The blobs were fungi growing on rotten wood. Sara's paw broke one, and the air was instantly filled with drifting motes of dust. She sneezed and then crowded her front paws against her nose. When she sneezed she had dropped the knife and that was dangerous. Quickly she picked it up again.

Any leaves which had fallen from the dead trees had long ago turned to dust, because the ground was bare black earth. She hated the slippery feel of it against her paws and, whenever she could, she walked along exposed roots or the trunks of fallen trees.

A human without a compass might have been lost in that maze where every tree copied its neighbor and the fungus lights confused the eye. But Sara's cat instinct took her without trouble toward the heart of this evil place.

She had not sighted any animal, bird, or insect. But she had a queer feeling that something lurked just beyond the limit of the eye, spying, waiting. And that Sara did not like at all.

Once she had to detour about a pool where the water was black and scummed. Bubbles rose slowly to the surface and broke. There Sara saw the first living thing, a pale, bleached lizard on a slimy rock, watching her with hard, glittering eyes.

At the other end of the pool Sara came upon faint traces of a path and she turned into it, eager to reach her goal. She had not forgotten caution, however, and it was with a cat's instant response to a danger signal that she halted at a faint sound. Was the lizard following?

Then she saw the enemy, not behind but to her right. A cluster of the fungus lights displayed its full horror. Sara tried to scream and the sound came from her furry throat as a hiss.

The thing ran along a tree trunk in a burst of speed she could not have bested and then halted. When it rested it was hardly distinguishable from one of the fungus lumps. Sara's claws dug into the ground as she flexed them. Warily she looked about, studying fungi which might not be fungi after all.

Her alarm grew. There were three, maybe four of the giant spiders drawing in about her. Had she not been alerted by the carelessness of the first, they might have surrounded her before she knew it. One she might attack, but not a whole ring of them.

A strand of thread floated lazily through the air. It drifted down, lay on Sara's furry back. There was another—and another! A web was being woven to enmesh her. But at that moment she feared the spiders themselves more than their handiwork and she planned desperately. She must allow herself to be trapped. Then, when they were sure of her, she would use the knife to escape.

It was very hard to do, waiting for the floating threads to coil about her. But Sara flattened her body to the ground, her paws drawn under her, the knife between them ready to be pushed forward. She shivered as the mat of threads caught on her ears and hurriedly shut her eyes.

Once the net covered Sara's back and head it fastened her tightly to the ground in a few seconds. She had to depend now on nose and ears to guide her. Legs raced across her imprisoned body and she shuddered as the spinners tested the silky bonds.

What if the spiders stung her now, left her paralyzed and helpless in the wrappings? She could smell their foulness, hear the faint rustle of their passing. They were circling, adding to the weight of the web.

Then a last tug on the smothering cover over her. The strong odor of the creatures faded. She strained to listen, to smell. If they left a sentry, there was no more than one. And one alone she could handle. Moving her paws against the ground, Sara pushed out the knife to touch her bonds.

There! Her right forefoot was free! Iron magic worked again. Sara arose from her crouch as the web broke and shriveled. She opened her eyes.

Facing her, standing erect on all its eight legs to challenge, was one of the spiders. It teetered back and forth and sprang. Sara struck with a front paw, knocked the creature to the ground, then swung the knife to touch it. She was not sure Huon had been right—that iron was poisonous here. She could only hope so.

The spider pulled its legs under it, becoming a white-yellow lump. Sara took the haft of the knife in her mouth and jumped, pulling the blade across the insect's round body. The spider wriggled in sharp jerks, its legs flexed, and then drew up again. Sara prodded it with the knife, not wishing to touch it with her paw. When it did not move again, she laid the knife on the ground, keeping one paw on it, and with her tongue cleaned the remnants of the web from her fur.

Then, carrying the knife, she circled the dead spider and went on. But she was alert for another meeting with the creatures, watching every near fungus cluster with suspicion. It was very quiet in the dead wood, for there were no leaves to rustle, nothing but damp soil underfoot. Now that earth was giving way to flat stones which might have been old, old pavement.

The path dipped with banks of tree-grown earth rising on either side. Sara kept to its center, for in between those trees were more thick webs.

That sunken road brought her to a stream. This was no scummed pond but brown flowing water running in two ribbons about an island.

The outer rim of the island was a wall of stone so old and overgrown with dead vines and shaggy moss that it was hard to tell it from native rock. Once there might have been a bridge connecting it to the road, now there was only a series of water-washed stepping stones.

Sara prowled back and forth on the bank eying the stones doubtfully. Though she had not been told, she believed that the island was the center of the wood and held what she had come to find, but how to reach it was a problem. She could see unpleasant-looking water creatures swimming or moving back and forth on the stream bed, and she did not want to battle them. But could she leap from one wet stepping stone to the next without losing her footing?

She crouched, balancing the knife carefully in her mouth, and jumped to the first rock. It was slippery but she held fast. The second was flatter and better footing. There she sat, the knife under her forepaws, to study the third—for that had a rounded top and was green with slime. However, the fourth was another flat one. Could she leap to that from here? She crouched again, her hindquarters quivering, and tried.

Her hind feet splashed in the water as she scrabbled for a hold with her forepaws. There was a sharp pain in her tail and she heaved up and out. A clawed creature was pinching her tail tip, and Sara growled, swinging the creature against the knife so it tumbled off limply into the stream.

218

Wet fur made her cat body miserable, but she could not pause here to lick herself dry. For there was now another and longer jump to reach the top of the island wall. Clenching her teeth upon the knife, she made it. The wet hair on her spine rose in matted spikes, her ears folded to her skull, and her tail swung as she stood stiff-legged staring down at what that circle of ancient wall guarded.

The spiders of the forest were nasty creatures which she hated on sight, but here was worse—a toad three times the size of her present cat shape. It squatted motionless in the exact center of the open space, but its yellow eyes were fixed unblinkingly upon her and Sara feared it more than the spiders.

Her small body was shaking with more than the chill of the water. Those eyes—they were bigger—bigger—they were filling up the whole world! They were open places into which she might fall!

Sara blinked. It was dark, night had settled in. But those yellow toad eyes were bright enough to light up the island. The huge stretch of lips below them was opening—

She made herself as small a target as possible, the knife in her teeth. But the toad was so large, and the power of its eyes held her still. A black lash of tongue flickered out from between those huge lips, striving to whip her into the waiting mouth. But it touched the knife and snapped back.

The toad shivered, its bulk quivered, its mouth shut. Then out from between those lips fell a round, glowing bead which rolled to the foot of the wall where Sara crouched. The bead was as clear as glass and at its core she saw a ring of dark metal.

The ring! In that moment she had to choose. She could not carry both ring and knife. If she took the talisman in her mouth she would have to leave behind her only weapon.

Sara moved quickly because she was afraid that if

she waited she would not be able to do anything at all. She tossed the knife at the toad and saw it land on the creature's broad back. The thing writhed and twisted, and then crumpled as might a bag from which air had escaped.

She sprang from the wall and snapped up the bead. It was hard to mouth but she held it.

"Kaaaw—" A black bird such as those which had followed her and the fox dived from the air, sounding its battle cry. Sara moved with terrified speed, making the passage of the stepping stones in bounds, returning to the shelter of the dead wood. She paused under that cover trying to plan, fearing to travel the spider-infested path without the knife.

She had dropped the bead between her paws and it was only at that moment she remembered that the ring itself was iron and so might be her protection. But first the glass shell about it must be broken.

Dropping it on a nearby rock did not crack the covering. She stood upon it with the full weight of her forepaws, but it only sank in the mold and did not break.

"Kaaaw—" One of the birds hopped along bare branches just above her and he was answered from the air. Sara took the bead in her mouth once more and ran at her best speed. As she went she bit at what she held, hoping her needle-sharp cat's teeth could crunch through.

With a leap she cleared the body of the spider guard where she had been trapped. Perhaps if she just kept running she could escape any harm. But there was the beat of wings in the air, a quick stab of pain in one ear. Sara backed against a tree trunk where a mat of dead branches made cover to keep off the birds. She would have to break the bead or she would never get out of the wood, she was sure of that now.

With her nose and forepaws she wedged the globe against a half-buried stone and then, finding another

such stone, she pushed it against the outer surface of
the bead with all her strength, moving it slightly so
that the globe was ground between the two rocks. She
was losing hope in her plan when with a small "pop"
the bead was gone. Some dust glittered on the mold
about the ring and that was all.

Sara mouthed the band, ready to run again. There
was a scream from above. The birds were rising, leaving. Sure that she had a chance now, Sara ran, not
realizing at first what was happening about her. For,
as she sped among the trees, change spread with her.

Lumps of fungus dwindled, fell away. There was a
cool wind rising, driving through the brittle branches,
bringing with it a sweet cleanness. As she flashed
about the pool where the lizard had lain, the water
was no longer dull and scummed. It bubbled and sparkled, moved again by some long-choked spring.

When Sara reached the spot where she had crept
beneath the web wall, she no longer faced the stretch
of murky stuff. The web was now only bits of patches,
for the wind was tearing at it, shredding it loose. So
she ran easily out into the moonlight to climb the
slope to where the fox waited.

At the top of the rise she paused to look back. All
the dead trees were bending and twisting in the wind.
Most of the web wall was gone. It was as if the strong
blast of air was sweeping away all the evil which had
hidden there, making it ready for life again. She saw a
whirl of birds rise up against the moon. They wheeled
as they flew toward her, uttering their hoarse calls.

Sara turned and ran at her best speed. Perhaps the
wood was free of evil now, but it appeared that the
black birds still had the power to hunt.

THE FOX GATE

BEFORE GREG WAS transformation indeed—change as great Sara had seen in the wood. The village that had lain under the witch's spell came to life again. Its people, freed from their animal shapes, worked busily about their ruined homes. Two of those who had run as wolves now stood erect as lord and lady of the tower, to press upon Greg and his companions what shelter and food they had to offer. But when they had rested for a short space, Arthur's knight urged that they ride on, and now Greg was as impatient as he.

Though they pushed on into the gathering darkness, they did not lose their way, for, as the gloom thickened, there came a glow of light from the hilt of the great sword resting across the saddle before Greg, a light that was reflected and fed by a similar beam from the fork-spear. And this lighted their path as well as if a torch were being carried before them.

Where did the mountain road lead? Greg had entered it through Merlin's mirror and he had no idea of where it went beyond that point. He noticed that those who rode with him had their hands close to their sword hilts and that they kept careful watch of the heights on both sides of the road, as if fearing some ambush.

They came to the place where Greg had spent the night in his half cave. There it was necessary to dismount and pass one at a time, leading the horses down the broken slope. When they were once more on level ground, Greg was almost too tired to climb again into the saddle.

"Mount, young sir!" Arthur's knight urged him. "Time passes. Even now the east and the west may be facing the enemy. And how may Pendragon ride to battle without his blade? Mount—we must hurry!"

Painfully, Greg obeyed and rode on, nodding with weariness, not aware that the knight had taken his reins and was leading the horse he bestrode. But he roused quickly when the knight shouted an alarm.

The moon had risen and before them was drawn up a force, a silent barrier across the road. There were men—or things that looked like men—and these were flanked by monsters. Along their ranks, pointed at Arthur's men and at Greg himself, were blades of smoky red flame. At the back of this dark company was a shimmering silvery curtain—Merlin's mirror?

"Ho for Pendragon!" It was the knight who raised that cry as he drew his dwarf-forged blade. Those of his band echoed the cry and showed their own weapons.

Greg's horse, when the hold on the reins loosened, cantered on toward the line of the enemy. The boy heard the shouts of Arthur's men, the pound of hoofs on the roadway. His own horse, frightened, began to gallop. Points of dark fire gathered before Greg in a menacing wall. He held Excalibur tightly to his body with his left arm, while in his right hand he lifted the fork-spear. And the moonlight, pallid and weak though it was, centered on that, making it a banner of white flame. The dark wall wavered, moved before him. Greg cast the fork-spear, and the enemy's line curled back from its touch, while the horse galloped on toward the misty curtain.

Behind that, Greg saw a man mounted on one of the winged horses. He was a big man, with a golden beard and a helmet topped by a carven dragon with eyes of fire as red as the surcoat which covered the man's back and breast. Behind him was a great host of knights and archers under a banner that crackled in a high wind.

The bearded man faced Greg and held up his hand in a gesture of both entreaty and command. Somehow Greg found the strength he needed. Raising Excalibur in both hands, he hurled the sword up and out. End over end the giant blade went through the curtain. Then, as if drawn to a magnet, it flew to the outstretched hand of Arthur Pendragon. Three times the Warder of the East whirled the sword over his head as the banner behind him dipped in salute.

Then Greg's horse was at the edge of the mist, and Greg himself was engulfed in a swirl of fog. From afar he heard shouting, the clash of blade meeting blade, the singing of bowstrings. Then he rolled across grass and opened his eyes—to see above him, plain in the warm sun of afteroon, a fresh blaze cut upon a tree trunk.

Eric shrank back from the water into which the sea-thing had rolled. His first plan for spending the night in the cavern no longer pleased him. All he wanted was to return to shore, get away from the island as quickly as he could. He launched the boat, hoping to be free of the cave before the light utterly failed.

He kept the horn on his knees as he used the spoon paddle, determined not to lose it again. It took him much longer to edge through the narrow passage to the outer cave, for he feared ripping the skin covering of the craft on a rock, and he inched along until he could see the gray of evening reflected on the water ahead.

Against the lap of the waves, the sound of surf, Eric strained to hear any other noise. The monster of the inner cave might not have been the only one of its kind abroad. Eric's worst fear was that something would rise from the depths to attack the boat.

It was more difficult to get out to sea than it had been to enter the cave originally. For then he had had the waves at his back and now he must head into them. Eric was so tired that every time he raised the spoon paddle his shoulders ached with the effort. But he made it at last, and gave a sigh of relief when he saw the island only a shadow on the sea, at his back instead of before him.

To Eric it seemed that that shadow reached in a black block from the island to the shore and that his path was covered by its gloom. The last red bands of the sunset were across the sky where it met the water, and in the air wheeled and called the sea birds.

They coasted on outstretched wings over the waves, skimming not far above his head. Surely they must be some of those that had perched upon the ledges to watch his battle with the monster. And now they followed him as if keeping watch. But for whom—for what?

Each slap of wave rocked the light boat. It would be so very easy for something to rise out of those waves, to turn the craft over. He must not think of that! His one bit of good fortune was that the shoreward wash of the waves carried the boat along, easing his paddling.

As the minutes passed and the beach drew nearer, Eric's confidence increased. So he was ill prepared for the trouble which did meet him.

The boat grounded gently and he jumped into the receding wash of the surf to draw it up. While the sea birds had seemed his enemies on the island, gathering to watch the attack of the giant bird, now they proved his friends. For, as Eric scrambled over the wet sand, the flock which had escorted him to land flew shrieking toward the dunes, uttering the same call they had given when he had leaped into the nest.

Eric spun around. The dunes made hills and valleys where the wind drove rippling sand. Coming out of several of those valleys were creatures no taller than he. They scuttled swiftly on webbed feet, moving to encircle him.

Their scaled skins gleamed wetly in the last glow of the sunset, the tangled mops of their green hair hung over their small eyes—which were fixed on Eric. If they kept on moving, they would push him back to the sea.

He held the horn and the spoon. The spoon had stood between him and the fury of the giant bird, had saved him in that battle in the cave with the unseen monster. Now it must clear a path through this mob of mermen. He twisted the sling of the horn through his belt, making very sure he could not lose it.

Then, holding the spoon before him, Eric moved straight ahead to meet the line of attackers. A swift dip of his odd weapon into the sand, a flip of grit into the faces of two of the creatures sent them wiping frantically at their eyes as they cried aloud in high, thin voices like the screams of sea birds. But others were closing in and Eric swung the spoon. It jarred against one of the mermen, who in turn stumbled against his nearest fellow, tripping him up.

Eric sped through the gap so opened in their line. He dodged into a space between two of the dunes, only to face the rising slope of a third. To climb the sandy hill at speed was, Eric discovered, a difficult feat. At any moment he expected to feel a webbed hand close about his ankle and pull him down. But with aching ribs and pounding heart he reached the top of the rise, still ahead of his pursuers.

A green paw was grabbing for him, and behind that leader the rest of the pack crowded close. Their clamor shrilled in his ears, bewildering him. Now they had ringed the foot of the dune, were advancing from all sides. Eric did not see how he could escape.

He chopped down at the first paw with the spoon, made the leader tumble back. Then, because he could think of nothing else, he hurled the spoon at the advance and brought the horn to his lips—to blow with all the breath remaining in his laboring lungs.

There was a thunderclap of sound. The green men froze, then charged at him, yowling. But a shimmering gray curtain was before him and Eric, desperate, leaped through it.

On a windy hillside he faced Huon, who stood brave in silver armor with a green surcoat, a helmet on his head. Behind him were the knights and archers from Caer Siddi and over their heads whipped in the wind the banner which had been on the castle tower.

Though Eric believed he had securely fastened the horn, it now left him, swinging up into the air. Huon snatched it. With one hand he saluted Eric, with the other he raised the horn to his lips. There was a second blast of sky-cracking sound and Eric was picked up by it, or by the wind, or by some strange force, and swept away.

Panting, he leaned against a tree. And before him, as tired and dirty as he was himself, Greg sprawled on the ground.

"Kaaaw—"

Sara leaped ahead, but a wing scraped across her tail. She kept her mouth clamped tight on the ring and fled at her best speed toward the marking of star and circle where the fox must be waiting. Now the black birds were attacking her as she had seen bluejays attack a cat, and she feared their sharp beaks and claws.

"Come! Come!" To human ears, that might only have been the bark of an excited fox, but to Sara it was a promise of help. The large red body of her woodsguide flashed down to circle her, snarling at the birds. But they were not to be driven off so easily.

Again Sara felt a sharp stab of pain as a claw raked her ear. She wanted to squawl her rage, but remembering the ring she held she kept her mouth shut and ran. Her pace was slowing, her throat was dry, her chest pained. There—there was the star-in-circle!

Now the fox was leaping into the air, battling the birds. Black feathers fluttered down. Her guide caught one body in his teeth and shook it limp. But the rest of them darted past him at Sara. She arose on her hind legs, striking out with unsheathed claws. Then she gave a last great spring and landed beside the picnic basket in the center of the star.

The fox barked and the birds swooped, still overhead.

"Use the ring! Change shape with the ring!"

Sara's mouth opened, the ring fell out upon the lid of the basket.

"Touch it and wish!" The fox bounded back and forth outside the circle.

Sara put up a footsore paw and laid it on the iron circlet.

"I want to be myself again," she meowed.

The fur on the back of her paw faded, the pads grew into fingers. Then, in a few more moments she was truly Sara again, outside as well as in, with a smarting scratch across her cheek, and so tired she could hardly move.

Once more the fox barked, but now she could no longer understand. He nodded his head vigorously toward the path in a way she could not mistake, and she got wearily to her feet. The ring! There it was on the lid of the basket. She picked it up and slipped it on her finger, doubling her fist about it for safekeeping. Then she hooked her arm through the handles of the basket and started after the fox.

The birds had drawn off the moment Sara had used the power of the ring. And, though she could still hear their harsh cries, they no longer flew to attack. But she was too tired to walk far.

However, the fox did not go with her on the woods path. Instead he slipped between two trees, giving reassuring barks and whines to urge her on.

They came to an opening in the woods where Sara could look through a frame of branches as one might look through a window. And she was not too surprised to see beyond the frame the room of the mirror where the tapestries still moved in the wind.

Merlin was there, facing her. He smiled and nodded, and held out his hand, palm up. Sara pulled the cold ring from her finger, glad to be free of it. She tossed it through the frame of branches and saw it fall into Merlin's grasp, his fingers close about it. Then the opening into the room of the mirror was gone and in its place was another stretch of woodland where Eric and Greg sat together under a tree, both of them looking very much as if they had been in a rough-and-tumble fight.

"Greg! Eric!" Sara broke through the bushes. She put down her basket and caught at her brothers to make sure that they were real and they were all truly together once more.

"Sara!" Both boys held her hands tightly. From behind came a sharp bark. The fox had followed her and now he trotted purposefully on, looking back over his shoulder in summons.

Sara was so used to obeying that gesture that she freed her hands from her brothers' grasp and picked up the basket again.

"Come on."

They threaded a way among the trees until before them stood an arch of stone covered inches deep with green moss, with the carven mask of a fox set to crown its high point.

"The gate!" Eric ran forward. "We're able to go back—"

Sara turned to the fox and held out her hand. The big animal walked to her and just for a moment her fingers rested on his proud head. Then he barked impatiently and Greg pulled her on.

But there was no going through the gate. They

could see no barrier though but it was there, an invisible wall between them and their own world.

"What's the matter?" Eric's head was up, his face flushed, he was shouting aloud to the trees about them. "We got back your talismans, didn't we? Then open the gate! Right now!"

Sara looked at Greg and her lip trembled. She was almost as frightened now as she had been in that wicked wood among the spider hunters. Would they never be able to leave Avalon? It had been an exciting adventure, but she wanted it to end—right now!

"Open up!" Eric aimed his fist at the space between the stone pillars, only to have his hand rebound from an unseen surface.

Then, to one side there was a shimmering of silver light. Sara caught at Greg's arm, Eric moved back. The tall column of silver broke into a mist of small, glittering sparks and in the midst stood Merlin.

On his robe the red lines twisted and climbed, blazing brighter than they ever had before, and the iron ring banded the forefinger of his raised hand.

Sara looked at the ring when she said, "We want to go home."

"Cold iron is master," he answered her. "You have left behind that which is not of Avalon and it binds you within this gate."

"The fork!" Greg cried out. "I lost it when we fought to reach King Arthur, back on the mountain road!"

"And the spoon," Eric broke in. "I dropped that on the dune where the sea people were."

"I threw the knife at the toad," Sara added. "Does that mean we have to go all the way back and find them again?"

"Iron, cold iron, answer iron—and your master!" Merlin turned the ring on his finger.

There was a tiny clatter and at his feet lay fork, spoon, and knife, their ordinary size again. Merlin beckoned with his ringed finger to Greg and the boy picked up the fork.

"Iron of spirit, iron of courage, making you the master of the dark and what may lie within it—the dark within, the dark without."

Then Merlin pointed to Eric, who took up the spoon.

"Iron of spirit, iron of courage, against fears within and fears without, waves and ripples of fear to be known no more."

It was Sara's turn, and as her fingers closed about the haft of the knife she heard Merlin's warm voice promising:

"Iron of spirit, iron of courage, mistress of fears whether they come gliding, crawling, or running on many legs!"

"Sir," Greg stood there, turning the fork about in his fingers, "what of the battle? Will King Arthur and Huon win?"

"Already they have driven back the enemy two leagues and ten. For this time Avalon still holds—and wins! Now"—he waved the ringed hand to the gate—"I conjure you, take your road and your cold iron with you. Also know this—Avalon gives thanks and Avalon cherishes her own. For you are now a part of her, which in time to come may be more to you than you can now guess. The gate is open. Go!"

Sara found herself running with Greg and Eric on either side. There was the mist curling about them and they were in the courtyard of the miniature castle once again.

"The door's gone!"

At Eric's cry the other two turned. All the stones they had picked out to make the passage were set back in place. And again the creeper wove a green veil there. Had they really gone through at all?

But in Greg's hand was a fork, Eric held a spoon, and Sara clutched the knife as well as the basket.

"Iron," began Greg and then corrected himself. "Steel magic."

A spider, very large and black, ran out of the vines, scuttled across the pavement by Sara's foot. She watched it go without withdrawing and said, half aloud, "Against fears whether they come gliding, crawling, or running on many legs." She looked again at the spider. Why, this creature was nothing at all compared to those she had fought in the webbed wood—nothing to be afraid of. It was just a bug! Iron of spirit, iron of courage. She wouldn't be afraid of the biggest spider in the garden from now on. Maybe Greg and Eric had not had time to try out their iron of courage yet, but she was sure it would work for them, too, and that they wouldn't need to carry spoon or fork to prove it.

"Hey!" Eric was already ahead of them, down the gravel bank leading to shore. "Hear that?" He kicked a stone into the lake defiantly—water was for drinking, washing—and for swimming. Water was only water.

A whistle—Uncle Mac's imperative signal.

"We're coming," Sara replied, clutching the basket tightly as she raced after her brothers.

OCTAGON MAGIC

Elegy for Sabina 1968

Now, sweet witch cat
Free from flesh,
May you hunt
Happily
in the fields of Heaven.

Composed by Grace Warren for Sabina.

∽ CONTENTS ∼

WITCH'S HOUSE

"CANUCK Canuck walks like a duck!"

Lorrie Mallard walked a little faster, staring straight ahead. She was determined not to run, but she could not shut out those hateful words. Two blocks yet to go, with Jimmy Purvis and Stan Wormiski and Rob Lockner all close behind.

"Canuck—"

There was a prickle in her nose, but she was not going to cry—she was not! And neither was she going to run so they could chase her all the way to the apartment house. Boys—mean, hateful boys! Staring and laughing and whispering about you in class, trying to pull your hair or trip you up or grab your book bag in the halls, trailing you home singing that mean, hateful song. Two blocks more . . .

Unless she took the short cut by the witch's house.

Lorrie turned her head, just enough to sight the beginning of the alley, the one where the tangle of overgrown brush hung in a big choked mass over the rusty iron of the old fence. It looked just like the jungle pictures in the social studies book, if the jungle had lost all its leaves in a storm.

Social studies! Lorrie frowned. Back home in Canada at Miss Logan's School they did not have social studies, any more than they had boys. They had *history* and she had done well in history. But now it seemed she had learned the wrong kind of history. She did not belong. If only Grandmother had not had to go off to England where her old friend could care for her after her operation.

"Canuck—"

Lorrie turned into the alley. You could see the top of the witch's house above all the trees and bushes. Was it just a big old garden filled up with trees and plants growing wild, Lorrie wondered. There was a gate opening onto the alley, but it had a chain across it as rusty as the iron fence. No one had opened that for a long, long time, she guessed. Of course, a witch wouldn't need a gate anyway. She could just fly over on her broom.

"Canuck—"

Lorrie gripped her book bag tighter. Her small pointed chin rose a fraction of an inch, her lips set stubbornly. A possible witch behind a locked gate was not nearly so bad as Jimmy, Stan, and Rob. Now she deliberately slowed down.

The boys and the girls were afraid, or said they were, of the witch's house. Lorrie had heard them daring one another to climb the fence, to rap at the front door. Not that anyone, even Jimmy Purvis, had ever done it.

On her right, on the opposite side of the alley, was a red-brick building with the glass all broken out of the windows, and boards nailed across them. It had once been a stable where horses and carriages were kept. Then came the end of the parking lot for the apartment house where Lorrie lived, all cold and bare with only a couple of cars in it at this time of the afternoon.

Wind swept up the alley. Leaves spun and rustled along with it. Most of the trees and bushes behind the fence were bare. Still one could not see in very far, the branches and trunks were so thick.

Lorrie did not really believe that a witch lived there, or that there was a ghost groaning inside either, even though Kathy Lockner swore it was so. Aunt Margaret had said it was just an old, old house unlike any built today. Octagon House they called it because it had really eight sides. And there was an old lady living there who could not walk very well, so she never came out.

Swinging her book bag to the other hand, Lorrie went up to the chained gate. The house *was* queer, what she could see of it. Now, greatly daring, she squeezed her arm between the bars of the gate, leaving streaks of rust on her windbreaker, and pushed aside two branches to clear the view. Yes, it was very different. She could see steps and a door, and an angled wall with very tall, pointed windows. Lorrie made up her mind.

She would take part of that dare, even though they had never made it to her. She was going to walk all around the witch house, see all of it that she could. Setting down her bag, she tried to brush off some of the rust marks. This was the end of the alley and she turned north on Ash Street, instead of south, walking slowly along the front of the house.

Here the brush-and-tree jungle was not as high or as thick as by the alley. There was an opening and Lorrie halted with a little gasp of surprise. The last time she had come this way she had been hurrying to keep up with Aunt Margaret, who always seemed to be a step or two ahead. That had been just after she had come to Ashton when there had still been leaves on all the branches, so she had not seen the deer, as big as a real one, but black and green—not brown—as if moss grew on him.

Lorrie pushed closer to the fence. The deer stood on a big stone block, and there was a brick wall, all the bricks laid crooked with green moss between them. Then came the house. It had tall windows—the ones she could see had shutters across them—and a door. Leaves had drifted high all over, as if no one ever swept them up to be burned.

Lorrie bit down on her lower lip. . . . Burning leaves in big heaps, the smoke that smelled so good. Once, they had put three big potatoes right in the middle of

238

the fire. Those became all black on the outside, but you broke them open and ate them with a little salt. And the squirrels had come up and asked for bits.

She had been only a little girl then. Why, that must have been five—six years ago. But she could remember it, though now she did not want to. Not when she lived here where there were no leaves to burn, nothing—where they called her a stupid, silly Canuck—though she did *not* walk like a duck!

Lorrie set her bag on the ground between her two feet so she could hold the bars of the front gate. There was no chain, but of course it was locked. All those leaves . . .

There was a big oak tree in the yard at Miss Logan's. You hunted for acorns and tried to find the biggest one. She never had, but Anne, her best friend last year, a whopper—almost as big as Lorrie's thumb. Miss Logan's—Anne—Lorrie fought the nose-prickling sensation again.

Everything had gone wrong for her here in Ashton. Maybe if she had arrived when school started and not come late when everyone had already made friends and she was alone—No, she was different anyway, she was a stupid Canuck, wasn't she?

Her troubles had started the day of the big test last month. There had been a substitute teacher—Mrs. Raymond had had the flu. And she had been so cross when Lorrie had not understood the questions. Could Lorrie help it if she came from Canada where they had taught different things? She had always had high grades in Miss Logan's School and Grandmother Mallard had been proud of her. She had never asked to come to Ashton and live with Aunt Margaret Gerson, who was away working all day, when Grandmother had had to go for her operation. All the things they taught at Miss Logan's seemed wrong here. When she had answered the first time in class, said, "Yes, Mrs. Raymond," and curtsied, they had all laughed, every one of them.

All those hateful boys bobbing up and down in the yard afterward and yelling, "Yes, ma'am, no, ma'am." There had been no boys at Miss Logan's—hateful things!

And she could not talk about the same things that Kathy and the rest of the girls did. Now Mrs. Raymond mentioned putting her back a grade, saying she was too slow in catching up. Put back—just because they had different lessons here.

Then Jimmy Purvis made up that song, and they all sang at her on the way home. She did not like to go home when Aunt Margaret was gone, and Mrs. Lockner kept saying she must come over to their apartment and not stay alone.

Lorrie blinked hard several times. The deer had looked watery and wavery, but now he was sturdy and strong again. She wished she could see him closer. There was a big leaf caught on the prong of one of his antlers and it flapped up and down like a little flag. Lorrie smiled. There was something funny about that. The deer was so big and proud, and kind of stern, but that leaf flip-flapped as if making fun of him.

In spite of the shuttered windows, all the dark trees and bushes and the big piles of leaves, Lorrie liked this house. It was not a scary place at all.

Or were there two kinds of witches? The mean, scary kind was one, and then there were those like the Princess' grandmother in *The Princess and Curdie*. A fairy godmother had magic powers. Only she made good things, instead of bad, happen. She could use a fairy godmother now, one to transform Jimmy Purvis into a *real* duck.

Lorrie grinned as she picked up her book bag. Old Jimmy Purvis with yellow feathers all over him and big flat feet—that was the first thing she would ask for if a fairy godmother, or a good witch, said she could have some wishes. She had better get home now. She could say she had homework to do so Mrs. Lockner would leave her alone in Aunt Margaret's apartment.

On impulse Lorrie lifted her hand in salute to the deer. The wind gave an extra tug at that moment and tore the leaf flag from his antler, soaring it over the gate to Lorrie's feet. She pounced upon it, torn as it was, and tucked it into the pocket of her windbreaker. Why, she did not know.

Then she turned south toward the apartment. She had just reached the mouth of the alley when she heard a thin cry. Something in that sound halted her.

"It went in there! Poke it, Stan, poke it out here and I'll catch it!"

Jimmy Purvis knelt by a bush growing near the old stable. Stan Wormiski, his lieutenant and faithful follower, thrust a long branch into a tangle of weeds, while Rob Lockner stood by. Stan and Jimmy were excited, but Rob looked a little unhappy.

"Go on, Stan, poke!" Jimmy ordered. "Get it out. I'll grab it!"

Again that thin, unhappy cry. Lorrie found herself running, not away from the gang this time, but toward them. Just before she reached the boys, a small black shadow burst from the weeds, dodged past Jimmy, and sprang at her.

Needle-pointed claws cut through her tights, then grabbed her skirt, and her windbreaker, as a frenzied kitten swarmed up Lorrie as if she were a tree. She threw her arm protectingly around it and faced the boys.

"Well, look who's here. Old dummy Canuck. That's a witch cat, Canuck, give it to me. Give it here, now!" Jimmy came at her, grinning.

"No!" Lorrie swung her book bag as a defensive barrier. Against her chest, under her other hand, the kitten was a shivering mass of fur, still crying with tiny shrieks of fear.

"Give it here, Canuck." Jimmy was still grinning,

but Lorrie was frightened. He did not look in the least as if he meant this for fun, not the kind of fun she recognized.

She turned and ran, away from that look in Jimmy's eyes. She could not gain the apartment before they caught up with her, of that she was sure. And if she did, with Aunt Margaret gone, who would take her side?

Maybe—maybe she could get over the fence, hide in the bushes. She used to climb a lot—in that yard of bonfires and happy times. There was the front gate, and the fancy curves in it ought to make good holds. Lorrie threw her book bag up and over, pushed the now feebly struggling kitten into the front of her windbreaker, and began to climb with a speed born of desperation.

Why the boys had not already caught up with her, she did not know. Maybe Jimmy Purvis would not dare follow her in here. But she wasted no time in looking around to see. Lorrie topped the gate, swung over and down, landing in an awkward tumble on the crazy pattern of the brick walk.

The kitten fought furiously for freedom, leaped to the path, and scuttled on among the leaves, heading around the house rather than to the front door. That, to Lorrie, looked as if it were never opened. Afraid that in its fright it might dash back to the alley again, she scrambled up to follow.

She saw the bright red of Jimmy's windbreaker, the soiled gray of Stan's. They were coming along the outside of the fence on Ash Street, but not very fast. Suppose they followed her in here?

Lorrie's retreat was as fast as the kitten's as she followed in its wake. It was several moments before she realized that, for all the piles of leaves through which she rustled, this was relatively clear ground. There was a walk of the crisscross brick going around the side of the house, and it was bordered by beds where stood stalks crowned by the withered heads of frost-killed flowers. The heavy growth of bushes and trees was only along the fence, screening this inner part.

She glanced at the house as she rounded one of its angles. The windows here were not covered by shutters, but the shades were drawn so she could not see in.

"Merroww—" That was the kitten. Lorrie hurried on.

Rounding another angle, she came to a place where the bordering flower beds of the walk widened out into squares. These were bare, as if whatever had grown there had been carefully harvested. More of the tall thin windows, but these were neither shuttered nor shaded. She saw the white of a curtain and an edge of dark red drape at one. If the front of the house had been closed, it was not so here.

Lorrie stopped running, and walked slowly and almost warily along the path. Leaves were here, too, blowing and gathering in heaps. In the center of the cleared beds was an empty pool. Centering that was a crouching thing, a dragon, Lorrie thought. It held its head high at a rather uncomfortable angle, with a small black pipe just showing in its wide open mouth, as if it had once spit water—instead of the fire storybook dragons blew at their knightly enemies—into the basin at its clawed feet.

"Merrow!" The kitten's voice pulled her on, around another angle. Here was the door she had seen from the chained gate. On one of the steps beneath it crouched the kitten, its mouth open to emit another small but piercing wail.

Lorrie stiffened at a creaking louder than the kitten's cry. She stopped short, to watch the door. It was opening, and as soon as a big enough crack showed, the kitten whisked through. But the door continued to open and Lorrie discovered she could not have run, not even if she had wanted to, for her feet seemed as firmly fixed as if she had stepped into a roadway surfaced with sticky tar.

It was dark inside the house. Though on this late fall afternoon lights had already appeared in the windows elsewhere on the street, none showed here. But the woman who stood in the doorway was perfectly visible to Lorrie.

She was small, hardly much taller than Lorrie herself, and her shoulders were rounded, making her bend forward. Her face had a large, broad nose and a chin that pushed up and forward in an effort to meet it. Above her dark brown cheeks and forehead, her black-and-gray hair crisply curled together, what showed of it, for she wore a cap with a frilled edge that made a stiff frame all around her head. Her dress was of a deep, dark red, and the skirt was very long and full under a large white apron that had a starched ruffle on the lower hem. With her hand on the latch of the door, the woman stood on the top step looking down at Lorrie. Then she smiled, and the droop of her nose, the sharp upturn of her chin, were forgotten.

"Hullo, little missy." Her voice was very soft and low. "Now, you, Sabina, where's you bin, an' what's you bin doin'—gittin' all frazed up this heah way?"

From beneath the edge of her skirt popped the kitten's black head. Its round blue eyes surveyed the woman for a long instant and then turned to stare unblinkingly at Lorrie.

"Some boys," began Lorrie hurriedly, "they—"

The head in the frilled cap was already nodding. "They was up to tricks, aye, tricks. But you saw Sabina came to no harm, didn't you, little missy? I'll tell Mis' Charlotta, she'll be mighty pleased. You come in. Have a ginger cooky?"

Lorrie shook her head. "No, thank you. It's late. Mrs. Lockner—she'll tell Aunt Margaret I was late getting home. That would worry her."

"Come again then." The capped head bobbed, the smile grew even wider. "Now, how did you git in, little missy?"

"I climbed the gate, the front one," Lorrie admitted.

"An' did all that to your nice clothes. My, my." A brown finger pointed.

Lorrie looked down at herself. There were streaks of rust on the sleeves and the front of her windbreaker, more on her skirt and tights. She tried to brush off the worst of the stains.

"Come along. Hallie'll let you out, all right an' proper."

Down the steps she came, slowly and stiffly, as Lorrie waited. Then Lorrie followed that wide skirt as it brushed up leaves around the corners of the house, back to the front where the iron deer held his head high and proud. Hallie put her old, wrinkled hands on the gate, touched the top bar, and gave it a quick jerk. There was a small, protesting squeak and it moved inward, not all the way, for it stuck on the uneven bricks of the walk, but enough to let Lorrie through.

"Thank you." The manners that Miss Logan's classes had so carefully drilled came to Lorrie. She ducked a small curtsy. "Thank you very much."

To her surprise Hallie's hand went to each side of the billowing skirt at which the wind was tugging, and the old woman made a stately, dipping acknowledgment that was far more graceful than any such gesture Lorrie had ever seen.

"You is welcome, little mis', entirely welcome."

Curiosity broke through good manners. "Are you— are you the—?"

Hallie's smile grew wider. "The ol' witch?" Her soft voice made that name sound worse.

Lorrie blushed. Not that she had ever been one of those who ran past Octagon House calling that name out, daring someone to go in and bang on the old witch's front door.

"The—the lady who lives here?" she stammered.

"I live heah, aye. But I'm Hallie, not Mis' Charlotta. Mis' Charlotta, she's Mis' Ashemeade."

Hallie made it sound, Lorrie thought, as if Miss Ashemeade was as grand a person as Lady Cartwright, a friend of Grandmother's in England.

And now Hallie's smile was gone and she sounded almost sharp. "Mis' Ashemeade, she's a great lady— don't you ever forget that."

"I—I won't. And I'm Lorrie Mallard." Lorrie held out her hand. "Very pleased to meet you."

Her fingers were enfolded in Hallie's. "An' I to meet you, Lorrie. Come again."

Lorrie trotted on down Ash Street. At the mouth of the alley she turned to glance back. But the gate was now firmly closed and Hallie was gone. What small scrap of house she could still see looked deserted.

It was colder and the wind blew stronger, pulling at her plaid skirt and cap. And the sky was dark, too, as if a storm were coming. Lorrie broke into a run, but she kept a sharp lookout. It would be just like Jimmy or Stan to hide out and pounce at her. She breathed a little easier as she skirted the parking lot. There were more cars there now, but none of them close enough to shelter lurking boys.

She clattered up the steps into the lobby of the apartment house. Mr. Parkinson was there, taking his mail out of the box. Lorrie slowed down and tried to close the door very quietly. Mr. Parkinson did not like children and he made that widely and forcibly known. There had been one afternoon when Kathy Lockner had thrown a ball all the way down the stairs and Lorrie picked it up, only to be accused of wild behavior, with threats of taking the matter to Aunt Margaret. She had avoided Mr. Parkinson carefully ever since.

He frowned at her now. Lorrie was very conscious of her rust-streaked clothing. And what would Aunt

Margaret say if the marks did not come off? Clothes cost a lot of money, Lorrie knew that. Maybe if she brushed very hard—

But if Mr. Parkinson made his opinion of dirty and untidy little girls very plain in his stare, he did not put it into words. Lorrie edged past him and climbed the stairs as slowly and sedately as she could. But as soon as she hoped she was out of his sight, she hurried, her book bag bumping first against the stairs and then the walls as she went. Then she was at their own door, breathing fast, hunting under her jacket for the key. The Lockner door across the hall was closed. Mrs. Lockner was not watching for her.

Lorrie turned the key and slipped inside, shutting the door quickly behind her. Now she fronted the big mirror on the coat closet door and she gasped. No wonder Mr. Parkinson had stared so at her. She looked more of a mess than she had feared.

She hurried on to the bedroom she shared with her aunt. Then she pulled off her clothes, spreading them on her bed while she put on an old cotton dress. With a brush she set to work, trying to erase the marks left by her adventure.

Lucky, oh, she was lucky! Most of them brushed off. And those left were not too visible, even when she held them right under the lamp. This was Friday, too, so she could have another go at them in the morning. Finally she hung them up in the closet and went to the dressing table where all Aunt Margaret's nice-smelling bottles and jars were set out in a line against the base of the big mirror.

Such nice smells. There were lots of good smells in the world—burning leaves was one. Lorrie stood still, looking into the mirror, not now seeing her reflection but a picture out of memory. . . .

Mother and Daddy raking leaves for Lorrie to pack into a big basket. . . . Lorrie shook her head. She did not want to remember that because then she had to

remember the rest. Mother and Daddy and the air-
plane that had taken them away from her forever. . . .

Lorrie closed her eyes and was determined not to
remember. Now—she looked at the mirror again—there
was her face, rather like the cat heads she used to
draw when she was little—a triangle. Her black hair
was straying out of its ribbon tieback as it always did
at this hour of the day. Lorrie set about remedying
that with the same will and force she had given to
brushing her clothes.

Greeny eyes—just like a cat's. Now suppose she did
have a fairy godmother, what would be her next wish,
after making Jimmy Purvis a big yellow duck? Yellow
hair and blue eyes like Kathy Lockner's? No, Lorrie
decided, she did not want those. What she had suited
her well enough. She made the worst face she could
think of at the mirror and laughed.

She smoothed down her skirt. What would it feel
like, she wondered, to wear yards of skirt the way
Hallie did? People all did in the olden days whether
they were grown up or just girls. Lorrie enjoyed leaf-
ing through Aunt Margaret's costume books to look at
the pictures. Aunt Margaret wrote advertising copy
for Fredericka's Modes and knew all about high fashion. But nobody wore such dresses any more, so why
did Hallie? Did she have only very old, old clothes?
But the red dress had not looked old or worn. Or did
Hallie wear just what she wanted to, and did not care
if it were stylish to have a skirt short, or long, or in the
middle?

Lorrie went on into the kitchen and began to bring
packages out of the freezer section of the refrigerator.
As she set the table in the dinette she thought of
Jimmy and his gang. Jimmy would not forget her, but
tomorrow was Saturday and then there was Sunday,
no school, no Jimmy. So she had two days before she
had to worry about him again.

If Aunt Margaret did not have to work overtime

they would go shopping together in the morning. Then Lorrie could stop at the library. If only Aunt Margaret would stop worrying about why Lorrie did not have any close friends. Who needed the kinds of friends one could find about here? Kathy Lockner with all her silly jokes, and whispering about boys and playing those screechy records?

It was getting harder and harder to evade Aunt Margaret's pushing. Lorrie laid a napkin straight. She was not going to tell her that she did not like Kathy, or Kathy's friends.

There were some girls at school Lorrie would like to know better. Lizabeth Ross, for example. Lizabeth did not go around much with others, either. But she was smart and she liked to read the same sort of books. Lorrie had seen a copy of *The Secret Garden* on her desk. She had wanted to ask Lizabeth what part she liked best, and if she had read *A Little Princess* too. But then at recess Mrs. Raymond had kept Lorrie in for a talk about math mistakes and she had never had the chance. And Lizabeth lived down by Bruxten Drive and had never said anything to Lorrie except "hi." But to spend good time listening to Kathy's stupid old records, fussing with curlers in her hair, and talking silly—no!

Grandmother had never worried about her. If she just wanted to sit and read, that was fine. And she had had the right sort of friend in Anne. Only that was all gone, along with Miss Logan's, and what seemed now to Lorrie all peace and contentment. It was easy to forget the shadows and remember just sunny days when one wanted to.

Think of something else now—quick! Not Miss Logan's, or Hampstead, or Canada, or burning leaves or—Mother and Daddy—

The Octagon House, Lorrie seized upon that. The queer house, and the black kitten—Sabina, Hallie had called her—and Hallie herself. Hallie had asked her to come back. Maybe if she got out of school fast, and ran a lot of the way, she could some day.

Lorrie sat on the dinette bench and thought about it. There was nothing scary about the house she had seen. Was it strange inside, she wondered. What were the rooms like—three-cornered as wedges of pie? She would like to find out.

There was the click of a key in the hall door. Lorrie hurried through the rooms. Should she tell Aunt Margaret about her adventure, or part of it? Perhaps, but not yet, she decided just as the door opened.

THE BAD WEEK AND OLD MISS ASHEMEADE

THE BAD WEEK began early on Saturday with a blustery wind and a lot of clouds, plus the fact that Aunt Margaret's alarm clock failed to go off. She had extra work at the shop, and now she was so late she had no time for a proper breakfast, only the cup of coffee Lorrie poured for her while she scribbled down her grocery list.

There would be no shared shopping trip today. Aunt Margaret must try to get all the things they needed on her way home.

"Sorry, Chick." She frowned into the mirror of the closet as she put on her coat. "With the Christmas rush coming up, I can't get out of going to work today. But Mrs. Lockner will be driving to the shopping center and she'll let you visit the library. You just ask. Now"—she gave a swift glance around—"I think I have everything. Goodbye, Chick, and be good. Ohh, darn that clock anyway! I'm hours behind.''

She was out and running down the hall, her heels click-clicking on the stairs, before Lorrie had more than time to blink. Slowly she went back to the kitchen and sat down to eat her cereal as she reviewed the ruins of all her plans. Outside the window, the dark clouds were already letting down spatters of rain and it looked thoroughly dismal.

Lorrie drank the rest of her orange juice. She was not going to say anything to Mrs. Lockner. A library visit with the Lockner clan was the last thing she wanted. Kathy and Rob had cards, or had had them. But they thought of the library as only another part of school where one was forced to go when the teacher said such and such a book had to be read. She had gone with them once and even now felt warm inside with remembered shame. Rob had been sent out for loud talking, and the librarian had warned Kathy and Lorrie, too, since Kathy had been talking to her. Kathy and Rob had both followed her around the shelves demanding what did she want *that* silly old book for; and saying every moment or so, "Come on! Hurry up, let's get going!"

To Lorrie a library must be enjoyed in peace and quiet, with plenty of time in which to choose a book. It took time to choose properly, since one was allowed to draw only two books at a time, and Lorrie was a fast reader. Most books lasted barely past Sunday afternoon, so size as well as subject matter was highly important. Only recently had she stumbled on pure treasure, a whole shelf of bound magazines, one year's issues all in one big heavy volume. They were old magazines, older than Aunt Margaret (though she had read some of them, too, when she was a little girl, because she had opened one and found a story she remembered), perhaps even older than Grandmother Mallard. But the stories in them were good.

Lorrie took her bowl, glass, and Aunt Margaret's cup and saucer to the sink, and washed and dried them.

Her books were due and she wanted one at least of those *St. Nicholas* magazines. One would be all she could carry if she went alone, because that was just what she was going to do. It was easy when you planned it. She could go down to the corner of Wilton and Ash and take the Woodsville bus. That let you off at the shopping center. There was a stop light there so it was safe to cross the street to the library. Then, on the other side, was the bus stop to use coming home. Bus fare was twelve cents for children and she had a quarter.

Lorrie had never been to the library by herself, but there was no reason she could see why she could not go. Aunt Margaret had never said not to. Of course, Lorrie had never asked her about it, but she decided to ignore that thought.

It was raining harder. She would have to wear her raincoat and boots, and she would wrap up her books in a plastic bag. Lorrie moved briskly, putting the dishes away, mopping up the drain board and sink with a paper towel. The library did not open until ten, and it would take at least a half-hour to go. She had better leave a little after nine, or Mrs. Lockner might come over.

Lorrie sighed. People who wanted to be kind and helpful could certainly complicate life. "Kind and helpful," were Aunt Margaret's words for Mrs. Lockner. But to Lorrie, at times it seemed far more like interfering.

Now that she had made up her mind, she was excited. Why, she could do this every Saturday, and it would not matter how long she stayed at the library. No one would hurry her through her book selection, and she could even sit and read awhile. The thought of such bliss made Lorrie move restlessly from room to room, wishing the hand to go faster around the dial of the clock.

She was all dressed and ready at nine, hovering by the door with a nervous eye on the Lockner apartment across the hall. Then, unable to wait any longer, her books in their covering bag held tight against her, Lorrie locked the apartment and scuttled down the hall, though she took the steps at a slower pace.

It was raining really hard by the time she reached the bus stop. But there was a shelter there and she stood waiting for what seemed hours before the bus appeared. Lorrie was pleased with her own resourcefulness when she got off at the shopping center.

There was another wait by the library door. She hunched over her books, hoping none of the wet would reach them, and her coat was damp across the shoulders when the guard opened the building at last.

Once inside, Lorrie forgot all but the delights she always enjoyed. She had all the time in the world to browse along the shelves, pulling out old favorites to read a sentence here and there, even though she knew the stories almost by heart. Time meant nothing until she became aware of a hollow feeling in her middle and glanced up at the room clock. Twelve o'clock! Surely that was as wrong as the alarm had been earlier.

Lorrie picked up the heavy, bound-magazine volume and with it her other choice, which she had read twice before, *Half Magic,* and hurried out to the charging desk.

"This is heavy to carry, isn't it?" asked the lady at the desk.

Lorrie shook her head determinedly. "I take the bus, I won't have far to carry it. Here"—She pulled the plastic cover from her pocket; she had wiped it off with her handkerchief and it did not seem too damp—"I can put this over them. They won't get wet."

"You won't need that, the rain is over. But I'm glad to see you know the proper way to take care of books."

Why shouldn't she, wondered Lorie. People always seemed to think you didn't know about such things, and were surprised when you did. But maybe they were right to worry. She had seen Jimmy Purvis throw a book, actually throw it. And, when Stan had not caught it, it had hit the wall, to fall with loose pages. And Sally Walters had drawn pictures on the page margins in one of hers.

The rain might be over but the wind was cold. There was no bus shelter here, and she was so afraid of missing the next bus that she had to stand out by the sign on the curb where the wind swooped.

"Lorrie! Lorrie Mallard! What are you doing here?"

A car had come out of the shopping center lot across the street to draw up by her corner. Now the door swung open as Mrs. Lockner called again sharply, "Get in this minute, Lorrie. You are blue with cold. Where have you been? Where is your aunt?"

Lorrie sighed, there was no escape now. Reluctantly she got in beside Mrs. Lockner.

"Aunt Margaret had to work this morning. I just came to the library."

"By yourself? Did your aunt say you might?"

"I came on the bus. It was all right," Lorrie said defensively. "My books were due."

"But, Lorrie, you must have known I was coming to the center, you should have come with us. My, look at the time! I must swing around by Elsmere and pick up Kathy at dancing class, then get home in time to see Rob off for the game! What a big book, Lorrie. Isn't that too heavy for you?"

"I like it, and I can carry it all right." As always Mrs. Lockner's voice did something to Lorrie. She asked a lot of questions, and for anyone else Lorrie would have answered them without resentment, or at least with not as much as Mrs. Lockner always aroused in her.

"I do hope Kathy will be ready." Mrs. Lockner

drove a couple of blocks before she turned right. "They are practicing for their recital and sometimes the class runs overtime. Kathy has a solo, she is going to be a gypsy."

"She told me," Lorrie said. "And she showed me her costume."

Lorrie did not envy Kathy in the least her Saturday mornings at dancing school, but that costume was another matter. Dressing up was fun, one of the things her friend Anne and she had shared in the old days when Grandmother had allowed them to dip into one of the attic trunks.

"There. Oh, thank goodness, Kathy's waiting! Just open the door for her, dear. We have to travel if we are going to get Rob off on time."

So Lorrie was swept up and carried away by the Lockners. She shared their lunch, her protests being brushed aside. But she refused to share Kathy's plans for the afternoon, to go to the double monster feature at the movies.

At Lorrie's plea of having homework to do, Mrs. Lockner shook her head. But, since she could not push Lorrie out of the door with Kathy, she accepted it. Once Lorrie was back in Aunt Margaret's apartment, she got out her school books and started in on her homework. The mathematics she did first, because she hated it so. Always get the bad out of the way, then you could enjoy the good.

The good today was to write a theme about fall for English. And Lorrie knew just what she was going to write this time, about leaves and bonfires. Leaves— that made her think about Octagon House. My, the big wind today must be whirling them around. Would Hallie ever try to rake them up? Maybe Lorrie could offer to help.

She was making a neater copy of her first draft when she heard Aunt Margaret's key in the door. She was so pleased with her labors that she went eagerly to meet her, the scribbled-over first sheets in her hand.

"Aunt Margaret, I—"

But Aunt Margaret was frowning. She balanced a big grocery bag against her side and walked past Lorrie into the kitchen.

"Shut the door, Lorrie, and come here. I want to talk to you."

Lorrie obeyed. When she came to the kitchen, Aunt Margaret had taken off her coat and was sitting on one of the dinette benches. She looked tired and the frown made two sharp lines between her eyes.

"Lorrie, Mrs. Lockner spoke to me just now. She told me that you went to the library alone on the bus and that she found you standing on a street corner near the shopping center."

"I was at the bus stop there," Lorrie protested.

"I don't know what to do with you, Lorrie." Aunt Margaret had taken off her gloves, was smoothing them back and forth between her fingers. "I want to spend more time with you, but I can't. Mrs. Lockner has been very kind. She is perfectly willing for you to stay over there with Kathy when I am not at home. She would have given you a ride to the library."

"I didn't want to go with the Lockners."

"Lorrie, you can't have your way about such things. It is not safe for girls your age to go about alone. All sorts of accidents can happen. And you are alone too much. Mrs. Lockner said that Kathy wanted you to go to the show with her this afternoon and you would not."

"It was an old monster picture and I don't like them. And I had my homework to do." Lorrie crumpled her papers in her hand.

"I am not going to argue with you, Lorrie. But neither am I going to allow you to continue in this way. From now on, when I am not at home, you are to go to Mrs. Lockner's—until I can make other arrangements."

Aunt Margaret stood up and picked up her coat.

She went to the hallway and Lorrie trailed her, appalled at this idea of a future spent always with Kathy, and Rob, and probably Jimmy Purvis, too, he being one of Rob's close friends.

As she passed the coffee table, Aunt Margaret paused by the library books.

"To make this clearer, Lorrie, these books are going into the closet to stay until you prove you can be trusted to do what is right." And she took them both.

Lorrie listlessly put her school books and papers together. It wasn't fair! Kathy was one kind of person and she another. If she had to be with Kathy all the time, she couldn't stand it! And—and she would never get to visit Octagon House again.

That was the beginning of the bad week, and it seemed to Lorrie that it was never going to have an end. She went to school with Kathy and had to take part in a basketball game, which she detested. Her awkwardness always brought down upon her the impatience of her teammates. She made a poor mark in math, and Mrs. Raymond said her fall leaves story was fanciful but had too many spelling mistakes. Jimmy Purvis sang his hideous song in the yard and some of the girls picked it up. And Aunt Margaret questioned her a lot about school and how many friends she had and why didn't she do this or that, even saying she was going to have a serious talk with Mrs. Raymond.

Lorrie felt as if she were tied up in a bag, with no chance to be herself. By Friday night she was so unhappy that she felt she could not stand much more.

But on Friday the worst of all happened. Because Aunt Margaret had said she must stay at the Lockners' after school, Lorrie had had to take some of her things over there. And this time she brought the small, old lap desk Grandmother Mallard had given her. She wanted to write Grandmother a very special letter, not a complaining one, because Dr. Creighton had explained to Lorrie carefully when Grandmother had

had to go to England that she must not be worried in any way.

Because this had been such a bad week, Lorrie had been afraid to write for fear some complaints might seep in despite her efforts. But she wrote Grandmother regularly and must not wait any longer. She had a first draft on notebook paper and must make another on the special paper Grandmother had given her with her name at the top of each sheet.

Lorrie laid her paper out on the card table Mrs. Lockner allowed her to set up. Then the phone rang and Mrs. Lockner called her to answer because it was Aunt Margaret saying she would be detained until late and to stay where she was.

There was no use in protesting, but Lorrie was unhappy as she came back. Then her eyes went wide and all the unhappiness of the week exploded inside her.

"Give me that!" She grabbed at what Kathy had taken from the desk.

"Let me look first." Kathy, laughing, jumped away, swinging her hand out of Lorrie's reach. "What a funny old doll. You still play with dolls, Lorrie? Only little kids do that."

In her grasp the old doll dangled too loosely. The delicate china head struck hard against the wall and smashed into pieces.

"Miranda!" Lorrie sprang at Kathy, standing disconcerted now over the broken bits of china. She slapped her as hard as she could. "Give me—!"

"All right, take it!" Kathy threw the headless body at Lorrie and it sprawled half in, half out, of the writing desk.

Lorrie scooped up desk and all and ran, out of the Lockner apartment. She was fumbling with her own key when Mrs. Lockner caught up with her.

"Lorrie, what is the matter? Tell me at once!"

Lorrie struggled against the hand on her shoulder.

"Let me alone! Can't you *ever* let me alone!" She was crying now in spite of her efforts not to.

"Why did you slap Kathy? Lorrie, tell me, what is the matter?"

"Let me alone!" The key was in the lock now. With a sharp jerk Lorrie freed herself from Mrs. Lockner's hold and got around the door. The writing desk and the paper fell all over the floor, but those did not matter now. What did, she still held in her arm tight against her chest.

Lorrie turned and slammed the door right in Mrs. Lockner's face, locking it quickly. She heard them calling, knocking on the door. Let everyone yell and bang—it wouldn't do them any good! Crying so hard she could hardly see, Lorrie made the bedroom and flung herself on her bed. She felt the hard lump of Miranda under her, but she could not bear now to look at that headless body.

Miranda had been extra special. She was not just a doll, but a person, and she was very, very old. Grandmother had played with her when she was little, very carefully, because even then Miranda was special. Grandmother's own grandmother had had Miranda. She was more than a hundred years old! Now—now—Miranda wasn't anything!

Lorrie rolled over on the bed and made herself look at the remains. The small arms and hands of leather were intact, and the black boots and legs covered with red-and-white striped stockings were as always. But, above the old-fashioned dress Grandmother had made, the head and shoulders were gone, only one little jagged splinter was left. Miranda was dead and Kathy had killed her! She would never, never speak to Kathy Lockner again! Nor would she ever go back to the Lockner apartment.

Still gulping sobs, she got off the bed and went to the chest of drawers. She found the handkerchief Grandmother had given her. That was old, too, soft heavy silk, yellow now, with a big, fat initial G and some marks over it embroidered in one corner. It had belonged to Grandmother's father.

Tenderly she wrapped Miranda in it. Miranda was dead and Lorrie could not bear to look at her again. They might even say to throw her out in the trash, just an old broken doll. But Miranda was not going into any trash can, she was going to be buried where there were flowers in summer.

And the place—the Octagon House! Lorrie put on her coat and cap. She opened the back service door and, with Miranda in her hand, crept down the back steps. It was getting dark out, but she did not have far to go. In her other hand was the big spoon she had picked up in the kitchen. She could dig a grave with that. She only hoped the ground was not frozen too hard.

Lorrie ran across the parking lot and out the other end, and came to the gate that she had climbed on her first visit. There were no lights at all in the house that she could see, and the bushes and trees made it seem very dark. But Lorrie was too unhappy to be afraid.

Hallie had done something to the upper bar of the gate to open it. But then Hallie had been on the other side. Lorrie had best climb again. She had laid her hand on the gate to do just that when it gave and swung a little, easier than when Hallie had opened it for her. Then she stood on the shadow-patched brick walk.

The flower beds in the back—they ought to be easier to dig in. Heedless of the shadows, Lorrie hurried to the place by the pool. There she squatted to dig with her spoon.

There was no wind tonight, so she heard the tapping sharp and clear. Lorrie turned her head to look at the house. There were the windows with the curtains. And now there was a light there, not bright, but enough to show the lady who was leaning forward with her face quite close to the glass. And it was not Hallie.

For a long moment Lorrie was startled, too startled to run as she might have done. Then she saw that the lady was not frowning or looking in the least cross as she might have been at someone digging in her garden. Instead she smiled, and now she beckoned to Lorrie, and pointed in the direction of the back door.

Lorrie hesitated and then got to her feet, still pressing Miranda close to her. Then the lady tapped again and once more pointed. Lorrie obeyed, walking along the brick path.

The door swung open before she had quite reached the steps, and Hallie greeted her. "Mis' Lorrie, come in, come! Mis' Ashemeade, she wants to see you."

Lorrie came into a hall that had darkish corners in spite of a lamp set up on a wall bracket. It was triangular in shape with a door in each wall. One opened into a kitchen, and Lorrie could see part of a stove. The other, to her right, opened into the room of the curtained windows. Hallie pointed to that.

"Go right in."

Lorrie suddenly felt very shy. The lady in the window had smiled and seemed friendly, but she had not invited her in.

It was the strangest room Lorrie had ever seen. The light there, and there was light in plenty, all came from lamps and candles that flickered now and then. There were red-velvet drapes at the windows over white-lace curtains, and a red carpet underfoot. A big table, which had two candelabra, was in the center of the room, and it had a great many things laid out on it. There was a fireplace to her left with a fire glowing in it, and before it on the hearthrug lay Sabina.

Between the table and the windows was a chair with carved arms and a high back. In it sat the lady. She wore a dress with a tight waist and a full long skirt like Hallie's. But this was an odd shade of green. And her long apron was not white and ruffled as Hallie's but made of black taffeta with a border of brilliant flowers and birds worked in many colored silks. Her hair was very white but thick, and was braided and then pinned about her head with a fluff of black lace and dark red ribbon fastened on for a cap.

She had a tall frame at her elbow as if she had just turned away from her work. And on that was stretched canvas with a picture half embroidered. But now her hands rested on the arms of her chair, and on their fingers were many rings, most of them set with the red stones Lorrie knew for garnets such as Grandmother had, but seldom wore.

A necklace of the same stones lay on the front of her dress, and earrings glinted in her ears. She did not look at all like any lady Lorrie had ever seen, but in this room she belonged.

"Come here, Lorrie. Let me see Miranda." She held out her hand and her rings winked in the firelight.

Lorrie did not find it odd that Miss Ashemeade should know just what she carried in her bundle of handkerchief.

Miss Ashemeade put one hand over the other, the package that was Miranda between her palms. For a long moment she sat so, then she spoke:

"There is breaking in plenty in this world, Lorrie. But there is also mending, if one has will and patience. Never be hasty, for haste may sometimes make a large trouble from a small one. Now, what do you think of that?"

She pointed to something that lay across one end of the table. Lorrie moved a little to see a length of lace, so delicate and beautiful that, though she would like to touch it, she did not quite dare. It was a cobweb, as if some spider had chosen to spin a design instead of her usual back-and-forth lines. But there was a breaking of threads, a tear to spoil it.

"Haste makes waste." Miss Ashemeade shook her

head. "Now much time and patience must be used to mend it."

"But Miranda can't be," Lorrie said. "Her head was all smashed, into little bits."

"We shall see." Still she did not unwrap Miranda to look. "Now, Lorrie, tell me, what do you see here? Take your time and look well. But"—now Miss Ashemeade smiled—"remember something that was a command of my youth—look with your eyes and not your fingers."

Lorrie nodded. "Don't touch," she translated. She might have resented such a warning, she was no baby. But somehow it was right and proper here. Now she began to look about her, moving around the room.

It was exciting, for there was a great deal to see. On the walls hung framed pictures, many of them too dim to make out clearly, though Lorrie saw some were strips of cloth and the painting had been done with needle and thread rather than paint and brush. Across the back of a sofa was a square of fine crossstitch, a bouquet of flowers. And the seats and backs of every chair were worked in similar patterns.

Over the fireplace was a tapestry that drew and held Lorrie's full attention. A knight and his squire rode toward a wood, while in the foreground stood a girl wearing a dress of the same shade of green as Miss Ashemeade had chosen. Her feet were bare, her dark hair flowed freely about her shoulders from under a garland of pale flowers.

"That is the Tapestry Princess."

Lorrie looked around. "Is it a story?" she asked.

"It is a story, Lorrie. And the moral of it is, or was, make the best of what you have, do with it what you can, but do not throw away your dreams. Once that princess was the daughter of a king. She was given everything her heart wished. Then her father fell upon evil days, and she was captured by his enemy and put in a tower. All she had left her was one of her christening gifts, a golden needle her godmother had given her.

"She learned to sew in order to mend her own old clothing. And so beautiful was her work that the usurper, who had taken her father's throne, had her make clothing for his daughters, the new princesses. She grew older and older and no one cared.

"Then she began at night to make the tapestry. First she fashioned the knight and squire. And then worked all the background, except for one space in the foreground. One of the usurper's daughters, coming to try on a dress, saw the tapestry and ordered the princess to make haste to finish it, that she might have it to hang on the wall at her wedding feast.

"So the princess worked the whole night through to complete it. And the maiden she put into the blank space was she as she had been when she was a young and beautiful girl. When the last stitch was set she vanished from the tower, nor was she ever found again."

"Did she go into the tapestry?" Lorrie asked.

"So it is said. But it is true she found some way of freedom and only her picture remained to remind the world of her story. Now, Lorrie, you have a story, too. And what is it?"

Without knowing just why, Lorrie spilled out all that had happened during the bad week, and some of the other things that had been bothering her for what seemed now to be a long, long time.

"And you say that you hate Kathy, you really do, my dear? Because she broke Miranda?"

Lorrie looked at the silken bundle in Miss Ashemeade's lap.

"No, I guess I don't really hate her. And I—I guess I'm sorry I slapped her. She didn't mean to break Miranda."

"Hate is a big and hard word, Lorrie. Don't use it unless you are sure. You have been unhappy and so have seen only unhappy things around you. You have been setting your stitches crooked, and now they must be picked out again. Such picking must always be done or the design will be spoiled."

"I wish"—Lorrie looked about her longingly—"I wish I could stay here."

"You do not want to go back to Aunt Margaret?" All at once there was a sharp note in Miss Ashemeade's voice.

"Oh, no, I don't mean that. I guess I mean I wish I could just come here sometimes."

Miss Ashemeade beckoned to her. "Come here, child."

Lorrie edged around the table, came directly before Miss Ashemeade, on one side of her the frame holding the unfinished work, and on the other a table whose top was set up as a lid to show many small compartments, all filled with spools and reels of brightly colored silk and wool thread.

Her chin was cupped in Miss Ashemeade's hand as the old lady leaned forward to look into her eyes. It seemed to Lorrie that all her thoughts were being read, and suddenly she was ashamed of some of them. She wanted to turn away her eyes, but she could not.

Then Miss Ashemeade nodded. "Perhaps something may be arranged. Now, Lorrie, I shall write a note for you to take to your aunt, that she will know where you have been. Miranda you shall leave with me, which is better than burying her in my herb garden, as you thought to do."

RIDE A WHITE HORSE

LORRIE shuffled her feet unhappily as she came up the hall of the apartment. But she knew what she had to do and pushed the button beside the Lockner door, feeling that if she did not do it at once she might turn and run. Then she was looking at Kathy and she said in a fast rush of words: "I'm sorry I slapped you."

"Mom, it's Lorrie! Hey, your aunt's here. They've been looking all over for you." Kathy caught at her arm. "Listen, Mom gave me heck for breaking your doll. I didn't mean to, really."

Lorrie nodded. Aunt Margaret now stood behind Kathy. She looked at Lorrie with no welcoming smile. Rather she put her hand out in turn and set it firmly on Lorrie's shoulders.

"Come, Lorrie. I believe you have something to say to Mrs. Lockner also, haven't you?"

Again Lorrie nodded. There was a tight knot of misery in her throat that made her voice hoarse as she said to Mrs. Lockner:

"I'm sorry. I shouldn't have slapped Kathy, or run away."

"No, you should not. But then Kathy should not have taken your doll either, Lorrie. Your aunt has explained that it meant a lot to you. Where is it? Perhaps it can be mended."

"No." Lorrie found it very hard to look at Mrs. Lockner. "I don't have her any more."

266

"I believe Lorrie has caused enough trouble today, Mrs. Lockner. We'll go home now."

Aunt Margaret's hand propelled Lorrie to their own apartment. Once inside, her aunt moved away from her, leaving Lorrie standing alone. Aunt Margaret sat down with a sigh. For a moment she rested her head on her hand, her eyes closed, and she looked very tired indeed. Lorrie fumbled with the zipper on her windbreaker, let it slip off her arms and shoulders. It tumbled to the floor and the small envelope Miss Ashemeade had given her fell from the pocket. Lorrie picked it up and stood turning it in her hands.

"I don't know what to do with you, Lorrie. This running away, and slapping Kathy Lockner. She was only interested in your doll. If you did not want to show her Miranda, why did you take the doll over there?"

"Miranda was in my desk. I took that over to write a letter to Grandmother."

If Aunt Margaret heard her, she did not seem to care. She sighed again and got up as if it were an effort to move.

"I am too tired to talk to you now, Lorrie. Go to your room and think about this afternoon, think about it carefully."

Aunt Margaret started for the kitchen.

"But I haven't set the table."

"I believe I can manage very well without your help. I want you to spend some time thinking, Lorrie. Now!"

Slowly Lorrie went to the bedroom. She had laid the letter on the coffee table. That did not matter now. Aunt Margaret was angry or, what was worse, hurt. Lorrie sat down on the bench before the dressing table and stared at her reflection in the mirror, and then she covered her face with her hands.

Think about this afternoon, Aunt Margaret said. It was hard now for her to understand what *had* happened, even harder to puzzle out why. She had not wanted to go to the Lockners', and then Kathy with Miranda . . . and the shattering crash of Miranda's head against the wall . . . her hand against Kathy's cheek. Then planning to bury Miranda . . . going to Octagon House, meeting with Miss Ashemeade— What had Miss Ashemeade said?

"Haste makes waste—"

Lorrie took a tissue from the box in the top drawer to wipe her eyes and blow her nose. She was sorry about Kathy and about causing Mrs. Lockner and Aunt Margaret trouble. But she was not sorry about meeting Miss Ashemeade—she was glad for that.

"Lorrie." Aunt Margaret called.

"Coming." Lorrie gave a last wipe to her reddened eyes.

Aunt Margaret was already seated at the table as Lorrie slid in across from her. Friday night was usually a night when they had special food and a happy time, but not tonight. Lorrie sighed.

"Aunt Margaret—" That knot in her throat was back, so big a lump that she could not swallow anything, even a sip of hot chocolate. "I'm sorry."

"Yes I believe you are—now—Lorrie. But being sorry now, will that last so something such as this does not happen again? You know I cannot be with you as I would like. And you cannot stay alone. Mrs. Lockner has been more than kind, considering your rudeness in return."

Lorrie choked, staring down at the plate of food she could not eat.

"Lorrie, I know that this way of living is very different from what you had with Grandmother Mallard. But to sulk because of that—I do not like it."

Lorrie felt for the tissue in her pocket.

"You cannot expect to have friends if you are not friendly in turn. When Kathy asks you to go places with her you always say no. You have not joined any of the school clubs. Mrs. Raymond tells me that at recess you sit and read a book, unless the playground teacher asks you, or rather orders you, to join in a game. I know that this was all strange to you when you came. But surely it is not so now and you should be making friends."

Aunt Margaret pushed aside her own plate as if she could not swallow any better than Lorrie. She drank her coffee slowly, the frown lines between her eyes very sharp.

"What did you do with Miranda?" she asked abruptly.

"I took her to the Octagon House," Lorrie answered, hardly above a whisper.

"The—the Octagon House?" Aunt Margaret sounded really surprised. "But why in the world?"

"I wanted to bury Miranda, not just throw her out in the trash. There's a garden there."

"How do you know that?"

Then Lorrie told about the kitten and the meeting with Hallie, and of today when she had seen Miss Ashemeade in her wonderful room. As she poured out her story, some of her misery eased and she could look at Aunt Margaret again.

"And she sent you a note—" Lorrie dashed into the other room, came back with the envelope, which she laid before Aunt Margaret.

Her aunt opened it. Lorrie caught a glimpse of the writing, very different from any she had ever seen, looped and curved as much as the decorations of the rusty iron gate.

Aunt Margaret read it twice and her frown became a puzzled look. She studied the signature again before she turned to Lorrie.

"Miss Ashemeade would like you to spend the day with her tomorrow."

Could she go? Lorrie did not quite dare ask. Not to go—that might be what Aunt Margaret would consider a suitable punishment for this bad week. Oh, if she could go, she would be willing to do whatever they wanted her to—go to a monster show with Kathy, play basketball, all the things she shrank from but which they seemed to think she should want to do. But she could not ask or promise, somehow she could not. She did not know the brightness of her eyes, the strained look on her face asked for her.

"Very well." Aunt Margaret folded the note to slip back into the envelope. "You may go." Then, as if that decision had lifted a big black shadow from the kitchen, she began to eat. Lorrie swallowed. The knot was gone from her throat too. Suddenly she was hungry and everything looked good.

She did all her homework that evening, being twice as careful with the math problems, while Aunt Margaret worked with her own papers and sketches on the other side of the table. Lorrie picked up one drawing that had somehow been mixed in with her scribble sheets. She looked at a chair that was familiar and then realized she had seen its like in Miss Ashemeade's room. Only this was painted with a golden covering, and she thought the needlework of flowers much prettier.

"Why don't they have flowers here?" She held out the sketch. "Miss Ashemeade does—pink, yellow, and green—a pale green—" For a moment Lorrie closed her eyes to picture the better her memory of the chair.

"You saw a chair such as this at Miss Ashemeade's?"

Lorrie opened her eyes. Her aunt was staring at her in surprise.

"Yes. She has two. They are by the fireplace. But hers have embroidered backs and seats."

"What colors did you say?"

"Well, the background is not quite light yellow, more cream. And the flowers are not bright, but you can see them. There are pink roses, and some small yellow bell things, and they're in a bunch tied with ribbon—the ribbon is pink, too. Then they have a circle of leaves, a kind of vine, around them, and it is a pale green."

Her aunt nodded. "Probably petit point. But it is an excellent idea—we want to use this chair as a background for a sketch of formal gowns. Lorrie, when you are there tomorrow look carefully at those colors, and the design. Do you know, from what you have told me, you are a very fortunate girl. Miss Ashemeade's house must be a treasury of fine old things."

"It's beautiful, simply beautiful!" Lorrie cried. "And the candles—the fire—It's just wonderful!"

Aunt Margaret smiled as she put her papers back in her briefcase. "I can imagine that it is. Now, you might try making tomorrow come the sooner by getting to bed."

Lorrie thought that it might be as hard to get to sleep as it was on Christmas Eve. But it did not turn out that way, for she was so quickly asleep that afterward she could not remember climbing into bed. And morning did arrive swiftly after all.

She managed her share of the morning work eagerly and then decided that a visit of such import demanded her go-to-tea dress. That seemed tight now and Aunt Margaret, looking her over before Lorrie put on her best coat, agreed that she must have grown since Grandmother had had it made.

Then she was free, speeding along Ash Street at anything but a decorous pace, toward Octagon House. Again the gate gave to her push and she walked more soberly around to the door, which Hallie opened promptly at her knock.

"She's havin' her mornin' chocolate, you go right in. There's a cup waitin' for you, too, Mis' Lorrie."

Then she was back in the red-velvet room. The drapes were pulled back to let in the fall sunshine. There was still a fire going, but no need for candles this morning.

Miss Ashemeade's chair had been moved closer to

271

the window, so the daylight fell across her frame and the contents of the table which held the silks and wools. But before her was another small table and on it sat a tall, straight-sided pot with violets scattered over its white sides and gold edging on its handle. Two cups matching the pot sat on a small tray, and there was a plate with a fringed napkin covering it.

"Good morning, Lorrie."

Lorrie had hesitated just within the door. Now she curtsied.

"Good morning, Miss Ashemeade." She must watch her manners. This was a room which welcomed only the most ladylike behavior.

"Give Hallie your coat and hat, my dear. Do you like chocolate?"

Lorrie wriggled out of her outdoor things. "Yes, please."

At Miss Ashemeade's gesture she sat down on a high stool across from her hostess. Miss Ashemeade poured from the tall pot, and took the napkin from the plate to display some small biscuits. Lorrie sipped her chocolate from a cup so light and delicate that she feared an incautious touch might break it. Then she nibbled at a biscuit that was crisp and not sweet, but which had a flavor all its own, one she had never tasted before.

"Do you know how to sew, Lorrie?" asked Miss Ashemeade as she emptied her own cup.

"A little. Grandmother was teaching me to make Miranda a dress."

"There was a lady in England," Miss Ashemeade replied, "who once said that it was as disgraceful for a lady not to know how to use a needle as it was for a gentleman to be ignorant of how to handle his sword." She wiped her fingers on a small napkin. Lorrie did not know just what was expected of her, but she said after a moment's pause:

"Gentlemen do not have swords any more."

"No. Nor do many ladies use needles either. But to forget or set aside any art is an unhappy thing."

Miss Ashemeade glanced around at the pictures, the rolls of material on the long table, to the tapestry over the fireplace. Then she picked up a silver bell, which gave a tinkle and brought Hallie in to take the tray.

For the first time Lorrie saw the top of the table on which the chocolate set had rested. Against a black background was a scene that held her attention. There was a gold castle on a mountain, its windows all pearl, while above it a moon of the same pearl peered out of golden clouds. Miss Ashemeade saw her interest and traced the scene with a finger tip.

"Papier-mâché, my dear. Once it was very popular. Now, Lorrie, suppose you put this little table over there, since we no longer need it."

The table was very light, Lorrie discovered, and she could easily move it. When she came back, Miss Ashemeade was bending over the table with all the small compartments under its top lid. She had pulled around before her the frame with the half-finished work, and now Lorrie could see that that was a picture, too, within a flower border.

"Do you think you can help me a little?" Miss Ashemeade asked.

"Oh, yes!" Lorrie was eager.

"You may thread my needles, if you will." Miss Ashemeade smiled. "I can no longer see as well as I once did, and needle threading is a trial at times. Now, here are the needles in this case. And I will use threads this long, from this, and this, and this." She pointed to the colored wools wound smoothly on reels of carved ivory.

Lorrie set to work. The needles were fine, but they had larger eyes than any she had seen before, so threading was not hard. There were quite a few needles standing up in the funny little ivory case made like a cat—you unscrewed its head to see them. But

273

that was not the only needle box in the table compartments. Miss Ashemeade took out the other one and opened it. Inside there was room for many needles to be stuck through a piece of green velvet, but only two were there. They were different from the ones Lorrie threaded, for they gleamed of gold in the sunlight instead of silver.

"These, Lorrie"—Miss Ashemeade's voice was serious—"are very special needles and not to be often used."

"They look like gold," Lorrie ventured.

"They are," answered Miss Ashemeade. "And they are very important."

"Like the magic needles the princess had?"

"Just so. You will not use them, Lorrie. Understand?"

"Yes, Miss Ashemeade."

As Miss Ashemeade closed that case and put it back, Lorrie noted that it was of a dark wood that looked very, very old, and it was patterned on the top with tarnished metal.

"Thank you, Lorrie. Now you may stick those all along the frame where they may be easily reached. You have been sitting still, which I know is hard for one of your years. So, now you are free to explore."

"Explore?" echoed Lorrie.

"Explore the house. You are free, Lorrie, to enter any room where the door will open for you."

What a queer thing to say, Lorrie thought. As if a door could choose of itself whether or not to open for her. But to explore the house, yes, that was exciting.

"Thank you."

Miss Ashemeade smiled again. "Thank me when you return, Lorrie, if you still wish to."

That, too, was puzzling. But Lorrie did not try to figure it out. She decided to leave by the door opposite the one where she had entered. Miss Ashemeade was bending over the frame, already beginning to stitch the canvas.

Lorrie went into the next room. This was dusky, behind the closed shutters. Unlike Miss Ashemeade's warm and welcoming chamber, this was chill and dark. No fire burned in the fireplace. All the furniture was covered by sheets. Lorrie glanced around. The room had let her enter, but there was very little to see that attracted her. Next was a hallway, and then another room, which must balance the red room. It was a bedroom and it was alive and open, only it was all green—as green as Miss Ashemeade's dress. The bed was very large and had carved posts and a frame at the top of them, from which hung pale green curtains patterned with vines in darker green, the same shade as the carpet under Lorrie's feet. There were chairs and a small sofa, all covered in light green patterned with the darker leaves. Almost, Lorrie thought, one could believe this a wood with things growing.

She stood by the foot of the bed, looking about her. Miss Ashemeade had said to enter any room that would let her. But Lorrie did not feel comfortable here.

"Merrow—"

Lorrie, startled, looked to her left. There were two other doors leading out of the room, and peering about the edge of the nearer was Sabina. She opened her small mouth again to utter a cry that sounded much too large for such a small kitten, almost, Lorrie decided, as if she were impatiently telling her to hurry.

As Lorrie went toward her, Sabina ducked around the door and disappeared. Then Lorrie entered.

She was in a very queerly shaped small room. The outer wall, which had a single window, met the longer wall to her right at a very sharp and narrow angle. But on the other side, to her left, it was square as an ordinary room. There were no curtains or drapes, so the light came through easily to show what stood there.

Lorrie gasped. The center of the misshapen room was occupied by an eight-sided dais or platform of

275

polished wood. Set in the sides of that were drawers, each marked by a gleaming brass keyhole and handles. And using that base for a foundation was a house of red brick with a wooden trim, an exact copy of the very home in which it stood. If it were a doll house it was larger and more perfect than any Lorrie had seen before. Taller than Lorrie herself, it almost filled the room.

Facing what was meant to be the front door of the house was a rocking horse such as Lorrie had seen pictured in the old volumes of the *St. Nicholas* magazines. It was big, nearly as large as a pony she had ridden at the park last summer, and it was white, with a silky mane. On its back was a red saddle. Only, Lorrie saw as she went closer, it was an oddly shaped saddle, not like any she had seen before.

She put out her hand cautiously. Why, the horse felt as if he were covered with real hide! Bolder, Lorrie stroked his mane, and under her touch he rocked back and forth with a faint creak-creak.

"Merrow!" Sabina was standing on her hind legs, as if she were trying to peep into one of the windows. But it was too high above her head. Lorrie went on her knees to look too.

It was as if she were viewing a real house through the wrong end of field glasses, making all smaller instead of larger. There was furniture and pictures, and carpets on the floor. She could even see a little tea table with a service set out upon it, just waiting for someone to pour. In fact, as Lorrie moved around the house, she had the oddest feeling that it was inhabited, and, if she hurried a little faster, she would catch sight of some person who had just this moment left the room into which she was now looking.

Miss Ashemeade's red-velvet room was different, for in the little house it was a dining room, the long table set with a white cloth and dishes ready for a meal. She crawled around to the kitchen side and then on to look into the green bedroom. Upstairs there were other bedrooms—three big square ones. And then there were three triangular rooms that had big cupboards in them, and another, oddly shaped room with a stair opening into it.

All of it was furnished and ready—so ready. The oven in the kitchen stove was half ajar and she could see the end of a loaf of bread.

Doll houses opened, so this must. How else could all the furniture have been put in? But when Lorrie tried to find any hinge or latch on the outside she could not. Baffled, she sat back on her heels. Then she tugged at the pulls on the base drawers. But not one gave to her urging. They had keyholes, perhaps they were locked.

Once more she circled the house. It was just a little taller than she was, counting the base. But the attic rooms were so dark she could not see in through their slits of windows. If there were any rooms behind those they remained a mystery. Maybe the house was to be respected as Miss Ashemeade had warned her, something to look at with the eyes but not with the fingers. And there was plenty to look at, tiny marvels in each room every time she peered anew.

Lorrie stepped back. She could not rid herself of the belief that this was no ordinary doll house to be played with. It was so much like the house in which it stood that somehow it was alive, really more alive than those parts of Octagon House she had found sheeted and covered. And there remained her feeling that all of the smaller house, not just part of it, was in use—by someone.

Used by what—whom? She hurried around the corner to look into another window, then raced to the next room. If she could just move fast enough to catch a glimpse of the tiny person who only that moment had gone out! Then she stood still and looked at Sabina, who had settled down in the full light of the window, to wash a back paw with deliberation and much attention to the space between two well-spread toes.

"It's—it's just a doll house, isn't it, Sabina? No one *does* live there. No one could."

Sabina did not even flick an ear in her direction. Lorrie took another step back and her shoulder struck against the rocking horse. He swayed, and under the rockers the floor creaked. Lorrie drew her hand down his mane. Just—almost as good as a pony.

She eyed the queer saddle. Why was it made that way? But—it would be fun to take a ride. Rocking horses were for little kids, but this was such a big one.

Lorrie climbed on and tried to sit astride the saddle. But you could not do that comfortably, it had bumps in the wrong places. Somehow, she did not know how, she found herself sitting the horse in another way, her knee hooked over a big horn, both of her feet on the same side of the horse. And he began to rock, faster—

There was a wind blowing and leaves whirled up— leaves? Lorrie blinked. This was not the room, it was a road with trees on either side and the wind in their branches. She was not on a rocking horse at all, but on a real one. And she wore a long skirt flapping in the wind. For a moment she was stiff with fright, and then that fright vanished. Dimly she had a strange feeling she had done this before, that this was just as it should be.

The white horse moved easily at a steady trot, and Lorrie rode him as if this was the most natural thing in the world. Not too far ahead was a brick house. The Octagon House! Lorrie's heart beat faster. Something, someone was waiting there for her and it was most important.

Then the horse flung up his head and shook it. He stopped beside a big block of stone by an iron gate. Lorrie slipped out of the saddle to the stone and then to the ground. She had to gather the long folds of her skirt up over her arm or she would have tripped on them. But she opened the gate and walked up to the front door.

There was a brass knocker there and Lorrie lifted it, letting it fall again with a loud bang. Only—there was no answer. No one came, and when she tried the door it was locked. Her happy excitement was gone, suddenly she shivered and was afraid.

The wind blew dust at her and she closed her eyes. When she opened them there was no big door. She stood in front of the doll house. Her long skirt had vanished, everything was as it had been. Lorrie blinked rapidly. It was a dream, that was what it had been. But—she looked about the room—she did not want to stay in here any more.

Nor did she want to explore any further. Swiftly she retraced her way back to the red room. There was only one threaded needle still unused at the side of the frame. Miss Ashemeade looked up as Lorrie hurried to the light of the window. It seemed to Lorrie as if in that glance Miss Ashemeade had learned all that had happened. She did not want to talk of the small house, or of the horse, not even to Miss Ashemeade.

"Well, my dear, see, I have almost finished my morning's stint. Do you know what a stint is?"

"No." Lorrie sat down on the stool.

"When I was young every little girl had a piece of needlework on which she did an allotted portion of work each day. That was her stint. It was an excellent way in which to learn both discipline and sewing."

She took up the last of the needles Lorrie had threaded. "Now, just this last small bit—"

"Oh!" Lorrie cried out in admiration.

In the picture there was now a small fawn standing beside the tree that had marked the edge of the filled space when she had come that morning. It was so real! Lorrie felt that if she put out a finger she would touch sun-warmed hide.

"You like it?"

"It is so real."

"Would you like to learn to do this?"

"Could I? Could I really make something—a picture?"

Again Miss Ashemeade gave her one of those long, piercing looks. "Not without a great deal of patience and hard work, Lorrie. And no haste, you must understand, no haste."

"Could I try?" Lorrie was only a little daunted.

"We can always try—anything," Miss Ashemeade answered. "Yes, you may try, Lorrie. You may begin this afternoon if you wish. But in the beginning you do not do this kind of work. Beginning is sometimes very dull and takes learning and practice."

"I would like to try, please," Lorrie said.

"Then you shall, and we will see if you have any gift for it. Now, dear, will you tell Hallie we are ready for lunch?"

PHINEAS AND PHEBE

AFTER that Saturday Lorrie found she was living two lives. But it was not confusing. In one she was Lorrie Mallard who went to school, who did her homework, who walked home with Kathy now and then, who had household tasks to do. But to be that Lorrie was not too hard because there was escape into Octagon House. She did not go too often, of course, though she tried to take the alley route by it each morning and evening, hurrying before and after that one stretch of walk so she could go more slowly there. And twice Hallie had been at the chained back gate with a note for Aunt Margaret, inviting Lorrie to more afternoons in Miss Ashemeade's big room.

Miss Ashemeade had been very right in her warning that to learn to sew was a task. The needles and silks and wools never seemed to prick *her* fingers or tangle when she used them. Sometimes she worked on the canvas in the frame, or again she mended lace or one of the pieces that lay waiting on the table. But she was never too busy to look over Lorrie's strip of linen on which were shaping rows of different kinds of stitches. That "sampler" would serve Lorrie later, Miss Ashemeade said, as a pattern for all the stitches one must know.

Sometimes as they worked together Miss Ashemeade told stories. And sometimes Lorrie talked about Grandmother Mallard and Miss Logan's, and once even about Mother and Father. And sometimes about school.

"I'm to be a Puritan," she announced on her third visit. "It's for the Thanksgiving play. I don't have anything to say. I just bring in a big dish of pretend corn for the table. We're supposed to be giving a feast with the Indians as guests."

Miss Ashemeade was working on the lace, using the finest of thread and needles. Even Lorrie's bright eyes had had trouble in finding the holes in those.

"Indians and Puritans. So you are beginning to learn your American history now, Lorrie? Perhaps with less trouble?"

"Some. I still get mixed up once in a while though. And then that Jimmy Purvis always laughs."

"Jimmy Purvis." Miss Ashemeade took another almost invisible stitch. "Ah, yes, he is the boy who chased Sabina."

"He's mean, just plain mean and hateful!" Lorrie burst out. Since she walked now and then with Kathy, Jimmy and his gang were not quite so much on her heels, but she still was a little afraid of him. "I don't like boys anyway, they're always doing mean things."

"How many boys do you know, Lorrie?"

"Well, there's Rob Lockner, he's always tagging

along with Jimmy, doing what Jimmy tells him to. Then there's Stan Wormiski. He's another. There're all the boys at school. But I don't bother with them—they're all mean."

"All mean," repeated Miss Ashemeade thoughtfully. "That is quite a severe judgment, isn't it, Lorrie? But perhaps you have reason to make it. Now—" She looked around. "Sabina seems to have vanished. I wonder if you would find her for me, Lorrie?"

Since Sabina came and went at will and apparently Miss Ashemeade did not care, Lorrie wondered a little at such an errand. But she obediently put aside her sampler and went to hunt the kitten.

Through the room with the shrouded furniture she called, "Sabina, Sabina!" with no mew of answer. Then the half-ajar door brought her on to the green bedroom and finally to the strangely shaped room of the doll house and the rocking horse.

Sabina was there, all right. She was standing on three legs, while with her right forepaw she patted at one of the drawers in the base. From the keyhole there something dangled, swinging back and forth. Lorrie got down to look. And Sabina jumped to one side, as if Lorrie's coming had caught her in some mischief that she must now pretend she knew nothing about.

What swung from the keyhole was a chain, a gold chain, and it was fastened to a key set in the drawer lock. On impulse Lorrie turned the key, and the drawer pulled out easily.

Two dolls lay within upon their backs, staring up at her. One was about five inches high, the other four, and their heads were modeled with very lifelike expressions. But they were not made of china, Lorrie noticed, though they were quaint enough to seem as if they were as old, if not older than, Miranda.

The taller doll was a boy with black hair. And his clothes were odd. He wore long trousers of gray material and a short jacket fastened with a single button under his chin. The little girl had her brown hair parted in the middle and pulled back of her ears where her braids were turned up and under, pinned in a coil. She had a dress that was wide across the shoulders and veed in a point from the yoke to the high waist, and there were small frills of lace showing at neck and wrist. The skirt was full but not floor length, and under it showed pantalets much ruffled.

With great care Lorrie picked up the boy doll. The clothing was so carefully made that, having become so conscious of stitchery, she marveled at the patience taken in its making. She was going to lay him back in the drawer when she heard a faint squeak and looked up to see Sabina claw at the side of the house.

"No—"

But Lorrie was too late. The little claws touched some hidden spring and half the house moved, swinging back—the walls that covered the green bedroom and the kitchen. It moved easily though Sabina did not touch it again, but sat back to watch.

Now Lorrie could see the interior in detail, much clearer than she had through the windows. And for a long moment or two she simply looked. One of the portions now revealed was the very room in which she sat. But it did not in the least mirror the modern room. There was no rocking horse in miniature, no second doll house. Instead, on the now empty shelves along the wall were tiny books, and rows of minute jars and crocks. There was one chair in the corner— could it be a copy of the high-backed one Miss Ashemeade now used? And on the floor was a painted design instead of a carpet or rug. That resembled a star, Lorrie thought.

But the oddest thing revealed by the opening of the outer wall was a three-cornered space between this room and the kitchen. When the house wall was shut that must be completely closed, as there was no opening into it from either this room or the kitchen. What was it meant for, Lorrie wondered. A cupboard? But then why no door to it?

The kitchen absorbed her attention the most. It was in such detail. There were even baskets of vegetables and eggs on the table. And she could see the bread waiting in the oven. All it needed was a Hallie busy there to bring it to life.

On impulse she put the boy doll by the fireplace. He was able to stand, Lorrie discovered, if you fixed his feet properly. Then she added the girl and lifted the egg basket from the table to hang on her arm. There!

Carefully Lorrie swung the side of the house shut and crouched way down to peer through a window. Why, they looked real, as if they were going to move about their own business any minute. They belonged somehow just where she had put them.

There must be a reason—

Not understanding why, Lorrie got up and went to the horse. It was easier to get into the queer saddle now and she settled herself on the horse with more confidence. Under her weight he began to rock. . . .

No wind blew today along the gravel road, but it was fall and leaves lay about. The white horse trotted toward Octagon House and again Lorrie felt that rise of excitement. Something was going to happen, something important—

This time when she slid off onto the mounting block she did not go to the front door that had refused to admit her before. But, gathering her skirt up over her arm, she took the brick walk around the side. The trees and bushes growing along the fence were smaller and not tangled all together, but they made a screen. And it was a dark day with heavy clouds hanging overhead, cold in spite of the lack of wind.

Lorrie came to the back steps and held her long skirt higher so she could climb them. But when she raised her hand to knock on the door it swung and she opened it. No Hallie stood there to bid her welcome.

It was the same triangle with the two doors, one to Miss Ashemeade's room, one to the kitchen. The one to the red room was tightly closed, and when Lorrie tried to raise the old latch, it did not move. She remembered what Miss Ashemeade had said:

"You may go through any door that will let you."

But Miss Ashemeade had said that about the other house. Or had she? Which was this, a doll house in the Octagon House, or the Octagon House itself in some strange way?

The kitchen door, on the other hand, was standing ajar and Lorrie took that for an invitation. She came into warmth and good smells, and a feeling this was a good place to be. There was a big black pot on the range and from it came a soft bubbling noise. Lorrie sniffed the odor of fresh bread, and an even more mouth-watering spicy smell. On the table were all the things laid out to make a pie—a rolling pin, a waiting plate, a jug, some butter in a dish, a bowl with flour in it. And a pan of apples stood ready for the slicing knife. But where were the boy and girl? Or the cook who must have been busy here?

Lorrie looked around, knowing once more the feeling that someone had just stepped from the room as she entered. There was another door, but it was shut, and when she went to it, it was as tightly closed against her as Miss Ashemeade's had been.

So, only the kitchen and the back wall were open to her.

Lorrie moved slowly around the room. There was a big, polished brass pan hanging on the wall and it was almost as good as a mirror. She saw a reflection in it and stopped short to view herself. Of course she knew she was wearing the long skirt, which seemed fit and proper for riding here (where was *here?*), but now she saw other changes in Lorrie Mallard. Of course, she still had black hair and greeny eyes. But that hair was tied in a tight, turned-up, half bun at the back of her neck, and she had on a hat with a wide, curly brim and a soft feather drooping in the back. And instead of a zippered windbreaker she had worn outdoors a couple of hours ago, she now had a brown jacket, tight fitting and trimmed across the chest with rows of red braid, buttoned from her chin to her waist. She looked so different she could only stand and stare at that rather murky reflection.

She was Lorrie Mallard, Lorrie repeated to herself, Lorrie Mallard, eleven and a half years old. She lived with Aunt Margaret in the Ashton Arms apartment and she was in the sixth grade, the last year at Fermont School—that was the truth.

A sound broke through Lorrie's absorption and she turned around. Something outside the window—surely she had seen movement there! Quickly Lorrie hurried around the table. My, how dark it was getting! A bad storm—no, it must be night! That could not be true, it was only the middle of the afternoon. But Lorrie had to believe it was almost night now.

The pot continued to bubble comfortably, but no one came to see how it was doing. Once more Lorrie went to try the other door of the kitchen, to find it as firmly fixed as ever. As she stood by it she again heard that sound. There was a tall cabinet here and it was dark in this corner. Lorrie pressed back against the door and watched the far window.

There *was* a shadow there! She could see it against the small panes of glass. Now—that sound—the window was rising a little at a time. Suddenly Lorrie crouched at the end of the cupboard. She did not know why she went into hiding, only that she was afraid and excited, and wanted to see without being seen.

For what seemed a long time to Lorrie nothing happened, except that the window was now open. Then a pair of hands gripped the sill, and behind them Lorrie made out a hunched outline that could be head and shoulders. Someone was climbing in!

It was darker in the kitchen than it had been when she had first entered. But there was a lamp on the table near the range. And, though its circle of light did not reach all the way to the window, Lorrie made out the figure huddled on the floor directly below the sill.

A boy! He had bare feet protruding below a pair of patched trousers all ragged at the ends. His hands and arms were bare almost to the elbow, and his shirt sleeves were tattered. There was no collar on the shirt, only a band fastened with a ragged strip of cloth. When he moved, it sprung open farther down his chest and Lorrie could see bare skin there also. He must not have anything on under that shirt, in spite of the cold.

His hair was an uncombed, unclipped mop that kept falling forward over his eyes, so that he was constantly raising his hand to push it back. And his face was very dirty. Around one of his eyes skin was puffed and dark and there was a greenish-blue bruise on the side of his jaw. Except to brush the hair out of his eyes, he had not moved since he dropped over the sill into the kitchen.

Now his head turned from side to side as he looked round the room. Lorrie thought he must be listening as well as looking, for now and then he stiffened and was still for a moment or two as if he could hear what she did not.

Then he got to his feet. He was very thin, his arms so bony and his waist—where his trousers were belted with a piece of rope—so flat that Lorrie thought he certainly had not had enough to eat for a long time. He reached the side of the big table in a single stride and grabbed at the apples, putting them one after another into the front of his shirt where they made lumps under the grimy material.

The bowl emptied, he made for the half-open door of the range. His hand went to jerk the door farther open. Then he cried out softly and held his fingers to his mouth, but kept turning his head as if in search of something. He took up a poker and reached within the oven, pulling the bread pan forward, and then a second pan from which came the spicy smell. As those reached the door the boy hesitated. To pull them farther would dump them on the floor and apparently they were too hot to hold in his hands.

Again he looked around for a tool and caught a towel from a wall hook. With the towel wrapped around his already singed fingers, he brought the pans to the top of the stove before he snatched the red-and-white-checked cloth from a smaller table. He dumped into it the loaf of bread and the sheet of gingerbread, digging the latter out of its pan in great broken hunks. His head went up and he looked to the hall door. Jerking the cloth into a bag, he made for the window through which he had come, bundled out his loot first, and dropped after it into the night. The window slid down and Lorrie was alone.

She listened. Whatever the boy must have heard, or thought he had heard, she could not. But she wanted to know more— Why had he come to steal food? That was somehow important. Though she crossed to the window she could see nothing. But the window slid up smoothly at her pull. Without stopping to think, Lorrie followed the boy, climbing up to drop to the ground behind a bush. Now she could hear crackling off to her right, around the next angle of the house. Holding up the long skirt of her riding habit, she followed as fast as she could.

There was a brush screen close to the house as far as the next angle. Now she must be directly below that hidden, closed-in space, because before her was the window of the room with the painted floor. And from it came a beam of light. She saw a black shadow slip across it.

Dark as it was, Lorrie discovered that she was able to follow the scurrying shadow as it flitted from one bush to another. Now it was heading for the fence.

The bedroom windows were above, but there were no lights there. Lorrie glanced back and up at the house. On the second floor was a pale gleam in one window, as if a single candle was not too far away, but the rest was dark.

There was a swaying of bushes and Lorrie saw a black figure climb over the fence. She began to run for the gate, but to climb in this long skirt was out of the question. She came to the mounting block. And for a moment she was daunted, for the white horse was gone. Then she heard a noise to her left, and, gathering up her skirt with both hands, keeping to the pools of the shadows, she moved to where the boy had gone over the fence.

He was still keeping to cover. Then behind her she heard a faint creak and she stood still. Someone else was using the gate, a figure not much taller than she. Who?

Lorrie was undecided. If she stayed where she was she would lose the boy. If she kept on with the unknown behind her—Lorrie did not like the idea of being followed. And that other moved as carefully among the shadows as she was doing, as if dreading discovery.

She began to advance in a crabwise fashion, trying to watch both directions at once, which could not be done as she soon discovered. This was not Ash Street but a gravel road, bordered on both sides by trees and bushes. Shortly the gravel disappeared, leaving only hard-packed dirt.

The one behind her made a sudden dart forward, which brought her level with Lorrie. For it was a girl, a girl who could not have been much older than Lorrie herself. She wore a long, hooded cloak, but the hood was pushed back far enough so Lorrie could see her face. The newcomer passed within hand's distance of Lorrie without looking, as if indeed Lorrie were not there. She ran lightly after the boy.

Lorrie followed. There was a stream with a wooden bridge over it. But the girl from the house did not cross that. Instead she stood very still, her head bent to one side as if she were listening. Lorrie listened too—

She could hear the very faint rippling of the water below. But there was another sound also—someone was crying. And someone else was talking, a murmur that rose and fell but never quite drowned out the crying. To Lorrie's surprise the girl turned her head and now her eyes looked directly into Lorrie's. She did not seem in the least amazed, but as if she had known all along that Lorrie was there. And also as if, Lorrie thought, they were sharing this adventure.

Her finger was at her lips as she nodded sharply at the bridge from under which that crying came. Lorrie understood. She remained where she was, but the other girl crept forward very softly, drawing her cloak about her as if she did not want it to catch on any of the bushes or dried weeds.

The sound of talking below stopped, but the crying, now a very weak whimper, continued. Then, so suddenly Lorrie cried out, a black shadow rose from the weeds and threw itself at the girl. There was a struggle and she fell, the shadow trying to hold her down. Only she pulled free, leaving her cloak half torn off. Her hair tumbled loosely about her face and she raised her hands to push it back.

"Don't be afraid," she said.

"I ain't! Not of no girl, anyway." It was a hoarse boy's voice that answered. "What you doin', sneakin' up on—"

The girl gave her cloak a twitch, settling it smoothly about her shoulders again.

"You are from Canal Town." It was a statement, not a question this time.

"We ain't nobody, missy. You gits yourself outta here afore you gits into trouble."

"Phin? Where are you, Phin?" The whimpering had become a wail, and in it was a fear so strong Lorrie shivered in sympathy.

The boy moved, but the girl from the house was quicker. She slipped down the bank, under the over-hang of the bridge. The boy scrambled after her, and now Lorrie dared go nearer.

"I am Lotta Ashemeade." That was the girl from the house, her voice calm. "You are afraid of something, bad afraid, aren't you?"

"Matt." There was a gulping sound. "Matt Mahoney. Dada died, and Matt, he says I must go to th' poor farm—"

"Close your trap, Phebe, close it tight! You want to be walked there straight off?"

"Stop it!" Lotta ordered. "You want to scare her to death, boy? She doesn't have to be afraid of me. Phebe, there's no reason to be afraid. Nobody's going to find you."

"No?" The boy again. "An' how kin you promise that, missy? You gotta army maybe to slow up Matt? Cause it'll take about that to stop him."

In answer the wail broke out louder than ever.

"I said to stop it!" There was authority in Lotta's voice and the wail became a whimper. "Come on, Phebe."

"An' jus' where're you thinkin' of takin' her, missy? Back to that big ol' house of your'n? Keep her there an' send for Matt. Or maybe, her bein' an orphan, send her to th' pore farm yourself?"

"She's cold and she's wet and she's hungry. Oh, I know you got food, out of our kitchen, for her. But see how she's shivering and she hasn't even a shawl. If she stays here tonight she'll be sick before morning."

"So—she ain't stayin'."

"How far do you think you can take her now?"

"What's it to you, anyhow? We're from Canal Town, we ain't big house folks. I'll do for Phebe, never no

291

mind from you, missy. Come on, Phebe, we'll jus' move on a bit."

"Phin, I can't. My foot hurts so. I jus' can't! You—maybe you better run for it. Matt, he said he'd take th' horse whip to you, 'member? Oh, Phin, you jus' cut along. Missy, Matt he wants Phin to work for him. Only Phin, he thought we might jus' find some movers goin' west and maybe hide in a wagon—or somethin'.''

"Spill it all now, will you, girl? Anyway, I has nowheres to go without you, Phebe. I keeps my promises. Ain't I always?"

"Then if you want Phebe to be safe, you'll come with me."

"An' why, missy? Why would you care?"

"I do."

She did, Lorrie knew that for the truth. Perhaps the boy recognized it also.

"Please, Phin."

"All right. Maybe I believe her, but there's other folks in that there ol' house an' they maybe ain't feelin' th' same way. Specially as how I helped myself pretty free to some o' their vittles a short while back."

"No one needs to know about you and Phebe. You'll be safe."

"What'd you mean, missy? You gonna fix us so no one kin see us, like we is ghosts or somethin' like?"

"Not that, Phin," Lotta answered. "But I do know of a safe place, at least for tonight. And it is warmer and dryer than under this bridge."

"Phin?" There was a pleading note in Phebe's voice.

"It ain't safe, I tell you."

"Please, Phin. She says it is. An'—an' I believe her, Phin."

" 'Cause you want to!" he flared up. " 'Cause you're cold an' hungry an' you want to! Ain't I told you a hundred times, it don't do no one any good to believe nothin' ner nobody?"

"I do her, Phin, somehow I do."

"All right. But I don't! You hear that, missy? I don't believe, an' I'll be watchin' for any tricks."

"Fair enough. Now help me, Phin."

They came down the road again, Lotta, with her arm around a much smaller girl wearing a torn dress and with feet as bare as Phin's. She limped along slowly, though Phin and Lotta supported her more and more as they reached the gate. Again they made the journey around the house. This time they did not go as far as the kitchen, but instead to the window of the doll-house room.

Lorrie heard them whispering together and then saw Phin push at the window. When he had it open he helped Lotta over the sill, and a moment later they had boosted Phebe through. Lorrie moved in closer. She could see them all inside. Phebe was squatting on the floor as if she did not have the strength to stand, and Phin was staring about him warily, a scowl on his face, as if he believed he was in a trap.

Lotta had gone to the side by the window, out of Lorrie's sight. Then Phin exclaimed aloud in surprise.

"What's that there? A cupboard?"

"Bigger than a cupboard," Lotta answered him. "It's a safe hiding place for now."

He strode forward, also to disappear from Lorrie's sight.

"A trap—maybe jus' a trap—" She could still hear his voice.

"Please." Phebe raised her head to look at Lotta. "I don't believe it, I don't believe you is goin' to send us back, missy. We ain't no kin to Matt. Jus' like Phin's no real kinfolk to me neither. Only he stood up to Matt when I got coughin' sick an' the shakes. An' Matt, he beat up Phin 'cause he traded some corn for medicine. Then Matt says he'd see I go to the pore farm. An' Phin says never, no to that an' we'd run. But we ain't far away and Matt he'll be after Phin does he stay here." She coughed, her thin body shaking with the effort.

Phin stepped back where Lorrie could see him again. "You ain't got th' little sense you was borned with, Phebe. Little missy here, she ain't a-carin' 'bout all that. Maybe Matt's got a poster out on me—Phineas McLean—ten shillin's reward—or th' like, but that ain't sayin' as how he'll ever lay his belt on me agin. 'Less missy here talks."

Lotta was at the door of the room. "If you truly believe that, Phineas McLean, you can go. The window's open." She gave him a long look and Phin made a gesture to push away his overgrown forelock but did not answer her. Then Lotta went out.

"Phin," Phebe choked out between coughs. "Phin, you'se always bin powerful good t' me. If you think Matt'll git you, you'd better go. Only I don't believe it—I don't. I think she's tellin' it true, we'll be safe here. I feel good, real good, right here. I truly, truly do, Phin!"

Once more he pushed back his hair, then he dropped on his knees beside Phebe and threw his arm about her shoulders.

"I ain't goin', girl. Leastwise, not tonight."

"Phin, don't you feel it, too? That this be a safe place?"

He was looking around, a rather puzzled expression on his bruised face.

"Maybe you is right, Phebe. Only it's right hard to believe in any place bein' safe for the likes of us— Canal Town trash, as they is always so quick to sing out."

"This is." Lotta was back. Across her arm was a quilt and a thick blanket. She nodded to the portion of the room Lorrie could not see. "Take these. And you had better get in there for now. I'll come when it is safe. And here—" Phin had taken the coverings from her, now Lotta picked up the tablecloth bag Lorrie had watched him fill. "Take this with you, I'll bring more later."

Wind was rising in the trees, the light in the room winked out. . . . Sunlight lay in a bar across the floor and in it lay Sabina asleep. Lorrie was not crouched down outside the window but she sat on the floor beside the doll house. Once more the side of the house hung a little open. She drew it the rest of the way to look into that small space with no proper door. It was empty.

In the kitchen the two dolls stood just as she had posed them. Carefully she took them out, knowing now who they were. Phineas McLean, no longer dirty, ragged, bruised—but she supposed that a doll would not look that way. His clothes were neat and whole, maybe this was meant to be Phineas truly safe and happy.

And Lotta—but no, this other doll did not have Lotta's features. This was Phebe, plumper, much happier looking. So maybe the house had welcomed them and continued to be their home. Why she thought that, Lorrie did not know.

She laid them back in their drawer and closed it. There was a click. The key on the chain—it was gone! When she tried the door again it was locked.

Phineas and Phebe were gone and the house— Now that she looked again Lorrie saw that the side of the house was once more tightly closed. Though she searched carefully for the latch, she could not find it.

Sabina awoke, yawned, got to her feet, stretched first front legs and then hind legs, and trotted to the door. More slowly Lorrie followed her, looking back once more at the baffling doll house.

A COLLAR FOR SABINA

"HEY, Canuck—"

Lorrie had paused at the mouth of the alley to take a tighter grip on the dress box. It was hard to manage that and her book bag too. Aunt Margaret had wanted to drive her to school this morning, but the car would not start. And Lorrie would have to hurry if she was going to get there in time.

It was just her luck that Jimmy and his gang were also late. Of course, maybe she could take refuge in the yard of Octagon House. She was somehow sure Jimmy would not follow her there. But such a detour would make her really tardy.

"Canuck, walks like a duck!"

Lorrie held the box tighter. It had her Puritan dress in it, and she had sewed a lot of that herself. Aunt Margaret had been surprised at how well she could do it. And Lorrie had pressed it and folded it neatly. She must not let it get wrinkled now.

"Canuck—"

Lorrie stared ahead. She was not going to run and let them chase her all the way to school. Boys—mean old boys!

She glanced to the house on her right. If only Hallie would come down to the back gate now. But every window was blank; it might have been deserted. Only—just looking at it—

What had Phin said? "Canal trash as they is so quick to sing out." Lorrie did not know why that flashed into her mind now. But for a moment it was almost as if she could see Phineas McLean pushing back his hair to glare at Lotta Ashemeade. She could hear Lotta's calm voice, see her refused-to-be frightened face when she answered him. Why, just a moment ago Lorrie had been ready to run to the house for safety herself.

"Canuck— What've you got in your box, Canuck? Give us a look."

Lorrie swung around.

Jimmy, yes, and Stan, and Rob Lockner. Jimmy in the lead as always, and grinning. For a moment Lorrie was afraid, so afraid that she thought she could not talk past the dryness in her mouth and throat. Then she thought of Lotta and Phineas, and Phebe who had so much worse to fear.

"My dress for the play." Lorrie hoped her voice did not shake as much as she thought it did. "Where's your Indian suit, Jimmy? You certainly got a lot of feathers for your headband."

"He sure did," Rob Lockner broke in. "Know what he did? His uncle knows a man down at the zoo, and the birds there, they lose feathers. So he got real eagle feathers, didn't you, Jimmy?"

"Sure. That's what Indians wore, eagle feathers." Jimmy answered, but he was looking at Lorrie oddly, as if before his eyes she had turned into something quite different.

"The zoo." Lorrie did not have to pretend interest now. "I've never been there."

"Me, I go 'bout every Sunday," Jimmy returned. "My uncle, he got me a chance to see the baby tiger last year. They keep the baby animals in a different place, see, and you have to look at them through a window. But if you know somebody there they'll let you. This year they got a black leopard cub and two lions. I haven't seen them yet, but I'm going to." Jimmy's teasing grin was gone, he was talking eagerly. "They're just like kittens."

Kittens! For a moment Lorrie had a fleeting memory of Jimmy hunting Sabina through the tangled grass. She gripped her box more firmly and made herself walk at an even pace. Jimmy fell into step with her.

"You ought to see the snakes," he continued. "They got one as long as this alley."

"Aw, it's not that big," protested Stan.

Jimmy turned on him. "You say I don't know what I'm talking about?"

Stan shrugged and was quiet. But Jimmy continued, "And the alligator, you ought to see him! I had a chance to have an alligator once. My uncle was in Florida and he was going to send me one, a baby one. Only Mom said we didn't have any place to keep it."

"Boy, you know what I'd like to have?" Rob broke in. "A horse, that's what. Gee, I'd like to have one just like they used to keep in that stable over there."

"Hey, you know what's still in there?" Stan pointed back to the tumble-down carriage house. "There's a sled, only it's for horses to pull. Neat, eh? Be fun to ride like that."

"It is," Lorrie agreed.

"How do you know?" Jimmy demanded.

"It used to snow a lot in Hampstead and there was a sleigh at school. We had sleigh rides sometimes."

"That true? A real sleigh with horses?" Jimmy sounded skeptical.

"Yes. It was old but they kept it fixed up and people used to rent it sometimes for parties. You'd ride out in it to the lake to go skating."

"Ice skating?" asked Rob. "You ice skate, Lorrie?"

" 'Most everyone did. I was learning figure skating." She thought that that was just one more thing she had lost.

"Hey"—Stan pushed up level with Jimmy and Lorrie—"there's the ice rink down by Fulsome. They let kids in Saturday mornings. Last year Mr. Stewart talked about it in gym, said we might like to learn. We saw a picture about the Olympic skaters in assembly. They sure were neat!"

"It's hard to learn the fancy things," Lorrie answered. "There was a girl at Miss Logan's, she was good. But she had been skating since she was five and she practiced all the time. I guess you have to, if you want to be good."

"We went to the Ice Follies last spring," Rob volunteered. "They had this guy, he was dressed up like a bear, see, and he chased another guy who was a hunter all around. Gee, it sure was funny!"

"Dad said he was going to get us tickets this year," Jimmy cut in.

They had reached the school crossing, and Lorrie looked to the clock over the main door.

"We're going to be late."

Jimmy followed her gaze. "Not if we zoom—"

"Yah, yah! I'm a Purple Hornet, zoom, zoom, zoom!" yelled Stan.

"Me, I'm riding the fastest horse on earth! Get going, Paint!" Rob took out after Stan.

"Gimme that. You're going to have to run, Canuck!" Jimmy grabbed at Lorrie's book bag.

They ran for the door as the clock boomed out and they heard the ring of the warning bell. And Lorrie was not sure how it happened that she entered the school with Jimmy Purvis carrying her book bag, somehow not minding at all that he had called her Canuck as he pounded along beside her.

The Thanksgiving weekend was exciting for Lorrie because Aunt Margaret had two whole days free. They went shopping for a new best dress for Lorrie, and had lunch in the big restaurant at the very top of Bamber's store, from which you could see all over the city. Aunt Margaret had gone out with her on the terrace to look down at the buildings and streets that made up Ashton.

"There will be some changes next year," Aunt Margaret said. "The new thruway will pass not far from us, you know. The world moves fast nowadays, Lorrie. See, down there—" She pointed to a narrow strip leading into the river. "That is all that is left of the old canal. And only a little more than a hundred years ago travel on that was as exciting as travel by jet plane is for us today. Why, Ashton was built because of the junction with the river."

"Where was Canal Town?" asked Lorrie suddenly.

Aunt Margaret looked surprised. "Canal Town? I never heard of that, Lorrie. Where did you hear it mentioned?"

"At Octagon House." Lorrie was alert to her mistake. She did not know why, but she was sure that her adventure with Phineas and Phebe was something to be kept to herself. Why, she had not even spoken of it when she had gone back to join Miss Ashemeade on the afternoon when it happened. Yet of one thing she was sure—Miss Ashemeade had somehow known all of what had happened to her.

"Yes, Octagon House," Aunt Margaret said slowly. "It is a pity."

"What is a pity?"

"They have not quite decided on the linkup with the thruway, but they believe it will cross the land on which Octagon House stands."

Lorrie held hard to the terrace railing.

"They—they couldn't take the house—pull it down—could they?" She stared out over the city, trying to see the house. But, of course, it was too far away.

"Let us hope not," answered Aunt Margaret. "Now it is cold here, isn't it? And I want to look at those blouses on sale, if we can get near enough to the counter. Most of Ashton appears to be doing their Christmas shopping this weekend."

Christmas—she wanted to get Grandmother's gift today. Aunt Margaret said it must be mailed this coming week. For a moment Lorrie forgot the threat against Octagon House.

"Lorrie," Aunt Margaret said that evening. "Do you suppose that Miss Ashemeade would care if I asked to see some of her needlework? You've talked so much about it that you've made me curious. Would you take a note over for me tomorrow?"

Lorrie was surprised at her own feelings. There was no reason in the world why Aunt Margaret would not want to see all the treasures in the red room. But—but it was as if her going there spoiled something—what? Lorrie could not say, and she knew, she told herself, she was being silly.

"All right." She hoped her voice did not sound grudging.

She wrapped Grandmother's scarf ready for mailing. Then she spread out all Aunt Margaret's gift paper and examined it piece by piece. There was one sheet she set aside. The background was green, not quite the green of Miss Ashemeade's dress, but close to it. And the pattern over that was a big golden-purple-green of peacock feathers. Lorrie was entranced by it. There was gold ribbon that was perfect against it. She slid the white handkerchief box onto it and turned the paper up and around with all the care she could. Then the ribbon was looped, as Aunt Margaret had shown her, in a special bow. Yes, it looked almost as pretty as she had hoped. And the handkerchief— she had been lucky to find it among all the rest—so many ladies had been picking and pulling them around. But this was white and it had a narrow border of lace with a big A in the corner. Lorrie had added a little wreath about that with her best stitches.

She went to put it away in the drawer that was kept for Christmas. There was one other thing among those already there. She had finished it last week and she hoped Aunt Margaret would like it, though now she wondered. In Octagon House when she had made it, it looked pretty and amusing. But in this room would a plump red-velvet heart pincushion with a white lace frill fit? Aunt Margaret liked old-fashioned things though. And Lorrie had a bottle of her favorite cologne, too.

Octagon House—and the thruway. Lorrie went back to the living room.

"When will they know?"

Aunt Margaret looked up from her book. "Know what, Chick?"

"Know about Octagon House?"

"There will be a meeting late in January, I believe. All the people whose property will be affected will have a chance to meet with the Commission."

Lorrie wondered if Miss Ashemeade knew. Could she go to the meeting? Twice only had Lorrie seen her walk. Both times she had moved very slowly, one hand on Hallie's shoulder, the other on a gold-headed cane. She never went out of the house, Lorrie knew. Once a week a boy came up from Theobald's grocery and got a list from Hallie. Lorrie herself had taken that list in when the boy had the flu. Hallie did not go out either. So what would happen if Miss Ashemeade could not go to that meeting and protest about Octagon House's being torn down?

"Miss Ashemeade's lame, she can't walk very much." Lorrie put her fear into words. "What if she can't go to the meeting?"

"She may send a lawyer, Lorrie. Most of the people will have lawyers to represent them."

Lorrie sighed. She hoped that was true. But tomorrow she would ask Miss Ashemeade, tell her about the need for a lawyer to go to the meeting.

Only, when she was settled by Miss Ashemeade the following afternoon, her workbox open beside her and Miss Ashemeade's regiment of needles all waiting to have their gaping eyes filled, Lorrie somehow found it hard to begin.

"You are unhappy." Miss Ashemeade adjusted the embroidery frame. It was dark outside, grayish, but she had candelabras, each bearing four candles, perched on high candle stands to either side. "Has Jimmy Purvis been a problem again?"

Lorrie drew the soft strand of cream wool through the needle and stuck it carefully on the side of the canvas.

"He still calls me Canuck, but I don't care any more.

"So?" Miss Ashemeade smiled. " 'Sticks and stones may break my bones, but names will never hurt me.' Is that it, Lorrie?"

"Not exactly." Lorrie added a needle with a burden of pearl-pink to the first. "Only I think he does not mean it the same way. He likes to talk a lot."

"And you do not find it hard to listen? When he's such a mean and hateful person?"

Lorrie carefully chose a strand of wool of rose color. "Maybe—maybe he isn't so mean and hateful any more. He's changed."

"Or you know him better and do not see only the outer covering. Things do change, Lorrie, and sometimes for the better. One time, many years ago, some people lived just a little way from here. The men had come to work on the canal. But they had come from another country so they spoke differently, they went to another kind of church than the one in the village. Because they felt so different they kept to themselves. And the village people did not welcome any of them who tried to be friends. Then there was often trouble —fighting.

"Some of these men later brought their families here because there was a famine in their own country and nothing left for them there. Others had wives from other parts of this land. But when they came here to live there was ill feeling. Because they did not know each other a wall grew higher and higher, until both the canal people and the village would believe any sort of evil of the other."

303

Lorrie put another cream-threaded needle into the side of the frame. "You're talking about Phebe and Phineas, aren't you, Miss Ashemeade?"

"Phebe and Phineas, and many others like them. Though they did not know it, the night they came here Phebe and Phieas made the first small break in that wall. They trusted someone on the other side. But it meant changes on both sides. People had to learn not to look for what they feared to see."

Lorrie unwound a strand of coral wool, measured the proper length, and cut it with small scissors fashioned in stork shape, the long bill being the sharp blades.

"You mean—I was afraid of Jimmy so I saw him that way. But why did he—"

"Begin to call you Canuck and chase you? Well, perhaps Jimmy thought it a joke at first and if you had laughed, that would have been the end of it. Then, as some people are very like to do, he found he enjoyed chasing you because you ran, or showed that you disliked and feared him. When you began to treat him as if you were not afraid, he stopped hunting you. You may not want Jimmy for a close friend, that is true. But I do not believe you dislike him so much."

"No, I don't." Lorrie chose a reel of golden tan. "Miss Ashemeade, what happened to Phineas and Phebe afterward?"

There was such a long moment of silence that Lorrie looked up in surprise, the needle in one hand, the end of the wool in the other. Miss Ashemeade was no longer smiling. Instead she was looking at something she had taken out of the sewing table, turning it around between her fingers. It was the box that held the golden needles.

"They made a choice, Lorrie, and thereafter they lived by it. Some can be so hurt by the world that they choose to turn their backs upon it. My, look at the snow!"

Lorrie turned to the window. Flakes were whirling down, to be seen in the crack between the lace edges of the curtains. There was a soft mew and Sabina leaped to the sill, to stand on her hind legs, patting the panes furiously, trying to get at those fluttering crystals.

"No more needles, Lorrie," Miss Ashemeade said. "I think there is other work to be done this afternoon. Sabina is very good at reminding one."

Lorrie helped her set away the frame and then watched curiously as Miss Ashemeade got to her feet with difficulty. She moved forward impulsively and Miss Ashemeade accepted her help, putting her hand on Lorrie's shoulder as she had on Hallie's arm.

They began a slow progress to the big table on which lay the materials, the various pieces of half-finished mending work Miss Ashemeade kept at hand. She did not pause by the lace, or by the moth-holed tapestry, or by the beautiful coat of silk that had the wonderful birds embroidered on it (and that Miss Ashemeade said had been made a very long time ago in China for an emperor to wear). Instead they came to the far end of the table where there were no pieces waiting for repair, but rather rolls of cloth and ribbon, each neatly packaged and tied with leftover twists of wool. Miss Ashemeade stood there for what seemed to Lorrie a very long moment. And then she said:

"That red-velvet ribbon, Lorrie, there next to the blue. That is what I need."

The velvet was very thick, but silky feeling. And the color was that of the garnets Miss Ashemeade wore. Once it was in Lorrie's hand, the old lady made a slow progress back to her chair. And when she was again seated she kept the roll of ribbon on her lap while she examined intently all the spools and reels housed in the compartments of the table top. Finally she lifted out a spindle of black wood. Wound about it was a glistening thread, as brightly silver, Lorrie thought, as the trimming of a Christmas tree she had seen in Bamber's.

Then Miss Ashemeade took up a little box from another compartment and when she moved it, there was a faint tinkling sound.

"Merrow!" Sabina jumped from the window sill, came in two leaps to Miss Ashemeade's side, and now stood on her hind legs, her eyes fixed upon the box that rang so.

Miss Ashemeade lifted the lid.

"Bells!" Lorrie had been as curious as Sabina.

"Bells," agreed Miss Ashemeade. She took out one about as big as the nail on her little finger and shook it gently. The tinkle was faint, but pretty. There were bells even smaller, but none larger. "Do you approve, Sabina?" Miss Ashemeade held the velvet ribbon in one hand, the bell box in the other, for the kitten to see and sniff.

It seemed to Lorrie that Sabina studied them carefully, as if they had a meaning for her.

"Merrow!" Sabina rubbed her head against Miss Ashemeade's hand, and then was back at the window again with a whisk of her tail.

Miss Ashemeade picked up the box that held the golden needles. As she opened it she spoke to Lorrie.

"My dear, will you play the music box for us?"

The music box had its own table. It was of polished, dark red wood, and its lid was bordered with small white blocks of ivory. You pressed a small lever after you raised the lid, and the music came. Like the bells it was a soft, tinkling music, but Lorrie loved it. She started it now and the tune filled the room.

"Quite right and proper—the 'Magic Flute,'" said Miss Ashemeade. "This is an afternoon for magic, Lorrie. Some days are, some days are not."

"Because it is snowing? I never thought of snow being magic."

"Much of the magic of this world does not seem to exist just because we are too blind, or too busy to look for it, Lorrie. Blindness and unbelief, those are the two foes of magic. To see and to believe—those who do have many gates to enter, if they choose."

She measured out the velvet ribbon, doubling it into two thicknesses when she had the length she wished. Then she cut off a piece of the silver thread.

"Do you want me to thread it?" offered Lorrie.

Miss Ashemeade shook her head. "Not this thread, not this needle, Lorrie. This can only be my doing at this time."

It was one of the golden needles she used. The thread went in smoothly and she began to stitch the ribbon double. Lorrie, so used to seeing her at the exacting work on tapestry or lace, had never watched Miss Ashemeade sew so swiftly. It was not a straight hemming stitch either, for the needle worked a pattern along the edge. Also, Lorrie thought, the gold needle was brighter in the candlelight than the silver ones, flashing in and out, so sometimes it appeared as if Miss Ashemeade was not using a needle at all, but a splinter of light.

Lorrie brought out her own sewing. This was for Christmas and she had been happy with it. But now that she looked at the simple design of white flowers across the red apron, she was not satisfied. The flowers seemed coarse and big, and she was not certain the pattern was even straight.

In the room the music box played and Miss Ashemeade's needle flashed in and out. Sabina gave up trying to reach the snowflakes and came back to sprawl out on the hearthrug. All at once, Lorrie, in spite of her misgivings about the apron, was happy. She was safe—safe—safe— There was warmth here, and happiness, and all the good one could wish for. Outside lay cold and dark, but here was warmth and light—

It was moments before she realized that the music box had stopped. But there was still a murmur of sound and it was Miss Ashemeade singing. Lorrie could hear what she thought were words, but she could not understand them. The song went on and on and the needle flew. Now every once in a while Miss Ashemeade chose a bell from the box, using only the smaller ones, and fastened it to the velvet strip to fringe it, and their tinkling was a part of the song Lorrie could not understand.

Lorrie's own stitches seemed to come faster and easier too, and her thread did not tangle. And somehow she found she was putting in her needle and drawing it out in time to certain repeated notes of the song. When she did it that way, her needle flashed almost as quickly as Miss Ashemeade's. She was humming and, though she did not know the words, she could follow the tune.

"Ahh—"

Lorrie started, pricking her finger on her needle.

Miss Ashemeade held up the belled strip of velvet so Lorrie saw it plainly for the first time.

"A collar?" she asked.

"Just so, my dear, a collar. Sabina must have a Christmas gift also."

"But will she want to wear it—some cats—" Lorrie knew that much about cats.

"Some cats are not Sabina, she is a very special cat. As for collars, this one she will want to wear, when the time comes. And—it is four o'clock. Hallie has some gingerbread and Chinese tea. I think we would be refreshed by both."

The golden needle was gone, the case that held it back in its compartment. Miss Ashemeade rang her little bell. Then she smiled at Lorrie.

"It seems you have spent the afternoon profitably also, Lorrie. Only a stitch or two more and your apron is complete."

Lorrie was surprised when she looked at her work. She *had* done most of it! And it had seemed so easy too, once she had begun. She folded it carefully into the lower section of the workbox.

"Miss Ashemeade," she said slowly, "do you know a lawyer?"

"In my lifetime, Lorrie, I have known several. Why? Are you now at odds with the law?" Miss Ashemeade smiled as she closed her worktable.

"Because—Aunt Margaret said that there was going to be trouble about the thruway—that—that they might want to run it right here!"

Miss Ashemeade no longer smiled. Her hands rested quietly on the top of the table.

"There has been such talk."

"But Aunt Margaret said they are going to have another meeting to talk about it, and that the people who couldn't go to the meeting could have a lawyer speak for them."

"I believe that is so. And you are worried about me, Lorrie? Yes, I see that you are. Well, we shall see what we shall see. I am not defenseless, Lorrie, not entirely defenseless."

Now she was smiling again. "And, Lorrie, if you wish, please come to tea tomorrow. And"—she motioned to the tall desk standing in a darker corner of the room—"if you will bring me paper, pen, and ink, my dear, I shall write a note to your Aunt Margaret. I should very much like her to come also."

Lorrie went to get Miss Ashemeade what she wanted, but she hoped as she went that Miss Ashemeade was right, that she had a defense against the thruway. Because—because—Lorrie could not bear that thought. Not this house—this room—to be pulled all to pieces.

OCTAGON HOUSE KEEPS CHRISTMAS

THERE had been more snow during the night, and in the morning too, while they were in church. But in the afternoon, while Aunt Margaret and Lorrie had tea in Miss Ashemeade's warm red room, the sun came out and made thousands of sparkles across the drifts. Sabina sat before the fire and purred to herself, a song, Lorrie thought, not unlike the one Miss Ashemeade had sung when she worked on the collar.

She dropped down beside the kitten and stared into the flames, another world all red and yellow trees and— Sabina purred while the fire crackled gently to itself.

Aunt Margaret and Miss Ashemeade were examining the framed embroidery pictures and panels on the wall. That is, Aunt Margaret moved about, looking at them, asking questions that Miss Ashemeade answered from her chair. There were lots of candles, all lighted, as well as the sun at the windows, so one could see. Lorrie heard the excited note in Aunt Margaret's voice after she had made the circuit of the room and came back to sit down again by the window.

"—museum pieces!"

"Perhaps in this day and age. Much has been forgotten. But they were made for pleasure and with pride of talent. They were fashioned because the urge to do so was great."

"Carolinian stump work! And those needlework engravings—the samplers! One reads of such things, but they are seldom to be seen. And the tapestries"—Aunt Margaret kept turning her head from side to side—"such needlepoint! It is fabulous. I have never seen such a complete collection—it must date back three hundred years—and such perfect condition!"

"Oh, thread and fabric wear through the dust of years. But there are precautions one may take, of course. I have reason to care for them since they give me pleasure and I do not go abroad nowadays. But all things pass with the years themselves. Perhaps the time will come when none shall care. And if there is no one to do so, then it is better such work vanish. But this is no day, with the sun bright and the snow all diamonds, to think of that, is it?"

She rang her bell and nodded at Lorrie. "My dear, I think that perhaps you may help Hallie. Dear Hallie, her baking tins and mixing bowls are to her what my needles and threads are to me, and she so seldom has a chance to show her skill nowadays. I think she has, perhaps, as the saying goes, outdone herself today. Company for Sunday tea is a pleasure we have not had for a long time."

Lorrie went to the kitchen. She had peeped within it several times as she went through the hall on her other visits. But somehow she felt shy about entering without Hallie's invitation. Just as she never entered the red room without knocking and waiting for Miss Ashemeade to call, "Come." Now she stared about her with frank curiosity. Why, it was almost exactly the same as that kitchen where she had hidden to watch Phineas steal the bread and the gingerbread. Only this time there were no preparations of pie making on the table.

Instead there was a shining silver tray and on it a silver sugar bowl, a cream pitcher, and another rounded container in which teaspoons with flower-patterned handles stood upright. Hallie was at the big range, filling the silver teapot with water from a steaming kettle. She smiled at Lorrie sniffing the spicy odors that all at once made her sure she was hungry.

"Come to help, Mis' Lorrie? That's fine. Hallie hasn't got her four arms, or five hands, or a little fairy wand to push an' pull an' fly things 'round for her. You take that cloth now an' put it on the tea table. They's napkins with it, don't drop them, child. Then, if you'll come back, we'll git along with the rest."

Lorrie could hardly believe this was meant to be a tablecloth, it was such fine material and bordered with lace. But she followed Hallie's instructions and then trotted again across the triangle of hallway with the napkin-covered plates Hallie gave her.

"Hallie," Aunt Margaret observed, when those napkins were gathered up to show such numbers of small cakes, sandwiches, things Lorrie did not even know how to name, "you are an artist! These look far too good to eat."

Hallie laughed. "Now, Mis' Gerson, that's what they's made for, an' it gives me a pleasurin' to have a chance to keep my hand in a-makin' 'em all. Mis' Charlotta, she don't eat no more'n a bird."

"I don't believe you have ever watched a bird, Hallie," laughed Miss Ashemeade, "if you say that. They eat *all* the time when they can find sustenance. As one grows old the sharpness of one's senses is curtailed. Taste and smell are not what they once were, and then half the pleasure of food has fled. So Hallie is enjoying herself today, having a chance to cater to more appreciative and larger appetites than mine."

Sabina mewed loudly, pressing her small body against Miss Ashemeade's wide folds of skirt. Though Miss Ashemeade's dress was made the same as the green one, today it was gray, with a wide collar of cobwebby lace lying on her shoulders. The ends of the lace hung to her waist. On her wrists were wide bracelets of black enamel with small pearl flowers set in wreaths on them. A big pin of the same workmanship, with a whole bouquet of seed pearls on it, fastened the collar.

Now one of the bracelets turned round and round as if it were made for a much plumper wrist, as Miss Ashemeade gently pulled her skirt from the claws Sabina was daring to lay in its folds.

"Not so, Sabina. You have tea, to be sure, but in the proper place. We have nothing here to interest small cats."

"Come on, Sabina." Hallie moved toward the door. "You's not forgotten."

Sabina scurried past Hallie, heading for the kitchen, and Miss Ashemeade laughed again. "Now there goes one who is certainly *not* unmindful of the pleasures of the table."

Later, when they were walking home in the early winter dusk, Aunt Margaret spoke suddenly:

"I felt as if I had been caught in a fairy tale when I was in that house. It has an enchantment, Lorrie. Time seems to stand still there—" Her voice trailed off as if she were thinking.

"They mustn't tear it down!" Lorrie voiced the fear that had been with her at intervals since Aunt Margaret had first mentioned the thruway.

"We feel that, Lorrie. But in the name of progress more than one crime is committed nowadays. I wonder just who will rejoice when the last blade of grass is buried by concrete, when the last tree is brought down by a bulldozer, when the last wild thing is shot, or poisoned, or trapped. Lorrie—" again Aunt Margaret hesitated "—don't set your heart on saving Octagon House."

"But—but where would Miss Ashemeade and Hallie and Sabina go?"

Aunt Margaret shook her head and did not answer. After a moment Lorrie said angrily:

"I don't believe it! And I'm not going to think it will happen!"

"Please, Lorrie." Aunt Margaret looked at her anxiously. "Hope for what you wish, yes, but you must learn to accept disappointment. Learn all you can from Octagon House, because it has a great deal to offer one who has eyes to see. But it belongs to another day, when time itself moved slower. We believe we have mastered time in some ways, but when one opens one's hand to grasp a new thing, one has to let go of an old. Do you understand what I mean, Lorrie?"

"I think so. But I don't believe it is good to put that street through here!"

"Maybe we don't believe so, Lorrie, but you wouldn't find many to agree with us. Anyway, there is still the meeting and a chance the plan will not go through. In the meantime, Miss Ashemeade has invited us to spend the afternoon of Christmas Day with her."

"Really and truly?" Lorrie grabbed at Aunt Margaret's hand and squeezed it as tight as the mitten and glove covering their hands would allow. "Are we going?"

"Yes. She is being very kind, for she said I might bring the camera and take pictures of some of those wonderful needlework pieces. They can't ever be copied, such work is not possible today. But some of the patterns might be adapted. Though"—Aunt Margaret sighed—"for anyone who has seen the originals, copies will be sorry substitutes."

The days until Christmas might have dragged, except there was so much to do. Lorrie was one of the Holly Chorus at school for the Christmas Assembly and went about singing "Deck the halls with boughs of holly" until Aunt Margaret said that she had no objection to carols but they did seem to ooze out of the walls at this time of year and were hard to think by.

Then she produced tickets for a special Walt Disney movie downtown. And Lorrie asked Kathy and Rob Lockner, and Lizabeth Ross, who was beside her in the Holly chorus, to go. They had lunch at Bamber's and after the movie a sundae at Walker's, with a trip through the Freeman toy shop at the end of the day.

"Gee, Lorrie, Miss Gerson, that was swell," Rob commented as they came upstairs.

"I loved it when the fairy turned them all into animals," Kathy said. "Thank you, Miss Gerson."

Lorrie agreed it had all been super. But back in the apartment she sat down in the first chair to take off her boots, and her face was sober.

"Too much show, or ice cream, or walking?" asked Aunt Margaret. "I will admit that pushing through crowds is rather trying."

Lorrie looked up. "You know," she spoke half accusingly. "Why—why wouldn't Kathy sit next to Lizabeth? She pushed me in ahead when I was being polite to let her in first. I think Lizabeth knew it too. She didn't talk much after that. It isn't fair! Lizabeth's nice, she's smart, and she's pretty. Kathy was mean."

"I don't think Kathy was being mean exactly," Aunt Margaret answered. "Kathy doesn't see things the way you do, Lorrie. For a long, long time there have been separations between people. That this is not right, we know now more and more. But when people stand apart and do not try to make friends, walls go up between them, and they believe all kinds of untrue things about the person on the other side of the wall The less they know about a stranger, the more ready they are to believe that he is bad in one way or another.

"I don't believe that Kathy ever in her life before spent an afternoon with Lizabeth or any little girl of another race or color. So she was feeling strange and did not know what to do, while Lizabeth drew back and did not try any more to be friendly after Kathy had snubbed her. Both of them had a chance to break down that wall a little, but neither made the attempt."

"But you tried to have them do it, didn't you, Aunt

Margaret?" Lorrie set aside her boots. "That's why you had them look at the stuffed animals together."

"Yes. And I think that next time Kathy will wonder if Lizabeth isn't like her after all. They both liked the big fox and the baby owls. When they forgot themselves, they talked about those, remember?"

"Then you don't think that—that Lizabeth will be mad at me?"

"Not in the least. And now, I am just a tired old aunt. Do you think you can get me a bite of supper all by yourself as a good, kind, obedient niece should?"

"One supper coming right up!" Lorrie jumped to her feet. It was about Phineas and Phebe she thought as she looked into the freezer for inspiration. They had not had friends either. Miss Ashemeade had said they had stayed on at Octagon House. Odd—Lorrie paused between stove and table. She had never spoken to Aunt Margaret about the doll house. Yet that was a bigger treasure than all the pieces of embroidery.

No—the doll house was something else. When had it been made? There was no miniature of it inside the smaller house. That room had only the chair, the painting on the floor, the shelves with their bottles and books, some dried plants hanging in bundles along the walls, and also that secret place where Lotta had hidden Phineas and Phebe.

Lotta lived in the house. But who else did? Lotta was only a little girl, not much older than Lorrie. Did she have a father and mother? Brothers and sisters? Who had baked the bread and the gingerbread Phineas stole? Was the doll house itself made for the Lotta of long ago?

There were so many questions. But maybe Lorrie could find the answers to a few of them. Only—again Lorrie stopped to think—she did not want to see the doll house often. Lorrie wondered about that a little. The first time—then she had been exploring as Miss

Ashemeade suggested. And when she had had the second adventure, Miss Ashemeade had sent her to find Sabina. She was sure that Miss Ashemeade knew both times about her visits back to that other time. Then, did Miss Ashemeade intend her to have those adventures. Why? And would she have any more?

Lorrie put down the butter dish she was carrying. She was not quite sure she wanted any more rides.

The school Christmas program was over and vacation began. Christmas was on Saturday, but Aunt Margaret had to work until the Wednesday before. The Lockners were going away on Tuesday and Lorrie persuaded Mrs. Lockner that she had Christmas presents to finish and wanted to work on them at home. But she dutifully went there to lunch on Monday and helped Kathy wash dishes afterward.

The next morning the boy from the grocery brought a note from Octagon House. Miss Ashemeade wondered if Lorrie would like to help with Christmas decorations. Aunt Margaret agreed, and by ten Lorrie was tramping along the snow-covered brick walk around to the back door.

She shed her boots, ski pants, and jacket in the hall. Hallie came to the door of the kitchen with two big bowls in her hands. One was mounded with cranberries, the other had fluffy popcorn heaped high in it.

"You're jus' in good time, child, to save old Hallie a couple of steps an' a minute or two. You take this in."

The cranberries were raw, even if the corn was popped. Did Miss Ashemeade mean they were to eat them so? But without asking questions Lorrie took the bowls into the red room.

There had been changes there. The sewing table was moved back against the wall, the embroidery frame pushed beside it. Another small table stood beside Miss Ashemeade's chair, holding only her needle box, a pair of scissors, and a very large spool of coarse white thread. On the stool where Lorrie usually sat

stood a box, its lid thrown back, and out of that Miss
Ashemeade was taking small bundles of old, much
creased tissue paper and cotton.

"You are in good time, my dear. Now, do you
suppose you can move up that other table? Put the
bowls over here, then just set this box on the floor.
There, we are quite in order now. What do you think
of the tree?"

It stood there, bare and green and fragrant, between the two windows. And it must have been placed
on a box now wrapped with green cloth, for it was not
a full-sized one. As if reading Lorrie's thought, Miss
Ashemeade shook her head.

"We used to have a proper tree, tall enough to top
all heads. But I did not believe we could manage to
trim such a one now. We shall have work enough to
dress one this size."

She was pulling away the paper and cotton wrappings from things she took from the box, setting each
with a gentle touch, as she freed it, on the table Lorrie
had moved close to her. There was a row of tiny
baskets, some with lids. Next came walnut shells,
gilded and fastened half open so that one could peep
inside. Lorrie did, to discover that they cradled tiny,
brightly colored pictures of flowers, animals, boys and
girls. Then there were flat ornaments of cardboard,
velvet-covered and edged with gold-and-silver paper
lace, in the center of each a larger picture.

Miss Ashemeade held some a little longer than others, as if they brought her memories. One of these was
a cage of fine golden wire, within it a bird fashioned of
tiny shells. And there were more baskets, made of
cloves strung on wire with a glass bead inset on every
wire crossing.

"Oh, I had forgotten, almost I had forgotten." Miss
Ashemeade held a small round box on her hand. "Look
at this, Lorrie. When I was younger this was a dear
treasure."

In the box was a set of four bowls, bowls so tiny Lorrie did not see how anyone could ever make them. But the greatest wonder was that in each of those minute bowls rested a silver spoon!

"So little!" marveled Lorrie.

"They are carved from cherry stones, my dear." Miss Ashemeade carefully set aside the box. "See, here are some similar carvings." She uncoiled a piece of thin cord. Fastened to it at intervals were baskets, only one or two as big as Lorrie's finger nail. "These, and these, are from cherry stones. And that—that is a hazel nut, and that an acorn. This is sturdy enough to hang on the tree. But the bowls—they are too easily lost."

"I never saw such things."

"No," Miss Ashemeade agreed, "perhaps you have not. You see, once people made all their own decorations. We did not have the fine glass pieces that were for sale. So we used our imagination and made our own pretty things."

"I like these better than the store things." Lorrie did not touch the peep-show walnut shells, the cord of nut baskets, or any of the treasures Miss Ashemeade had set out. She wanted to, but she did not quite dare.

"So do I, my dear. But then I have known them for a long, long time and old things grow into one's heart and memory until one cannot lose them, even when one can no longer do this." She picked up one of the walnuts and smiled down at it. Within a dove fluttered white wings above blue and pink flowers.

"Now." She put aside the walnut and picked up a needle case from the other table. "We shall need some long thread, Lorrie, as long as might go around the tree at least once."

Lorrie cut the thread and put it through the needle eyes. Miss Ashemeade took a cranberry and speared it neatly, drawing the thread through it. Three more cranberries went on and then a grain or two of popcorn before more berries.

"That is the way to do it," she said.

Eagerly Lorrie set to work with another needle. As they made the chains Miss Ashemeade told stories. They were Christmas stories and now and then she touched some ornament on the table as she spoke.

So many Christmases, all in this house. And every one Miss Ashemeade spoke about as if she remembered it for herself. But to Lorrie that did not seem strange, though surely Miss Ashemeade could not be as old as that!

But though she talked of the house and the things in it, of how this or that was made or used, she never spoke of the people in the house. She only said "we did" this or that.

They had quite a pile of chains finished and all the cranberries were gone from the bowl when Hallie came in with a big tray that she set on one end of the long table.

"Here they all is, Mis' Charlotta. An' they turned out jus' fine."

"I see they did, Hallie. The red eyes for the mice were an inspiration! What do you think of Hallie's contribution to the tree, Lorrie?"

"This ain't all—" Hallie was already on her way back to the kitchen. "I has the candies for the baskets, an' the gingerbread—"

But Lorrie hardly heard her. She was too amazed by the tray on the table. Mice, three rows of white mice, all with red eyes, small pink cardboard ears, and string tails! And behind them another three rows of pink pigs!

"Sugar mice and pigs." Miss Ashemeade laughed. "They are good to eat, too, Lorrie. Hallie has always been a master hand at mice and pigs for the tree. We shall make some ribbon collars for them to hang by. That very narrow red-and-green ribbon over there ought to do. And I think, I really think, Lorrie, you might test Hallie's proficiency by tasting one of each."

Lorrie selected a very plump pink pig and nibbled up its hind legs. It was sugary and good, so good the rest of the pig vanished very fast indeed. But she set the mouse aside to look at, determining to take him home to show Aunt Margaret.

While Miss Ashemeade measured and cut lengths of ribbon, Hallie brought in a second tray. There were gingerbread men wearing coats of white frosting, trousers of red, with currant eyes and squiggles of chocolate frosting for hair. And gingerbread ladies in their company with skirts striped red-and-white and blouses of white with red buttons. There were horses with frosting manes and tails, and half a dozen cats with frosting whiskers and eyes of bits of candied green cherry.

"Well, Hallie, these are the best yet!" Miss Ashemeade put aside the ribbon and leaned forward in her chair.

"I thought as how it should be, Mis' Charlotta—considerin'," Lorrie heard Hallie answer.

"Quite right, Hallie, quite right. I do not think we shall try to hang these, Lorrie. But we can set them about in the branches."

"I'll get the candies now, for the little baskets—" Hallie was gone again.

Lorrie continued to study the gingerbread people. "I never saw anything like them. They're precious!"

"Very dashing, those gentlemen," Miss Ashemeade commented. "Quite the beaux. But the ladies, they look flighty to me. However, elegant, very elegant. They all have quite an air of high fashion, I would say."

"Here's the candies." Hallie came back with a third tray, even larger than the first two. And Lorrie quickly moved a pile of folded material to make a place for it on the table.

Just as the mice, pigs, and gingerbread company, here, too, works of art were set out. Tiny sugar flowers, miniature chocolate drops, a wealth of little things, too many for Lorrie to see all at once.

Miss Ashemeade pulled toward her some of the small baskets.

"They go into these, Lorrie. Let me see now, it was always the peppermint drops in the green baskets, and the chocolates in the white and the sugar flowers in the red—"

"An' the candied peel in the clove ones," Hallie added. "But maybe better have lunch now, Mis' Charlotta, before packin' all those."

By twilight the tree was trimmed and Lorrie sat on her stool, pleasantly tired from stretching, bending, walking around and around it to set some basket, ornament gingerbread piece, or cranberry string in just the proper place.

It did not look very much like the trees one could see in other windows up and down Ash Street. There were no lights, no sparkling ornaments, no trickling tinsel strips. But to Lorrie it was the most wonderful tree anyone could ever imagine. She said so.

"I think so, too, my dear. But it is out of another time and perhaps it has no place in the world outside these walls." Miss Ashemeade's hands lay quietly in her lap as she also looked at the tree. Sabina sat at the edge of her mistress' skirts, staring round-eyed at the strings of cranberry-popcorn, at some spinning ornaments that turned now and then, hanging beyond the reach of her claws.

Lorrie heard the chime of the mantle clock. Reluctantly she stood up. Then she looked from the tree to Miss Ashemeade.

"Thank you, oh, thank you!"

It was not only for the fun of trimming the tree, but also for this whole, long, beautiful day. Lorrie was not quite sure of her feelings, but she knew that she would remember all of this, and that memory would be something to treasure.

"Thank *you,* Lorrie. Yes—" again she seemed to read Lorrie's confused thoughts "—some memories are very good. They are a fire to warm one's heart. Do not forget, Lorrie, Christmas is coming."

"Christmas is coming," echoed Lorrie. Why had Miss Ashemeade said that? Of course, Christmas was now only three days away, everyone knew that. But the way Miss Ashemeade said it, it sounded as if she were making a promise.

Lorrie said good night and struggled into her ski pants, jacket, and boots in the hall. Hallie had the mouse in a little bag and she let Lorrie out into the bare garden where the unhappy dragon pointed its snout at a dark sky.

As Lorrie came opposite the windows of the room, she stopped for a last glimpse at the tree. Several branches were in her range of vision. A gingerbread lady leaned on one of them, her rounded arm looped in a cranberry strand to anchor her firmly on that perch, though she must view with alarm the close-by swing of a white sugar mouse.

Lorrie chuckled. The gingerbread lady had a surprised look on her flat face. Hallie had given her very arched eyebrows of frosting above her eye currants. Perhaps she was just about to swing away from the menacing mouse, using the chain for transportation. What would Miss Ashemeade or Hallie think if the lady gave a screech and flew out into the room?

A cold wind reached Lorrie. She trotted on along the brick walk. In the front yard the deer had a ridge of snow on his back, some touches of it in the curves of his antlers. But that did not seem to bother him. He seemed as proud and important as he always was. Lorrie waved her hand to him and closed the gate carefully behind her. The Christmas tree lights were bright along the street. If she hurried she could arrange a surprise for Aunt Margaret, a live-looking sugar mouse under her supper napkin! Lorrie began to run.

CHOLE AND NACKIE

"**O**F COURSE, properly trimmed, there would be candles," Miss Ashemeade's voice made a calm whisper in the room. "But such candles would be difficult to find, and even more difficult to guard against fire. We used to keep a bucket of water standing on hand, just in case."

The firelight was warm, the many candles in holders about the red room were warm too, friendly with their light. Miss Ashemeade's table and frame were still against the wall, well out of the way. Now the room seemed centered about her and the tree.

Again she had changed her usual green dress for another. This was of garnet velvet. The wide skirt hung in soft folds over her knees, about the chair, to drape a little onto the floor. The lace collar was about her shoulders again, with cuffs to match at her wrists. She had no lace cap perched on her braids, but a high comb set in garnets winked there. And more of those red stones sparkled on her fingers and in the brooch pinning her collar. Nor was she wearing her black apron today. She looked, Lorrie thought, exactly as a fairy godmother should.

"But it is just perfect as it is!" Aunt Margaret sat on a footstool, aiming her camera at the tree. "I only hope that these pictures *do* turn out well. Those gingerbread figures and the ornaments— If I can *only* get a good shot!"

Lorrie nibbled at a piece of Hallie's candied peel, and blinked rather sleepily. She watched Sabina, a small black shadow, slip under the tree to where some parcels were laid, and reach a black paw for one.

"No!" Aunt Margaret cried and tried to wave the kitten away.

Sabina stared unblinking at Aunt Margaret for a moment, and then turned back to her own concerns. She took the package delicately between her teeth, brought it back to the hearthrug where she began to remove its wrappings in long strips of shredded tissue paper. Miss Ashemeade laughed.

"That one knows her own mind. Well, perhaps she is right, it is time for the gifts. You know, one used to give presents on New Year's Day. Christmas was for churchgoing and family gatherings. On New Year's one's friends came visiting and then presents were exchanged. And, my, how cold some of those visitors might get on the way! It was usually the gentlemen who came, ladies stayed home to do the receiving. Afterward young ladies counted their cards, to see who had the most and the prettiest—all pictures and silk fringe—"

Miss Ashemeade was looking at the tree, but Lorrie thought she was really seeing things she remembered.

"What kinds of presents were there?" Lorrie asked after a pause.

"Presents? Oh, when one was very young a jumping rope with wooden handles, or a porcelain slate. Dolls, to be sure, and a bangle bracelet. Once, Lorrie, that workbox you use now, all correctly fitted with scissors, silver thimble, stiletto, needlecase, penknife, thread— Once the music box. And always candy, maple cakes, animals of barley sugar, gingerbread people—

"Then, when one grew older, there were other things." But Miss Ashemeade did not list those. Instead she reached out with her cane and neatly snared one of the packages under the tree by placing its tip through a ribbon bow. Balancing it with ease, she held it out to Aunt Margaret.

"See what tricks infirmity can teach one? I am proud of such sleight of hand." She slid the package off her cane to land on Aunt Margaret's knees.

"Now, let us see if I can continue to do as well." She fished to catch a second bow, and with the same success transferred to Lorrie's hold another package.

Miss Ashemeade's gifts for them were wrapped in white tissue and tied with bright red ribbons. Lorrie laid hers carefully on the floor and went to take those she and her aunt had brought with them from under the tree. Two she handed to Miss Ashemeade, the other two she carried to Hallie sitting in one of the chairs beside the fireplace.

"Ah." Miss Ashemeade held up the one wrapped in the peacock-feather paper. "These new gift papers are works of art, are they not? Peacock feathers—those recall memories, do they not, Hallie?"

"Nackie's mats, Mis' Charlotta. It's easy rememberin' those. They was the sun 'n' moon 'n' stars to Nackie, an' maybe he was right."

Sabina growled. She had brought a catnip mouse out of what she plainly considered entirely unnecessary wrappings and was tossing it high in the air, to be pounced upon and shaken vigorously.

"Sabina! Sabina, remember in this room you are a lady!" But the kitten paid no attention to Miss Ashemeade's warning.

"Alas, who among humans has ever impressed his will upon a cat." Miss Ashemeade laughed again. "We must just ignore her bad manners."

Moments later Lorrie stared down at the contents of the package Miss Ashemeade had handed her. Miranda? No! Miranda's body, yes, with Miranda's dress upon it. But not Miranda's head. For Miranda, for all her age and her dearness to generations of small girls, had been just a doll, with staring blue eyes, rigid ripples of painted hair, a rather expressionless face.

Lorrie touched the cheek of this new Miranda. It

was as smooth to feel as Miranda's china had been, but it was far more like her own skin in color. And the hair on the small head, braided and looped somewhat in the same style as Miranda's modeled and painted locks had been, was, or felt like, real hair. The expression was real. Now she looked like one of the doll-house people—a little like Phebe—as if she might suddenly come alive, shake free of Lorrie's hold, to move and speak for herself. Lorrie drew a long and rather shaky breath, then she looked to Miss Ashemeade.

"No, not Miranda." Miss Ashemeade said. "Miranda has had her life and she was very old and tired. I think she deserves her rest, do you not? This is someone else. I will let you decide just who—you will know, when the proper time comes."

"Why—" Aunt Margaret stared at the frame she had unwrapped. "You can't mean to give this—it is too much of a treasure!"

"Treasures are born of cherishing," Miss Ashemeade spoke almost briskly, as if she wanted no thanks, did not even consider it polite for Aunt Margaret to offer them.

Aunt Margaret met her eyes for a long moment. "This shall continue to be cherished."

Miss Ashemeade smiled. "Did you believe I needed such assurance? Ah." She slipped off Lorrie's carefully tied ribbons, unfolded the peacock paper with small deliberate movements of her fingers. Then she lifted the handkerchief. The lace and the big A—they had been on in the shop. But the wreath about that A—did any crooked stitches show? Lorrie frowned anxiously. "Thank you, Lorrie." Miss Ashemeade tucked the handkerchief in her belt, frilled up its edges, and Lorrie was content.

Hallie admired her potholder, with its marching line of little figures, each carrying a bowl, or a knife, or a

fork, a spoon, a kettle. She drew her finger along
under them.

"My, this heah's a whole army of cooks. Can't never
say now I need me some help in the kitchen!"

It had been dark and dreary when they had come to
Octagon House, but now the sun flashed through the
pointed spears of icicles hanging over the windows.
Aunt Margaret caught up her camera and turned it
upon Miss Ashemeade.

"May I?" she asked.

There was again a smile on Miss Ashemeade's face.
"If you wish to."

Sabina startled Lorrie by rubbing against her. Having so attracted the girl's attention, she made for the
door to the hall and pawed at it, looking back at
Lorrie, her wishes made very clear. Lorrie went to
open it and Sabina flashed across the hall, to paw at
the kitchen portal in turn. Once more Lorrie obeyed
her urging.

But the kitchen did not content the kitten either.
She was through that in a flash, and the door she now
wanted to open was the one Lorrie had found locked
during her back-in-time visit.

She followed Sabina on into a short hall from which
spiraled the stairway hugging the big central chimney
of the house. But Sabina called with a note of irrita-
tion in her "merrow" at another door.

Now they were in the green bedroom and Lorrie
realized she had made the other half circuit of the
house. The door of the doll-house room was Sabina's
goal and Lorrie hurried to that.

There was no fireplace in the doll-house room, yet it
did not seem cold in there, in spite of a huge icicle and
several small ones half barring the one window. It was
light, also, though there were no candles or lamps
here and the sun shone on the other side of the house.

Lorrie looked about her. The other times she had
been here the horse and the house had claimed and

held her attention. Now she was trying to see how like was this room to the one into which Lotta had brought Phineas and Phebe. There was no chair, but there were still shelves fastened to the walls. No books or jars, crocks, bottles were there now. No bunches of dried plants hung on strings. She looked at the floor. The house and its base took up a large portion of the room, the horse more. But she still could see the faint outlines of the painted design that had been so much clearer in the doll house.

A faint tinkling drew Lorrie's attention to the house. Once more Sabina pawed at a chain dangling from one of the drawers. Lorrie moved forward, as if Miss Ashemeade were telling her she must do this. She knelt and turned the key, and pulled open the drawer. It was not the one that held the Phineas and Phebe dolls, but the next. And Lorrie was not in the least surprised to find another pair of small figures.

One was taller than either Phineas or Phebe, the other much smaller. She lifted out the larger one. The skin of the face and hands was a creamy brown, and the hair, just showing a little under a ruffled cap such as Hallie wore, was black and curly. The dress was like Hallie's too, except for the color, for this was a pale yellow and scattered over it were white flowers hardly larger than the head of a pin. Like Hallie she wore an apron that reached almost to the hem of her full skirt.

The second, smaller doll was a boy, much younger than Phineas. He wore a red-and-white shirt of minute checks, and blue jeans, with a red handkerchief tied, three-cornered about his throat. He had the same creamy-brown skin as the woman doll, and his head was covered with tight black curls.

Lorrie laid the woman doll on her knee and took up the boy. Again the fine stitching on the clothes amazed her. How could one sew so perfectly on such small things? There was a small creaking sound—

Lorrie looked up. Perhaps Sabina was not responsible this time, but the side of the doll house swung slowly open. Once more Lorrie faced the kitchen, the green bedroom, and the small room of the painted floor, twin to the one in which she sat.

There were no preparations for pie making on the table now. Instead it seemed as if a dinner must be in progress, with a course waiting ready to be served. Dishes and platters were set on the big table and on a smaller one on the side. The top of the stove was covered with pots and pans.

Lorrie put the woman doll by the tall dresser with its burden of dishes, and tried to stand the boy by the stove. Only he would not, or could not, stand. At last she settled him on a small stool.

About her a whirling flurry of snowflakes drove between her and the house. Then the snow cleared and Lorrie found she was not on the back of a horse as she had thought she would be, but cuddled down in a sleigh. There was a white fur rug pulled up almost as far as her shoulders, and her head was snug in a fur-lined hood. She shared the seat of the sleigh with someone else, and Lorrie turned her head quickly to view her companion.

She, too, wore a fur-bordered hood. In the late afternoon that shone red, the ruff of fur about her face white. Lotta was driving the sleigh with practiced ease. It was a small sleigh in the form of a swan with a proudly curving neck and a high-held head. The horse speeding alone before that curve of swan neck was white too, but his harness was as red as Lotta's hood, and tassels and silver bells bounced and rang as he trotted briskly along. There was a smell of pine from some boughs resting across their laps, a Christmas-y smell.

"Merry Christmas, Lorrie!" Lotta's voice was clear even above the ringing of the bells. She was not a little girl any longer, but a young lady. But she was still Lotta, and Lorrie smiled back.

"Merry Christmas!"

It was so exciting, this dash along the snowy road with the ringing of the bells, the smell of pine, and all the rest of it. But ahead Lorrie did not see the rise of the red-brick walls as she expected. If they were bound for the shelter of Octagon House, they still had some distance to go.

" 'Deck the halls with boughs of holly,' " Lotta sang. "We have pine if not holly, Lorrie. Ah, this is a good day."

"Yes!"

The snow spattered up from the horse's flying hoofs. Some of it stuck against the arching wings of the swan that protected the riders. It was crispy cold, but all but the tip of Lorrie's nose was cheerfully warm. She wriggled her hands and discovered that under the sleigh robe they were not only mittened but also protected by a muff.

"Where are we going?" Lorrie dared to ask when Octagon House still did not come into view, though they rounded two curves and could now see a good stretch of open country through which the road was a pair of ruts deep cut in the snow.

Lotta shook the reins as if to urge the horse to a brisker pace. "I—" she had begun when there sounded a long mournful howl. Their horse neighed. Two dogs bounded toward them, and behind rode men on horseback. Again the bells on the harness tinkled as Lotta pulled on the reins. The horse slowed to a walk and finally stopped.

Lorrie felt a chill she had not known earlier. There was something about those dogs, the mounted men behind them— She did not know why she had that shiver of fear, but she heard Lotta say softly:

"It is their thoughts you feel, Lorrie, reaching as shadows across the snow, darkening, spoiling it. It is what they have done, and what they would do, that we see coming before them—a taste on the wind."

There was a puff of wind in their faces and Lorrie smelled what was a ghost of an old and evil odor. Lotta continued:

"What you smell is the seed of fear, Lorrie. Never forget that fear has a seed, and it is cruelty. There are hunters and hunted, those who run and those who pursue."

One of the hounds had almost reached the sleigh. It raised its head and bayed. Lotta whistled, only a note or two, high and shrill, and the hound whined and leaped away.

"Your servant, ma'am." Lorrie had been watching the hound so closely she had not seen the first rider gallop forward to Lotta's side of the sled. The man in the saddle leaned forward a little as if to see them both better.

He wore a broad-brimmed hat tied on his head with a scarf that went over the top of his hat and down over his ears, being then wound and tied about his throat. His thick coat had the collar well turned up, and he had heavy gloves on his hands.

"Your wish, sir?" Lotta had given him no greeting.

"Not to disturb so lovely a pair of ladies, ma'am." He had a mustache that curled up at the tips stiffly as if, Lorrie thought, he had used hair spray to set it so, and a little pointed beard that waggled up and down before his checkered muffler as he spoke. "Have you passed anyone on the road?"

"And your reason for asking?" Lotta counter-questioned.

"Miss Ashemeade, ma'am." A second rider had come up to join the first. His face was round and reddened with the nip of hours in the cold. Some spikes of fair hairs stuck out raggedly from beneath his fur cap, which was old and had bare and shiny spots where the hair had fallen out.

"Constable Wilkins," Lotta acknowledged.

"We'se huntin' runaways, ma'am. These here are lawmen from down'cross the river. Two o' them runaways, ma'am, a woman an' a boy. It's the bounden duty of all law-bidin' folks to turn 'em in, ma'am."

It seemed to Lorrie that Mr. Wilkins was uneasy and grew uneasier still as Lotta continued to look at him calmly, just as she had once looked at Phineas when he had raised suspicious objections to her offer of help.

"We have been advised of that law several times, Constable Wilkins. A woman and a boy, you say. This is cruel weather through which to be hunted."

"By their own choice, ma'am," the other man broke in, "entirely by their own choice. You have not seen them, of course." But Lorrie thought that was not quite a question, it was almost as if he expected Lotta to say no, and refused to believe that she spoke the truth.

"We have seen no one. And now, the hour grows late, and the wind grows colder. If you will permit me, gentlemen." Lotta slapped the reins, and the white horse settled to his collar. Lorrie thought that the man wanted to say more, but the sleigh was already on its way again. When she looked inquiringly at Lotta, she saw that the happy look had vanished from the older girl's face.

"It seems that trouble does walk the world, even on this night, Lorrie. And we are summoned to take a hand. So—" She clicked her tongue and shook the reins again and the white horse quickened pace.

Lorrie looked back. She could still see the men as black dots and she heard the dogs yelping. The trees of a long finger of woods were reaching out for the sleigh. And as the sleigh came into their shadow, Lotta pulled in the horse to a walk.

"Watch for a tree that is storm-split, Lorrie," she said. "That is our trail marker."

Lorrie saw it to their right among others and called out. Then they turned off the road into a way where the snow lay soft and unbroken, but where there must be some sort of trail, for Lotta drove confidently forward.

"A short cut, Lorrie. I do not think they will backtrack to follow us, but if they do we shall have an excuse for taking this way. Now—" She began to sing. That tune—Lorrie thought she had heard the tune— but the words she did not understand. Only, after some moments she found herself humming the melody. Up scale and down went those notes as they drove out of the woods again, down a slope, and turned into another marked road. Now they turned right, taking a direction that led back the way they had come.

Still Lotta sang, sometimes so low her voice rose hardly above a murmur, sometimes louder than the chime of the bells. Then, all at once, she stopped, and Lorrie thought she was listening, as if she expected some answer from the bushes and trees lining the road ahead.

Once, very far away, there was the bay of a hound. And then there was a faint smile about Lotta's lips for an instant. But still she watched the way before them intently. They pulled up a hill and paused on its crown for a moment while the horse snorted and blew clouds of white breath, bobbing his head up and down.

The road sloped again before them, crossed a bridge, and then—yes, to the left ahead Lorrie saw familiar red bricks. That was Octagon House. And when she sighted it, the small nipping fear that had been with her since they had met the horsemen vanished.

"Slowly, Bevis!" Lotta called.

As if he understood her, the horse neighed and nodded his head vigorously. They went down the far side of the hill at a much slower pace. And still Lotta looked as if she were listening, expecting to hear something besides the thud of hoofs on the packed snow.

"Bevis!" They had come close to the bridge when Lotta's voice rang out and the horse halted. Now Lotta flung aside the fur robe in the sleigh and climbed out. Though she did not summon Lorrie to join her, the girl pulled out of the tangle of cover to follow.

Lorrie's long skirts dragged in the snow as she tried to hold them up, moving far slower and more clumsily than Lotta, who was peering down into the shadows beneath the bridge, just as she had on that other night when Phineas and Phebe had taken refuge there.

Lorrie heard no crying this time. But there was something else. Just as she had sniffed that evil smell when the riders had met the sleigh, so now did she feel fear—not her fear but one that spread to her from the dark by the water. And she stopped, uneasy.

"They are well away—" Lotta's soft voice carried. "Their hounds are running straight now on the wrong scent. Come out while there is time."

There was no answer. It seemed to Lorrie that the fear wave came more strongly. Now it hit her so that she could not move. But Lotta held out her hands to the dark pool of shadow.

"You need not fear us. Come while there is time. I can promise you a safe hiding place. But how long we have, I do not know."

Again silence. Then Lorrie saw a flicker of movement in the shadows. Out of them crawled a bent-over figure, hands and knees in the snow. It dragged behind it what might have been a cloak or shawl on which lay a heap of rags.

"I'se got to believe." It was a cry of pain. "I'se purely got to believe that, mis'."

Lotta ran forward, her outstretched hands falling to the shoulders of the crawling figure. "Lorrie!" she called, and Lorrie struggled through the drift to join her.

Together they brought to her feet a tall skeleton of a woman, who shivered with great shudders running all through her too thin body.

"Nackie! Nackie!" She tried to stoop again to the bundle on the shawl and nearly fell until Lotta steadied her.

"Come!" she urged. "We have so little time! Lorrie, bring the baby."

Baby? Lorrie looked down at the bundle, which had neither stirred nor cried. Baby? Not quite believing, she stooped awkwardly and picked up the heap of rags on the snow-wet shawl. She *did* hold a small body and there was a tiny movement against her shoulder as she struggled against the weight of her skirts back up to the sleigh.

Somehow they all crowded into the seat and Lotta snapped the reins. Bevis trotted on, across the bridge, up the lane, turned past the horse block to come to the door of a stable. Someone ran through newly falling flakes of snow to meet them.

"Miss Lotta?"

"Take care, Phineas. We may have visitors later."

The boy nodded. "If they come, I'll have some answers for 'em. Do you need help?"

"Not now. You're better out here for a while."

Lorrie still carried that small light bundle as she went up a shoveled path behind Lotta and the woman they had found to the back door. Light shone in the windows and, as she came into the back hallway, she heard the murmur of voices. They turned into the kitchen. From beside the stove a girl turned to face them. Her eyes widened as she saw the woman Lotta supported. Then she ran to open the other door into the hallway, asking no questions. They made a swift journey across the green bedroom, then were in the room with the shelves and the painted floor. Lotta lowered the woman into the chair. For a moment she was limp, and Lorrie was afraid she would slip to the floor. Then with a visible effort she straightened up and held out her arms.

"Nackie—give me my Nackie!" Her demand was

fierce and she stared at Lorrie angrily. Lorrie hastened to lay the baby in her arms.

Only, as the woman pulled the tattered coverings from around that small body, Lorrie saw it was not a baby she had carried. It was an older child, with large eyes in a pinched face. He put up his hands and stroked the cheeks of the woman bending over him, and he made a sound, a rasping little cry that was no word or any normal child's call.

"Nackie!" The woman rocked back and forth in the chair, holding him close. Lotta went to the door. The girl from the kitchen—it was Phebe—stood there holding a tray with a bowl and a mug on it.

Lotta brought them to the woman. "Drink. It is hot and nourishing and you need it."

The woman stared at her and took the mug, sipped from it, then held it to the child's lips. He drank greedily, and over his head she looked again to Lotta.

"We'se runaways, from 'cross th' river."

"I know. But here you are safe."

It was almost as if the woman could not understand. "Nackie—they was goin' t' sell me 'way from Nackie! They never did want him. He can't talk ner walk. He couldn't live weren't he with his ma. But he ain't trash like you throw 'way. He can do things with his hands. Looky here, mis', jus' looky here. Nackie made this all by his ownself!"

She took the cup away from the boy and put it on the tray Lotta still held, to search in the front of the shapeless garment she wore. Then she brought out a small square of woven mat. Its edging caught the light to glisten brilliantly. Feathers, Lorrie saw—peacock feathers.

"Nackie—he made me that—made it all by himself for his own ma who loves him! He ain't lackin' in th' head, no, he ain't! No matter what ol' mis' said. I ain't losin' my Nackie! I heard 'em tell as how they was goin' to sell Chole—that's me, mis'. An' so I jus' took Nackie an' I ran—I ran as far an' as fast as I could."

"There will be no more running," Lotta said. "Now drink this good soup in the bowl, Chole. You are safe here."

"Is I, mis'? Be there any safe place for me an' Nackie?"

"There is." The firmness in Lotta's voice was convincing. "Lorrie, will you take this to Phebe?" She held out the tray with the now empty mug and bowl.

Lorrie went back to the hall. There were no candles or lamps here—it was very dark. She was a little afraid of that dark, for it seemed to move about while she stood still. Then the dark was gone and she sat on the floor before the doll house once again.

STORM CLOUDS

"AUNT MARGARET." Lorrie held open on her lap one of the costume books her aunt kept for reference. "How old do you suppose Miss Ashemeade really is?"

Aunt Margaret glanced up from her sketching pad.

"I haven't the slightest idea, Lorrie. From things she says—" Aunt Margaret's voice trailed off, and she looked puzzled.

"Look here, see this dress? It's like those Miss Ashemeade wears. But the book says it was worn in 1865! And that's over a hundred years ago. Why should Miss Ashemeade wear a dress over a hundred years old?"

"Probably because she wants to, Chick. But her dresses are not over a hundred years old, they are just made over from the old patterns. Miss Ashemeade does not go out, you know. Perhaps she likes dresses of older periods and sees no reason why she cannot suit herself and wear them. They are very beautiful. And materials such as those cannot be found nowadays."

"Then where does Miss Ashemeade find them?" persisted Lorrie.

"Perhaps she has stored lengths of material to use. It was often the custom to buy dress material by the bolt and store it for future use. In a house as old as hers, there must be a good supply of things from the past. Octagon House was built back in the mid-1840's."

"Who built it?"

"The Ashemeade family. Miss Ashemeade is the last of them now, at least the last of that name in Ashton."

"Hallie wears dresses like these, too." Lorrie went back to her first line of questioning.

"Hallie greatly admires Miss Ashemeade, and she must be as old, so she likes the same styles. I must admit, on both of them those dresses are very becoming."

Lorrie turned back the pages of the book and looked at another illustration and at the date beneath it. Miss Ashemeade wore a dress of 1865, but the little girl in this other illustration had a dress like that of the doll Phebe. And the date under it was 1845.

She began to turn the pages carefully in search of something else. The full skirts were common and she could see no small detail to date the dress Lotta had worn during that journey by sleigh. And—who was Lotta?

Once or twice Lorrie had believed she knew. Only that could not be true! Or—could it? She turned back to the page of Miss Ashemeade's dress.

"What a wonderful house!" Aunt Margaret was no longer working, but looking rather at the wall where hung her Christmas gift from Miss Ashemeade. It was a picture of a lady and gentleman standing stiffly in a garden where flowers grew stiffly also. The gentleman had long curls that hung down on his shoulders, and a sword at his side. Aunt Margaret explained that it was stump work, a kind of embroidery very seldom seen, and that the picture must be close to three hundred or more years old. "It is really a museum, Lorrie."

"Then, why doesn't someone make it one? They couldn't tear it down for the thruway if it were a museum, could they?" demanded Lorrie.

"Perhaps." Aunt Margaret picked up her sketching pencil again as if she did not want to talk about that. "Don't you have some homework, Chick?"

Lorrie put the costume book back in its proper place. "Math," she said briefly and with no relish. But it was hard to think of math when this other idea had taken root in her mind.

If Octagon House was made important they could not pull it down. How did you make a house important? A story in the paper—maybe talking about it on TV? But how did one get a story in the paper, or someone to talk on TV? Did you just write a letter and ask?

"Lorrie, you don't seem to have done very much," Aunt Margaret observed as she gathered her own papers together and slid them into her brief case. "I don't believe Mrs. Raymond will accept such scribbling. If I remember rightly from my own school days, once Christmas was over it was back to work, and hard work, before the end of the term."

"Yes, I guess so." Lorrie tried to push Octagon House out of her mind and concentrate on the dreary figures that she never liked.

But in bed that night she thought again about Octagon House. Suppose she, Lorrie Mallard, could write a letter to the newspaper, all about the house and Miss Ashemeade, and the wonderful things—

Wonderful things— Lorrie's enthusiasm about her budding idea was sharply checked. The doll house— Miss Ashemeade had never mentioned the house to

Lorrie, just as she herself had never spoken of it to
Miss Ashemeade, or to Aunt Margaret. It was—it was
something very private, Lorrie knew without anyone
telling her so. But it was part of Octagon House and if
that were turned into a museum— Miss Ashemeade
and Hallie—where would they live? Did people ever
live in museums? But what if—if the house were torn
down—then where would Miss Ashemeade and Hallie
go? And where would the doll house and Bevis and—
and Sabina—go? Lorrie sat up in bed. What *would*
happen? She had to tell—to ask Miss Ashemeade.
Tomorrow she would get away from school as fast as
she could and—

Oh—tomorrow they had the class meeting. But that
did not matter, not now. She simply had to see Miss
Ashemeade and ask her about the museum idea, about
whether it could be done.

Lorrie was impatient. All her life she had always
wanted to do at once anything she had planned. But
now she must wait through the night, and most of
tomorrow, before she could see Miss Ashemeade. She
twisted uneasily on her pillow as she lay down again.

She dreamed that she saw the house and over it a
big storm cloud. In the shadow of that the red-brick
walls began to shrink smaller and smaller until Lorrie
was afraid that they would vanish altogether. She ran
forward, trying to reach the house before it disappeared.
But suddenly the front door opened, and Miss Ashemeade stood there. She was not leaning on Hallie's
arm, nor was she depending on her cane for support,
but she held out both hands, waving Lorrie back. And
she was smiling as if all were well.

However in the morning her plan still filled Lorrie's
mind. Kathy pounded on the door and they went off
together, taking the shorter way that did not go down
Ash Street. Kathy chattered busily as usual but suddenly she broke off and said in a sharper voice:

"Lorrie Mallard, I don't think you've heard one

single, solitary word I've said. Where are you anyway? Right here, or about a billion miles away?"

Lorrie was startled out of her own thoughts. "Here —at least I'm walking along this street."

"You'd never know it to look at you! You're more like one of those robots Rob keeps reading about. I was talking about the Valentine Fair and Open House, Lorrie—THE VALENTINE FAIR!"

"But Valentine Day's in February, and this is only January."

"Boy, are you ever a real drippy dope, Lorrie. The Valentine Fair is about the biggest thing at school, it surely is. We're the seniors this year, and that means we plan most of it. And today they are going to elect both committees—girls' and boys'."

"You ought to be on it, Kathy."

"I sure hope so. Look here, Lorrie. Deb Collins said she'd nominate me. Now, will you second it?"

"You mean get up in class and say I want you for the committee?"

"You just say, 'Second the nomination.' Lorrie, you've heard them do it before, there's nothing to it. I've some dreamy ideas and I think I have a chance to be chairman. So, you'll do it, won't you?"

"But—I wasn't going to stay for the meeting."

Kathy stared at her. "Whyever not? And, don't be stupid, Mrs. Raymond won't let you miss it, anyway. Being seniors we're supposed to take an intelligent interest. Don't you remember what she said last week? Or weren't you listening then either?"

"I have something important to do," protested Lorrie.

"I'm telling you the truth, it's got to be the best excuse in the world or Mrs. Raymond isn't going to take it. You'll be there, Lorrie. Now, will you second me for the committee?"

"Yes." Lorrie's heart sank. Kathy was probably right, she so often was in such matters. And if she had to stay for the class meeting, she would have no time for a visit to Octagon House tonight. But it was so important!

Kathy was right. Lorrie tried her excuse of an important errand after school. But when the questioning revealed to Mrs. Raymond that the errand was Lorrie's idea and not Aunt Margaret's, she was told that participation in class activities was far more important.

Lorrie returned to her seat with a rush of the same unhappy feeling that had been hers when she had first come to Ashton. She was hardly aware of Bill Crowder's calling the class to order as president and the rest of the talk at the front of the room. But she came to with a start when she was conscious of a sudden silence. Several of those around her were glancing at Lorrie as if they expected something from her, and she had a sudden thrust of panic—as if she had been called upon to recite and had not heard the question.

Then two seats beyond, Bessie Calder stood up and said, "I second the nomination."

I second the nomination! Why, that was what Kathy had asked her to say! Kathy! Lorrie glanced quickly at Kathy and met an accusing stare in return. Kathy had asked her, and she hadn't done it. Kathy must believe she kept quiet on purpose!

Again Lorrie ceased to listen to what was going on as she thought furiously of how she could explain her lapse to Kathy. She would have to tell Kathy about Octagon House and the thruway. Now she shifted impatiently in her seat, waiting only for the end of the meeting so she could get to Kathy and explain.

Only Lorrie was not to have the chance, because, as she started toward Kathy's desk, the other girl called:

"Bess! Chris! Wait up! I've some groovy ideas. Just wait until you hear them!"

Lorrie pushed her way determinedly to Kathy's desk. "Kathy—Kathy!" she called, intent on making Kathy turn her head and acknowledge her being there. She made some impression, for Kathy did turn and look around. But her face was set and cold.

"What do you want, Lorrie Mallard? You broke your word. Think I want you on *my* committee now?"

"But Kathy—"

"I said"—Kathy leaned over her desk—"get lost, Lorrie. You wouldn't help me, I don't need you—and don't you forget it! Come on, gang, we've got a lot to do!"

With that she joined a waiting group of girls and was gone. Lorrie pulled her book bag back to her locker. There was no hurry now, she did not have time enough to go by Octagon House, and she was not about to leave so fast Kathy would believe she was trailing along behind her. As Kathy had pointed out, they did not need each other—not at all. Lorrie kept holding to that thought as she zipped up her ski jacket. Someone banged the door of the locker next to hers and she looked up.

"Lizabeth—"

"Out in the cold again, Lorrie?" Lizabeth asked. "What did you do this time to upset her royal highness?" There was such sharpness in Lizabeth's voice that Lorrie was startled.

"She asked me to second her nomination for the committee and—well, I was thinking about something else and I forgot all about it. She has a right to be mad."

"Now"—Lizabeth set her hands on her hips and looked at Lorrie—"now just what could be more important than this committee? What deep thought, Lorrie?"

Lorrie felt a little embarrassed. Lizabeth did not like Kathy, not one little bit. And she made it so clear now. Lorrie thought back to the theater party and her own uneasiness about how Kathy had acted over the seating. Lizabeth had so quickly withdrawn then into a shell of her own.

"I was worried." Suddenly she had to talk to someone and she liked Lizabeth, or the usual Lizabeth, not this sharp-tongued one. "Lizabeth, do you know the Octagon House?"

"That old place over on Ash Street? Sure. Daddy says it's the only one of its kind anywhere around— has eight sides. What about it?"

"They say it's going to be torn down for the thruway."

"Yes, the line runs through from Gamblier Avenue to the State route, and that's three blocks beyond Ash."

"How do you know so much?"

"Daddy's on that project, he's an engineer with the highways. But what about you, why do you care where the thruway goes?"

"They can't tear down Octagon House!" Lorrie protested. "I thought— Suppose people wrote to the papers and said not to— Or someone talked on the TV about it. Wouldn't that stop them?"

"They've been doing that for over a year now," Lizabeth returned. "Oh, not writing about Octagon House, but about other houses. This Friday they're having a big meeting about it before the Commissioners. But it isn't going to do them any good. There's a river underground a little to the north, and they can't build the thruway over that, so it will have to go this way."

"A river?" Lorrie repeated. Was it perhaps the stream that the bridge had spanned in the past, under which the fugitives had hidden?

"Yes. It used to be above ground, just like any other. Then they began to build more and more houses out here. So finally they put the river in big pipes and built right over it. But they can't lay the thruway over that."

"But Octagon House—"

"And what makes that so wonderful? They're going to tear down the old Ruxton House too. And Mother says that's a shame. A man came all the way from England more'n a hundred years ago to plan that. It's beautiful."

"So is Octagon House," countered Lorrie stubbornly.

"Now? It's an old wreck on a piece of wild land."

Lorrie shook her head. "It only looks wild from outside the fence, Lizabeth. Inside there's a garden, and in the house— Oh, Lizabeth, it's wonderful!"

"How do you know? Lorrie Mallard, have you been *in* the witch house, have you really?"

"There's no witch!" Lorrie flared. "There are Miss Ashemeade and Hallie and Sabina! And my aunt says it's like a museum there. Yes, I've been in, and so has Aunt Margaret. I go there to learn sewing from Miss Ashemeade, and Aunt Margaret's been there to Sunday tea, and we were there on Christmas. It was wonderful! You ought to have seen the tree and Hallie's gingerbread people and—" Lorrie launched into a confused description of Octagon House, its inhabitants and treasures—all but the horse Bevis and the doll house. And Lizabeth listened with flattering interest.

"You girls there—time to get out." It was Mr. Haskins, the janitor, shouting at them down the hall. Lorrie slammed shut her locker.

Why, it must be late. Everyone else had gone. She looked up to the big clock at the end of the hall just as its minute hand made a full sweep—ten after four!

"Look here," Lizabeth said, "Mother's calling for me. I'm supposed to go to the dentist. We can let you off at the end of Ash and you don't have far to go from there, do you?"

"Mother," Lizabeth announced as they reached the waiting car, "we can drop Lorrie off at the corner of Ash, can't we? It's late."

"As I was just about to observe. What kept you, Lizabeth? Of course, Lorrie, hop in."

Lizabeth wriggled into the middle of the front seat. "Mother, Lorrie's been in the Octagon House, she knows Miss Ashemeade. And they had a Christmas tree with gingerbread people."

"So you know Miss Ashemeade, Lorrie?" Mrs. Ross's

voice cut through her daughter's excited speech. "That is a privilege, Lorrie."

"Do you know her, too, Mrs. Ross?"

"When I was a little girl, I went there twice with my aunt. Her father's aunt lived there—Hallie Standish."

"Hallie's still there!" said Lorrie eagerly. "She made the gingerbread people for the tree and all the little candies."

"But—" Mrs. Ross looked startled. "But she can't be! Why, Auntie would be in her late eighties if she were still living. And Hallie—why Hallie Standish would have to be over a hundred! It must be her daughter. Though," Mrs. Ross looked thoughtful, "I didn't know she had a daughter. But I do remember my visits there and Miss Ashemeade—she must be very old now."

"Mrs. Ross, what will happen to Miss Ashemeade and Hallie if they tear down Octagon House? And can't they save the house? Aunt Margaret says it is like a museum."

"Nothing is decided, it won't be until after the Commissioners' meeting. Most of the people will be represented by lawyers. Surely Miss Ashemeade will. Oh, here's your corner, Lorrie."

"Thank you, Mrs. Ross." Lorrie watched the car draw away and then she started down Ash Street. When she reached the fence about Octagon House she slowed. She could see the deer, who had snow piled high about the base on which he stood but none now on his back, and the shuttered front windows, the closed door. She put her hand to the gate, and tried to work the catch. But it did not give under her fingers and somehow she knew this was not the time to climb into territory closed against her. Unhappily Lorrie went on toward the apartment house a block away.

Kathy—she must explain to Kathy, Lorrie thought as she went down the hall, though she was uncomfortable as she pressed the button of the Lockner doorbell. Rob answered.

"Kathy? No, she's over at Bess Calder's for supper. She's really flipped over this Valentine Fair. Valentines!" he laughed. "They're for girls."

"Tell her I want to see her," Lorrie said. She was sure, though, that if she did see Kathy it would be by her own efforts, with no help from Kathy.

And her fears proved true. The next morning she lingered, waiting for Kathy, not quite daring to go to the Lockner apartment again. But no Kathy appeared and Lorrie was almost tardy, making her desk only a second or two before Mrs. Raymond closed the door. Kathy was in her place but Lorrie had no time to speak to her.

Recess was just as bad. When the bell rang, Kathy asked permission to hold a committee meeting in the room and Lorrie had to go out with the others, leaving Kathy and her friends in a group about Mrs. Raymond's desk. Toward the end of the day, as Kathy continued to avoid every attempt Lorrie made, Lorrie lost her temper. So, let her think what she wanted to! She, Lorrie, was through trying to explain! She had more important things to think about and today she was going to stop at Octagon House. If the gate was shut, why she would just climb over it! But she had to see Miss Ashemeade—she had to.

However the gate did swing open slowly and gratingly under her push. Lorrie was breathing fast, as she had run most of the way from school in order to have time for this visit. But surely Aunt Margaret would understand if she were a little late getting home. Aunt Margaret was concerned too. The meeting with the Commissioners was this week, and Miss Ashemeade must have some way to make them understand the importance of Octagon House.

Lorrie ran around the house and knocked on the back door. For the first time Hallie did not answer. A little frightend, Lorrie tried the latch and it lifted. She came slowly into the hall.

"Hallie?" she called.

The door to the kitchen was shut, but the one to Miss Ashemeade's room a little ajar.

"We are in here, Lorrie."

Lorrie tugged at zippers, pulled off at top speed the ski suit to hang pants and coat on the wall pegs and set her boots under. Then she went in, only to stop just inside the door and look ahead with startled eyes. Hallie was working by the long table. She was flanked by tall cartons with detergent advertisements stamped on their sides (they looked as out of place in this room as a pile of dirty boards).

Sabina stood on her hind legs scraping her front claws down the side of one box, trying vainly to see into its interior. Into the next one Hallie was carefully packing all the rolls of material and ribbon that had lain undisturbed on that end of the table ever since Lorrie had first come here. There was the rustle of tissue paper as she rolled each one in that covering before fitting it into the carton.

Packing—Hallie was packing things away! Was—had Miss Ashemeade given up? Was she planning to move? But there was nowhere else for Miss Ashemeade, and Hallie, and all the treasures of Octagon House. This was where they belonged. They could not live anywhere else and be the same!

"Housecleaning, Lorrie." Miss Ashemeade was busy, too. The length of tapestry that had been in the frame, for which Lorrie had threaded so many needles of wool, lay across her lap, and she was folding it carefully in a piece of protecting muslin. "Things accumulate so, and every once in a while they must be put to rights. It is an offense against thrift to hold onto what one cannot use to any profit. Hallie's box is going to the Ladies Aid of the Gordon Street Church. They can put all those pieces to good use, better use than they will be here, attracting dust and getting creased and faded. Why, what is the matter, my dear?"

"You're—you're not packing to move? You're not leaving Octagon House—"

Miss Ashemeade raised her hands and held them out, and Lorrie was drawn to her as if those hands had reached clear across the long room to her. When she stood beside Miss Ashemeade's chair, they came to rest on her shoulders.

"You need never fear, Lorrie, about that. I shall not leave Octagon House, nor shall the house—the real house—ever leave me."

"The real house—"

But Miss Ashemeade was shaking her head. "The time will come, Lorrie, when you shall understand that. So, you thought we were moving, not cleaning up a bit? Ah, Lorrie, were we to move, I am afraid we would have to pull up roots so long and deep set that there would be a major disturbance in the world. Is that not so, Hallie?"

" 'Deed so, Mis' Charlotta, 'deed so." Hallie chuckled. "Cleanin' up, that ain't movin', Mis' Lorrie. Now, looky heah, Sabina, you take's your claws outa that right smart. Them fixings was never meant for pullin' about thataway."

Sabina was backing across the carpet, pulling after her a long trail of golden ribbon that uncoiled as she went. She tried to jerk it free from Hallie's fingers when Hallie caught the other end. But Hallie won that tug of war and rewound the ribbon, to put it in the carton.

"Housecleaning is an excellent occupation for at least once a year," Miss Ashemeade continued. "And not only houses need cleaning. But, Lorrie, you are still troubled. Now tell me what it is."

"Tomorrow night is the meeting with the Commissioners, Miss Ashemeade, about the thruway."

"And you are wondering if I shall be represented there. Yes, there is a Mr. Thruston who will see to my interests."

"I've been thinking, if people wrote letters to the papers, maybe talked on the TV and the radio—Aunt Margaret said this house was a museum. Museums are important, they can't go knocking those down. Maybe Octagon House might be a museum if people wanted it."

Miss Ashemeade smiled slowly. "A museum, yes, that is what it has become through the years, Lorrie, but not one that everyone can enjoy. Museums have no real life, they are full of things frozen in time, so stand always as they are. There are those who enjoy visiting them to see the past, but those who feel true kinship with the past grow fewer and fewer."

She looked about the room. "There are treasures here, Lorrie, as your aunt saw, which perhaps do belong in a place where they may be cared for and shown to those who appreciate them for their history and their beauty. But this house holds other treasures that cannot be reckoned by the measurements of the world outside its walls. No, good as your plan is in its way, my dear, it cannot be used to protect Octagon House. Now"—again she looked at Lorrie—"do not carry this worry as a burden, my dear. There is a solution, believe me there is. You have nothing to fear for Octagon House, nothing at all."

And Lorrie believed. She gave a sigh of relief. Mr. Thruston must be an extra-special lawyer.

"Now, Lorrie, how goes the world with you? You may put these wools to rights while you tell me."

Lorrie sat down on her old place on the stool and began to untangle and rewind the odds and ends of wools left from the tapestry, tucking the loose ends under neatly. She found herself talking about Kathy and the trouble her own absent-mindedness had caused.

"Valentines," Miss Ashemeade said. "A Valentine Fair to raise money for the school. Lorrie, see that large scrapbook over there, on the bottom shelf of the case? Bring it here, child."

Lorrie brought over the large book. It was bound in leather of dark red, embossed and stamped with a design that combined small, plump hearts and wreaths of flowers. And in the creases of the design there were still faint lines of gold.

"Take it with you, Lorrie. And tonight tell Kathy you have something very special to show her. Tell her also, that if she is interested, to do what comes into her mind and that you will help her."

"What—?" Lorrie started to open the book, but Miss Ashemeade shook her head.

"No. Open it with Kathy, my dear. And remember— tell her you can help her. That is all. Now, perhaps you had better go, it is getting late. Let Sabina out for her run as you leave. Do not worry about us, Lorrie. We are going to manage splendidly."

She was so certain that she made Lorrie certain of that, too.

CHARLES

THE BOOK was big, too big to put into Lorrie's bag, and she had been afraid she would drop it in the snow, so she gave a sigh of relief when she reached the apartment lobby.

"Then I'll see about the cookies—"

Lorrie halted just inside the door. Kathy and Bess were there. They both turned around to look at her as she came in.

"Hello, Lorrie," Bess said, as if she did not know just what to say and chose the easiest words.

"Hello." Lorrie marched straight for Kathy. Maybe Kathy would turn and go upstairs, with Bess seeing and listening to everything. But this was the best chance she had had since the unfortunate class meeting to talk to Kathy. "This time, Kathy, you have to listen."

"I don't have to," Kathy interrupted. But Lorrie stood right in front of her now, and her refusal trailed into silence.

"I wasn't trying to be mean, Kathy, when I didn't second your nomination at the meeting. I was thinking about something else, something important, and I really forgot what was going on."

"Forgot!" Kathy looked unconvinced. "As if you *could*—"

"I did, and that's the truth, Kathy Lockner, the whole truth!"

"I don't see what could be so important that you'd forget like that." Kathy's protest sounded less certain.

"It was important to me, Kathy. Now"—she held out the book—"I have something for you to see. Miss Ashemeade said you should."

"Who's Miss Ashemeade?" Kathy demanded, but she was looking at the scrapbook.

"The lady who lives in Octagon House."

"She means the old witch!" broke in Bess.

Lorrie spun around. "You take that back, Bess Calder—right now you take that back! Miss Ashemeade's nice. She had Aunt Margaret and me there for Christmas, and it was wonderful. And Octagon House is beautiful."

"It's an old eyesore, my father says so," shrilled Bess. "And the city's going to tear it down and put a street right over it, so there, Lorrie Mallard! You'd better take your old witch's book and get out. Kathy and me's talking committee business and you're not on the committee. Kathy wouldn't have you after what you did!"

But Kathy was still looking at the book Lorrie held. "What is it?" she wanted to know.

"A scrapbook. I haven't looked in it either. Miss

Ashemeade said to wait for you. Come on up"—she hesitated and then added to Bess—"both of you and let's see."

"All right," Kathy agreed. "You, too, Bess. Call your mother and stay for supper if she lets you. It's almost five anyway."

"But what right's Lorrie got pushing in? She isn't on the committee."

"Who said anything about this being for the fair? Miss Ashemeade said to show it to Kathy."

"How did she know about me?"

"I told her about what happened and how sorry I was that I forgot. And I am sorry, Kathy, but you wouldn't let me say so before."

"All right. Come on, Bess, let's see—won't hurt us."

Lorrie unlocked the door and went to lay the book on the coffee table. A moment later she turned the thick leather cover to the first page.

"Valentines!" Bess exclaimed.

Valentines they were, fastened to each page, but such valentines!

"See this round one!" Kathy touched with a finger tip. "Those flowers, they're really embroidered in silk! And look at the darling little cupid holding up the wreath of roses!"

"And that one. It must be a paper doll, isn't it, Lorrie?" Bess added her voice to Kathy's. "But the dress—it's so old-fashioned!"

"Look at this one! The center is satin and the lady's painted on—with the butterflies." Kathy had found another wonder. "Why, Lorrie, I never knew they once had valentines like these—all lace and flowers, with birds and butterflies."

"They're a lot prettier than the kind we have now. Oh, here's one that's an open fan with a lot of pictures at the top and a cord and tassel at the bottom!"

"They're old," Lorrie said thoughtfully. "But that

lace, it's rather like the lace you see now in paper mats. Aunt Margaret has some for cake plates."

"These flowers and birds." Bess touched one blue-bird. "Don't they have little books at the bookshop—the gummed-stamp ones? Some are flowers and some are birds. You know, the first graders get them pasted on good papers at school."

"This one has real lace on it." Kathy bent closer. "I've seen edging at the fabric shop that looks like these tiny pink roses."

"Did you see Lizabeth's Christmas cards? Wait a minute, let me show you." Lorrie put down the book and went to get a card from the desk drawer. "She made them herself. I asked her where she got the pictures for them, and these gold stars and leaves, and she told me about a store that has all kinds of these. They come from Germany. Now, doesn't this little angel look a lot like the cupid on that card?"

Kathy took the Christmas card to make a careful comparison.

"It does," she admitted, but Lorrie thought she did so reluctantly.

"Lizabeth could show us the store."

"You and Lizabeth are not on the committee!" Bess sat back on the couch. "Kathy?" She looked to her in appeal.

Kathy was still studying the pages before her. "See here, Bess, we want to make money for the senior gift, don't we? Well, we have a cooky table, just as always, and a candy table. But this kind of thing, we've never tried before. And I'll bet it would be something even the grownups would like. You know, Mother and I went to visit a friend of hers, a Mrs. Lacy who lives up on Lakeland Heights. And she had a coffee table with a glass top. Under that were some valentines like these."

"But those were real old ones, like those in this book," Bess pointed out, "not like those made today."

"But they were pretty, so people saved them. Listen, Bess, how many valentines from last year did you save more'n a few weeks?"

Bess thought. "A couple."

"Because someone special sent them to you, not because they were so pretty. Now isn't that so?"

"I guess so."

"All right. But you offer some copies of these old ones for sale and perhaps people would keep them longer."

"We can't use these."

"No, I said copies." Kathy studied Lizabeth's card again. "Lorrie, you say Lizabeth knows a store that sells these cutouts. Could you ask her where it is?"

"You ask her, Kathy," Lorrie answered calmly. "Lizabeth made that card, so she must know a lot about such work." She thought Kathy looked flushed and a little ill at ease. Then the committee chairman lifted her head with a little toss.

"All right, I will! As of now, Bess, we are going to expand the committee. Lorrie comes in and Lizabeth, if they will."

"The rest of the girls aren't going to like it," Bess protested.

"Why not? We want to have the best Valentine Fair ever, don't we? And here's something no other class ever had before. The boys are going to put on a puppet show and run the pop booth, and Jimmy Purvis will show his animal slides. But they've always had something like that—as they always had the candy and cooky sales. Now, this is something new and I think it's good!"

"But asking Lizabeth—"

Kathy turned sharply. "All right, Bess, just go on and say it! Say you don't want to be on a committee with her."

"You said it, too, and other things—" Bess stopped

short under Lorrie's accusing stare. Kathy was very flushed.

"Yes," Kathy admitted in a low voice, "I did."

"And now—just because you think she can do something for your old committee, you're ready to ask her!" Bess returned.

Lorrie looked from Bess to Kathy, who was very red now. Maybe that was the truth. But she remembered what Aunt Margaret had said—walls rose because people did not really know each other. If they did get to know, the walls began to crumble.

"Lizabeth's nice," she said, "and she's clever. She's one of the smartest girls in the class and you both know it. She should be on the committee anyway and, I think if Kathy asks her in the right way, she will."

"And what's the 'right way'?" Bess wanted to know.

"Tell her that she has something the class needs," Lorrie said slowly. "That's really what a committee is, isn't it. People all working together, each doing what he can, even if they don't all do the same things?"

Kathy nodded. "All right, I'm going to ask her. Maybe it's because she can work. But some people don't care for Sandra Tottrell very much, and we asked her because she makes super fudge. Isn't that so, Bess?"

Bess was frowning. "It's your committee." She sounded grudging.

"It's our fair," Kathy returned. "Lorrie, would Miss Ashemeade let us borrow this book for a while, so we could copy ideas from it? We would promise you could take charge of it and we would be very careful."

"I'll ask."

"You might go through it tonight," Kathy continued, "and make a list of things we need, lace paper and flower seals and ribbon. Then maybe Saturday we could see about buying them. And tomorrow at recess, if you could bring the book, Lorrie, we'll show the girls and decide."

"I'll see if Miss Ashemeade will let me."

"Come on, Bess, you have supper with us, and then we'll do some phoning to the committee. Thanks, Lorrie, and thank Miss Ashemeade too."

But when Aunt Margaret came home and Lorrie showed her the scrapbook and explained, Aunt Margaret shook her head.

"Lorrie, these old valentines are what they term 'collectors' items' now and are undoubtedly worth a great deal of money. I don't like your bringing them here, and certainly you should not take them to school tomorrow."

"But Miss Ashemeade gave me the book, told me to show Kathy—"

"To show Kathy in our home, not to carry it to school where an accident might happen. No, Lorrie. And I do not think we should keep it here. As it happens I have some of the Christmas pictures back from the developer and I want to give Miss Ashemeade a set. So, after supper, we shall return the book. It is far too precious to be handled carelessly. Miss Ashemeade may not realize its value."

Hurriedly Lorrie leafed through the pages and tried to list the supplies Kathy wanted. But could they do anything without the samples in the book to copy? Maybe she had made Kathy believe something that now could not be carried out.

The front of Octagon House was very dark when she and Aunt Margaret arrived before the gate. But the latch gave under Lorrie's push and, as they took the walk around the house, they saw the gleam of lamp and candlelight in the windows of the red room. Also it seemed that they might have been expected, for Hallie opened the back door at their first knock.

"Come in, come in. This is a chill night!" She welcomed them heartily. "Go right in with you now. An' git close to the fire, toast your fingers and toes!"

Aunt Margaret knocked on Miss Ashemeade's door and, at her low call went in, the scrapbook in her hand. She had carried it from the apartment in a plastic bag, as if she feared something would happen to it. But when Lorrie would have followed her, Hallie set her old wrinkled hand on her shoulder and gave her a little push toward the kitchen instead.

Surprised, Lorrie went. This room was warm and welcoming also. Sabina sat upright in the chair by the stove. Hallie moved to the table and lifted a hot cooky from a sheet on the tip of a turner.

"Seems like I was jus' knowin' someone would be along tonight. Now you wraps your tongue about this, child, an' then you lets me know how it does taste."

Lorrie obediently tasted, until the cooky was all gone. "Mmmmmm, extra, special good! That's what it is, Hallie!"

"You ain't th' furst as has said that, Mis' Lorrie. You, Sabina, what is you up to now?"

Sabina had jumped from her chair and was crying by the other kitchen door, the one that led to the hallway.

"Let her out, child. She has her own night ways, an' they ain't ours."

Lorrie opened the door. But somehow she already knew what Sabina wanted. The doll-house room— Sabina was leading her to the doll-house room. Licking the last crumbs from her fingers, Lorrie followed.

Moonlight fell very bright and clear on the house, made Bevis' hide coat silvery. Lorrie moved around the doll house. Oddly enough she could see illumination in the rooms. There were faint glows from the small lamps and candles, though she could not see any flames. And she was so intent upon peeking in an upper window that she struck her shin against an unnoticed, half-open drawer in the base.

This was a smaller drawer, set just under the room with the painted floor. Unlike the other two she had opened, this one held a single doll. Lorrie lifted it out and held it into the moonlight.

It was a man doll and it wore a uniform with a small sword at the belt. Lorrie saw a gray jacket with an upstanding tight collar, and scrolls of very fine gold on the sleeves. A Confederate soldier! He had a thin face with prominent cheekbones and rather long dark hair, and his eyes seemed alive, as if he were looking intently back at her.

Lorrie tried the back section of the house, supposing it would swing open as it always had before. But this time it was firmly set. She walked around to try the other side. That gave, pulling out to show the parlor, the front hall, and the dining room, which was now Miss Ashemeade's day room.

In the parlor no cloths covered the furniture, the fire was built up in the grate. Carefuly Lorrie set the soldier beside the fireplace, and knew that was where he belonged. She swung the side of the house back into place and went to Bevis. But this time she did not climb into the saddle, because that curious whirlabout came before she had time to. She heard Bevis' snort by her ear and turned her head. She had been in a moonlit room and she was still in moonlight. But this was outside and the moon was bright on snow. Bevis stamped and snorted again.

They were by the stable and there was a lantern there, hung over the main door.

"Miss Lotta, they're out beatin' th' river banks. You ain't goin' down there!" The voice in the stable was raised in hot protest.

"Not by the river, no, Phineas. I am going to the village."

"But you'll have to pass them, Miss Lotta. An' they're a rough lot. Let me go, I can take a note t' the rector."

"Phineas, what if I hadn't gone on a night we remember, or on another night Chole tries hard to forget?"

"But, Miss Lotta, this here's a Reb, outa prison. He's desperate and dangerous. They say as how he kilt a man as tried to stop him."

"They say, they say! Always *they* say many things, Phineas. No one has managed however, I notice, to mention the name of the man who was killed or even repeat the same story twice. At least not in my hearing. No, I'll ride to the village, Phineas, and what happens thereafter is a matter of fate and fortune. Do not fear for me, Phineas, never for me."

There was a muttering and then the door swung open. A white horse, twin to Bevis, came through, on his back a woman riding sidesaddle. She did not seem in the least surprised to find Lorrie in the lane, but smiled in greeting.

"A chill night, but light enough, Lorrie," she said. "Shall we ride?" She brought her mount close to Lorrie and reached down to aid her into the saddle. But Lotta did not speak again as they trotted to that other road, which wound much as Ash Street would run some day.

In the direction of the river, Lorrie saw bobbing lights and once or twice heard a distant shout. She shivered. Again it was as it had been with the men and the hounds who had hunted Chole, a fear cloud touching them even this far away.

"They say that man is the most dangerous animal of all, Lorrie. But this night the hunters and not the quarry are the dangerous ones."

"Whom are they hunting?"

"A prisoner escaped from a camp in the North, a beaten man trying to make his way home to ruins and a lost cause."

"Do—do you know him then?" Lorrie asked.

Lotta looked at her in silence for a long moment. "I

know what he is, I can guess what made him so. The man himself I do not know."

"But you are going to help him, as you did the others?'

"Perhaps—only perhaps, Lorrie. For I cannot govern the choice of the house. It offers shelter by its own desire, not mine. My people have some powers, Lorrie. We can bend and weave, twist and spin. But there are other arts, equal but apart, and these we cannot influence, though we must abide by their results."

"I don't understand."

Lotta was smiling again. "Not now, Lorrie, not now. But the time will come that you do. If you were not what you are, then the house would never have opened to you even this much. For it chooses its people. A last choice, however, remains yours. Now, I think we shall ride the woods path. For those are very noisy hunters down there, and they must have long since driven any game within hearing into other hiding."

She raised her whip and with it held aside a drooping branch, then turned her mount to the right. Lorrie followed and the branch fell back into place behind them. This was a very narrow way, so narrow they must ride single file, so shut in by trees and bushes that, leafless though those were, they made two walls. Now and then Lotta stopped. In that shadowed place Lorrie could not see what the older girl did, but she thought that she listened.

All at once Lorrie turned her head. Did she really hear a thin, far-off cry? Or— Again she shivered. Lotta was bearing right, where the brush was thinner. They had to ride bent low in the saddles for this was no path, merely a seeking through the woods. At last they came out by a fence made of rails laid crisscross in angles, and Lotta followed this.

Lorrie dropped Bevis' reins and held her hands to her ears with a gasp. That shrill cry was inside her head and it hurt! It was too close, much too close.

She heard Lotta speak a word that had no meaning. The harsh sound ended as if silenced by that word. Again Lotta spoke in a kind of singsong, not as she had the night they had found Chole, but in another way, as if she were calling with a firm intention of being answered.

The snow in the field beyond the fence was unmarked by any trail. But farther along, in one of the fence corners, something stirred. Lorrie could not help being afraid. When she had been in the sleigh that other time she had known the fear broadcast by the hunters, by Chole, but this was something else. It was as if Lotta, so close Lorrie could almost reach out and touch her, was not there at all, but that Lorrie was alone while something very strange crawled out to meet her.

Now that stirring in the shadows became a man, who pulled himself up to lean heavily against the rails. He did not try to move toward them, but waited for them to come to him.

Lotta did, but Lorrie remained where she was, though she was not too far away to hear Lotta's voice as she leaned forward a little in her saddle to ask:

"Who are you?"

"Who has the Call?" a hoarse voice answered. "Not what you think I am, I am afraid. I was given the Call to use when all else failed me, as this night it has. But any power was not mine, but another's. I do not claim to be more than I am."

"Which is well for you. To make rash claims to such powers—"

"Could not bring me into more danger than I know, lady. Raise your voice a little and those louts beating the river banks will be up to dispose of the problem I am. And at this point I do not believe I care very much any more."

"Can you walk?" To Lorrie, Lotta's voice sounded cold and demanding.

"After a fashion, ma'am. I've run and I've crawled, perhaps there is enough strength left in me to walk—but not far."

The shadow lurched away from the fence, stumbled toward Lotta, caught at her skirt. There was a ripping sound as the man almost went to his knees. Lotta reached down and caught at him.

"Hold to my stirrup!" There was a note of command in her voice. "Lorrie, go back to the road, watch— See that they do not come from the bridge without warning."

Lorrie edged Bevis around in the narrow space between the edge of the wood and the fence. Could she find her way back to the road? She was not at all sure. But Bevis started confidently on and she thought she might leave it to him. That choice proved right, for he went through the trees to that very narrow path. Lorrie listened for any shouting, any sound that the searchers by the river were moving up to the house. She reached the screen of boughs that hid the entrance to its path, and looked down the road.

Torch lights moved together, as if the men who carried them were gathering into a single party. What must she do if they started up toward the house?

"Lorrie?" came a soft call from the path behind her.

"They are gathering together by the bridge," she answered.

"We must cross the road before they come any closer. It is only a little farther, you *must* make it!" Lotta must be talking to the man.

"Tell that to my legs, ma'am. This is a case of the spirit being willing, but the flesh very weak."

"Hang on. Lorrie, move Bevis between us and the bridge as a screen. Do you understand?"

"Yes!" Lorrie caught up the branch marking the end of the path. Lotta moved into the open, her horse coming step by cautious step, that dark figure stumbling painfully beside her. Then they were on the road, and Lorrie came to the other side, Bevis matching step to Lotta's horse so that the stranger staggered between them.

Back they went to Octagon House. When they reached the lane that led to the stable, Lorrie could hear the man breathing in harsh gasps, saw him wavering as if he could hardly stand. Lotta kept a grasp on his shoulder.

"Get Phineas," Lotta ordered. Lorrie broke away, urged Bevis into a leap forward, scrambled out of the saddle by the stable, and ran for the door.

"Phineas!"

He came out in a rush, passing Lorrie as if he did not see her, but ran down the lane to Lotta.

"Here!" He was beside the stranger, pulling at him.

"Lorrie—the horses—into the stable! They are coming!"

Lorrie caught the reins of Lotta's mount as Lotta dismounted and held to the stranger's other side, turning him with Phineas' help to the garden path that led to the back door. She took Lotta's horse and Bevis, pulling them into the stable, shutting the door on them, before she ran back to that slowly moving trio on the walk.

Now she could hear only too clearly the voices on the road. Lotta was right, the hunters were coming.

"Up here!"

"I can't—"

"You must!" That was Lotta.

Somehow he must have found the strength, for they did get him up those four steps, through the door into the back hall.

"Hurry!"

They pulled him on, Lorrie following. Something dropped to the floor as they came into the kitchen and Lorrie caught it up. Chole stood by the table, but at the sight of them she ran and pushed open the door to the back hall, went before them to open the way into the green room, and then to the chamber with the painted floor. Phineas and Lotta lowered the man into the chair and his head fell back against its high back, his beard-matted chin pointing to the ceiling. He was heavily bearded and his eyes were deeply sunken. Under dirty rags his body was very thin and he shivered as if he had not been really warm for a long time. Lotta turned to Phineas.

"Look to the horses!"

"I will that—" And he was gone.

Then she spoke to Chole. "Some soup—and blankets—"

But Chole stood staring at the half-conscious man. Then she looked at Lotta.

"He's—one of *them*."

"So? In this room, in this house, do you question, Chole?"

For a moment they stared at each other, and Lorrie had the feeling that though they made no sound, yet they spoke together in a way she did not understand.

"Would he be *here*," asked Lotta in a less stern voice, "if what you wish to believe was true?"

Slowly Chole shook her head. Then she, too, went.

Now the man in the chair seemed to rouse a little. He moved his feet, and Lorrie saw there were great holes worn in his boot soles. His hands lifted from the arms of the chair and went to the front of his coat, which was tied together with bits of string through holes.

"Where—where—" He opened his eyes and pulled at the front of his coat as if he hunted for something he carried there and now could not find. "Where—"

For the first time Lorrie glanced down at what she held in her hands. It was a very shallow wooden box or tray, about six inches square. Glued within it were shells, a great many small shells, along with shiny seeds. It was a picture, a heart of brown-red seeds surrounded by flowers of shells and, in the middle, spelled out by seeds, two words: "Truly Thine."

"Is this what you want?" Lorrie held it out to him.

His eyes opened wider as he looked at what she held. Then his lips twisted and he made a queer sound.

"We—cling to things," he said. "Too long sometimes. To make something keeps a man alive. Even in the hell camp it kept my mind alive. But—no—not any more. There is no need now." He took the shell-and-seed picture from Lorrie.

With it in his hand, he sat a little straighter in the chair and looked about him, last of all at Lotta. "For what it is still worth in this mad, troubled world," he said, "I am Charles Dupree, at your service, ma'am. And I believe, unless I have totally lost all count of time, that this is something of a feast day." Ragged scarecrow that he was, he leaned forward in a gesture that had the ghost of grace about it. "Perhaps"—he coughed and then smiled at Lotta—"perhaps, I should now say it. Madam, will you be—my valentine?"

Lotta caught the shell picture as it fell from his hand. And he would have gone to the floor if she had not pushed him back in the chair.

"Lorrie—the wall!" She was holding Charles in the chair. "Press the two ends of the middle shelf, both of them together!"

Lorrie stretched her arms wide, her finger tips just touching the points Lotta indicated. She pressed as hard as she could. Then she jerked back as the wall moved. There was a tiny triangular closet beyond with a very thin slit of window.

Chole stood at the other door. She carried a mug from which a curl of steam rose. And then there was a heavy rapping that echoed through the whole house.

"*Them!*" Chole flashed across the room and set the mug in the closet, dropped a blanket from her shoulder to the floor, was back again. "Leave him to me, Mis' Lotta. You go an' talk t' *them!*"

Lorrie started forward to help Chole, but she never reached the side of the chair. Light and dark whirled to become moonlight and shadow around the doll house. She turned slowly to face the other wall. There was no opening there. But—she had to know. Slowly she went to the empty shelf where books had stood it seemed only seconds earlier. She put her finger tips and pushed, then moved back. There was no quick outward swing this time, but the shelf wall *had* moved a little. Lorrie put her fingers into the new crack and pulled.

There it was—a bare little three-cornered closet, empty of all except shadows. But it was there. Lorrie pushed the wall back into place. All at once she was cold and the shadows seemed larger and blacker, the moonlight strip thinner and weaker. She wanted real light and real people. So she ran, Sabina streaking before her, back into the house of her own time.

ONE GOLDEN NEEDLE

"**F**OR YOU, with all the thank you's from the committee." Lorrie held out the tissue-wrapped package to Miss Ashemeade. "And here is the scrapbook too. The girls were all very careful. We know it is a precious thing. You were kind to talk to Aunt Margaret about our borrowing it."

Miss Ashemeade smiled as she took the package. "If I had not known you would cherish it, Lorrie, I would not have lent it to you. Nothing, child, is too precious to give or lend to one who has need of it, always remember that. And now, let us see what this is."

She drew off the ribbon, put aside the tissue paper, and looked at the offering from the committee.

"It was the prettiest one," Lorrie said. "We all worked on it."

Miss Ashemeade held the valentine up so that the sunlight fell across the lacy paper and the center bouquet of flowers, touched the golden letters Lizabeth had so skillfully cut from the gilt paper in the shape of a twisted rope.

"To Our Valentine," Miss Ashemeade read. "You have done well, all of you, Lorrie. I shall give you a note for the committee. And so these are what you are going to offer for sale at your fair?"

"We made fifty," Lorrie answered with pride. "Oh, they're not all as large as this one. But we tried to copy the ones in the book we liked best. And Mrs. Raymond said they were 'works of art,'" Lorrie quoted.

Miss Ashemeade set the valentine carefully up on top of her embroidery table. Lorrie watched her and then paid more attention to the room. It was different. Now, with a sharp stab of fear, she knew why. The long table was bare, there were no longer any piles of materials and ribbons, any piece of work waiting the repairing needle.

The embroidery frame was empty and put back against the wall. Though there was a fire on the hearth this late Friday afternoon and Sabina lay curled before it, and there were candles lighted, for the first time Lorrie did not feel the old safe welcome. She looked to Miss Ashemeade troubled.

"You aren't cleaning now—" She wanted that to be a question, but it sounded more a statement of a fact she did not want to believe.

"No, Lorrie, the cleaning and the clearing are almost done."

"The house! Miss Ashemeade, that meeting— Couldn't

369

the lawyer do anything to help you? They are not going to tear down Octagon House! They can't!"

She had been so busy with the committee, with end of the term lessons and tests—she had been too busy to care! Maybe—maybe she could have done something— There had been her idea of trying to get people interested in saving the house. If she had only paid attention, tried— The chill within Lorrie spread. She shivered as she looked about the room again and noticed all the familiar things now gone from it. What— what would happen now?

"Lorrie." Miss Ashemeade's quiet voice drew her attention from the room to its mistress. "In this much you are right, the time of Octagon House is fast drawing to a close. But that is the natural course of life, dear child. Nothing remains unchanged, unless it withdraws from life itself. By man's measurement Octagon House has had a long life, well over a hundred years. It has seen many changes around it, and now it shall be changed in turn."

"It will be torn down! Gone—not just changed. It's—it's all wrong!" Lorrie had jumped to her feet and that denial came out of her in a shrill voice.

Miss Ashemeade no longer smiled. She gazed at Lorrie very soberly and intently.

"Lorrie, one cannot say no to life and remain the same. When you first came here, you were trying to say no to change. You thought you could not find anything good in a new way of life, was that not true?"

She paused, and Lorrie tried to remember back to the days before Octagon House opened its doors for her.

"Then the house had something to offer you. It is, and it has always been, a refuge, Lorrie. Do you understand what I mean?"

"A safe place," Lorrie answered.

"A safe place. And some who found their way here, child, were so beaten and hurt by life that this refuge became a home. In this house there is a choice one may make—to re-enter life again, or to stay. You thought you were unhappy and alone. But were you ever as unhappy and frightened and alone as Phebe and Phineas, Chole and Nackie, and Charles Dupree?"

Lorrie did not know quite what Miss Ashemeade was trying to tell her. "They came—Lotta brought them—because they were being hunted—people after them—"

"They were hunted, yes. Two orphan children, and two escaped slaves, and a prisoner of war. The house chose to shelter them, and in turn they chose to remain in the house. You thought you were being hunted, too, but what were you running from, Lorrie?"

"Jimmy Purvis—the boys—" Lorrie began slowly, trying to think why. Somehow it all seemed so silly now. "And I guess everything else—missing Grandmother and Hampstead, and being lonely. I was silly and stupid"—she felt her face grow hot—"just as they said I was."

"These things seemed big to you then, Lorrie. But how do you find them now?"

"Small," Lorrie admitted.

"Because you have learned that time can change some things?"

Suddenly Lorrie asked a question of her own. "Miss Ashemeade—the doll house—this house—are they the same?" She herself did not know quite what she meant, yet it was important.

Miss Ashemeade shook her head. "That I cannot tell you. It's not that I *will* not, but I truly *cannot*. But know this much: if you had not had the power within you that opened the doors, you would not have seen what you did. The house chooses, it always does. And now that you have seen some things, there is reason to believe that time may open more doors for you, if you wish."

"Miss Ashemeade, if Octagon House must go, where will you and Hallie live?"

Once more Miss Ashemeade smiled. "Dear child, that is a worry no one need have. And now I believe you have one last row on your sampler to finish. Shall we sew for a while?"

She put aside the valentine and opened the top of her table. Lorrie picked up her own workbox and got out the strip of linen with its rows and rows of stitches. A little surprised, she surveyed the record of her learning. Why, it was longer than she had thought, beginning with simple outline stitching and French knots, and going on to featherstitching, chain stitching, into more complicated work.

Miss Ashemeade had taken a small package out of one of the table compartments and was unfolding a strip of cloth.

"Will you set the music box, Lorrie?" she asked.

As the tinkling notes sounded through the quiet of the room, Lorrie was not surprised when Miss Ashemeade began to sing in that unknown other language. But she was not stitching tapestry, or mending lace, or making a collar—

Collar, thought Lorrie in sudden surprise. Miss Ashemeade had made that velvet colar for Sabina for Christmas. But Sabina had not worn it then, nor had Lorrie seen it again since the day it had been fashioned.

What was Miss Ashemeade making now? Lorrie leaned forward a little to see, for it was small. Yes, that was the golden needle flashing, though there was no sun to light it today. But—she was making a doll dress!

And as she sewed on, she glanced now and then to a small picture that had been wrapped up with the material. By leaning forward just a little farther Lorrie could see the picture clearly, and with a start of surprise recognized the lady in it.

That was Lotta as she had seen her last with Charles. Only instead of a riding habit she wore a lovely dress of lace that spread out in rows of ruffles from her small waist. And Miss Ashemeade was copying that dress, sewing on such tiny ruffles that Lorrie would not have believed anyone could make such invisibly small stitches unless she had watched them in progress. Miss Ashemeade sang. Again Lorrie found her own needle moving in time to that singing, with ease and pleasure in what she was doing.

When her last row of sampler stitches was completed, she folded the length of material and placed it neatly in the bottom of her box, beneath the tray that held the needlecase, reels, and spools. She sat quietly, content to watch the flashing of the golden needle in and out, and then she found herself repeating the words of the song along with Miss Ashemeade, not knowing what they meant, except that they were a very necessary part of what Miss Ashemeade was now doing.

How long they sat there Lorrie did not know or care. For her the warmth and the safe feeling had returned to the room. But at last Miss Ashemeade set a final stitch and cut her thread. The dress was finished. She smoothed it with her fingers and then further unrolled the large square of material. Within lay a second dress of soft rose-pink and with it a ruffled apron.

"Oh!" Lorrie cried in distress. "You broke your needle—the gold needle!"

Miss Ashemeade no longer sang. And as she put down the needle it no longer flashed. It was broken in two, and somehow it no longer seemed gold, but lay in dull pieces, as if the stitching it had just done had drawn out of it all the life it had once held.

"Its work was done, my dear." Miss Ashemeade did not sound sorry. "It was very old and its usefulness was finished."

Lorrie eyed the doll dresses. She wanted to ask why Miss Ashemeade had made them, but somehow she could not. It was as if such a question would have been rude.

Miss Ashemeade put them away, rolled up in the material. She shut down the lid of the sewing table.

"Now, Lorrie, if you will fetch pen and paper. I do want to thank the committee for their charming gift."

As Miss Ashemeade wrote, Lorrie moved to the fireplace. Sabina sat up and began to wash. It was so quiet in the room that the faint scratching of pen on paper could be heard, even the lick-lick of Sabina's rough pink tongue against her black fur. Suddenly Lorrie did not like that quiet. Hallie—where was Hallie? She listened for any noise from the kitchen. But perhaps the walls of the old house were too thick, for if Hallie were busy, no sound could be heard here.

Miss Ashemeade sealed her envelope with a small wafer, and then brought out from some inner pocket of her wide skirt another envelope.

"Lorrie, I am going to ask you to do something that is very important to me. And I shall also ask you not to question it. I believe I can trust you."

"Yes, Miss Ashemeade."

"As you leave here tonight, you will find the key in the lock of the back door. You will lock the door, then you will put the key into this envelope, seal the envelope, and mail it at the corner post box."

"Miss Ashemeade!" Lorrie dared to catch and hold the hand offering her the envelope. "Please, Miss Ashemeade, what are you going to do?"

"I said no questions, Lorrie. And do not be afraid, because there is nothing to fear, that I promise you. I told you once that belief was needful. Believe me now."

Lorrie took the envelope. "I do."

"And now, Lorrie, it grows late."

But Lorrie did not turn at once to the door. "Please—I *will* see you again?"

Miss Ashemeade smiled. Sabina came running lightly across the room and jumped into her lap.

"I believe you will, Lorrie. Remember, belief is very important—belief and the need for seeing with the heart as well as with the eyes. Always remember that. And now, goodbye for a little while, Lorrie."

"Goodbye." Lorrie could linger no longer after that dismissal, but somehow she was almost afraid to go, afraid that if she went out of this room she would never see it again. She turned as she reached the door to look back for the last time.

Sabina lay at ease across her mistress' lap and Miss Ashemeade was stroking her. The shadows were gathering darker and darker in the far corners of the room, beginning to creep out toward its center.

"Please, may I say goodbye to Hallie too?" Lorrie asked.

"Of course, my dear, if you can find her."

Lorrie closed the door and crossed the hall to the kitchen. The door was shut and did not open to her pull. What had Miss Ashemeade once said, on her first exploration of the house—go anywhere the doors will open. This one would not.

Lorrie rapped on it, but there was no answer. But she must say goodbye to Hallie! Somehow, tonight especially, that was important. With her knuckles still resting against the stubbornly closed panels, Lorrie called:

"Goodbye, Hallie, goodbye!"

Still that did not seem enough. Alarmed, why she was not quite sure, Lorrie turned to the door through which she had come only moments earlier. She would ask Miss Ashemeade. But that door could not now be opened either. She lifted her hand though she did not knock. After her last goodbye, Lorrie somehow felt she must not disturb the mistress of Octagon House again.

She put on her wraps and boots. The key was in the lock, just as Miss Ashemeade had said it would be. She let herself out, then turned the key. For a long moment she stood on the top step, holding it in her hand. She had locked Miss Ashemeade and Hallie inside—why? The key was big and old and heavy. But perhaps they had another key. Maybe Hallie was tired and had gone to rest, and Miss Ashemeade wanted to spare her having to come and lock up.

But then why put the key in an envelope and mail it? Lorrie turned the envelope over in her hand. There were papers inside to make it fat. She dropped the key in quickly and licked the flap shut. The name and address on it—it was meant to go to a Mr. Ernest Thruston—the lawyer!

Belief was important, Miss Ashemeade had said—and don't ask questions. But questions buzzed in Lorrie's head as she walked to the mailbox and dropped in the heavy letter.

Lorrie continued to think about that key and the big envelope while she got supper for Aunt Margaret, who would be late tonight. She kept remembering things that made her more and more uneasy, just why she was not sure. Miss Ashemeade's precious golden needle, dull and broken. And the locked door when she left—Miss Ashemeade certainly could not have risen and walked across the room all by herself to lock the door of the red room in the short time Lorrie had been at the kitchen door! Then who had? Hallie, coming around the other way through the unused parlor?

But always her thoughts came back to the key and why Miss Ashemeade had wanted her to mail it to Mr. Thruston.

Where *would* Miss Ashemeade, Hallie, and Sabina go? Lorrie could not think of them living anywhere else than in Octagon House—they did not belong to the world outside its doors. And what would happen to all the treasures? Would Miss Ashemeade be able to take them with her?

Lorrie glanced about the very small kitchen of the apartment. Imagine Hallie trying to work here! Her beloved stove could not fit in. Suddenly Lorrie wanted to race back through the dusk, knock on the back door—that locked back door—and find Hallie, and the red room, and Miss Ashemeade just the same as they had been through all the months she had known them. Months, wondered Lorrie. Yes, part of October, all of November, and December, and January, and one week in February— But it seemed to her now that she had been a visitor to Octagon House for far longer than that.

What would become of Bevis and the doll house? Or—for the first time Lorrie's thoughts winged in another direction—*was* there now a Bevis and a doll house? Had there ever been at all?

But Miss Ashemeade knew about Phebe and Phineas, Chole and Nackie, and Charles Dupree. She had said this afternoon that they had chosen to remain in its safety. Did that mean they lived there forever and ever? Lorrie looked at the clock and at the coffeepot put on to perk. Believe, Miss Ashemeade had said.

Lorrie drew a deep breath and stood still. She was staring at the wall but not seeing the brightly polished copper molds hung there to brighten up the dark corner beyond the dinette. There was a new warm feeling inside her. Now—now she believed that Miss Ashemeade, and Hallie, and Sabina were safe too. No matter what would happen to Octagon House, they would be safe—forever!

"Lorrie?" She had not heard Aunt Margaret's key in the door. Now she turned, startled.

Aunt Margaret still had on her coat and hat. She looked unhappy. "Lorrie, I am so sorry—"

"Sorry for what?" Lorrie was jolted out of her own thoughts.

"About Octagon House." Aunt Margaret had the evening paper in one hand. "The thruway—" She hesitated.

"I know. Miss Ashemeade told me."

"Those poor old ladies. Something must be done for them. Wherever will they go? Lorrie, I think I had better go up there this evening and see if there is any way I may help."

"Miss Ashemeade said they would be safe."

"Safe? Oh, yes, you were there this afternoon. But maybe she did not really understand, Lorrie. The Commissioners announced today that the appeal failed. All those who objected will have to move. Miss Ashemeade is very old, Chick. And sometimes old people do not understand how things can be taken this way by the city."

"She does know, Aunt Margaret. She told me there was no place for Octagon House now."

Aunt Margaret slipped out of her coat. "But there should be!" she said almost fiercely. "We must see what can be done! At least for those poor old ladies."

"Aunt Margaret," Lorrie asked slowly, "do you really think they are poor old ladies?"

Aunt Margaret looked at Lorrie in surprise. Then her expression became thoughtful.

"No, you are right, Lorrie. Miss Ashemeade may be old, but I do not believe that she would allow anyone to make decisions for her. And she told you she has plans?"

"Yes and—" Lorrie told her about the key and the letter.

"Lock the back door behind you and mail the key—and you did it? But, Lorrie, leaving the two of them locked in and— Why, whyever would they want that? Lorrie, you stay right here—understand?"

Aunt Margaret pulled on her coat, ran out into the hall, and was gone, not quite shutting the door behind her. For a moment Lorrie's amazement was part fear. And then the certainty of moments earlier returned to reassure her, and she knew there was no need to worry about Miss Ashemeade and the other inhabitants of Octagon House. She went on with supper preparations, listening for Aunt Margaret's return.

And return she did before not many minutes had passed. There was an odd expression on her face as she came once more into the kitchen.

"I don't know why," she said. "I got as far as the gate and then, why, then, Lorrie, I just knew it was all right with them."

Lorrie noded. "I know it too."

But Aunt Margaret still had that strange look on her face, as if right before her eyes something had happened that she could not believe, even though she saw it happen. Then she shook her head.

The letter came the following Friday. But as that was the day of the fair, they did not open it until late. Aunt Margaret had come to the P.T.A. supper, and she and Lorrie did not get back home until after nine. The envelope was waiting in their mailbox, a long white one with a business address in the upper corner and it was addressed to them both: Miss Margaret Gerson, Miss Lorrie Mallard.

Aunt Margaret, very puzzled, read it aloud. They were to go to Octagon House on Saturday morning at eleven, and it was signed Ernest Thruston.

"Miss Ashemeade's lawyer," Lorrie explained.

"But why?" Aunt Margaret read it through a second time, this time to herself. "I can't understand—Well, it sets one's imagination to working, doesn't it? Luckily I am free tomorrow."

It was snowing a little when they opened the front gate of Octagon House the next day. Again the proud deer had a small ridge of white down his back as he stared over their heads. Lorrie looked at him a little sadly and hoped he would find another home when they took away his lawn and garden.

There were tracks in the snow on the walk, as if someone had gone around the house not too long before, and they followed those to the same back door they had always used. Aunt Margaret rapped and the door was opened, not by a smiling Hallie, but by a man who said at once and a little sharply:

"Miss Gerson?"

"Yes, and Lorrie."

He brought them into the red room. But Lorrie shivered. There was no fire on the hearth. A lamp and some candles had been lighted, but all the warmth and cheer had gone out of the room. The tall back chair was empty. Aunt Margaret asked the question that Lorrie could not voice.

"Miss Ashemeade?"

"She has gone. Of course, she has always been a will unto herself. The key and her instructions were mailed to me. Brrr—these old houses without central heating—nothing but damp and cold! If you don't mind." He glanced about him as if he did not care for the room or the house, and would like to be away as soon as possible. "Miss Ashemeade has made certain dispositions of her property that I am empowered to carry out. Your niece, Lorrie Mallard, is to have the contents of the toy room. If you will please come with me."

"The toy room?" echoed Aunt Margaret. "But—"

It was a strange house, Lorrie thought as they went from shrouded parlor to bedroom, where now covers were also draped all over the furniture. Then Mr. Thruston pushed open the last door and they were in the room with the painted floor.

There were Bevis and the house, just as they had always been.

"Why, Lorrie! A doll house, and a rocking horse—" Aunt Margaret stared at those. But there was more in the room now, Lorrie noted. The box from which Miss Ashemeade had unpacked the wonderful Christmas ornaments stood to one side and on it rested both the workbox she had used and the scrapbook of valentines.

Aunt Margaret walked slowly around the house, peering into its windows.

"This—this is a museum piece, Mr. Thruston. And—and we do not have room for it in the apartment."

"I believe Miss Ashemeade foresaw that problem, Miss Gerson." Mr. Thruston held a piece of paper. "It has been arranged that most of the furnishings of this house, having historical value, be presented to the Ashton Historical Society. The doll house and the horse may be placed on loan with them also, a loan that may be terminated upon demand at any time by your niece. They will have safekeeping, and they will doubtless be enjoyed by the public—I believe the school classes make yearly visits to the Society. But whenever she wishes, she may reclaim them. And now, I dislike hurrying you, Miss Gerson, but there are certain articles left to *your* care. If you will just come and see—"

"That wonderful house— Yes, I'll come," answered Aunt Margaret.

Lorrie waited until they had left and then she stepped around to the side of the house where the dining room was—the room Miss Ashemeade had made so much her own. In spite of the gloom in the room, she had caught a glimpse, a glinting sparkle against the base.

Now she knelt on the floor to see it better. Yes, she was right! There was a gold chain, and strung on it seven small keys, while an eighth stood in the keyhole of the drawer.

She turned that key and drew open the drawer. It was one of the wider ones.

"Lotta." She did not need to touch the beautiful lace dress she had seen Miss Ashemeade make, nor the doll who wore it. "Hallie." No longer bent and old, but young as Miss Lotta—wearing the rosy dress. "Sabina." Small, quiet, with her silver-belled collar. "Hello." Lorrie bent closer to whisper. "Now—all of you—wait for me."

Softly she shut the drawer and turned the key in its lock. Why had she said that? Wait for her—how? —where? Until someday when she had a house big enough to hold the doll house? When again there might be a chance to visit it, meet again those who would live there for always and always?

One, two, three, four drawers with their occupants. What lay in the other four?

She tried a key in the next and opened it—nothing. Then a second and third—they were empty. But when she pulled out the fourth—Lorrie looked closer. It was the wooden needle box. She picked it up and opened it. One golden needle was left, thrust firmly into the velvet. Lorrie did not touch it, but put the box back and locked the drawer.

Then she tried them all. They were safely locked. The house, yes, let them put the house in the museum where anyone who wished might look in it. But the people of the house—let them be as safe as they had chosen to be.

Lorrie dropped the chain with its keys into her workbox, and took that up with the scrapbook. She could get the ornament box later. Holding the box and the book, she went to Bevis and stroked his arching neck. Thump, thump, he rocked back and forth, but he did not change. Lorrie was not disappointed. That was as it should be—for now.

She went to the door and then looked back at the waiting house, at Bevis. Wait they would, house and horse, as long or as short—as time.

"Goodbye," said Lorrie very softly, "for a while. Goodbye—"

The floor creaked. Had or had not Bevis rocked to nod her an approving answer?